TERESA F. MORGAN

I live in sunny Weston-super-Mare, trying to hold onto my Surrey accent where I was born and bred. For years I persevered with boring jobs, until my two boys joined my nest. In an attempt to find something to work around them, and to ensure I never endured full time boredom again, I found writing. I am at my happiest baking cakes, putting proper home cooked dinners on the table (whether the kids eat them or not), reading a good romance, or creating a touch of escapism with heroes readers will fall in love with.

http://www.teresamorgan.co.uk/

@Teresa_Morgan10

One Fine Day

TERESA F. MORGAN

Harper*Impulse* an imprint of
HarperCollins*Publishers* Ltd
1 London Bridge Street
London SE1 9GF

www.harpercollins.co.uk

A Paperback Original 2015

First published in Great Britain in ebook format by Harper*Impulse* 2015

A catalogue record for this book is
available from the British Library

ISBN: 9780008124618

Automatically produced by Atomik ePublisher from Easypress

One Fine Day is dedicated to my mum – who needs another book to read.

I would like to say a big thank you to Liz Wood, June Bastable and Jacquie Franks for their tremendous writery-support.

And to all my friends and readers who enjoyed my first book, Plus One is a Lucky Number, and have given me encouragement and praise; I really hope you like this one even more.

Prologue

Steve Mason grinned and waved, stepping out of the air-conditioned limousine, the evening summer heat engulfing him. Then he gallantly held out his hand to help Erica Kealey out of the car with grace. She emerged looking stunning, wearing a sparkly, silver sequined evening gown which accentuated her slim figure – too slim, Steve had sometimes worried – and the press went berserk; snapping cameras and shouting questions. Even in her four-inch heel Jimmy Choos she was still slightly shorter than him. They walked the red carpet laid out in front of the five star Hollywood hotel, and he kept one hand on the small of Erica's back, protective and loving. They briefly posed for photographs, but Erica felt tense in his embrace. They faced a barrage of paparazzi questions.

"Have you set a date?"

"When will the engagement be announced?"

"Have you thought about a location for the wedding?"

They didn't stop to answer tonight; they were questions Steve couldn't even answer, yet. He kept on smiling and walking with Erica who was in a rush. She'd hardly said a word to him in the limo, and now in front of the press her smile appeared strained. Only he could see it though, she was a brilliant actress. But Steve knew.

A slight niggle in his subconscious told him Erica was behaving oddly. She appeared ever gracious, knowing the paparazzi were eager to snap celebrity couples, but something was bothering her. Rumours could spread fast if the paparazzi detected any friction. He checked his tuxedo pocket; the ring box was safe. He wanted to quash any rumours. He wanted the world to know the love he felt for this woman.

Entering the hotel, he relaxed, the cooler air refreshing him, and they followed the throng towards the ballroom. The glitzy, Hollywood birthday party – a black-tie affair – was for their director in *Perfection*, Jimmy Petersen. The big man had big movies behind him and practically every A-Lister in Hollywood was attending. Steve was almost used to walking among them, but still had to pinch himself occasionally – he'd earned the right to be with the stars. Erica fitted with this crowd naturally as her father, Robert Kealey was a well-known actor and director so she'd been born into stardom,

As they entered the busy ballroom, Steve grabbed two champagne flutes from the nearest waiter. He turned to find Erica had wandered off, and he weaved through the guests, nodding and saying hello to familiar faces as he caught up with her.

"Erica, do you want to tell me what's wrong?" Steve said, frowning as he handed her a glass. Her bad mood was rubbing off on him and he hated the distant feeling between them. Erica smiled weakly, looking troubled, staring into her champagne flute. Steve stroked her arm tenderly with the back of his finger. "Are you all right?"

"I have something on my mind." She shrugged and sipped her drink. "That's all."

"You look like you need cheering up," he said more happily, feeling excited suddenly. "I didn't want to mention it in the limo, I wanted to surprise you." With his right hand, he fished out the ring box from his pocket, and flicked it open to show her the large solitaire diamond set in platinum. "I picked up the ring. Thought we'd make it official. We could do it tonight—"

"No!" Erica hissed, shielding the box from view of others. "Put it away."

Steve frowned, quickly snapping the lid shut and pocketing the box, all of his enthusiasm draining. "I thought with the press outside, we could use it to our advantage."

She mumbled something but Steve didn't quite hear. Or did he? His stomach churned and his mouth became dry. He swallowed some champagne, but a lump had already formed in his throat. "What did you say?" She couldn't look him in the eye. "Erica, is everything okay?"

She took a deep breath, and spoke fast, "I'm sorry, Steve. But I can't marry you. It's over." She dumped the half-full champagne flute on a table and headed for the exit. Steve stood mouth open, all the air whooshed out of his lungs as his world imploding. What had just happened? He glanced around; guests stared at him, whispering, pointing. Then mentally shaking himself back to reality – *how long had he stood there, dumbfounded?* – he hurried after Erica.

Her elegant shoes clicked along the polished walnut floor in the corridor, the party in full swing behind them.

"Wait, Erica!" Steve said, discarding his empty glass on the tray of a passing waiter. "Can't we even talk about this?" He grabbed her arm to stop her, turning him to face her. "We can fix this. I love you." He reached to stroke her face.

"I don't love you!" she snapped, pushing his hand away. Steve froze, shocked at her words. Her eyes glistened and her lips trembled before she spoke more calmly, "I'm sorry, Steve, it's not what I want. I'll get my PA to come pick up my belongings from yours tomorrow." She'd never properly moved in, they'd each kept their own homes. She owned a property in Beverly Hills, and tomorrow, her assistant would remove all traces of Erica's existence from his life out of his rented luxury apartment. He remained silent, unable to think straight. What words could he say to make this better? This couldn't be happening. An hour ago he'd been blissfully happy, now his life had been shattered like broken glass. Thousands of tiny shards inside his chest.

She started walking again.

"What do you want?" he said, pacing beside her. "I thought I was everything to you. That's what you told me."

"That was then. Things have changed."

"Tell me what I have to do to convince you, and I'll do it, Erica." Steve combed a hand through his hair, hating that he sounded desperate, but he was. "I love you. Only you." Everything about her was beautiful. Her auburn hair fell onto her shoulders, framing her perfectly made-up face. Erica stopped and frowned. They were in a quiet corridor, with a door leading out to the back of the hotel. A doorman waited outside as if on guard.

Erica looked around, then at Steve, hesitant. "These past few months have been hard," she said, lowering her voice. "You've been filming *Nothing Happened*. I've been half way across the world filming too. We've drifted apart, Steve."

"We can make this work, I know we can," Steve said, reaching to touch her hand, but she shifted her weight so he couldn't.

"Steve, our schedules won't gel." Shaking her head, she pulled out her phone from her purse and made a quick call. "Yes, I'm round the back." She hung up, but remained clutching her phone as she focussed on Steve again – he hadn't taken his eyes off her. "One of us would have to sacrifice our work. I'm not prepared to do that, and you're not either."

"How do you know? I'd give it up for you."

"I don't want you to give it up for me. You're on the verge of being the hottest new star in Hollywood. You should be happy."

"I am but I want to be happier – with you." He couldn't believe he'd never hold this woman again, never kiss or make love to her. The thought made him miserable. He couldn't imagine life without Erica Kealey. How did he make her see they were perfect together?

"I'm sorry," she said. "I never meant to hurt you." Then, hesitantly, she gently kissed him on the cheek. The doorman pulled open the door, and Erica confidently sashayed out the back of the hotel to her awaiting limo. There were a few opportunist photographers, held back by some security. Like strobe lighting effects, camera flashes followed her. Steve watched her elegantly step into the limo, disappearing into its blackness. Tomorrow the whole world would know Erica Kealey had dumped Hollywood heart-throb Steve Mason.

As the limo drove off, the pressure building in Steve's chest rose to his throat and his eyes stung. The last time he'd cried was at his mother's funeral, and even then, he'd hidden his grief from prying eyes. In the privacy of his apartment, he could allow his emotions to show, but not here. He needed to return to the party.

How was he supposed to appear happy, when the woman he had planned to spend the rest of his life with had just walked out of it?

Chapter 1

Steve stretched and yawned. He was only half way through his eleven-hour flight to London. At least, travelling first class, he could sleep for some of it, but he never truly allowed himself to fall into a deep sleep. He had to keep his wits about him, especially as he'd left his bodyguards behind. The stewardess had come along and put a blanket over him and constantly checked he was comfortable.

Of course she would do, he *was* Steve Mason, after all.

Like all stewardesses, she wore perfect make-up and precision styled hair. She looked pretty, but he did wonder what she'd look like with the cosmetics removed. Yet it made the flight pleasant. He wasn't going to complain when a pretty girl gave him attention. She had to be around her mid-twenties. Some of the flight attendants were older, but this particular stewardess was his, it seemed. All the other travellers could whistle; she only had eyes for him.

When he couldn't snooze he put his nose in a book or watched the in-flight movies. His latest movie, *Perfection* was available but he skipped that one. How vain would it look to be watching your own movie?

However, a glimpse of Erica would have been nice.

He couldn't believe how much he still missed her.

"Are you ready for some breakfast, Mr Mason?" the stewardess said, in her beautifully British accent, which was from somewhere around the London area.

"Yeah, sure," he said, sounding very American. He adjusted his chair with the ever-helpful stewardess assisting. He checked her name badge. "Thank you, Suzie," he said, giving her his best smile. He had been fortunately blessed with straight teeth.

"So is this trip for business or pleasure?" Suzie placed a breakfast tray in front of him. She was flirting, he knew that, the way she looked at him out the corner of her eye, the smile in her voice. He was used to women flirting with him, he preferred it to them reacting oddly, acting either incredibly shy, or throwing themselves at him, claiming they loved him and wanted to have his babies.

At least she hadn't done that yet.

He used to get plenty of attention from the ladies before he was famous – now it was a given. He was up there with Robert Pattinson, having women's underwear thrown at him.

"I'm going to see my sister."

"You have a sister in London?"

"Not quite in London, no." Maybe it was best not to give Ruby's location away, he didn't need the press chasing after him. The idea was to lay low for a bit. "But not far."

"Well, I hope you brought your winter jacket, we're having a cold October."

"Yeah, I've packed my sweaters." He winked, and she coyly smiled.

Suzie attended to another passenger – who had been huffing loudly at all the attention Steve had been getting – then returned with a coffee pot. Steve had started eating his breakfast, welcoming the food. For some reason, although he found others complained a lot about it – especially the celebrities – he really liked in-flight food. But then he'd been brought up never to be fussy – and to clear his plate.

"Coffee, sir?"

"Please, need something to wake me up."

"You know, I'm sorry you and Erica Kealey didn't work out. I thought you made a beautiful couple," Suzie said, pouring him a cup of coffee. Steve's expression must have shown surprise. He closed his mouth and blinked. "Oh, I am sorry." Even with her heavy make-up Suzie couldn't hide her blushing – he watched her neck flush pink.

He laughed and waved it off. "Hey, I wasn't expecting someone to comment, that's all. The whole affair wasn't too pretty."

And he wasn't quite over Erica. He still missed her – loving her, and being loved back. He'd hoped she'd be the one. She'd left a huge void in his life.

"I'm sure you won't be on your own for long." Suzie said, not quite meeting his gaze.

His stewardess was persistent, he'd give her that. But he didn't mind, she was actually talking to him like he was a human being and not a god. She was prying, but then, they were all nosy when it came to fame and fortune. Suzie, albeit flirty and unprofessional, was still pleasant to talk to.

"No," he said, laughing it off. "If I was, wouldn't you know? The press know our secrets before we do." He raised his eyebrows knowingly as he dabbed his mouth with a napkin.

"Oh, you celebrities have a way of hiding things, you never know what to believe in the press. I don't read the papers myself."

"Yeah, I wouldn't. Most of it isn't true."

"Or it's blown out of proportion," she said.

"Yes, that's true." He sighed. "Basically, I need a vacation. Preferably without the press hounding me."

He never thought he'd say this but he needed time out of LA. He needed time away from Hollywood and the limelight. His popularity had erupted suddenly and he still hadn't adjusted. Hopefully, in the UK he might fade into the background a little, if he kept a low profile. Even his agent had suggested him taking a couple of weeks off, seeing the fallout from Erica's betrayal.

He'd just finished filming his next movie, *Nothing Happened*, which was due out next summer, plus all the other stuff that went with a movie release. He'd still had to do the rounds for *Perfection;* TV chat shows, magazine interviews, radio shows. His schedule had been hectic over the last few months, and he wanted to remove himself from it, slow things down.

Steve had locked up his Hollywood apartment, handed the keys to his personal assistant Marie, and told her he was taking a vacation. While he sneaked out of LA, his PA arranged for a guy who'd doubled for him on *Perfection* to spend a couple of weeks sunbathing in the Caribbean at an exclusive resort with a private beach, in the hope of fooling the tabloids. Steve had some time before he started shooting his next movie, so this was a good time to get away and catch up with Ruby.

He'd last seen her at their mother's funeral, and that had been fleeting. Although the paparazzi wouldn't gatecrash the wake, he'd had to return to LA, back to filming, so he hadn't stayed as long as he'd have liked. Ruby felt like a stranger to him.

For a moment sadness and regret filled him. His mother. He'd hardly seen her in the last fifteen years, intent on making it big in Hollywood, plus flights home weren't cheap when he hadn't been making money. And then it had been too late, cancer took her in her prime.

He clenched his fists, reliving his anger. *He should have been told sooner. He would have come home.*

Thankfully, Suzie left him to eat his breakfast in peace, remembering that there were other first class passengers to attend to – especially the huffy old dear a row behind him – letting him dwell. The flight wasn't busy – there weren't many people flying in first class. He hadn't made a fuss, wanting to retain a low profile, and it had worked. The cabin crew had been very surprised when the actual Steve Mason had boarded their plane.

After the breakfast trays had been cleared away, Steve must have dozed off, because he was gently woken by Suzie checking his seatbelt was fastened, and telling him they were approaching Heathrow.

About to disembark, Steve slipped his hand into his jacket pocket and felt a piece of paper in there. He didn't remember having anything in his pocket. He took it out and read it: a note from Suzie, apologising for being unprofessional but providing him with her number, 'in case he was staying anywhere near Richmond and needed company.'

He turned, winked, which made her blush and giggle, then walked off the plane.

Nothing personal, but he wouldn't be calling Suzie, although he couldn't just throw away her number, so he left the note in his pocket for now. He'd discard it later, discreetly. However much he would like to find love again, he knew Suzie wouldn't be the one. She was in *love* – well, lust – with the star, the glamour, the money; not the real Steve Mason.

In pursuit of his luggage which he'd put through fast track, Steve tried Ruby's work number. She was manager at a small hotel in the posh end of Bristol, as she'd put it.

"Good afternoon, Durdham Lodge, you're speaking to Lydia. How can I help you?"

"Oh, hi, could you put me through to Ruby Fisher, please?"

"I'll try her number for you. Who's calling please?"

"I'd rather not say, I want it to be a surprise." Steve wondered if he should have waited until he was out of the airport, the noise and bustling of people was making it hard to concentrate. He held his hand over his other ear. He'd wanted to call before boarding his plane, but with the time difference and everything, the need to just get out of LA, (he was the prime example that men couldn't multi-task) – it had been the middle of the night in England – he had decided to leave it until landing.

"I'm sorry, sir, but I do need a name to transfer you. It's company policy. What is the call regarding?" What did Ruby do that ensured her calls needed to be vetted? Even his own PA, Marie wasn't this tough on private callers.

"I wanted to surprise her. Lydia, it is Lydia, yes?"

"Yes." She had a soft voice. She sounded young, and he imagined her to be pretty... as pretty as Suzie, but telephone voices could be deceiving. Probably about fifty, married and looked like a dragon, knowing Steve's luck. He'd have to ask Ruby about Lydia.

"My name's Steve, and I'm family. We've not seen each other in a while; I'd like to surprise her, even if it is on the phone," Steve said, trying to convey his smile down the line. "Can you trust me on this one? I'll owe you big time." A loud tannoy sounded over the arrivals lounge.

"I'm sorry, I didn't quite hear you. There's a lot of noise in the background," Lydia said.

"Sorry, I'm at the airport. I've just landed."

"Oh, okay." Steve had to hand it to Lydia, he understood why she was doing her job properly. He'd often relied on a good receptionist's vigilance to keep the prying paparazzi from finding out he was staying in a hotel. "So you're definitely not trying to sell something?" She giggled. It was infectious. If only she knew who she was really speaking to, would she be so at ease?

Steve chuckled. "I promise, hand on my heart, I'm not trying to sell her anything."

"Okay, I'll try her line for you." There was silence, then Lydia came back on the line. "I'm sorry, sir, she's not in her office at the moment. Would you like to leave a message?"

"No, no, I'll try again later." Steve grabbed his case as it finally passed him.

"She'll be leaving around six tonight. Try her at home after then, maybe?"

"Yes, I'll do that, thanks for your help. Oh and please don't mention that I called. Like I said, I want to surprise her."

"Your secret is safe with me," Lydia said, then, more hesitantly, "Will we get to meet you?"

"Um, I'm not sure yet. That'll be up to Ruby. But if we do, I

11

owe you a drink. Thanks for your help, Lydia. It's been nice talking to you." Even though disappointment lingered in his thoughts, his spirits had been lifted with his brief conversation with Lydia. She hadn't known who he was, so had reacted to him normally. If only life could be that simple, maybe he could find a girlfriend.

Steve slipped his phone into his inside pocket and headed through passports and customs. When planning his journey, he'd thought about catching a domestic flight to Bristol, but instead decided he'd hire a car. Driving on the motorway was a better way to stay low and get lost in a crowd.

Steve had ensured he'd drunk enough coffee to keep him awake for the two hour car journey. He needn't have worried. Concentrating on staying left whilst fighting his way onto the M4 was enough to keep him fully alert. He didn't remember the British as maniac drivers. Wasn't the speed limit seventy?

How come they were all doing ninety?

He turned the radio on, tuned into Radio One, and although he no longer recognised the DJs, turned up the volume. It wouldn't be long, and he'd be home.

***

Alone in his hotel suite Steve took his phone out of his pocket, and checked for messages. None.

Why did he keep thinking he'd see something from Erica? For Christ's sake, he needed to get a grip. Erica didn't want him back, she'd moved on. So should he.

Maybe this proved his skin wasn't thick enough, he wasn't used to being a celebrity yet. His fame still hadn't sunk in. Which was ridiculous; he'd had three big movies now – okay, so he'd only been the male lead in one of them, *Perfection*, which had increased his profile. It had taken a while to get there, some bad films, some bit parts, his career starting with television shows and adverts initially, earning him a keep, but this was it. He'd just finished filming another lead role, and he had another film lined up on the horizon. His agent promised him filmmakers would be knocking on his door wanting Steve Mason, the new Hollywood hunk, in their movies. He'd never be out of work.

Perfection had been a mixture of action and romance, a box office smash putting him up there with the best of them. Instead of chasing for parts, film makers were chasing him. He'd finally done it after a damned hard slog.

His fame would only grow further now. At the moment, he still had an element of freedom; not everybody knew the face of Steve Mason like they knew Tom Cruise. His name was only starting to spread around Hollywood, and that's why it was important to see Ruby now. His next movie, *Nothing Happened* was due out next year and after that, everyone would know Steve Mason's face.

A quick glance at his watch told him it was half past six. His sister should be home from work. He dialled, and waited, praying it wouldn't go to her answer phone.

"Hello?" The voice sounded dubious. He was lost for words, momentarily, and she cut in, "If this is one of those bloody sales calls, will you just piss off!"

"No, it's not a *bloody* sales call." Laughter laced his words.

"Who's that?"

"Ruby, it's me."

"Who's *me*?" she said impatiently.

"Steve."

"Steve ... Where are you?"

"The Hilton in Bristol."

"No you're not. Where are you really?" she said dryly.

He laughed. "I am. I swear, The Hilton, Bristol."

"Which one?" She still didn't believe him, her tone dubious.

"The one just off the M5." He sighed, losing his patience.

"Bloody hell! I'll be right over. I assume you'd prefer to be tucked away in your room?"

"Yeah, for now. We'll have dinner here, I've got a suite."

"Oh, um, what name should I ask for?"

"You won't need a name, just come up." He gave her the room number and ended the call, then started unpacking his things. Not that he'd be able to stay here long. Someone would work out who he really was and before he knew it, the paps would arrive.

***

"Where's my British brother gone? What's with the accent?"

Ruby had turned up half an hour later and hugged him. She'd changed so much since the last time he'd seen her. Lost some weight, and cut off all of her hair. It suited her though; she looked like a younger version of their mother with her tomboy hairstyle.

"Well, you tend to pick it up ... and I needed to sound less British to get better parts. I have been living in LA fifteen years."

"Don't I know it, and you're brown as a berry." She gently prodded him. "Is it fake tan?"

"No."

"Oh, well, you'll soon lose that here. It's turned so cold. So, what brings you home?"

"You."

A stab of guilt hit him, realising his agent had encouraged him to visit Ruby. It hadn't come from Steve; hadn't entered his thoughts initially, as he was still carrying a slight niggle of resentment about his mother's death. Damn, he was really glad to be here.

"Me?" Ruby said with disbelief.

"Let's order some food and then we can talk," Steve said, finding the room service menu. This was going to be tough. He hardly knew her now, but he wanted to get some time back with her. Catch up, talk about things. Mum, even Erica. Could he tell Ruby about Erica?

The room service arrived and Ruby and Steve sat around the

14

small table. Ruby insisted she didn't want wine, she'd drive home as she needed her car for work the next morning.

"So," Ruby put her fork down and rested her elbow on the table, "when does your next film start?"

"Starts shooting in three months. Marie will let me know when they send the revised script through."

"Marie?"

"She's my personal assistant."

"Is she pretty?"

"She's forty-nine and married with two teenage kids." He looked at her dead pan.

Ruby rolled her eyes. "Okay, so for someone who's worth a million dollars, you're looking pretty miserable. What's up with you?"

"You read the papers, right?"

"Not really – full of tripe most of the time. Quick glimpse at *OK* or *Hello* when I'm in the hairdressers, but that's about it. Oh, and I might catch the front pages of the newspapers before they head up to the rooms. But I don't like reading stuff about you." She shrugged.

"I was seeing Erica Kealey. We met filming *Perfection*." During the making of the movie a passion had been ignited within them – it hadn't helped they'd had a lot of love scenes. On and off the set, they couldn't get enough of one another. Steve had believed Erica was his soul mate.

"*The* Erica Kealey? Wow! I did see you were going to marry your leading lady and was wondering where my wedding invite was, admittedly." Ruby scowled.

"Yeah, well, we broke up." Over a year later, when they'd made wedding plans for next spring – albeit loose ones, then she'd ended it all. She hadn't even given him a backwards glance.

"When?"

"About two months ago – and now it appears she has a thing for her current leading man." After their sudden break up, Erica had drifted to another man's bed. She had moved on easier than Steve.

"Oh." Ruby patted his knee. "I'm sorry."

They finished their meal, then headed over to the couch, Steve pouring himself a large scotch. Ruby insisted on an orange juice.

"So, is that what's bothering you? Erica Kealey? She's your reason for turning up on my doorstep – sort of." She gestured to the four-star hotel suite. "Do you still love her?"

"Yes, and no. I had the Hollywood bug, didn't I? We're so rich, so independent, we can leave a relationship at a drop of a hat. See it happening all the time." Steve looked at his sister, and sighed angrily. *Perfection* had given him millionaire status, but even before that, his income had been increasing nicely over the past few years. From years of struggling, he'd gone to the other end of the scale. "I had hoped I'd be married when success knocked on my door. How am I going to find someone to settle down with now?"

Ruby frowned. "You want to settle down?"

"Yes, of course. Why is it so hard to believe I don't want to play the field? I want to find love. Real love – like our mum and dad had." He ran his hand through his hair. "Maybe I'm being stupid—"

"Ha! I didn't say that."

Steve scowled at her interruption. She buttoned her lips then sat rock still. "I want to find a woman who wants to get married and have kids. I want a family, like we grew up in. If I fall for an actress, she's as busy as me, we have no time for one another, and then there's the added stress of neither of us really committing. I mean it's so easy to get out of a relationship in Hollywood rather than actually work at it." He sipped his scotch, and slouched further on the couch, sighing heavily. "I want a marriage where we don't need to discuss pre-nups."

"You'd need to do that whether you married Miss Plain Jane or not. Otherwise they could take you to the cleaners."

"Exactly! If I say who I really am, how do I know someone's marrying me for *me*, and not my money? Not the person they see in the press. I need them to fall in love without all that getting in the way."

Ruby chewed her lip, as if in deep concentration. Steve watched, depression deepening. Telling Ruby hadn't lightened the weight on his shoulders as he'd hoped, just darkened his thoughts. He realised that he might not ever find the perfect woman. He was destined for a life of one Hollywood romance after another – and oh, how the press would love the gossip. It would be okay, but he was thirty-five now, and ready to settle down. He didn't want to grow old and lonely. He wanted to find someone he could share his life with, as his mother and father had done.

Maybe Ruby didn't remember, but their parents had been so in love. To this day, he remembered the tears his mother shed over their father's grave.

"I've got it." Ruby nudged him, shaking him out of his reverie. "What you need to do is be normal for a while."

"Normal?"

"Yeah, be normal – like me."

Steve raised his eyebrows. "You? Normal?"

Ruby scowled and nudged him with her elbow. "You know what I mean. Maybe if you take away your money, and flash looks, you might find someone."

"But won't I get recognised?"

"In London maybe, but here in Bristol... You can get a haircut," she combed her fingers through his Hollywood hair, "lose the designer stubble, maybe we can get you some glasses." She wiggled her finger at him.

"Like a disguise?" he asked warily.

"Yeah!" Ruby sounded excited, chirping up, almost bouncing off her seat. "Some people are going to say you look like you, but you can deny it. Change your clothes – you can't wear Armani."

"Not sure I like *that* idea."

"If you want to fit in, and be *normal*," she quoted with her fingers, "and want someone to love you for *who* you are, not *what* you are, you're going to need to make some changes. And don't flash your money around."

"Hmmm... I'm seeing your point of view here."

"You'll need to get a job, because sitting around in a fancy hotel isn't going to work either."

"Yeah, I could get a job." But how? Steve rubbed the stubble on his chin.

Ruby frowned. "Interviews are tough though, everyone will need references."

"What about where you work, could you get me a job?" He smiled his Hollywood smile, looking her in the eye, knowing the true effect of his blue eyes – it always worked.

"That smile and those eyes don't work on me. I'm your sister, remember?"

Hmm... He'd forgotten his sister was immune to him trying to get his own way. "But as I'm your brother, you could get me a job?"

Some time ago, he'd received a letter, an update from Ruby. She'd told him about her life and work, how she was happy running a small hotel on the outskirts of Bristol.

Managing meant hiring and firing, right?

She let out a deep breath. "Yes, I could get you a job, I suppose. But it's only a small hotel; we don't really need anyone at the moment—"

"I don't need paying, just get me in so I'm doing something – meeting people, making friends."

"Sure," Ruby said, mimicking an American accent with a sly smile.

"Stop doing that!"

"What?" She did it again, drawing out the word in an American accent. A poor American accent, Steve might add.

"I don't sound like that."

"Yeah, you do."

"It's not funny, Ruby." He looked at her sternly, giving her the 'big brother hating being teased by his little sister' glare.

"I'm sorry, but you sound all American," she reverted to her

Bristol tone, laughing. She nudged him. "So how long can you stay in the UK?"

"Three months – max! I've got three months to find the woman of my dreams, then I'm back to Hollywood."

"Make the most of tonight." She chinked her glass of orange juice against his tumbler of scotch. "It's your last night as a Hollywood hunk."

Chapter 2

Steve cupped Erica's face, his thumb gently rubbing her cheek. Out the corner of his eye, he could see on the horizon the dust rising into the sky. Flores and his men were coming. He shoved the car into drive, and was about to kiss those perfect, ripe lips, when his phone started ringing.

He didn't have his phone – did he? That wasn't in the script.

The image of Erica disappeared as he fumbled for his phone on the bedside cabinet.

"Hello," he said gruffly, his voice not quite woken up.

"Right, I'm coming to get you. I've been thinking about this all night. The longer you stay there, the quicker you'll get found out. And once the press find you, then we can't do this."

"Can't do what?"

"You know! But you can't stay in the hotel. Someone is bound to blab."

"Ruby, what time is it?" Steve rubbed his eyes. He was semi-aroused, dreaming of Erica. Luckily, he softened with reality, and his sister's voice.

"It's seven a.m. Not that early. I've managed to get the day off work, so make the most of it. Get dressed, and get packed, I'll be there in twenty minutes."

She'd hung up before he could argue. Last night, Ruby had left him full of ideas on how he could become *normal*, and he'd gone to bed, nicely warmed by the scotch inside him, wondering whether he would actually find the woman of his dreams while here in the UK. He'd told Ruby he could stay for three months – maximum. He'd have to return sometime in January. The Oscars were in February – he'd have to be back for those, and then the filming for his new movie would start after. However, his agent, Karl, still expected him back in LA in two weeks' time... Steve would worry about that later. He'd make sure Marie cleared his diary.

This meant he had until the end of January to find the perfect woman.

But he didn't want perfect. 'Perfect' he could pick up in Hollywood tomorrow. He wanted someone who didn't have to look immaculate every time she stepped out of her front door, didn't need to worry about image – at least no more than the next woman did. Erica had been perfect, and look what had happened there. Every day she'd worried about her dress size and what she ate, following a special diet. Dinner in a restaurant had been hard work at times. No, he wanted to find someone ordinary, normal, who he could settle down with. Someone he could love, and who would love him back.

Steve wanted all the things his mum and dad had had. He wasn't looking at this with rose tinted glasses either. He remembered their arguments, the tough times, more than Ruby would, but they'd always come out the other side, still in love. Dad coming home with flowers to apologise, Mum baking Dad's favourite lemon drizzle cake. He had fond memories of his mother standing at the sink doing the washing up, soap suds to her elbows and Dad surprising her from behind, kissing and hugging her.

He jumped out of bed and slipped on his clothes. The scruffier he looked, the better. He'd grab a shower at Ruby's. Rubbing the sleep out of his eyes, and combing a hand through his hair, he looked in the mirror and decided he'd do. Luckily, he hadn't unpacked much, so he was ready by the time Ruby knocked on his door.

Steve checked out quickly and as discreetly as possible, and was soon dragging his case behind him, out into the grey British rain, towards Ruby's waiting car. Somehow, after Ruby had thrown some carrier bags of shopping (new shoes and clothes) into the back seats, his luggage fitted into the small trunk – thank heavens he'd packed light.

With the two of them in the car, the front screen misted up quickly. Ruby switched on the blowers and eventually they blew out warm air. Thanks to the typical British weather, he hadn't seen the sun once since landing at Heathrow. He squashed the thought of missing the LA warmth quickly. This is what he wanted; to come home. He'd just forgotten how miserable the weather could be, he thought, tousling his hair to remove the rainwater. Used to the leg space in limousines, Steve sat cramped in Ruby's little car – he could almost touch his ears with his knees.

Okay, note to self; for her next birthday buy Ruby a bigger car.

"So, where am I going to stay, if I can't stay in a hotel?" Steve said, as he adjusted the car seat for some leg room. Instead, the chair tilted, throwing him back. Cursing under his breath, while Ruby giggled, he up-righted himself and worked out the seat eventually.

"You can stay with me."

He looked at her, surprised, his eyebrows raised.

"Don't look at me like that. I could change my mind," Ruby said, taking her eyes off the road for a second.

"I thought maybe I could stay at your hotel."

Ruby shook her head. "No, it's too small, we'll need the rooms. I'm taking a big risk as it is, and I don't want the staff questioning it. I've got a spare room, so you can crash there. It'll be the safest place for you."

"Can I shower there, too? You didn't exactly give me time."

"Sure, we'll drop your stuff off, have some breakfast then head for the Mall at Cribbs Causeway – it's got everything under one roof, even hairdressers."

Steve really didn't like how she kept mentioning hairdressers.

She grinned, stunning Steve by how much she reminded him of their mother. The last time he'd seen Ruby, she'd had mousy long hair. Now, it was cut short with hints of gold and blonde flattering her face and showing off her delicate ears and slender neck. His sister had turned into a woman, a very pretty one – if he looked at her objectively – and he'd never really seen the transformation. His mother had regularly sent updates, photos, but those had stopped when she'd died, and even they were nothing like seeing the real thing.

With eight years between them, he'd always been Ruby's really big brother. She'd been only twelve when he'd left home to find fame and stardom. A slight, skinny girl. Now, she had womanly curves, confidence, and a cheeky sense of humour – God, he was going to find it hard to meet her boyfriend and not give him the third degree. She didn't talk to Steve like she was on eggshells either – in fact she was bossing him about. She acted normal around him exactly how a sister should. His celebrity status meant nothing to her. It felt fantastic. He was breathing again, relaxing. He could fart and it wouldn't make front page news. He realised Ruby was one of the few people in his life he could trust.

She pulled up onto her small driveway and they both got out. He gazed up at the house.

"It's not much, just a two-bed end terrace, but it does me," Ruby said, opening the front door.

"Why don't you stay at Mum's – your home?" He looked around, frowning. The stairs were immediately in front of them, a small hallway with just enough floor space to dump shoes and her bag. He remembered something mentioned in an email about her moving out of the family home, but at the time he'd been too busy to persuade her not to. He hated the idea of selling it, so he'd employed contractors to oversee the maintenance of the house, through Marie, and the furniture had gone into storage, the house remaining empty.

"Because it was too big for just me to rattle around in, and besides ..." Her voice faltered and she ran up the stairs. He followed, lugging his case and holdall.

"Besides, what? I'd pay the bills, Ruby, if it got too much. That's why I sent you money."

"It wasn't that, Steve. There were too many memories of Mum. I found it too upsetting." She didn't look him in the eye, but showed him to the room at the front of the house. "This is my spare room, you can sleep here. I cleared it out last night."

He wouldn't push her about the house, their family home, for now. Instead he studied his new home, a pale-yellow box room, containing a futon along the side wall – *at least it was a double* – and on the other, a small desk where Ruby's computer sat, and a wardrobe. His bathroom back in LA was bigger than this, but he would make do. His heart lightened at the sight of family photographs in different frames hung on the wall in a higgledy-piggledy fashion.

Mum, and occasionally Dad; Ruby, growing up slowly, some with her teenage friends. Steve was in some of them, but he noticed, like his father, he wasn't in as many as Mum and Ruby. His presence was missing. His father couldn't be helped, he'd been dead twenty-odd years. As for Steve...

"Right, I'll let you get settled in. I keep the duvet and pillows in the wardrobe." Ruby pointed to the pine wardrobe. "I'll go and put the kettle on." She thudded back down the stairs, and Steve stowed his case between the wardrobe and desk where it fitted neatly. He opened the wardrobe, and there were pillows and a duvet, and clean sheets on the shelf above the rail. Only a couple of items were hung up – coats mainly. There was enough room for him to hang his clothes. He'd unpack and pull the futon out tonight. He looked out the window, seeing the street below – still raining. It looked a quiet neighbourhood, similar style houses to Ruby's lining the street. At least Ruby hadn't moved out of the area, had stayed around Westbury-on-Trim where they'd both grown up.

Checking he had his wallet, phone and his sunglasses inside his leather jacket, he headed back down the stairs to the smell of toast.

"Jam or marmalade?" Ruby called out.

"Marmalade, please." *No pancakes and bacon with maple syrup here.*

Ruby's kitchen was small, so he took a seat at her dining table. The lounge-diner was a good size, for someone living on their own. Behind the three-seater sofa, a wall of books and CDs stood in a large shelving unit. Ruby had always had her nose in a book from an early age, but when he'd left home, she'd just been finding music, much to Mum's annoyance.

He could fit this whole house in his living room. He hadn't lived in his apartment quite a year yet, but it was amazing how he'd got used to the space.

He was having a wake-up call to normality.

He remembered how, as his money poured in from the increasing film work, and the fame too, he'd instantly needed a more secure apartment. Being famous had its drawbacks. When your face is plastered over a movie screen, and then glossy magazines, women fall in love with your character, or you. It could get a bit scary in public – as he was starting to find out. He'd thought he was used to female attention – and had a rude awakening. It very soon became apparent he needed a bodyguard, to stop the girls from hurling themselves at him.

Hopefully, now in England, he'd left the crazies behind.

Hopefully.

Ruby plonked a plate of marmalade on toast in front of him, and a cup of black coffee. She came out with the sugar bowl and milk jug. He frowned.

"You don't have to do anything special for me."

"Don't get too excited, it's instant." Ruby held her hand up in defence, noticing Steve's look of distaste. "Hey, you sprung this on me. If you'd called, I'd have got stuff in special, proper coffee, even baked a cake."

Steve poured some milk into his coffee mug, and took a sip. It was wet and warm at least.

"But I wasn't sure how you liked it, or what you were used to. You're not some weird celebrity with silly OCDs now, are you? You don't have to wash your hands every time you touch something?"

He laughed, putting the mug down. "No, but I always wash my hands after using the bathroom."

"You never used to! Not as a teenager, anyway."

"Please don't tell the press."

"It'll cost you."

Then, there was an awkward silence, as though their joking had run out of fizz. Like they didn't really know what to say to one another. Strangers.

"God, I've missed you," she said, as if reading Steve's mind, wanting to remove their silence. Ruby threw her arms around his neck, and he hugged her back, surprised by her sudden outburst.

"I've missed you too, Roo."

She smiled. "Right, enough of the soppiness, we need to get you transformed." She let go of him. There was a brief change in her expression as she regained composure, and then she finished her own toast.

"Is this really going to work?" He wasn't liking the word *transformed*.

"Yes, I'm positive. As long as you stick to the rules, and keep your head down, it should be fine." Steve frowned as she spoke. "It worked for Clark Kent, it can work for you."

"This is how I'm going to find my Lois, huh?"

"Absolutely." Then, she looked him up and down, hand to her chin, contemplatively. "Hmmm... take your watch off."

"What?"

"It looks expensive. I don't doubt it is expensive. So take it off. You're hardly going to blend in wearing a watch that costs more than most people's wages. This is about changing your image. We'll buy another one later."

Steve did as he was told and removed his Jaeger-LeCoultre watch, sighing heavily. Luckily, he'd pulled on some jeans, a T-shirt and his leather jacket, trying to make sure he didn't stand out.

"And you better lose the designer stubble."

"Hey, I can't help the shadow. Something Dad passed on to me."

"Well, you're going to have to shave regularly – not once every five days."

"I could do with a shower," he hinted.

"Okay, grab a towel from the airing cupboard, I'll clear this lot up – and make sure you shave," she said sternly.

"Yeah, yeah."

Steve quickly finished his toast and took his coffee with him. When he returned thirty minutes later, clean-shaven, Ruby had cleared the breakfast things and had her hands in the sink, washing up. Her tiny kitchen had no space for a dishwasher it seemed. He dumped his dirty mug into the washing up bowl and she cleaned it, putting it on the draining board with the rest of the things. Drying her hands, she gave Steve another look up and down.

"Okay, you'll do for now. Let's go shopping."

He couldn't remember Ruby being so bossy. He was starting to think it wasn't a good thing.

Chapter 3

The first thing Ruby did was park up in the high street and took Steve to a cash point. "Take as much out as you can. The less you use your credit card the better – it's got your name on it, I assume."

"Yeah ..."

"Right, well, we don't need someone questioning anything, so use cash."

When had she got so bright, so street-wise, so mistrustful? Had she watched too many thriller movies? Next she'd be donning dark glasses and constantly looking over her shoulder.

"How much am I going to need?" he said, pulling out his wallet.

Ruby put her hand on her hip, and looked again at Steve, speculatively. He could almost see the cogs turning as she worked it out. "Well, you're going to need a new wardrobe, haircut, *and* you can buy me lunch." She grinned, flashing her straight, white teeth. *Wasn't he supposed to be the one with the persuasive smile?*

Once he'd withdrawn his maximum cash limit, from two credit cards, Ruby grabbed his arm, and they walked down the quiet high street. Steve secured his favourite, well-worn LA baseball cap on his head. He found that if he kept his nose to the ground the cap hid his face well.

"First things first, let's fix your hair before we head over to Cribbs."

"I like my hair."

"Yes, but it looks very Steve Mason," she said, lowering her voice when she got to his name. "We need to change your image from gorgeous actor to mediocre man."

Steve frowned warily.

"It's nice, bit longer than the last time I saw you. Maybe we need a short back and sides."

"But I've got a film in three months."

"It's hair! It'll grow back. Trust me."

"Why don't we get a bowl and just cut round that," Steve said dryly.

"Don't tempt me. But we do need to keep you semi-respectable otherwise you won't attract anyone." She dragged him towards a hairdressers. She walked inside then stopped. He'd seen it too. He tugged the cap down further over his face. A coffee table laden with glossy magazines, old issues – one with Steve Mason on the front page with Erica Kealey. Giving Steve an apologetic smile, Ruby pulled on his arm and they walked back out before anyone noticed, and continued further down the high street – Steve more sombre than Ruby – to a barbershop. Men only. No glossy magazines, and if there were, it would be cars, cars, cars. And the odd issue of *Nuts*.

Did he really have to cut his hair? He'd grown it for his last movie, where he needed to play the smooth hero. It was around the nape of his neck, and if un-gelled like today, it had a mad unkempt look.

"Isn't there somewhere more... designer?" Steve swallowed, looking up at the barber's sign over the door – specifying cheap cuts. Would they make a mess of his beautiful hair? He liked his hair – just the way it was. He had a particular barber he visited in LA who he trusted, who cut his hair the way Steve preferred. It cost him but he didn't care.

"There's nothing wrong with this place." Ruby grabbed his arm.

"And you know this because...?"

"Friends come here all the time." Steve raised his eyebrows. "Male friends. It's got a good reputation, honest. But anyway, we're not really here to get you a good haircut. Just a haircut. The worse it looks, actually, the better."

Steve's mouth fell open. *How would looking bad help him find the woman of his dreams?* But before he could reply, Ruby tugged him into the barbers, and smiled at the young man behind the desk.

"Haircut for my brother, please. Nice and short, and maybe spiky on top. Nothing too fashionable." Ruby's expression was stern, and the young man in his early twenties with pristine, gelled black hair looked at her as if she was mad. Ruby might as well have asked for the clippers to do the job herself. Then, the man gave an inquisitive glance towards Steve. Would he recognise him, or not believe his luck? Sometimes people could be too gobsmacked or embarrassed to ask.

Steve rolled his eyes, not wanting to let the guy dwell on who he was. The quicker he was in and out of this place the better. He hoped.

"Do as she says, otherwise we'll both be paying for it." Pulling the baseball cap off, he slumped into a chair, faced the mirror, and the man placed a gown around him. Remembering the happy photograph he'd just seen of himself and Erica smiling blissfully, reminded Steve why he was doing this. Ruby was right; the hair would grow back. It was a small price to pay if he did find true love.

Very quickly, Steve watched the hair he'd grown slowly come off. It wasn't long as in trailing down his back, but it had a mature length to it. The natural wave was starting to show now it had some length. Slicked back or left a little unkempt, he had a good head of hair. It was cut and styled with scissors rather than, as the young barber was currently doing, using clippers. He was getting a 'short, back and sides' like his own father used to order when he was a boy.

The barber worked in silence. Usually there would have been banter, but with Ruby standing there, her arms crossed and expression firm, he probably didn't dare make light conversation. Steve kept quiet too, for fear of giving the game away and he watched his transforming image in despair.

With every buzz of the clippers, Steve felt sickened. A couple of years ago someone in the industry had advised Steve to grow his hair, and by doing so he'd been surprised that instantly he seemed to become popular in Hollywood. He'd lost his boyish looks and become rougher, a harder looking, mature man. Something the filmmakers wanted. The roles he was offered changed, or the ones he went for, he got. No longer the supporting role, he'd become the leading hero.

And he'd always liked how Erica used to run her hands through it while they made love...

"Oh, and thin it out a little, so it's not so thick," Ruby added, hovering over the poor guy who clipped and cut his way through Steve's light-brown hair. "I was wondering if you should have some highlights—"

"Highlights?"

The barber jumped back at Steve's outburst, apologising for nearly cutting Steve's ear.

"But it's lightening up as he's using the thinning scissors on it. Relax, Bro." She nudged Steve, and he gave her his best-unimpressed smile. He noticed she hadn't called him Steve once in front of the barber or the other salon workers.

Once the barber had finished, he stood behind Steve with a mirror so that he could see the back of his head. Steve looked at his reflection properly for the first time throughout the ordeal. His slightly longer, wavy crop was gone and in its place a shorter, choppier style that did indeed transform him. Whether it was the sort of transformation he wanted he wasn't entirely sure.

He paid for his haircut, plus some hair wax Ruby insisted he purchase, tipped the guy (he deserved it for tolerating Ruby) and they walked out. Weirdly, his head felt lighter by the lack of hair. He could also feel the bitter cold wind around his neck and ears more so. At least it had stopped raining. He went to put his hand through his hair and quickly stopped as soon as he felt the gel.

"You do actually look younger," Ruby said. They headed back towards her car.

Steve scowled. Was this really going to be worth it? Would he really find his not-so-perfect woman in three months? "Man, I had it like this about three years ago when I was in a sitcom."

"*Man, I had it like this about three years ago when I was in a sitcom*," Ruby mimicked his accent.

"Shut up."

"Shudd-up," Ruby did it again and giggled, but Steve scowled.

Steve could not help glancing in shop windows as they walked, catching his reflection, his new look.

"Your hair will grow back. You didn't actually have that much cut off. It's only about an inch in places, two maybe on top." Ruby sighed. "The way you're looking at me it's as if I asked you to have a number one all over."

"I can't believe I paid eight bucks—"

"Pounds—"

"For a haircut," Steve continued, ignoring Ruby's correction.

"Oh, how the other half live," she said. "Having a cheap haircut makes you normal. Now stop complaining. Let's buy you some clothes. You can't go around in your designer gear. You're looking too trendy."

"I like some of my *designer* gear."

"You can't wear it, or if you do, tell people it's fake."

Crammed back into Ruby's car – Steve really was contemplating buying her something bigger, possibly today – she drove them to the Mall at Cribbs Causeway on the M5. Two floors of wall-to-wall high street shops, with a light and airy feel from the glass rooftop. It was unbelievable that when he'd left for LA, fifteen years ago, this building had just opened. He'd only seen the development phase. Steve admired the tall palm trees as he walked past the shops, reminding him of California, where they could grow that tall without being under glass.

They hit the shops, thumbing through T-shirts, shirts, jeans, everything on a hanger. Ruby had bypassed some of the fashionable shops advertising designer labels, in search for the cheaper stores.

"Pick out what you like. Remember you could be staying for a while. You need a new wardrobe."

Ruby had picked him out a new watch, which cost all of twenty-five pounds, and insisted on a pair of sunglasses. They were in the sale as it was October. He had sarcastically argued he didn't really need a pair.

"But you can't wear the ones you do – even driving. Says film star all over them."

"I won't need sunglasses. I haven't even seen the sun yet."

"This time of year, the sun is really low – when it does come out – so actually you will."

He'd agreed, handed over the cash, luckily no customer assistants asked any questions. In fact, at one point he thought he saw empathy in one guy. He must have thought Ruby's henpecking intolerable, however Steve, for some reason, enjoyed his sister's fuss, even if she was overbearing. Any other woman would not be getting away with this sort of behaviour, obviously, but as it was Ruby and she seemed happy to boss him about, he let her.

He had fifteen years to make up for.

Although, buried resentment reminded him he hadn't altogether forgiven Ruby yet. But today wasn't the time to dwell. They were all that was left of their family. And she was doing him a favour.

He just didn't like how she was taking pleasure in it. She was way too smug. This had better work.

Laden with the bags containing Steve's new wardrobe, Ruby stopped abruptly, looking at a dress in a shop window and sighed. Maybe it was time to make it up to her the only way he knew how.

Build a few bridges, Steve.

"Come on, all this shopping was for me; I'll treat you now."

"Oh, no, you don't have to."

"Yes I do." Steve grabbed her elbow, and escorted her into the shop. Twenty minutes later – Ruby had tried on a few dresses in the end – they left the shop, Ruby grinning gleefully.

"'Oh, you don't have to,'" Steve said sarcasm lacing his words, "'but is it okay if I try on this one, and this one and this one?'"

Ruby elbowed him playfully in the ribs. "Thank you, I'm very grateful. I'm not used to being spoilt."

Steve winked. "Not a problem, Roo."

"Just don't make a habit of flashing your money around though," she said more sternly.

"Okay," he said, then mumbled, "I try to do a nice thing…"

"You were nice, now how about a coffee. I'm all shopped out and need a rest."

Steve couldn't agree more. The jet lag was catching up with him. He needed a boost.

They stopped at a coffee shop in the middle of the Mall which had a seating area under the escalators.

Steve chose a table tucked away, while Ruby ordered the coffees. He grew anxious as he looked at the clothes in the bags. If the press got hold of this, would they make it out as an early midlife crisis on his part? He started to imagine the headlines; 'Mediocre Man Mason.'

Steve watched the shoppers passing him by. No one was taking a blind bit of notice of him. Maybe the people of Bristol were less likely to believe a Hollywood star would be right under their nose, whereas in London his cover could have easily been blown.

He wouldn't get too excited yet. This was the first day. If he did get discovered, he'd have to say goodbye to Ruby, or she'd be swept up in it all. Luckily, he'd changed his name to his mum's maiden name as he tried the rounds in Hollywood. An agent had suggested that Mason had a better ring to it than Fisher. This helped Mum and Ruby, when things had started to warm up for Steve on the fame front. They were able to keep a low profile, without being

34

instantaneously linked to the new actor on the scene. It helped they lived in the UK, too. But he'd kept them private as much as he could and it seemed to work. Ruby had led a normal life as far as he could tell.

Although, was she happy with this normal life? He'd ask her one day. Today she was too keen to be his personal shopper.

"Large cappuccino for you, skinny vanilla latte for me." Ruby placed the coffees on the table. "We'll have these, shop some more, then you can buy me lunch." She grinned.

"I was hoping you'd say we could go home. Haven't I got enough clothes? I don't have to get them all today."

"Oh no, the next stop is the opticians."

"I don't need glasses."

"You do now."

She sipped her coffee, and winced, it was still too hot. He'd tested his own, but could drink it napalm. His mother had always said he had an asbestos mouth, drinking tea practically from the kettle. Fascinated, he watched Ruby stir her latte.

"What? Have I got milk on my lip or something?"

He laughed. "No. You just remind me so much of Mum."

"I do?"

"Yes, your mannerisms, the facial expressions. Your eyes."

"Yeah, they're this a dull sludge colour, great."

"They're green. They're not dull."

"So where'd you get the pretty eyes from, huh?" She was referring to the light blue eyes that had now become one of his assets as an actor. That and his smile. Oh, he knew if he looked some women straight in the eye, he saw an instant transformation from calm and collected to a nervous jelly mess. He'd seen the state it could create a thousand times. Especially now he was Steve Mason – the Actor and Hollywood Hunk. He'd learnt in his teens he could make girls giggly and shy. He even used his eyes on his own mother to get away with murder.

"Dad, apparently," he said. That's what his mother used to say;

he was the spitting image of his father.

"Great, Dad passes on the pretty eye gene to just you," she said, cupping her latte glass and pouting.

"Your eyes are pretty."

Ruby snorted. "They don't sparkle like yours. So annoying! And don't look at me like that, either." She wagged her finger. "It won't wash with me. And don't forget it."

They people-watched while finishing their coffees.

"Shall we go?" Ruby said, draining the last of her drink and pushing the cup away.

"Damn it, when did you get so bossy?"

The next thing Steve knew he was being lead into an opticians.

"We need glasses," Ruby said to an assistant that approached her. She was a pretty blonde, who immediately took a shine to Steve who was trying on different pairs of glasses.

"Aren't you—?"

"No!" Steve laughed it off, keeping a pair of frames on his face.

"He gets that all the time." Ruby stood in between them. "That's why we were thinking some glasses."

"Do you need your eyes tested?"

"Nothing wrong with my eyes, twenty-twenty vision," Steve said, beaming his million-dollar smile at her. Ruby pinched him. He rubbed his arm, scowling at Ruby, then looked back to the assistant. "I've got a job interview, thought glasses would make me look more professional."

The assistant nodded. If she believed that, she'd believe anything.

"Here, try these." Ruby picked out a pair of glasses, thin silver frames and handed them to him. He put them on, looked in the mirror, then looked at her, she frowned. "Hmmm... Not enough."

"Remind me why I'm doing this again?" he said quietly so only Ruby could hear.

"Clark Kent." Ruby pushed another pair into his hands, putting the other pair back. "No one realised he was Superman, did they? Not even Lois." She whipped the next pair of glasses off his face.

"Not nerdy enough."

She found another pair. Steve knew what she was doing; she was trying to find frames that didn't quite suit him, yet didn't want them to look so ridiculous no one would fancy him. He put the glasses on. They were bigger frames, though fashionable, but they didn't quite complement his face, so would hide his looks, at least a little. His heart still palpitated every time he glimpsed his new haircut in the mirror, let alone the spectacles on his face. What *was* he doing?

Early mid-life crisis was definitely what it looked like. The press could not get wind of this.

"Perfect!" Ruby clapped her hands together. "Can we buy these, please?" she said, approaching the assistant, who'd watched dumb-founded for the last ten minutes. She'd tried helping but Ruby hadn't allowed her to express her expert opinion. The assistant's face said it all. These glasses were all wrong, which meant they were right for their purpose.

"Well, uh, they're our display." The assistant hesitated. "It takes a few days for them to come through usually—"

"We were hoping to take them today – as he only needs plain lenses."

Steve got out his wallet, pulling out twenties. "Here," he said, winking at the assistant, young enough to use his blue-eyed charm on, plus she wasn't his sister. "I'm sure this will do it. Just not a word now." He tapped his nose.

"Okay, okay." *Works every time.* The assistant hurried off, ran it through the till, having a word with the manager. She put the glasses in a case and handed them to Steve, keeping hold of his hand for a brief moment.

"You know, I'm free tonight—"

"I'm sorry, but he's gay." Ruby rushed in, grabbing Steve's arm. The assistant looked taken back.

"What?" Steve said, astounded.

"Come on, Bro," Ruby said sternly. "Bruno's waiting for you."

"Bruno?" Steve mouthed, still wearing a confused expression.

Immediately leaving the opticians shop, Ruby took the glasses out of the case and started cleaning them and removing the tags. "Put these on."

"Now?"

"No, next week." She rolled her eyes. "Yes, she was on to you then."

"I thought this whole idea was for me to find a date."

"You can't start using your charm like that. Not until we've fully agreed on your identity."

Steve's phone buzzed inside his pocket, he pulled it out, frowned and shoved it back. He'd deal with messages later.

"Phone!" Ruby said, stopping abruptly, holding a shopping-bag-laden hand in the air, as if pointing to a light bulb appearing above her head. "We'd better get you a phone. Nothing too fancy mind, but you're going to need to give out your phone number, and you don't want to give out that one." She tapped his arm, pointing to a phone shop ahead. "Get a pay as you go. That'll do you."

Twenty-five minutes, and some mild arguing later, Steve walked out of the shop with a brand new phone. Nothing too flash, as Ruby had insisted, something to make calls and take text messages. Ruby strolled behind him with a satisfied grin. Steve had wanted the all singing and dancing latest smart phone – even he didn't have it yet – but Ruby had a point. Unfortunately.

"You want someone to think you're poor and still love you, right?"

"Why did I let you talk me into this?" Steve muttered, momentarily annoyed by her smug happiness. He stood in the middle of the Cribbs, by the fountain, trying to work out his new phone and put Ruby's number in it. Ruby threw a coin into the fountain and closed her eyes. He hoped she was wishing this plan of hers would work.

Ruby nudged him. "Oh and, you know, I was thinking, you've got to ditch your accent."

"I've worked fifteen years to get this accent. I have to sound American, only way to get the best parts, *kid*."

"Hugh Grant does okay."

"Hugh Grant gets typecast."

"Point taken." She nodded. "But you still need to lose it. Otherwise they won't believe you're not Steve Mason. You're an actor, act British. Or something." She waved her hands in frustration. "Pretend this is your next big role."

"Okay, okay, I'll try. I'm sure hanging around you will bring my accent back slowly." *Plus make me swear profusely.*

"You say it as if it's a bad thing."

He wrapped his arm around her shoulder, and hugged her closer. "No, it's far from a bad thing. I just can't believe my baby sister has grown up... to someone really bossy."

"I'm assertive, not bossy." She elbowed him in the ribs, and he groaned.

"Right, yes, assertive. So where am I taking you to lunch?"

Chapter 4

With paranoia setting in, Ruby decided to leave the Mall for lunch and drove Steve to her favourite local café.

They were sitting in a corner making idle chit-chat whilst perusing the menu. Ruby had checked out the dessert menu first – as well as the cake options deliciously displayed on the counter. It always helped her choose what she wanted as a main. The café was quiet, with hardly any customers, which she hoped meant fewer chances of someone realising who Steve really was.

Would he fly straight back to LA if he was spotted? She liked him being here; it had been so long. She was trying to hold in some of her excitement at having her brother back in her life, for fear of scaring him away. She hadn't believed it was Steve on the phone until she'd seen him in the flesh at the hotel, but she needed to rein in her forceful nature, otherwise surely he'd up and leave? Was he used to being talked to like this? Hollywood-bred divas were not used to being told *no*. Would Steve be the same?

She couldn't help it, this is what she'd become. At work, she played her role firm but fair. She couldn't afford to look weak; if her staff didn't keep the hotel residents happy, she was just as likely to lose her job as any of the others.

Since her mum had died she had no one else but herself, so she'd toughened herself up and didn't take shit – this part she stuck to particularly after a few failed relationships with lousy boyfriends.

She watched as Steve turned over the menu, looking at the choices, utterly relaxed. He appeared down to earth and laid back, like he'd been as a teenager, so maybe Hollywood hadn't *ruined* him yet.

Steve looked up, catching her staring. "What?"

"Nothing," Ruby said, smiling. "Can't believe you're really here, that's all."

The waitress approached the table and took their order, placing two glasses of iced water down that they'd ordered when first seated. Steve had probably been a bit Hollywood Diva-ish insisting on the slice of lemon. At least he hadn't insisted on it being sparkling. This kind of café served water from the tap unless you were willing to pay for a bottle. Ruby felt strongly that there was nothing wrong with tap water, so why buy it? Even in the restaurant at the hotel she insisted on jugs of water being made available at the table. Admittedly, they did have ice and lemon too.

Once the waitress left, Steve sipped his water, then sighed with a frown, and said quietly, "Sometimes, Ruby, I think there is a price to pay for fame. It's called loneliness."

"Wow, you have got it bad," Ruby said, tucking the menu back into its holder to tidy the table.

"I'm happy, don't get me wrong. My dream came true and I've found success."

"But?"

"I'm not where I thought I'd be with life. You know… kids, family, a wife."

"Maybe you can't have both."

"I want to say nonsense, but now money and fame has arrived, maybe it's true."

Steve's success had started slowly, with minor character roles in television programmes, bigger parts started coming his way. Heavens, Mum and Ruby hadn't realised how famous he would get. Their mum had died before the release of *Perfection*, and the interviews on chat shows and in glossy magazines had intensified. Ruby was reminded of him very often, though eventually she'd stopped watching or reading, because she didn't like what she read. It impaired the memory she had of her big brother, her hero.

As Steve had become more successful, Ruby remembered Mum had wanted the family to stay out of the limelight. At the time, Ruby hadn't realised why. At the grand age of twelve, she'd boasted to school friends about her big brother going off to Hollywood to become an actor, and as he'd got small parts, usually in adverts, she'd shared the news. Good job that was before Facebook and Twitter. Those days, as a proud teenager, she wanted to stand in Cribbs Causeway with a megaphone, telling everyone who her brother was because she'd been so thrilled for him, but as Steve was finding now, she'd learnt people weren't always true to you. They could have a hidden agenda.

Fortunately, she'd lost touch with most of her school friends now – she wasn't a major fan of social media, not after Terry – so no one would know about Steve. Nowadays she didn't tell people she was the sister of *the* Steve Mason – she'd learnt the hard way. The people she worked with certainly weren't aware. As Steve understood, it was hard to trust people if they knew you were related to someone rich and famous. Were they hanging around because they liked you, or wanted to meet your brother?

She'd had her fingers burnt good and proper only two years ago in the early years of Steve's fame. He knew nothing about it and she wanted to keep it that way. Bitterness still lingered in her heart over that sordid affair – how naïve she'd been. It grated on her to this day, the memory of her stupidity. She wouldn't fall for it again.

Now, regretfully, she also carried a smidge of jealousy. He'd been able to follow his dream. Ruby had not – not that she truly knew what she wanted to do. When she'd felt ready to start her own adventure, Mum had got ill.

And now they were together, changing Steve's image, trying to make him fit in, so he might stand a chance of finding someone to love. Maybe there was nothing to be jealous about?

"So what type of girl are you looking for?"

"I don't know." Steve shrugged, leaning on the table. "Someone I can take to a restaurant who doesn't have to order salad so she can stay a size zero." Steve quickly held up his hands defensively as Ruby stared, reproachful. "Sorry, I don't mean it like that. Don't get me wrong, I know that actresses work hard and it's a major pressure for them. I have that pressure too, but nowhere near the same level. I suppose, what I'm trying to say is, I want to find someone who doesn't have to worry about appearing 'perfect.'"

"Okay, fair point." Ruby nodded. Strict diets and no chocolate for life were not her idea of fun, she thought as she eyed the scrumptious chocolate fudge cake at the counter. And the size of the door-stop sandwiches heading towards them were not for the strict dieters either. *Imagine the carbs.*

The waitress placed the sandwiches in front of them, with salad and a pile of crisps on the side.

Steve smiled his thanks at her, then when she'd gone continued the conversation with Ruby, "I want a woman I can laugh with, too. A good hearty giggle. About silly stuff."

"A woman with curves, and a good sense of humour," Ruby said aloud, as well as making mental notes.

"Of course."

"How fussy are you? Does she have to be pretty? Because you're not going to find that many gorgeous girls to sweep you off your feet in Bristol," Ruby joked. "Yes, there are plenty of attractive women, but we can't all afford to have impeccable beauty treatments."

Steve shook his head. "I know. There are immaculately groomed women lining the streets of LA but none are suitable." He sighed. "There has to be an attraction, obviously, but I want someone I can ... love, and who'll love me. And maybe start a family."

"Can't make you any promises, Bro, but we'll try. When there is a time limit, too, it makes things trickier."

"I know."

"There's no guarantee this will work."

"It had better work! You made me cut my hair, ditch my designer clothes, and made me wear glasses," he said, narrowing his eyes. The corners of his mouth curved to a smile and Ruby chuckled.

God, she hoped this worked.

***

"I'll be home soon," Ruby said to him, keeping the car running, as he unloaded bags from the trunk – Ruby had corrected him with 'boot'. "I want to pop into work to see what I can sort out."

Steve, feeling weary from traipsing around the shops, but happy about the time spent with Ruby, carried the shopping bags upstairs. There was little point emptying his case now; he hung up his newly bought wardrobe instead. Ruby wouldn't allow him to wear his *old* clothes, anyway.

Considering Steve hadn't seen Ruby since their mother's funeral, over a year ago, he was pleased they were getting along. At the funeral, he would have liked to have stayed for longer, but his work schedule had been tight, and he'd had to leave Ruby to grieve on her own. Thankfully, the press had stayed away and honoured his family's privacy.

He'd grieved on his own. Maybe that's why he'd fallen so hard for Erica, his emotions so bare and raw. Neither Steve nor Ruby had really mentioned their mum today. Maybe they were too scared to bring to the surface the emotions it might evoke. Fifteen years had put distance between Steve and his family, yet he would never forget his mother. She'd been the one insisting he followed his dream, supporting him through thick and thin. Unfortunately, when the time came and he could truly repay her, she was gone.

So he would do all that he could to help Ruby.

He raked his hands over his face, then headed back down to the kitchen. He stared into one of the overhead cupboards and spied, sitting on the top shelf at the back, a cafetière gathering dust. Unfortunately, after checking the rest of the cupboards, he couldn't find any ground coffee. He could take a quick trip down to the shop, he'd seen one on the corner. It wouldn't harm.

He grabbed the key and strolled down the hill. Ten minutes later, he was meandering around the shop with a basket, picking up essentials, which included a bag of ground coffee. He preferred to buy fresh beans and grind his own coffee, for ultimate taste, however he wasn't sure whether Ruby had a grinder or not. Trawling the aisles had a certain normality to it that Steve hadn't enjoyed in a while. Usually someone did this stuff for him, delivered his groceries – he had a team of people doing his day to day tasks. He hated the word, but yes, he had an entourage. But today, going around this small shop didn't feel menial. It felt great, liberating.

Freedom.

Like the good old days.

Near the checkout stood the newsstand. Anxiety slowly crept up his back, but deciding it was best to keep up with the news, he selected a couple of newspapers and a glossy magazine that followed the ins and outs of A-listers. He'd need to keep an eye on this. One whiff that he was near Bristol and he'd need to tell Marie to make sure his double was seen holidaying somewhere hot and far away from here.

The middle-aged woman in her smart, blue uniform didn't bat an eyelid, too busy scanning the items in his basket and shoving them into a carrier bag. She only looked him in the eye when she asked for his money. Maybe she didn't follow the world's top ten sexiest men – Steve was voted tenth last month. But it was a good thing she didn't, Steve quickly remembered, irritated that he'd felt a moment of disappointment that she hadn't recognised him. When had he got so cocky? Confidence was more attractive than cockiness.

He didn't want to get recognised. It would give him more chance of finding someone.

Steve strolled towards Ruby's house, her car still not on the driveway. Her neighbour's front door opened and an elderly lady slowly emerged, smartly dressed as though off to church. She wore a hearing aid over one ear and used a wooden stick.

"Oh, hello," she said, cheerfully beaming at Steve. "Has our Ruby got herself a young man at last?"

Steve laughed and shook his head, approaching the woman. "No, no, I'm her brother." He put his shopping down and held out his palm to shake hands with the woman.

"Ruby never said she had a brother. Well, well, what a handsome young man." The woman took his hand with her frail fingers and patted it, rather than shake it. "It's good she's got company. I'm Daphne. I'll see you again then?"

"Yes, I'm staying for a while." Steve hesitated, unsure whether to give his own name or not. They hadn't agreed on an identity. A name. He'd probably have to use a different one.

Daphne wandered off down the road, very slowly, and Steve let himself into the house. He flicked the kettle switch again, and it wasn't long before he was sitting at the dining room table with a decent mug of coffee, thumbing through the papers.

No mentions of him being anywhere near Bristol. Though, to be honest, today must be a good day. There were no mentions of him at all. This was British press though. He'd check with Marie what the Americans were saying, too.

***

Ruby had entered the hotel by the back doors and headed straight towards her office. She thought this would minimise her chances of being seen as she didn't wish to be in the hotel any longer than necessary. Her days off were precious at the best of times.

She worked all hours God sent at times in this place. She loved it, but she also needed a break from it too, and with Steve home, she wanted to spend time with him.

"Ruby, have you got a minute?"

With her face hidden behind her monitor looking at the staff roster, she grimaced and cursed to herself. *Too good to be true.* Sometimes her open door policy was a pain in the arse. She looked round and smiled, knowing damn well it looked fake, "What is it, Alice?"

Alice stood nervously in the doorway holding a piece of paper. She wore a sleek black spa uniform with a mandarin collar. Her chestnut hair was pinned into a neat bun, with a couple of spiralling tendrils down the side of her perfectly made up face.

"Pete hasn't approved the order I put through. I need some more supplies for the spa. I'm running low. I can't massage without oil."

Pete was Ruby's assistant manager, and not particularly good at his job. Ruby hadn't hired him. She hired most of the staff, but he'd been transferred from another hotel in the chain. She wondered if he'd been so shit at his job they'd decided to sweep him under the carpet by sending him to a smaller hotel where he could do less damage. Only it meant more work for Ruby.

"Alice, we have budgets. You're going to have to manage your stock better. Look, can we discuss this tomorrow. I'll take a proper look at it then – I'm on my day—"

"But I need this stuff!"

"It can wait until tomorrow," Ruby said, sternly. Lydia appeared at the door. "What now?" Ruby cringed. That was louder and sharper than intended.

"A customer was asking to see the manager," Lydia said, entering the office. "I was looking for Pete, but I can't find him. I thought I'd try your office but I wasn't expecting you to be here."

"I'm not supposed to be."

"Are you catching up with your brother today?"

"Yeah...." Ruby said warily. "How do you know?"

47

"Oh, gosh, totally forgot, I wasn't supposed to say anything, but he called yesterday from the airport."

"Did he?"

"Airport, huh?" Alice chimed in, nudging Lydia. "Did he sound hot?" Lydia blushed as Alice asked Ruby eagerly, "What's he like? You never said you had a brother. Will we get an introduction? Where's he been?"

God, where *had* he been? Steve and Ruby would need to organise a cover story.

"He's been away." How lame does that sound? She should have said working abroad, but daren't stumble too much over it now. "Erm, so, I need to get on. Alice, we'll talk budgets and orders tomorrow."

"Um, while you're here, did you want to see this customer?" Lydia asked, grimacing.

"Not particularly. Are they complaining?" Ruby closed down her computer and shoved some papers back into the top drawer of her desk – harder than intended, the contents slamming to the back.

"No, I don't think so. They didn't seem to be in a bad mood," Lydia said.

"Right, well, get Pete to deal with it. If they start moaning get Callum to give them a complimentary drink, or something. It's my day off and unless it's urgent, I'm leaving. Tell Pete I'll be in early in the morning."

Lydia nodded and Alice opened her mouth, about to wave her order form at Ruby, but Ruby didn't give her a chance, she grabbed her handbag, and darted out of there.

Usually she gave the hotel one hundred and ten percent of her attention. But not today. She didn't know how much time she had with Steve, so she needed to make the most of it.

***

As Ruby entered the house, the atmosphere changed. The door slammed, she huffed and puffed.

"I am so pissed off," she said, removing her shoes and dumping her handbag on the couch. Steve chose to remain silent. He'd learnt a long time ago to let someone rant when they needed to. "I got cornered by a member of staff. What part of 'it's my day off' do they not understand?"

Steve made Ruby a fresh coffee in the cafetière, and put it in front of her.

They definitely needed a coffee machine – it would have been ready and waiting in the carafe to be poured. He lived, breathed, survived only because of his coffee machine. Sitting at the table, Ruby muttered language that truly shocked him, drumming her fingers along the wood. Yes, he heard curses a lot, but not from the mouth of his dear, sweet, baby sister. She used to shout, "oh, poo," when angered, not every expletive under the sun.

"Who's Pete?" With Ruby's face looking like thunder, Steve would hate to be him.

"My assistant manager and he's a total waste of space. Probably why Lydia couldn't find him. Skiving off chatting up a waitress, knowing him. There have been rumours he takes naps in a room if it's available."

Steve chuckled. "Ruby, can you give me a job?"

She screwed up her face. "Do you really want a job?"

"How else am I going to meet people? I can't stay cooped up here. I can't just wander around Cribbs Causeway."

"There is Cabot Circus."

"What?" Steve frowned.

"It's another shopping centre, but never mind." Ruby shook her head, gesturing for Steve to continue.

"I need to make some friends, get out and socialise, and work is the best way. Isn't it?"

"Yes, I suppose so." She rested her head in her hands, slumping onto the table. "I can't pay you – as I said, there's just no budget right now. You'll just have to keep it quiet that you're not actually on the payroll. It's a bit dodgy, but I don't think anyone will question it."

"I don't need the money. I want an excuse to get up every morning, that's all. Lead a normal life."

"Okay." She sighed. "This is the best I can do; cleaner or bar staff?"

"Bar staff, that's a no-brainer!"

"You're sure? Some would rather clean."

"How many women am I going to meet with my head down the toilet?"

"Good point. But still, I bet you come begging after a week."

"I'll be fine. I've worked in a bar before. I can practise my cocktail making abilities." He shook an imaginary cocktail shaker.

"Tom Cruise has already done that film! A very long time ago."

"They might remake it, like they've done *Footloose*."

Ruby sank her head into her hands. "Oh God, I hope I don't get the sack for this."

"You won't, but if you do, I'd make sure you were okay. I can afford to." He patted her arm.

"That's not the point. I actually like my job."

"You were cursing it only five minutes ago. I think I heard every swear word in the English language. French, too."

"Oh, shut up." Ruby finished her coffee. "Coffee tasted good by the way. Is this real coffee?" She looked at him speculatively.

He grinned. "I went shopping."

Her eyes widened with horror. "You did what?"

"Relax. No one took a blind bit of notice. I've even got us some dinner in."

"Oh, yeah, I've failed to get to a supermarket this week."

Steve stood, clearing the table. "So when do I start my new job?" he asked, taking the mugs out to the kitchen.

"You can start tomorrow. You'll have to do some training first, about the facilities, hygiene awareness and general hotel procedures."

"Awesome."

"You've really got to work on the accent."

"I am!"

"You're an actor for Christ's sake. Pretend it's a part you're playing, a role."

Steve opened the fridge and started taking the ingredients out he needed to make dinner.

"*You're only supposed to blow the bloody doors off!*" he said, in his best British accent.

"Ha! Ha! Very Michael Caine. Just tone it down a little."

Steve felt a sting on his right ear where Ruby flicked it.

"That hurt." He rubbed his head and scowled. "Make yourself useful and peel the potatoes."

"Pardon?" Ruby raised her eyebrows, as if waiting patiently.

Steve cleared his throat. "Please can you peel the potatoes," he concentrated on sounding more British, "*Darling*? Ouch!"

***

"Okay, thinking about tomorrow," Ruby said, tucking into her plate of food. "I think you might want to act a little clumsy or nerdy. It worked for Clark remember?"

Between them they'd knocked up a simple dinner with lamb chops and lashings of mint sauce. Damn, had he missed mint sauce. This was what living an ordinary life was about.

"More acting required, huh?"

"Yes, and I was thinking that we should change your name."

Steve nodded. She had a point and he had thought this too.

"What about Stuart, it's close to Steve? I wondered about Stefan, but would that be too close?"

"Stuart is good. Not so keen on Stefan." Steve pulled a face.

"Then, Stuart it is. If I start saying Steve, at least I can correct myself. Also, as you're my brother you'll have Fisher back for your surname."

Steve nodded. "Stuart, Stuart, Stuart," he said, more to himself. Would he remember he was using a different name? Maybe he really did have to look at this as just another acting part. But there'd be no camera on him.

"Oh, and we've got to come up with a back-story, for why you've been away. You phoned from the airport."

"How'd you know about that?"

"Lydia let it slip."

"Will I get to meet Lydia? Is she cute?"

"I don't know, she's not my type." Ruby rolled her eyes. "She's quieter than Alice. But I'm not getting you a job so you can shag half the staff. You're going to have to pull your weight, Steve, otherwise the others will start moaning. You have to work."

"Yes, I know, boss."

Chapter 5

Ruby parked in the staff car park – as a manager she had her own space. Steve looked up at the quaint hotel, getting out of the car. Ivy grew up the corner of the brickwork and around some of the signage. Durdham Lodge. His insides jolted.

Nerves?

"It's four stars, but it's a small, manageable hotel," Ruby said as she locked her car. "You'll be fine."

Since landing, he'd been sure someone was going to shout out, "Hey, that's Steve Mason," and draw attention to him. Fortunately, it hadn't happened yet, and with a telephone call to Marie yesterday late evening, she'd reassured him the tabloids believed he was still holidaying in the Caribbean getting over his break up with Erica.

But was this foolish?

No, if he wanted to find a woman to love him sincerely, for him, not his looks, fame or fortune, then he had to give this a try. However mad it seemed.

What if he didn't find anyone?

Then he'd given it a go. At least he'd have had quality time with Ruby...

"In the week it's mainly people staying overnight on business, and at weekends we have spa breaks and tourists on city breaks." Ruby chatted as they walked in through the staff entrance, at the back of the hotel and along a narrow corridor not for the viewing of the paying public. It didn't have the luxurious decor expected in a four star country hotel, just dirtying magnolia walls. They passed a waiter and a chambermaid, and a small room that looked like it was for the staff, with smells of coffee wafting from it. Ruby swung open a door, they hit the plush red carpet, lavish decor and the aroma of freshly cut flowers. They were inside the hotel. A telephone was ringing in the background. Steve pushed his new glasses up on his face and slouched a little.

Ruby held open a door to an office – her office – and closed it after them. Steve breathed a little more easily.

"I warn you now, this is not as glamorous as producing a film," she said.

Steve chuckled, straightening his back. "You'll be surprised. A film set can be far from glamorous at times."

"Oh, yeah, I'm sure it's really boring." Steve laughed again at Ruby's sarcasm. He was starting to get used to her British wit again.

"Actually it can be very boring."

"Yeah, yeah... We're in early, but the hotel is staffed twenty-four seven."

No shit early. Ruby had him up and out before seven a.m. this morning. Okay, he was used to early starts on set, and very long days, but this morning he'd found it hard to get out of bed, as if his body wanted to recoup some sleep. It had only been a couple of days since landing. Jet lag would still be taking its toll. It hadn't helped it was still dark outside, either.

A photograph of Ruby and Mum rested on Ruby's desk, which Steve picked up and studied, smiling at it. She took it out of his hand, scowling, and put it back in its place, then dumped her bag in the bottom drawer of the desk. How long had she been doing this job? He hadn't even thought to ask her. All he knew from a letter she sent a while back, before Mum's funeral, was that she was a hotel manager. "Right, I'll show you around, give you a quick tour and find you a uniform."

On their way down the narrow staff corridor they met a young man wearing chef whites, adjusting his hat. "Hi, Ruby," he said.

"Oh, this is Brett," Ruby said and smiled. Under his chef's hat poked coal-black hair. He wore glasses and had a diamond stud earring in his left ear. "He works in the restaurant."

Steve held out his hand and smiled. "Hello."

"This is my brother... Stuart," Ruby said, after a deep breath.

The young man, probably of similar age to Ruby, took Steve's hand. He had a firm handshake, which surprised Steve, because Brett was slim built. Maybe the chef whites masked his true appearance.

"Hi, I'm the sous chef."

"Nice to meet you, Sue," Steve said, and winked, internally cringing – the joke had come out all wrong. He'd sounded American then. *Need to concentrate on the accent.*

Luckily Brett laughed. "So what you doing here? Ruby has never mentioned a brother."

"She's giving me a job until I find my feet," Steve said the first thing that entered his head. *Act. Remember to act.*

"Right, well there's lots to see, talk later, Brett," Ruby said quickly, grabbing Steve's arm.

Steve waved a friendly goodbye to Brett, who watched Ruby with a happy expression, then nodded at Steve.

Phew, one down, the rest of the staff to go. Maybe he could do this.

Entering a staff area full of lockers, Ruby rummaged through a cupboard. She handed Steve some clothes and pointed to where he could change, providing him with his own locker key.

"The rule is to get changed here," Ruby said. "Not to wear the clothes out of the hotel."

"Why's that?"

"So that you don't go down the pub wearing your uniform, and get drunk and give the company a bad name." Ruby smiled. "Leave your belongings in the locker too. You're not allowed a mobile phone or any money on you." Steve nodded. "Meet me back in my office when you're changed."

Steve fixed his tie and pulled on the three-quarter length jacket over his waistcoat. There was a lot to be said for tailor-made suits – and he wanted his back, now. The grey uniform trousers with their starched crease down the front were a little short in the leg, especially when sitting, and the shirt, like his burgundy polyester jacket, fitted across his broad shoulders snug but was too big in the waist. This added to the dork factor, supposedly, but he was pretty sure Clark Kent's clothes had fitted him.

Once he was as happy as he could be with his appearance, he found Ruby's office.

"Right, I'll show you around the hotel, introduce you to some of the staff and then leave you at the bar. I have a hotel to manage. I'll try to make your shifts tally with mine, otherwise I'll have to drop you in or something, if you have to come in when I'm not working." She chewed her lip.

"Roo, don't worry about it, I'll go with the flow. You're doing me a huge favour."

"Okay, let's do this. Gosh why do I feel nervous?"

"I don't know, you're not the one pretending to be Clark Kent."

"Stuart, Stuart, Stuart," Ruby mumbled as she left her office.

***

Steve was going to look at all this as experience. Research. *You never know when something like this might be needed for acting.* He followed Ruby out of her office, his heart beating faster with nerves, his palms sweating. His polyester-cotton mix shirt was making him hot and uncomfortable. He pushed the glasses up. The damn things were hurting behind his left ear and across the bridge of his nose. Did he risk returning to get them adjusted? He needed them to be comfortable as he couldn't risk not wearing them.

How hard could the work be? It had to be pretty straightforward and he'd do the job adequately. He did worry he'd let Ruby down. All his life he'd acted, though admittedly, he'd done every job imaginable before the acting had taken off. He'd done those successfully, too. Dredging through his memory, he'd done all sorts from waiting tables, serving drinks to working for a pizza delivery company. All in between bit part acting and gigs. Where did fifteen years go when you looked back on them?

"Okay, you're predominantly going to work in the bar area. You'll need to learn how to work the coffee machine too, I'll get Callum to show you." Ruby spoke as she walked and Steve nodded, running a finger around his collar. "And at quiet periods you may need to man the reception desk. We're a small hotel, so we have to muck in where we can. You'll have to work otherwise the others will complain, you understand?"

"Yes, boss."

She scowled at him.

"Stuart Fisher," Ruby said, more to herself than Steve as they headed towards the reception desk.

"Stuart Fisher." He nodded and placed an arm on her shoulder. "Relax, Roo, it will be fine."

"Yeah, why am I the nervous one here? Just remember to act nerdy, you know, like Clark."

"Yeah, yeah, but I don't want to be too clumsy..."

Lois hadn't fancied Clark – not initially.

"Yes, but too confident and they may see through the disguise. And work on your accent." Her eyes narrowed. "Right, I need to find Alice," she mumbled.

They almost bumped into a skinny lad with mild acne as he walked out of the lift.

"Ah, Callum, I want you to meet Stuart," Ruby said, as Steve held out his hand. As Callum returned the handshake, tucking the tray he carried under his other arm, he wore a puzzled expression, as though he'd done nothing so formal in his life. "He's going to be working with you behind the bar."

"Hi, Stuart." Callum looked from Steve to Ruby.

"He's my older brother," she said.

"Yeah, Ruby's helping me out. I need a job for a while." Steve tried very hard to lose his American accent but at the same time not sound like Benedict Cumberbatch. He remembered Ruby's advice, and his memories of the old Superman movie, trying to mimic Clark, to make his gestures jittery. Clark never stood as tall and straight as Superman.

Steve was naturally confident from years of girls falling at his feet, so now he needed to look less secure about himself – especially standing in front of a guy barely out of his teens.

"Ruby never said she had a brother." Callum frowned.

"Well, I've been away, um, travelling for a while," Steve said, not really sure where it had come from. Stupidly, they'd never managed to get around to making up a back-story. Maybe they should have thought harder about a past for him.

"Yeah, and he didn't leave on a good note so I didn't like talking about him," Ruby added, "but we're over that now. We've cleared the air."

"Oh, right," Callum said, scratching his head. "Nice to meet you, Stu." Steve frowned. "Oh, you don't like Stu?" Callum grinned wickedly.

"No, no, Stu's fine." Steve rubbed the back of his neck and chuckled. He'd have to get used to 'Stu' from now on.

"Well, you're Stu now," Callum said, laughing. The two men joked for a bit, the nervous atmosphere ebbing away, and Steve was able to relax. He wasn't looking at him as if he was a Hollywood film star. *Phew!*

"I'm going to introduce Stuart" – Ruby almost said Steve, but he was the only one to notice – "to some more staff then I'll bring him over to the bar."

"Yes, boss." Callum saluted, then turned on his heel and marched away. Ruby rolled her eyes as Steve smirked at Callum's cheek. Steve had said the same thing and clearly Ruby didn't like it.

"Firstly, I need to see Alice about some order issues she raised yesterday, so you can come with me," Ruby said, patting Steve's arm for attention.

Ruby led Steve along a corridor and through some double doors with a sign above them reading "Tranquillity Relaxation Centre". Instantly a lemony and floral fragrance hit him. The interior had changed from the hotel's rich colours, to soothing natural pastels, as if he'd walked into another world. The reception desk had a huge vase full of fresh flowers in yellows and whites. To the right of the desk there was a cream leather couch for guests to wait. A glass coffee table sat in front of it, with a neat pile of glossy magazines. Steve gulped. He hoped he wasn't inside one of them.

Being early, the place was deserted, including the reception desk.

"Where is she?" Ruby said, impatience lacing her words as she drummed her fingers against the desk.

"I'm here! Just made myself a coffee," called a woman Steve could only assume was Alice. "Though don't tell the guests, because to them I only recommend herbal teas."

Now Alice was Steve's type of girl. She strode across the wooden floor, and arrived in front of Steve with a steaming mug of coffee in one perfectly French manicured hand. She had chestnut hair, clipped up, with loose tendrils framing her attractive face. As she approached Steve, she smiled a million dollar Hollywood smile.

"Hello," Alice said, fluttering her long black eyelashes. Big, chocolate eyes looked him over. Her dark eyes were enhanced by black eye-liner and thick mascara lashes, and her pouty lips were glossy. The spa uniform accentuated her figure perfectly – beige trousers and a matching lotus tunic with a mandarin collar. Even though the tunic wasn't revealing Steve could still appreciate the swell of her breasts.

Hello, Alice!

The woman had curves, and knew how to show them off. She wasn't wearing a wedding or engagement ring. *Result!*

"This is Stuart." Ruby nudged him, and then looked at Alice

sternly, reminding her that Ruby was the boss. Alice kept her eyes on Steve, the corner of her mouth twitched. She really wasn't listening to Ruby.

"Hi, I'm the new boy." Steve returned with his own million dollar smile, and then remembering Clark Kent, albeit probably too late, slung his hands into his pockets as if nervous.

"He's my brother, and will be working here for a while. I'm just showing him around. I've come to discuss those orders with you."

"Oh, yes." Alice led Ruby over to the reception desk, leaving Steve to mull around in the spa.

Would Alice recognise him? She had a stack of glossy magazines on the coffee table after all. In her line of business she would be up on fashion and looks. She was the type of woman to take care of her appearance. The type of woman to follow what celebrities were up to.

Just deny everything. You're Stuart Fisher. You've been travelling for the past few years and now you're home. Or something like that.

Really should have worked on a back-story.

He'd iron out the details at home, later.

Steve nosed around, finding the pool and gym, then waited patiently for Ruby to finish up with Alice.

"Right, let's take you to reception," Ruby said. Steve shared a worried new-boy expression with Alice.

"Don't worry, Stuart, we'll look after you," Alice said, almost in a purr. "You're in safe hands. You should enjoy working here." Steve swallowed. He imagined Alice's hands were far from safe. He glimpsed a brief scowl from Ruby, a hint that she didn't approve of Alice, but he couldn't see why. She was friendly, bubbly and confident. And beautiful.

Heady from the spa's heavy scents and perfumes – or was it Alice's effect on him? – Steve walked in step with Ruby back to the main part of the hotel, leaving Alice in her relaxation centre.

"Can staff use the pool, Roo? And the gym?" Steve hoped so, it would be one way of keeping up his fitness. He couldn't shuck all his responsibilities as a Hollywood hunk.

"Yes they can, but only when they're off duty." Ruby said. "However, I'm not sure if it's wise for you to be in there."

"I'll make sure I wear really unattractive sweat-pants."

"Whilst swimming?" Ruby raised her eyebrows.

He smirked. "You know what I mean. However, I'm not taking this nerd look to the point of wearing Speedos."

"I so hope not!"

In the main part of the hotel, they headed towards a young woman, smartly dressed in similar uniform to Steve; burgundy jacket, and cream blouse with a silk scarf around her neck. They waited at the reception desk for her to finish with a customer, before Ruby spoke, "Hi, Lydia, I want you to meet my brother, Stuart." Steve smiled at Lydia, adjusting his glasses. "He's joining our team."

"Hello, Lydia." Steve shook Lydia's hand, more delicately than the way he'd grasped Callum's. So she was the owner of the voice at the end of the phone the other day, and she turned out to be pretty and young, not old-enough-to-be-his-mother as he feared. He would enjoy working here.

Lydia frowned. The penny had obviously dropped for her too. "You said you're name was Steve."

"Ha, yes, I did," – had he? God, he had – "well, I was worried you were going to ruin the surprise, so I made up a name..."

For a moment Lydia eyed him suspiciously, then nodded. "I wouldn't have said anything."

"I couldn't be sure. And so by giving you the wrong name, if you had said anything it wouldn't have rung true for Ruby." Steve anxiously chuckled. Oh, God this was awkward. Luckily, the telephone started ringing – saved by the bell! – and so Lydia gave a delicate, apologetic smile, tucking strands of blonde hair behind her ear and answered it, talking into the microphone on her headset. She had layered, bobbed blonde hair. She was probably Ruby's age. Steve noticed there were no rings on her left hand either. It had become a habit, checking out for wedding rings, as he'd been surprised at how many supposedly happily married women had thrown themselves at him as his fame increased.

"I know you're predominantly going to work in the bar, but sometimes you will need to help out on the reception desk, so I'm going to leave you with Lydia for a bit first."

Steve stopped studying Lydia – she was pretty – drawing his attention back to Ruby, and nodded.

"The fastest way to learn reception is when it's busiest."

The hotel was buzzing with more people around now. Everyone had woken up, had breakfast and were checking out, or getting on with their business.

Not for the first time that day did Steve feel the anxiety crawl up his back. How hard could it all be?

"Lydia, could you please show Stuart the ropes as occasionally he'll need to help you out." Ruby turned her attention to Steve, smiling. "And when you're ready, Stuart, you can take a call, but Lydia will listen in and help you if you get stuck."

Lydia nodded. "Don't look so nervous, you'll be fine."

He took a deep breath. Man up, Steve, it's a telephone, not a bomb.

"I'll come get you later, to show you the bar," Ruby said. Actually, was she smirking at him, enjoying this?

Lydia tapped him, to get his attention. "Listen and watch me. We have to man the phone and deal with customer requests face to face." She adjusted her headset, the phone softly rang, and she answered the call. Steve listened carefully to her, the patient tone she took with the customer. Her voice could melt butter, warming and gentle. He noticed the pad in front of her where she'd scribble notes while listening, or occasionally doodle. Little cherub like faces. Happy, sad or mischievous. All incredibly cute. As she spoke, she flicked through the computer system to check hotel availability.

An hour flew quickly as he watched and listened to Lydia and helped her where he could.

"It's time for my break, so let's get a cuppa, then you can have a go answering the phone and dealing with the customers who come to the desk."

"Oh, uh, okay." Steve's nerves were real. Why so much fear over a telephone? It's not like the people at the other end could reach down and throttle him if he got things wrong. They certainly wouldn't recognise him.

"This is Maxine, she also works on reception."

"Hello," Steve said, nodding friendly. Maxine was in her early fifties, with short brown hair. As she smiled the creases in her face deepened. She faintly smelled of cigarette smoke mingled with her perfume. He wouldn't need to act too dorky around Maxine, but then would he? What was he thinking? He couldn't let anyone realise who he was, not just the pretty women who were potential love interests. He had to stay on the ball and not let this act slip. He had to convince everyone. One word of who he really was and the game would be over. He'd be back in Hollywood before you could say shooting stars.

Lydia led Steve down the narrow staff corridor, although he was starting to learn his way around. He had a good sense of direction, and the hotel wasn't huge.

"The staff room," Lydia said, entering, the very small room. "I know it's a bit of a joke." It contained two tables with orange plastic chairs tucked underneath them and a vending machine. A fridge sat under the counter, while the basic kitchen appliances sat on top. Lydia continued, "This is where you come to take all your breaks. Do you want anything to eat?" Lydia asked, slotting coins into the vending machine and pressing the button to retrieve some biscuits.

"No, I'm all right thanks."

"I'll share my biscuits. Tea?"

"Yes please."

Lydia showed him where the tea and coffee was, with an urn full of hot water. "If you want posher coffees, you have to pay for them." She gestured to a machine where you could push buttons for cappuccinos, lattes etc. But they were powered milk variety and not the real thing in Steve's opinion. Tea would be just fine.

"Sugar?"

Steve grinned. "No, I'm sweet enough as I am."

Lydia giggled and he watched her cheeks redden as she concentrated on adding milk and removing the teabag, and not making eye contact with him.

Maybe he should lay off the flirting. It was only the first day. He was a natural charmer though, his mum had always said so. From about the age of three, he'd had old ladies eating out the palm of his hand. He only had to look at his teachers doe-eyed when he'd been cheeky and he'd get away with it. For now he'd turn down his charm-o-meter.

As they only had fifteen minutes, Lydia and Steve didn't get to talk much. She'd run through the basic chit-chat when two people don't really know one another and don't know what to say. Steve had decided to let her talk, and listen. She'd only worked for the hotel a year. It wasn't a career move, just a job to pay the bills and allow her to live. She lacked confidence, but it could have been an element of shyness, Steve decided, plus he was a stranger. Maybe he'd get her to open up more with time.

Lydia suddenly glanced up at the clock. "Oh, we better be getting back."

They swallowed down the last of their drinks, and pushed the orange chairs with a scrape under the table. Lydia took both mugs and placed them on a rack with other dirty dishes.

Back behind the reception desk, Lydia handed Steve one of the two headsets. He grinned, realising he was still nervous. She giggled.

"It's not that bad, honest," she said.

He was actually going to do this. Actually answer the phone and deal with queries, and serve any customers who came to the desk. Was he having an early midlife crisis – or something worse? His life was in LA, making movies...

Think Clark Kent... trying to find Lois.

He felt more nervous than being butt naked in front of a film crew doing a love scene. This shirt was doing nothing for him. He felt hot and awkward. The heating in this hotel needed turning down. He wanted air. In fact, he could just bolt. He didn't really need to do this job, he wasn't even getting paid. He could go back to LA... His comfort zone.

He'd find someone eventually, amongst the gold diggers. Not.

Running away, because he had the money to do so, was not an option. He wasn't a coward, he chided himself. If he wanted to find someone to love... and who loved him, he did need to try this. He had nothing to lose. If the press got wind, he could always say he was working undercover for research purposes. Anything. It would probably give his PA, Marie, the biggest headache of her life but he could get round it. He'd give her a pay rise.

He took a deep breath, and pulled up his sleeves. "I can do this."

"You'll be fine, and I'm here. If you get really stuck just say you're handing over to a colleague and I'll take over." She squeezed his arm and when the phone started ringing his heart sped up. Taking another deep, calming breath, he answered it.

Chapter 6

Ruby put the phone down then glanced at her watch; quarter past ten. Steve had done a long enough stint on reception for one day. He could do some more tomorrow. She'd take him to the bar where she wanted him to work most of the time. She felt guilty really, making him work, but there was no way she could have him here doing nothing. She'd have all of her employees complaining, or worse, walking out.

"How was your morning?" Ruby said, leaning against the reception desk, watching Steve fill the printer with paper.

Steve nodded confidently. "Good. Didn't make too many mistakes did I?" He nudged Lydia.

"Oh, no, you were fine," Lydia said. Then her smile dropped. "There was just that one time... Sorry, Ruby, we might have a complaint coming in—"

"Shhhh..." Steve's expression was mischievous, revealing the dimples in his cheeks, "I told you not to tell Ruby about it."

"About what?" She frowned quizzically.

"Nothing..." Lydia giggled. "Don't panic, he's pulling your leg. He told me to say it. I'm a terrible liar."

"I never!"

Ruby narrowed her eyes at her brother. He'd always teased her as a kid, and here he was winding her up again, getting Lydia to do it, too. *Swine.*

His flipping smile and sparkly eyes. Whether he was famous or not, they'd get people to do his bidding. *I give him a job and this is how he repays me.*

"Oh, Ruby," Lydia reached under the desk and pulled a book out from under it, "here's that book I said I'd lend you."

Ruby took the hardback, admired the cover then tucked it under her arm. It was sweet of Lydia to remember the book. She'd only mentioned it in passing a couple of weeks ago. "Thanks. You'll have to pop over sometime and take a book off my shelf."

"There's no need."

"No I insist." Ruby turned her attention to Steve, whose expression sobered. "There's some time before lunch, let's show you this bar. By the end of the day, I want you producing the best cappuccinos this side of Bristol."

"See you later, Lydia," Steve said, and joined Ruby in step as they headed towards the bar.

"How was it really?" Ruby asked, once out of the earshot of Lydia.

"Not bad. I was nervous the first time I picked up the phone."

"Hopefully you won't have to man reception too much, only quiet periods when the girls need to take their breaks etc."

"It was fine, honestly. I'm clocking it up as research." He chuckled. "And Lydia's really nice."

They walked into a room just behind reception. This was Ruby's favourite area of the hotel, where they usually held their functions. Because the hotel originally was an old Georgian house, this room had a large fireplace. In the winter she always ensured the fire was lit day and night, providing a cosy refuge from the cold for her guests. Two large leather sofas, the colour of caramel, sat in front of the fire, with a low coffee table made of solid oak between them. These were the most popular seats in the room. Scattered around the bar were other comfortable sofas and armchairs, tucked around small tables. Soft music played in the background. It all came together to provide a relaxing atmosphere. At the back of the room was the bar area, where Callum stood wiping glasses and placing them on the back shelf. Ruby was relieved to see he was actually working.

"Callum, would you mind showing Stuart how to work the coffee machine, and where everything is in the bar. Show him how room service works and the general routines." *See, there, didn't stumble over his name.*

"Yes, boss." Callum saluted and Ruby scowled.

"Callum, less of the cheek, please. You'll be working with my brother a lot, so I need you to go through your job and what you do – sensibly." She kept her expression stern, then she turned to Steve. "I'll leave you here with Callum. I'll come find you and we could have lunch together?"

"Yeah, Roo, that'll be great."

***

"Roo?"

"She's my sister. You call her that and she'll probably fry your balls," Steve said firmly to Callum.

Callum held his hands up defensively. "But I'm okay to call you Stu, right?"

"If you must." Steve wasn't enthralled about the name Stu, but as it wasn't actually his name, he'd let Callum off. Plus, he needed to make friends not enemies, and Callum was young and impressionable. Callum was trying to be 'cool', or so he thought.

In the time leading up to lunch, Callum had shown Steve the bar, what drinks they sold, how to work the till, where the cellar was for changing the barrels – they had a couple of beers available on tap. It was all stuff Steve knew through working in bars at Callum's age. The guy had to be in his early twenties. His attitude sometimes was immature, but generally Callum was a good guy. Steve had probably been the same, though he'd had more confidence with his looks. He'd never been struck with acne like Callum, and being sporty meant he had filled out early on.

"All right, Stu, let me show you how this big boy works." Callum patted the coffee machine and grinned.

Callum was scrawny, talked a lot about games on his PlayStation, and whenever a pretty girl entered the bar, whether hotel staff or a guest, he'd give Steve a nudge and wink. Again, Steve let Callum talk while he worked. The less Steve spoke the better, he thought, while he was getting used to his new role. This way he reduced the chance of giving something away.

"We get more room service orders in the evening, but sometimes during the day, guests want a posh coffee sent up." Callum had to raise his voice over the noise as he frothed milk in a stainless steel jug. He wiped the nozzle, then gently tapped the jug on the counter to send the froth to the top. He poured the foamy thick milk into a cup of espresso, sprinkled it with chocolate and grinned. "A perfect cappuccino is one third coffee, one third milk and one third froth."

"I know." Steve drank enough coffee to know how he liked it.

"You do?"

"Yeah, I can't live without coffee."

"Oh, I can't stand the stuff. Don't like tea either."

"So who's this for?" Steve pointed the coffee. Callum found a tray under the counter and placed the cup on it.

"Room 106. Come on, I'll show you."

When they returned from delivering the coffee, Ruby was standing at the bar waiting.

"Hey," she said, smiling at Steve. "Did you want to get lunch together?"

Steve's stomach rumbled as if on cue. "Yeah, that would be good."

"I'll bring him back to you after lunch, Callum."

Callum nodded as he went back behind the bar to serve an

approaching customer.

Steve held the door open for Ruby to enter the small staff room. Unwrapping two food parcels, Ruby placed one in front of Steve. They had a mouth-watering club sandwich each, doorstop sizes with lashings of mayonnaise. Steve's stomach gurgled with hunger.

"Where'd you get these?" Steve asked, bringing the thick granary bread to his lips.

"Brett makes me up a lunch," Ruby replied nonchalantly.

"Hmmm..." He nodded and swallowed. It tasted good. "Does he now?" He raised his eyebrows.

"It's not like that." Ruby dabbed her lips with a napkin which had also been provided. "He offers, and I can't say no. He only does it because I'm his boss."

"If you say so." He'd noticed how Brett had looked at Ruby earlier, even if she hadn't.

"So how's your morning been?" Ruby asked, deliberately changing the subject, Steve thought.

"Not as scary as I thought."

"Good, I just hope your cover doesn't get blown."

"Relax, Ruby, I'm feeling confident about this." For good measure, he pushed his glasses up the bridge of his nose, which he'd almost forgotten he'd been wearing. "I even broke a glass to appear clumsy."

"Don't break too many!" Ruby stared, horrified. "Or I'll have to fire you."

***

"Ready, Bro?" Ruby arrived at the bar, coat over her arm.

Steve nodded, wiping a glass and placing it on the shelf behind him.

At times, she found it easier to stick to calling him Bro rather than Stuart. Butterflies fluttered inside her stomach every time she thought about this little lie, and whether she'd let his true name slip. So far, Steve had managed a whole day in the hotel and everyone he'd worked with or spoken to seem satisfied. To her relief, no rumour floated around saying 'Steve Mason is in the building.' She realised, with a pang, she didn't want him to leave. Not yet, and if his identity was revealed he'd have to. This game had to work. For her sake, she thought selfishly, as much as Steve's.

She was the least worried about Callum – he wouldn't know a celebrity if they whacked him in the face with a script. Lydia was fairly quiet, kept herself to herself – that's why she'd chosen her to train Steve on reception duties. Only someone like Alice could be the real problem. Even with Steve's disguise, he was still a handsome man.

Disguise? Was she kidding herself by giving Steve a boyish haircut and a pair of glasses? It had worked for Superman, but that was fiction. Comic or film. It wasn't real.

Callum and Brett, and the rest of the hotel staff did not call Alice 'Man Eater' behind her back for nothing.

Dear God, that woman practically had a new conquest every weekend – or at least it felt like it the way Alice would talk of who'd taken her out to dinner. She was always dating – compared to Ruby who was never out. Ruby didn't know where Alice found the time, considering she worked as a beautician privately too. She had a lot of private clients she tended to on her days off and evenings.

She was the female version of Steve. She had assets and knew how to use them. Would Steve fall for Alice's charm? Alice was nice enough – in small doses – but she didn't seem as though she was ready to settle down – yet. Which was what Steve wanted, wasn't it? He could pick up a party girl in LA. Alice would look good on his arm though. A handsome couple.

What if Steve fell for the wrong woman, and had his heart broken all over again? Was this a good idea?

He's a grown man, Ruby. He'll be fine.

"Yeah, now I'm ready," Steve hung up the towel and walked

round the bar to greet Ruby, giving her a big bear hug.

"Hey, not at work." She blushed. "The staff will be walking all over me."

They separated at the locker rooms; Steve heading into the men's. When he came out, he was changed into his normal clothes, shrugging on his coat. Callum and Brett walked out with him.

"Hey, shouldn't we go down the pub for a pint, to celebrate Stu's first day?" Callum said.

"Yeah." Brett nodded, glancing at Ruby.

"Oh, it's up to Stuart, he hasn't got a car." Ruby flustered, then turned to Steve "I can pick you up later, though – if you want to go."

"You can come, too," Brett said, hesitantly, removing his glasses and smiling nervously. Ruby noticed Callum's groan. They didn't usually include 'the boss' in the pub invitation. "You're part of the team, too."

"Oh, I don't know."

"Ruby, come on, we could do with winding down. Let me get to know these guys a little better," Steve said, trying that twinkle with his eyes lark again. "You're coming, too. Lydia?"

Lydia and Alice had come out of the ladies' changing room.

"Okay, yes, I can come for one drink."

"Alice?"

Alice already had her lipstick reapplied. "You didn't even need to ask, gorgeous."

Ruby buried her anxiety. *Don't panic.* Alice called everyone gorgeous – except for Callum.

***

Steve bought the first round in the busy pub, full with after-work drinkers. Ruby had muttered in his ear, "Don't flash your money around."

He had to remember not to try too hard to fit in.

And not to drink too much, too.

The British were alcoholics compared to the Americans, and Steve had steered clear of too much drinking behind the scenes of the film industry, where it was laid on after a long shooting session. He'd witnessed first-hand the mess it had got some younger actors into. And older ones. Steve had kept clean and sober, not wanting to be in rehab before he was thirty. Luckily, he was the sort of guy who enjoyed life, and didn't need to get drunk or stoned to have a good time. Maybe that came from confidence. He could socialise with anyone, laugh at anecdotes, and had learned to bite his tongue to those he didn't quite gel with, walking away at the first opportunity, and not looking back.

Steve hadn't set foot in a proper English pub in years. While savouring his ale he observed his new friends.

His first day – without wanting to jinx things – had so far gone without a hitch. Callum and Brett were a duo, though Callum was more the clown than Brett. In fact, Brett had gone quiet, Steve noticed, and he looked at Ruby a lot.

Alice remained close to Steve, and he'd get wafts of her floral perfume occasionally, which wasn't overpowering. He'd be quite happy to breathe it in all day.

He listened to them all chat, getting to know them a little better, telling him their tales of work. Their best and worst guests. Callum and Alice were the real talkers of the group.

Ruby sloped off to the bathroom, and Callum nudged Steve, almost spilling his pint.

"We call her Miss Whiplash, coz she's so bossy," Callum said and Steve chuckled.

"She's not that bad," Brett said, finishing his pint.

"You're going to have to tell us some stories," Callum continued, ignoring Brett, "so we can tease her. What was she like as a kid?"

"Oh, no." Steve shook his head. "Don't get me involved. Ruby's doing me a favour."

Brett went to the bar to buy the next round and the conversation turned to the worst topic Steve wanted.

"You know, you remind me of someone," Alice said, as she studied him. Every time Steve had caught her eye, Alice had been staring at him. Steve pulled a face as if to say 'who?' He tried to remain calm and ready to be very blasé, in the 'I don't know what you mean' type way.

"Oh, I know, has someone ever told you, you're the spitting image of Steve Mason?" Alice brushed his chest with her hand.

Steve nearly choked on the drink in his mouth. Fortunately, he swallowed then coughed. He put his pint down on the table they were standing around, for fear of dropping it. Luckily, the pub was noisy. If it had been quiet, and she'd been heard, maybe others would have confirmed that he *was* Steve Mason.

"He gets that all the time." Ruby had returned from the ladies' loos and to his rescue in the nick of time.

"Yeah, yeah." Steve shrugged, shoving his hands in his pockets, jiggling the change, deliberately not meeting anyone's eye. His brain ticked on overtime to think about how to answer. Usually he had no trouble responding.

"Who's Steve Mason?" Callum said, glancing questioningly at Brett.

"You know, that American actor? His latest film with Erica Kealey. *Perfection* wasn't it?" Brett said, handing out the next round of drinks; most of them softies now, as they all had to drive home.

Okay, so Brett knew his stuff. Damn it.

"Isn't he British?" Lydia, who'd been quiet all evening, spoke up. Lydia knew her stuff too. Shit.

"No, he's American," Ruby added quickly, giving a subtle look to Steve.

"Oh, yeah, *Perfection*. That was one hot film, if you know what I mean?" Callum said, gesturing his approval of the film coarsely. Brett smirked and shook his head.

Steve's heart raced with panic. There had been a few racy scenes in that film. He prayed Ruby hadn't seen it. That's how he

74

and Erica had fallen in love. On and off the screen. Even with a whole film crew surrounding them, they'd worked very closely and it had driven them crazy, to the point they had to find each other off the set.

Ruby rolled her eyes but Alice laughed. "He is hot." She gave Steve another once over.

"Well, I'm not him. Wouldn't want to be either," Steve said, remembering the glasses on his nose, and giving them a push, Clark Kent style. Maybe if he dropped his drink? He was going home to watch Superman, one, two and three, to get some hints on how to hide behind a flimsy disguise.

He knew this would never work. Why had he let Ruby talk him into it? Might as well book the flight home now.

"Erica Kealey is hot with a capital H. Imagine her hanging off your arm every day of your life." Callum chinked his glass with Steve's. Steve feared he looked as white as ghost. He certainly felt the colour drain from him. "There's no way you'd be standing here now, that's for sure! Steve Mason is one lucky bastard."

"They've broken up now, haven't they?" Lydia said, frowning thoughtfully, and Alice nodded, eyeing up Steve.

Please stop looking at me.

"Nah, you're not as hot as him," Alice said.

Thank God.

And thank the magazines who Photoshop out the imperfections.

"You'd like his money, though," Callum said, elbowing him, nearly spilling his drink – again!

"Who wouldn't?" Brett chimed in and Steve was grateful the conversation changed to what they'd spend their millions on if they won the lottery.

Steve started breathing easily again. The one person he hated talking about, or thinking about, was Erica Kealey. That's why he'd flown home after all. Every time he heard her name – even in the crass way Callum had spoken – it felt like a knife stabbing his heart. He'd bitten his tongue so he wouldn't stand up for Erica, because it would have given the game away, and he knew Callum was just fantasising. He hadn't meant his words maliciously. Steve had once been like that about the stars, pop idols or actresses – he had a thing for Daisy Duke - until he'd become an actor.

When Ruby said it was time to go, he felt relief, glad to leave. Acting not in front of a camera was hard work.

***

Steve blew out of his mouth, scratching the back of his neck. "Phew! That was close," he said, getting into Ruby's car.

"Yeah, I think we got away with that one."

"I'd never have guessed Lydia knew her stuff. I thought Alice, if anyone, would see through my disguise." He took his glasses off, rubbed his eyes, putting the frames into the top pocket of his now-clingy cheap shirt. He had to endure this for possibly three months. Would he last?

Steve noticed Ruby hadn't headed straight home.

"As it's late, fancy fish and chips for tea?" Ruby said.

"Do I really have a choice?"

"Not really. I can't be arsed to cook."

Ruby pulled up outside the local chippy. The smell of batter, vinegar and oil, made his mouth water and his stomach grumble. Ruby dashed in and returned with their order, then drove them home while Steve held onto the hot packages, eager to pinch a chip.

First a real pub, now proper fish and chips. Steve Mason was home.

They sat around Ruby's dining table eating out of the paper wrapping. Ruby added more salt and vinegar to her chips, while Steve spread lavish amounts of tartar sauce over his battered cod.

"Is this regular guy stuff?" Steve licked his fingers.

Ruby nodded, chewed then swallowed. "You need to make sure your American twang stays hidden," Ruby pointed the wooden chip fork at him, "otherwise Alice really will put two and two together.

But at least she's in the spa. You shouldn't see her that often."

Did Ruby even own Superman on DVD?

Ruby went into the kitchen and returned from the fridge with two cans of lager. "So what's *Perfection* about?"

"So you haven't seen it?" Steve felt partly relieved. His biggest film to date, which was about to rocket his fame factor up a notch, had included a lot of nudity, putting him on that top ten of sexiest men list.

"No. I don't like watching things you're in. Feels odd. Especially if there are love scenes." The can hissed as she opened it, then she winced after taking a sip, reacting to the coldness. Steve opened his, too. "I mean, I know it's not real, but it's bloody close. Watching my brother make love is not an image I want."

"It's only pretend. I'm not actually, you know, doing it."

"All the same, I'm sure it comes pretty close to what you look like when you are actually *doing it*."

"Okay, I get your point. Did you watch *The Blackest Day*? There's no sex in that film. I don't even kiss a girl." It was one prior to *Perfection*, a step up the ladder on the acting, still only a supporting character.

"Only the trailer, but friends told me your character got tortured and died. I didn't fancy watching that either. I don't need to see you dying. I made the mistake of going with Mum to see one of your first films. Mum blushed, and then wept. I was horrified."

"Mum watched *Bad News*?"

"Yes, we both did. And decided never to do it again!"

In his first Hollywood film, he'd only been a side-kick. His character had had some raunchy action, before being gruesomely killed off. "Okay, I can see why you don't want to watch my films." He smirked, and they both laughed. "I won't make you if you don't want to."

"Good." Ruby grinned. "So how was your first day? Did you enjoy the work?"

"It was okay..." he dragged out. The work was monotonous at

times. He'd ended up cleaning the bar because it had been so quiet. "I think I will go back to acting afterwards, though. This certainly isn't a career change for the better." Ruby laughed; it was beautiful to hear her chortling again, as he always used to clown around trying to make her laugh when she was little. "But it wasn't as bad as I thought it would be. Especially the reception desk, once I got used to picking up the phone. That's actually scary. I like to look at these things as life experiences. Who knows? Might get to use it one day in my acting."

"Oh, like method acting."

"Something like that. Yes."

"Well, the staff have taken to you, so that's good. I thought they'd be the best crowd to introduce you to, bit more fun and all of them are single."

"I'm not dating Brett or Callum!"

"I know, stupid. But you need single male friends, too, so you can go out and socialise with them, right?"

"This is true. Ruby, when did you get so clever?" He winked, then screwed up his fish and chips wrappings, feeling very full and worried he'd overdosed on grease – cod and chips were not on the Hollywood diet.

"Maybe I did inherit something from Dad – he gave you his looks, but me his brains." Ruby gave an infectious giggle as Steve cleared the table.

"Actually, you're so much like Mum, it's unbelievable."

Ruby sobered. "She was clever too, though."

"Of course. And she was incredibly strong-minded. She kept it together even with Dad dying."

"Yes, yes. I don't remember Dad dying so much, but I do remember her strength."

"I can see that strength in you." Steve squeezed her shoulder. It was great to chat to Ruby like this, talking about their parents, talking about anything without fear of words being misquoted, or used against him, or read into wrongly. He hoped this would work, and he could lead an ordinary life – just for a while, because if nothing else, it meant he got to spend some quality time with his sister.

Chapter 7

Early the next morning, Steve crept out of the house, without waking Ruby, and went for a run before work.

He liked running. It cleared the cobwebs out of his head and let him enter his own bubble. It was something he usually did when on location, if he could. It enabled him to work on his character inside his head. He would have his personal trainer with him, and maybe a bodyguard. They were part of his small entourage.

Today he wouldn't be running with a bodyguard or trainer.

But he could think about his new character; Stuart Fisher.

Joining a gym wasn't an option. It was bad enough going around busy shops and worrying he might get spotted. He'd planned initially to move to a better hotel, and have a few pieces of gym equipment installed in his suite, rather than use the hotel's gym facilities, to keep a low profile. However, since Ruby's ingenious plan for normality, and therefore an even more important need to lie low, a run would have to do.

Being October, the sun wasn't even up. With his iPod tucked in its pouch around his bicep, he pushed in the ear buds, did some stretching and warmed up, then began a gentle jog, bringing up the pace. He started up the story he'd been listening to and it took him a moment to remember where he was in the thriller. He preferred to listen to books sometimes, rather than music, because the beat of the song affected his pace, either slowing him down, or making him run too fast. It was okay if he had his personal trainer with him, because he'd set the pace. But as there was no one setting the pace today, he'd stick to narrative rather than music.

By the time Steve returned to Ruby's house, sweat poured from him and his chest heaved as he drew in deep breaths. He'd run for an hour and wasn't even sure of the distance. Quietly, he entered the house, and did a warm-down in the lounge, stretching out his calves and hamstrings, then started sit-ups, crunching his abs, then press-ups, counting them out, his breathing heavy, his chest and biceps burning as he pushed.

"What are you doing?"

Steve jumped at Ruby's voice, unbalancing, and he groaned, landing in a heap on the floor. "Push-ups. What do you think it looks like?"

"Far too energetic for this time of the morning, it's not even seven o'clock." Ruby wrapped her dressing gown tighter, padding into the kitchen, and Steve carried on his exercising, hearing the kettle switch flick on.

Ruby came back out, and frowned. "I told you to act normally."

"Regular people exercise, Ruby. Besides, no one saw me – it's pitch black out there." Steve stood up, and wiped the sweat out of his eyes with his T-shirt.

"Would it harm if you put a bit of weight on? It would change your appearance." She poked his stomach, her expression surprised when she felt how solid he was.

"I'm filming in three months."

"Isn't it a romantic comedy?"

"Yes, but it has bedroom scenes—"

"I'm getting the picture, loud and clear." Ruby quickly held her hands up. "Coffee?"

"Not yet, I'll take a shower."

For the next two weeks, this was Steve's life. Every other morning he'd get up early and go for a chilly run before work. Autumn deepened, with icy winds making it harder for him to breathe. His head would ache as if he'd eaten ice cream too fast. He wasn't used to running in the cold in sunny LA.

Work treated him well, too. He fitted in. No one questioned who he was. Only Alice worried him, as she kept up to date on celebrity news with all the glossy magazines in the spa. Callum and Brett let him enter their small gang, and they'd joke childishly about bloke stuff. Cars, women and football. He hadn't had the time to follow football in the US so he swotted up on the Premier League, watching *Match of the Day* – luckily sometimes they had it on in the bar – and reading the sports pages of the newspapers. He went with supporting Manchester United as he vaguely remembered Dad supporting them, and as Brett did too, it made the conversation easier – and less meant rivalry. He used the excuse that with travelling he'd not been able to follow the football so easily, so his lack of knowledge was accepted. Remembering Ruby's advice, too, whenever with Callum and Brett, he kept up his nerdy, dorky appearance. He was getting used to the glasses now, even forgetting they were on his face at times.

Right now, Brett was sitting with them in the small staff room drinking coffee, and they were discussing gaming. Callum played Xbox a lot. Brett too – though he seemed a fan of his Wii.

"We should have a boys' night in," Callum said, ladling sugar into his coffee. Steve watched, trying to hide his grimace. He remembered the days when he used to take sugar in his drinks. He'd weaned himself off it, and was now grateful. Unwanted calories, plus he enjoyed the flavour of the coffee.

"Yeah, I can't afford to keep going out. I want to move out of my parents' place," Brett said, grumbling. The three of them were wedged around a small table.

"You're still living at home?" Callum teased.

"Yeah, after my ex dumped me, I moved back a couple of months ago so that I could save for a deposit on a property." Brett scowled at Callum. "And one day I want to open my own restaurant."

"Come on over to mine," Steve said, before even thinking it through. The place wasn't his. It was Ruby's.

Brett frowned. "Won't Ruby mind?"

"Nah, believe it or not, I've got her wrapped around my finger."

"I don't know," said Callum, "Won't it be a bit weird? I don't think Miss Whiplash likes me much."

Brett punched the top of his arm and Callum winced, a look of 'what did you do that for?' "Keep calling her that and she won't like you. Besides, she's not that bad. She's only doing her job. If you didn't fuck about, she wouldn't have to nag."

Callum rubbed the top of his arm, then brought his mug to his lips. "So what have you got, an Xbox or a Wii?" Callum turned to Steve, changing the subject back, and Steve's mouth opened, then shut.

What did he have?

"Um, both. Only bought them the other day—" He shouldn't have said that.

"Whoa! How much exactly is Ruby paying you?" Callum eyed Steve suspiciously.

"Oh no, I mean..." Steve laughed as he spoke, scratching the back of his head, hating the fact he couldn't run a hand through his gelled hair, but getting used to it. "I only unpacked them the other day. I've had them in storage for a bit." Luckily, the lads didn't seem to question it and Steve let out a relieved sigh as they walked back down to the office with their hot drinks in hand.

"So we'll come over with the pizza and beers – tonight?" Callum scraped his chair along the floor as he stood up.

"Yeah, why not. It's Friday," Steve said. "Do you guys have work tomorrow?"

"Not till later," Brett said shaking his head.

Shit, what was he doing? He didn't own any games consoles. Trip to the Mall required urgently – he'd slip out at lunchtime.

Callum smiled eagerly. "Perfect."

***

As soon as Steve arrived back home, he started setting up the games console in Ruby's lounge, plugging it into her TV. He'd hidden the boxes so they didn't look just bought. Ruby stood there, hands on her hips, and he knew he'd have to do some sweet talking. She didn't think his charm worked on her, but it did.

"What the hell is that?"

Steve tapped the boxes. "Xbox. I can play with Callum then." He grinned, showing off perfect teeth.

Ruby rolled her eyes. "Is this why you borrowed my car at lunchtime?"

"Yep. You wanted me to be ordinary, so that's what I'm trying to do. Mr Mediocre Man is into computer games."

"Mediocre man?"

"Yeah, you called me that when we were shopping that time, and it stuck. By the way, they're coming over at seven with pizzas."

"What? Who?"

"Brett and Callum. I couldn't ask you in front of them, how un-cool would that look?" he said, his expression and tone wry. "Sometimes I need to look as if I wear the pants."

"I'm your sister, not your wife."

"I know, and a bossy one, too. But because I need to make it up to you, I'm letting you boss me about." He winked, then continued with getting the TV set up.

"And the word is trousers. Ditch the American."

"Trousers." Steve nodded.

"Right, so I need to make myself scarce?" Ruby puffed cushions on her sofa and tidied the lounge so it looked uncluttered, stacking CDs, putting books back on the shelf and magazines in the rack.

"No, you like pizza, join us. It'll be fun."

"But ... I'm their boss," she said, hesitantly.

"Ruby, you don't have to be their boss after hours. Relax and let your hair down."

She flicked her fringe out of her eyes and slumped onto the sofa, Steve sat beside her with the remote controls.

"How much did this set you back?"

"Don't ask. I bought the Wii too."

"Well, make out you've had them a while, not you've just bought it."

"That's why I'm sitting here trying to work the damn thing out!"

Ruby huffed and disappeared upstairs, and Steve fiddled with the equipment, trying not to get frustrated. Why had he agreed to tonight? He'd played on the things, occasionally, because they were available in hotels and on film locations, as a way to kill time while waiting around during filming. But they were already set up, he just had to press a button and go. Steve plugged both the Xbox and the Wii into the TV. Even kids used these game consoles, so it couldn't be that hard to set up.

Steve was about to throw the remote control at the television when Ruby snatched it out of his hand.

"Oh, give it here. Luckily for you I've had a few ex-boyfriends who were addicted to these things." She pressed a button and the Wii's welcome screen appeared.

"A *few* ex-boyfriends? Not one or two?"

"Don't look at me like that. I'm twenty-seven. I carry baggage."

"Do I need to go visit any of these ex-boyfriends?" Steve said, seriously, eyeing her suspiciously. Every now and then he'd get that pang of guilt that he'd been missing from her life, not looking after her. When Dad had died, he'd promised himself he'd be the father figure for Ruby. He'd failed.

Ruby laughed, punching his arm softly. "No, I'm over them."

The doorbell chimed, interrupting Steve's thoughts.

"Oh, Christ, is that the time already?" Steve glanced at his watch. No, even for a cheap watch, it kept time perfectly. It was just him losing five minutes here and there. He hated running late, and so did Callum and Brett, apparently, because they were early.

"Ha, you'll have to wing it now. No time to practise." Ruby leapt off the sofa, and answered the door. Steve, finding his glasses and putting them on, hastily threw any remnants of packaging behind the sofa and followed. Callum and Brett stood bearing gifts; pizza, computer games and cans of lager.

"Sorry. Pizzas didn't take so long at the takeaway, hence we're early."

"Yeah, there wasn't a queue," Brett added.

"Hello, Ruby," Callum said, entering the house holding two large pizza boxes as Ruby beckoned them in. "All right, Stu."

"Hi," she replied.

Both wore casual clothes, which for a moment made them unrecognisable out of their work uniform.

"Stuart, shall I put the beers in the fridge?" Brett asked. He wiped his feet on the doormat, and once he'd removed his shoes, walked into the lounge.

"Yeah, just through to the kitchen," Steve said, pointing, used to being called Stu or Stuart now. Ruby tended to stick to calling him Bro when anyone was about. Would she remember tonight? She needed to be careful if drinking as she didn't want to get sloppy and blow Steve's cover.

Once settled, eating pizza direct from the boxes and drinking lager from the can, except Ruby, who had got herself a glass, they started playing the games.

There was a lot of laughing and jeering. Depending on the game, they either played individually or teamed up. Ruby and Brett versus Steve and Callum. "Good job my neighbour's partially deaf," Ruby said, her words slurring a little. "The noise three men make over a game."

Steve, pleased Ruby was relaxing, gave her a hug. "See, this is fun."

"Yeah, it is." She plopped herself next to Brett on the sofa and nudged him. Steve noticed his nervous smile.

In the early hours of the morning, Callum and Brett's taxi arrived to take each of them home. Ruby, a smidge drunk, gave them both a hug before they walked out the door.

She'd had real fun tonight, and it had been nice getting to know the two men a little better outside work. Maybe Callum wouldn't be so off-ish with her now.

"Night, Stu. Night, Ruby," Callum called out, waving, then walked towards the taxi.

"Thanks for coming, it was fun." She paused, hugging Brett, liking the sensation of him holding her. It had been a while since she'd been held. He didn't feel so scrawny now while she cuddled him. Was it her imagination or did he hesitate in letting her go?

Ridiculous!

He smelled rather nice, too, she thought, catching his aftershave, which she had been smelling occasionally.

Probably the alcohol, it was making her delirious.

"Thanks, team mate," she said as he let her go, and waved them off, Steve standing beside her. He'd done brilliantly tonight, too. They'd had fun, and Callum and Brett, though younger than him, had accepted him as a friend. Her plan was working, though a boys night in was hardly a way for Steve to find his true love. However, he had to begin somewhere, and friends were a good start.

Chapter 8

Monday 28th October

On Monday, Steve had a later shift to Ruby. She'd been scheduling their shifts to match most of the time, including their days off, but she had a meeting this morning, and needed him in later. He hated the idea that she was at work, and he was stuck home. He didn't know how long he had in the UK, so he wanted to spend as much time as possible with his sister. But there was nothing he could do. He had a few hours to kill, so he dropped her off, then went home to play the Wii. He particularly liked the golf. Brett was rather good at it too, and the competitive streak in Steve wanted to improve his technique.

This is when they found it difficult with one car. He felt tied, limited. He could just buy a car, but Ruby kept nagging about him splashing his money around and to live normally. She insisted they would share the car. Or he could take the bus.

In fifteen years, the public transport system really hadn't improved. He'd rather take a cab. He could afford a cab.

He'd just tell Ruby he'd got the bus.

Steve headed to the hotel early as Ruby would need the car to drive home. Plus being stuck indoors playing Wii was not going to help him find the woman of his dreams.

Uniform donned with his name badge 'Stuart' in place, he knocked on Ruby's office door even though it was open. Looking up from her desk, she smiled, then glanced at the clock on her wall.

"You're early," she said, frowning. He walked in and handed over her car keys.

"I know, but I was bored at home. I'm going to sit in the staff room for a bit and read the paper." He gestured to the paper tucked under his arm.

In the staff room, Steve looked up from reading his paper – he liked to keep an eye on the media – to see Lydia arrive. He'd worked with her on and off now and was getting to know her slowly. He smiled at her.

"Do you want another tea or coffee?" she asked.

"No, no." He coughed, realising his American twang was back since he hadn't spoken to anyone much that morning, and cleared his throat. "I'm fine, thanks. But come join me."

Lydia returned with a mug filled with tea and sat opposite him. He grinned, always the charmer. "Are you on your break?"

"No, I start in half an hour. I was over at the Mall, and I'm not a great window shopper. I get depressed looking at things I can't afford to buy, and didn't really have enough time to go home," Lydia said, relaxing into the chair. "I like to get a tea before I start, too."

She pulled out a small black sketchpad from her duffle bag and some pencils.

"Do you draw?" Steve closed his newspaper.

He watched as her cheeks flushed pink, her skin flawless without makeup. "Yes," she said, shyly. "I want to be an illustrator."

"For books?"

"Yeah, children's books really." She flicked open the pad, and showed him some drawings on a page, mainly of cherub like children and a couple of animals similar to the ones on her doodle pad.

"Cool – so this is just the day job?"

"It's my only job, until I make it," she said, emphasising the 'make it'. Steve knew all about making it and the long, lonely, broke path it led to. Until you did make it of course... and even then not everything was perfect. After all here he was now hiding behind an idea of Ruby's, her version of Clark Kent, Mediocre Man. He fumbled with his glasses – remembering Clark's clumsiness made him look less confident. When of course, Clark was confident, he was Superman for Christ's sake.

Steve was far from Superman, yet, fame and money could give you no limitations. He just couldn't fly, unless he had a green screen behind him and some computer graphics. He quite fancied a superhero role.

"You know, you really do have the most amazing eyes," she said, looking him right in the eye.

Steve frowned. Had he been staring into space?

"Oh, sorry." She blushed again, and Steve couldn't stop watching her. Lydia, although quiet and reserved, actually was very pretty when he took a closer look.

He used the modest approach. "Yeah, well, they're pretty good for seeing out of." He widened his eyes, and pulled a face, so she giggled. He liked that sound.

"No, seriously, I'd love to paint them, get their colour right. But I think it would come out wrong."

"Yeah, like you'd paint them green." He rolled his eyes and smiled playfully.

"Stop it." She nudged his arm, giggling. "Can I take a closer look? Purely for occupational reasons," she said and tucked a loose strand of her blonde hair behind her ear. "I want to see what colours are mixed in there. I have a boy character who could do with light blue eyes."

Steve shrugged. "Yeah, sure. If it's for professional reasons, why not?"

Their knees touched as Lydia pulled her chair round closer. Inches away, Lydia looked at one eye then the other. He could feel the warmth of her breath on his face.

"Can I?" She gestured towards his glasses and he nodded. As she removed his glasses, Steve couldn't register the feeling that occurred, only it was pleasant. Why had his groin suddenly come to life? She could remove every single piece of clothing from him like that...

Just not here at work...

With her expression serious, studying him, Steve crossed his eyes and pulled a face, making her laugh again. She tapped him playfully on his arm and he put his glasses back on, glad to be replacing his disguise, albeit a feeble one.

"Get what you want?"

She nodded, and scraped the chair back round to the other side of the table. She flicked open a black notepad and started sketching.

"Can I see?"

"No." She shook her head.

"Ah, come on, let me see. I did show you my eyes."

"I'd rather keep some of them to myself." She shielded the paper with her arm, like a kid taking an exam.

"Lydie, if you can't show me, how an earth you going to get them published?" He reached over to grab the notepad, still thinking they were playing a game. But sweet, quiet Lydia clutched the pad to her chest and scowled.

"No, Stuart, please, they're just scribbles. I've shown you what I want you to see." And she wrapped the band around the notepad and tucked it back into her bag. "And it's Lydia, not Lydie."

That's me told.

"Hey, Stu," Callum arrived. Brett following behind him. Both were in uniform ready for work.

"Hi, guys." Steve glanced at Lydia. She'd picked up her bag and walked out of the staff room. He didn't like the awkwardness between them; he'd wanted to encourage her, not upset her. He'd try talking with her later.

"Tea?" Lydia asked. She was at the urn filling a mug. It had been the first word she'd uttered to him since their little disagreement earlier on. He'd been tucked away in the bar, and hadn't had a chance to see her on reception.

"Thanks," he said softly, putting a thumb up.

This wasn't a chance meeting. He'd seen her go for her break and had made an excuse to Callum. He'd followed her into the staff room, relieved they were alone. One plus side to working late. He stood watching her make the tea.

"Hey, Lydia, I'm sorry," he said. "I called you Lydie, like I call Ruby, Roo."

"I shouldn't have got tetchy about it. Sorry." She still hadn't looked Steve in the eye once. She blushed and Steve felt the heat of the kitchen too, rising around his neck.

"I only wanted to look at the pad because I was interested, artist to artist. Not to ridicule you."

"You draw?" Lydia asked and Steve frowned at her. "You said artist to artist?"

"Oh, uh, no ... not really. But you were studying me, and—"

"Sorry, did you say tea or coffee?" Lydia put her tea aside and grabbed another clean mug from the shelf by the urn.

"Oh, yeah, tea please." he said, remembering he needed to look as if he'd come into the kitchen for a break. He dropped a teabag into his mug and she filled it.

In silence, she poured the milk and put it back in the fridge.

"Look, I don't want an atmosphere, I won't call you Lydie again. I didn't realise you didn't like it."

"Actually ... I did like it." She looked straight at him as he stepped aside and she rushed past him and Steve felt the whoosh.

Thursday 31st October

A few days passed and Halloween arrived. Every year the hotel held a masked ball. It was organised for most of the staff as an early Christmas party, because with the run up to the festive season, it got too busy with other events so this was the best time of year to hold a party. Ruby would rota the staff, so who worked the previous year got to party the following year. Some volunteered, happy to work for the overtime. The guests were invited too. This way there could be no complaints about the noise. Or at least, they'd be kept to a minimum. This year it was on Thursday, so it meant with the restaurant closed especially, the hotel would be fairly quiet and could run on minimum staff.

Steve hurried around in the afternoon, cleaning glasses and filling the fridges with bottles of wine, beer, and mixers. He and Ruby were going to be working that night, but she assured him it was just as good fun. It meant other staff who deserved the night off would get to party.

Callum and Steve had cleared most of the furniture out of the bar, making an area available for the band, and a temporary small wooden dance floor had been laid.

"Have you got a costume?" Callum said, huffing and panting with the sofa between them.

"Ruby's organised it," Steven replied as they lowered the sofa into place out in the hallway. They'd moved some of the tables and chairs to the edges of the room, and around the dance floor so that there were areas to sit and put drinks down.

"So you don't know what you're wearing?"

Steve cringed. No, he didn't.

***

Steve stared at his reflection in the mirror. Had Ruby taken this a step too far? Was this some kind of joke?

Superman. He was wearing a goddamn Superman costume. And he had a mask of Christopher Reeve's face. To get into character, he'd slicked his hair so that it had the quiff at the front and looked darker.

"Come on, Steve. We need to be there by seven thirty," Ruby called up the stairs.

Maybe it was a good job he was working because he wasn't sure where he was supposed to store his wallet. He stood at the top of the stairs, hands on his hips.

"Couldn't you have found me a better costume?"

"The theme is film stars and characters. And I left it a bit late. That was really the only thing in your size. Besides, I think it's apt." Ruby, unrecognisable dressed as Wonder Woman – including the black wig of hair – stood at the bottom, matching his stance. They were both getting into character, obviously.

"Apt! More like tight."

"Shove a pair of socks down there if you're worried."

"I don't need to put socks down there. Thank you very much." That certainly wasn't his problem. He wondered if this took his disguise to another level. *Oh, the irony.* But wasn't he supposed to be dorky, and here he was showing off his toned physique. Maybe he should have laid off the exercise... Would a cardboard mask of Christopher Reeve really hide who he was?

"I thought a masked ball was a glitzy affair. Big dresses and tuxedos."

"We did that last year. The staff wanted a bit more of a fancy dress theme – which is optional."

"Couldn't I have worn a tuxedo?"

"No!"

"And what am I supposed to do about my glasses?" Steve had tucked an arm of the frames down his costume, so they hung at his chest.

"Take them with you, and see how you get on. Everyone will be drunk by the end of the night."

The doorbell rang. Steve froze.

"Oh, an early trick or treater!" Ruby said excitedly, clapping her hands then opening the front door. *Saved by the bell.*

"Trick or treat," said a chorus of tiny voices. Two cute little witches and a three-foot skeleton.

Ruby dished out the sweets then shut the door.

"Come on, Superman," Ruby shouted.

"Maybe I should have the costume under a suit... and play Clark Kent."

"We don't have time. You look brilliant. Come on, my Man of Steel."

"Isn't that a different actor?"

If it hadn't been so dark, the car journey would have been more interesting. Steve and Ruby did get a wave at the traffic lights, and someone flashed their headlights. Oh and a middle-aged man crossing the road nearly tripped over – which made Ruby giggle. By then, Steve had pulled his mask on.

This better not get in the press.

The band was setting up and testing the microphones when Ruby and Steve arrived at the hotel. All the tables, covered with black tablecloths, had a scattering of pumpkin- and skeleton-shaped glittery confetti. The bar, adorned in Halloween decorations, had cobwebs hanging between the spirit bottles and spiders hanging from the ceiling. Outside on the terrace, lanterns were lit and the patio heater was fired up, ready for the smokers to gather. Other staff working the event were also in costumes. From James Bond – *easy, a damn tux! Couldn't he have worn that?* – to Mary Poppins. Steve tried to work out who was who. He'd been at the hotel a few weeks now, and was easily able to put names to faces, but the idea of a masked ball was to have some anonymity. There was more irony to this party; Steve in reality had met some of the faces on the masks.

Some of the partygoers had, like Steve, cardboard masks of their characters to hide their identity, and others wore the masquerade masks, some beautifully decorated and ornate.

"All right, Stu?" A man dressed as Robin slapped his back, then punched his gloved fists together before placing them on his hips, rehearsed true Robin style. He wasn't the 'film' Robin, but the old TV show that Steve had watched reruns of as a kid. Callum wore a red and green costume with a bright yellow cape. Even though he wore Robin's black mask he was still recognisable. *See, flimsy disguises don't really work. Who was he kidding with a pair of glasses?* Besides, Callum was the only person to call Steve, Stu.

Steve was relieved he wasn't the only guy now wearing tights.

Batman (Adam West rather than Christian Bale) appeared by his side-kick, Callum, and it took Steve a moment to realise it was Brett. Although a slim build, the man wasn't so scrawny out of his chef whites.

"Are you working tonight?" Steve asked them.

"I am," said Callum.

"I'm not." Brett raised a pint of beer and grinned. It was the only part of his face showing. Now he was wearing the right kind of costume – one that had a great mask. *And another guy wearing tights.* "Good job Ruby closes the restaurant, as I can't work in a kitchen dressed like this."

Steve chuckled. No, a kitchen certainly wasn't the best place to wear synthetic materials. "Holy bat mobiles, you mean you aren't carrying a fire extinguisher in your utility belt?"

Brett laughed, then his smile faded as Ruby approached. It was becoming DC Comics Superhero Central.

"Nice costume, Ruby," Brett said. "Are you working tonight?"

"Sadly, yes, someone needs to keep an eye on you lot."

"Maybe I can buy you a drink later then?"

Steve noticed a hint of confusion in Ruby's expression as she waved it off with a, "Yes, yes, maybe later. Thank you." Did she realise it was Brett? "Right, Robin, to the bat cave, bring me some more ice, please. Superman," she turned to Steve smirking, "there are Hollywood stars starting to arrive at the bar."

"Now I know why you chose Wonder Woman," Steve said.

Steve lifted the hatch, and went behind the bar. As he wiped down the counter, an impressive Yoda approached.

"What can I get you, sir?" Steve said, frowning. He wasn't sure if he liked the idea of everyone hiding behind a mask or not. Whoever it was under there was short – well, shorter than Steve – and so suited the costume.

Yoda lifted his mask to reveal a grinning Pete. He was Ruby's assistant manager, and because Steve worked most hours with Ruby, he didn't see him much. Ruby constantly moaned about the man and his incompetence.

"Fosters, a pint of, mate," Pete said in Yoda style.

Steve poured the pint and between them they shared some corny Star Wars jokes. "May the Force be with you," Steve said handing Pete his drink.

At nine o'clock the band kicked off, playing covers of the latest hits. More and more film characters and stars arrived. The iconic characters were popular. Steve served a few Darth Vaders. There were storm troopers, an Avatar, Spider Man and even a Scooby Doo. Everyone's costumes were brilliant; they'd gone to town on the details. There was an Elvis, and his mask was a pair of huge Seventies style sunglasses. He had the quiff and the sequins, and became the centre of attention on the dance floor with his swinging hips.

Callum gave Steve a nudge, and he looked in the direction Callum gestured.

"Who is that?" Callum said.

Catwoman walked towards the bar. It could have been Michelle Pfeiffer, only a little more curvier. The mask covered most of her face. She was unrecognisable. It had to be Alice. Only Alice would wear a black cat suit so confidently.

"Hi, a glass of white wine, please," Catwoman said. She could have been purring. Over the noise of the band, Steve couldn't even make out the voice. It didn't help that his brain had travelled south.

"Sure, Pinot Grigio or the Chardonnay?"

"The Pinot, please."

Steve must have been frowning, because she smirked. He could see blue eyes, heavily lined with black kohl and mascara. He recognised the eyes, but could not place them to a face. And didn't Alice have brown eyes?

Steve handed her the glass of wine. She went to pay, but he winked. "This one's on me."

She flirtatiously smiled her full, glossy red lips, raised her glass and gave a seductive purr that rumbled all the way to Steve's groin, then walked off.

Steve watched, trying to gather clues as to who the woman was. All her hair was tucked up into her mask, so he couldn't even tell her hair colour. She joined some girls on the dance floor. Some were waitresses in the restaurant, even Brett was there. Maybe she worked in the restaurant, too. Who was she?

"Stop ogling, and keep working." Ruby appeared in front of Steve with some empty glasses.

"Hey, the whole idea is for me to meet a woman." Shaken from his reverie, Steve cleared the glasses off the bar straight into the dishwasher.

"This is true."

"Hey, Ruby, who is Catwoman?" Callum asked the question Steve was dying to know the answer to.

Ruby smirked, hands on her hips in a true Wonder Woman manner – maybe she had the acting gene too – and said coolly, "For me to know, you two to find out. Now get back to work."

If only Steve did have x-ray vision...

Once Ruby had disappeared into the crowd, Callum said into Steve's ear, "Am I allowed to tell you your sister looks hot in hot pants?"

Steve scowled at Callum. "No." Then smiled, and slapped him on the back playfully. "Who do you think Catwoman is? Alice?"

"It's definitely not Alice," Callum replied.

"Why?"

"Because she's stood at the bar looking a lot like Lara Croft."

Steve turned, and sure enough, leaning against the bar was Alice. She wore simply a tight, dark brown T-shirt accentuating full rounded breasts, and shorts, with gun straps around her legs and arms, and her long, chestnut hair was woven into a plait, with a couple of tendrils at the front. In her well-manicured hands – unlike how Lara Croft's would look like climbing caves – she held her masquerade mask. She didn't hide her face though, so Steve didn't pull his mask down.

"Hello," Alice said, giving Steve an appreciative look up and down, unnerving him. His costume was so tight he might as well be stood there in his Calvin Klein's.

"What can I get you, Miss Croft?" Steve said, hiding his anxiety by broadening his smile.

"Bacardi and coke, please. Make it a double."

When Steve returned with her drink, Alice asked, "Where are your glasses?"

Steve tapped his chest. They were gone. Then he remembered he'd stuck them by the till. "Oh, they were getting on my nerves with my mask."

"But can you see okay?"

Yes, he had perfect vision but he couldn't tell her that. "Just about. Probably have a headache at the end of the evening."

"And not through a hangover," she giggled and sipped her drink. "You should think about wearing contact lenses."

Now Steve was nervous. Alice was the one person he feared would recognise him. He wanted to pull the mask down over his face, but how suspicious would that look? "I can't bear the thought of trying to stick things in my eyes," he said, screwing up his face.

Another person arrived at the bar, he excused himself and Alice disappeared into the crowd. When he went to put the cash in the till, he discarded the mask and he slipped his glasses on. The mask was getting on his nerves, because it hindered his peripheral vision – he had a Catwoman to find. He'd rather tolerate the glasses, feeling the need for some sort of disguise, however flimsy. *Just in case.*

Rushed off his feet all night, Steve ventured out to the reception area, where it was cooler and quieter, to collect some glasses. Hans Solo and Princess Leia were huddled together in a corner behind a small palm, embraced in a kiss, oblivious to their surroundings. Darth Vader walked by mumbling, 'Get a room'. Steve chuckled and nodded a hello to Maxine who was covering reception. She wore her hotel uniform, and didn't look very busy, flicking through a magazine behind the desk. By the photographs on the cover, it looked like a baking magazine, and not one that would contain Hollywood's sexiest men.

"You didn't fancy this tonight?" Steve said.

"No, it's for you youngsters," Maxine said, chirpily. "Besides, I'm having fun watching the shenanigans." She subtly gestured in the direction of the kissing couple.

Steve made the most of this time away from the bar trying to find Catwoman. He'd caught a glimpse of her earlier on the dance floor, but couldn't get away from serving drinks at the time to get a closer look. But where was she now?

Scanning the room, he couldn't believe how hard it was to find one woman. But with everyone dressed as a superhero, or a Hollywood star or character, it was proving difficult. Then, he spotted her. Catwoman stood by the fireplace. Steve dumped the glasses he was carrying on a nearby table and was about to head towards her when he paused. Another character, Indiana Jones by the looks of him, joined Catwoman, giving her a glass of white wine.

Damn it.

What should he do? He could still go over... some empty glasses needed collecting from the mantelpiece.

"I like your costume." A middle-aged woman wearing a blonde wig, stepped in front of Steve, her face hidden behind an ornate masquerade mask. She was dressed as a voluptuous Marilyn Monroe, the trademark white dress plunging low to reveal her cleavage. It fitted well. "Care for the next dance, Superman?"

She wobbled on her heels, possibly aided by too much alcohol, and Steve caught her glass, cupping her hand also. "Sorry, I'm working tonight."

As Marilyn stroked Steve's hand which he had unwittingly given her, he peeked around her towards the fireplace. Catwoman was gone. Steve cursed under his breath. With a firm grip, the woman dragged him towards the dance floor.

"You must be allowed one dance," Marilyn cooed flirtatiously.

"No, no, I really must get on—"

"Oh, there you are." To Steve's relief, Ruby taped him on the arm. "Some idiot has dropped their pint on the dance floor. Can you go grab the mop and bucket, please?"

"Yeah, yeah, sure, just a minute." He turned to Marilyn, and tried to look disappointed, shrugging his shoulders apologetically as he spoke, "My boss needs me."

"I'll take a rain check, sweetheart." She seductively dragged her fingernail gently under his chin, then kissed him full on the lips. Steve's eyes widened as he jerked away.

"Hurry up, Bro, I don't want someone falling over."

"Yes, I'm on it, Ruby," Steve said, frustration creeping into his tone. Did she think he really wanted Marilyn hitting on him? The woman had even had the audacity to slap him on his backside as he turned away.

While mopping the floor to dry up the spill, Steve continuously looked for Catwoman but he couldn't find her. Where had she gone? Had she already left?

Midnight arrived very quickly, and the band played their last song. As soon as the lead singer said 'Good night', the main lights were switched on as a clear sign to ask everyone to leave. There were some lingerers. Callum, Steve and the rest of the staff worked to clear away the glasses, removing the tablecloths and stacking away tables and chairs as the band dismantled the equipment. Ruby instructed she wanted it back to normal ready for the morning.

"Stuart, give us a hand with Alice," Batman called. It took Steve a minute to realise he was talking to him. Brett still had his mask on – impressive. He must have been roasting under there. He held onto Alice who was unsteady on her feet. Between them, they escorted Lara Croft, to a waiting taxi she'd pre-booked.

"Thank you, Superman," Alice said, her palm to Steve's cheek. "Can I be your Lois?" She planted her mouth on Steve's, and he quickly pulled away. The kiss pleasantly surprised him. "I'd love to wake cuddled up with you tomorrow morning."

"Alice, you're a little drunk," Steve said, lightly, helping her into the taxi. "Maybe another time."

They watched the taxi drive out of the gates, then strolled back into the lobby.

"Did you see where Catwoman went?" Steve asked, feeling the need to change the subject over Alice kissing him.

Brett shook his head. "I think she left early, something about working tomorrow morning."

"Who is she?"

Brett chucked. "I don't know."

"Is she one of the waitresses?"

"I don't think so."

"Hmm... maybe she's one of the chambermaids." They strolled into the bar, and Brett helped clear up.

"Hey, you're off duty tonight, you can go home," Steve said.

"It's all right, Callum's giving me a lift home," Brett glanced at Ruby as he spoke, "plus many hands make light work and all that. It'll help the rest of you get home earlier too."

Ruby approached, wig removed and looking rosy cheeked and hot. "Hey, how's it going? Did you enjoy yourself, Bro?" As she spoke, Brett removed his mask, also looking flushed. "Oh, it's you, Brett," she said.

He nervously smiled, Steve observed. Did Brett have a thing

102

for Ruby? He glanced at Ruby.... hmmm... did she have a thing for Brett?

"Thought I'd help out while I wait for Callum to finish." Brett shifted from one foot to another.

"Thanks for the drink earlier."

"Callum did deliver it then?"

"Yes, he said it was from Batman," Ruby said, giggling. "I wasn't sure who that was, so thank you."

"No problem."

Steve coughed.

"Oh, yes, not too much to do now, the band are nearly packed away," Ruby said getting back into boss mode. "Brett could you help Ste... Stuart move the sofas back, please?" She'd stumbled over his name. "Oh, on second thoughts, you're not actually working so you're not insured. I'll get Callum—"

"It's okay, I can help Superman. Though, he should be able to lift them all by himself."

"Ha ha ha! You mean you don't have something in your utility belt?" Steve said, slapping Brett on the back. "Come on, then we can head home."

Chapter 9

Friday 1st November

Steve had arrived into work with Ruby, and although it was later than usual, he could have done with another hour in bed. He wearily polished glasses and tidied the bar, removing further traces of last night's Halloween party. Also, Friday meant the hotel would start getting busier with weekend travellers, the City-Breakers as Ruby referred to them, so he made the most of this quiet time to catch up with chores ready for this afternoon's busy rush. He'd been in the UK nearly four weeks now. The time was well spent with Ruby, but would he really find his perfect – or not so perfect – woman in two months?

The phone at the bar rang, waking Steve out of his tired reverie.

"Hi, you're through to The Terrace Bar how can I help you?"

"Oh, you're American," said a cheery voice.

Steve coughed, shaking his head. *Concentrate!* This happened when he hadn't spoken a word all morning. "No, sorry, I'm not, I'm just working on my accents. Forgot myself for a minute."

"What others do you do?"

"Sorry?"

"Accents. Are you an actor?"

He laughed. Good job the caller couldn't see his expression.

Get out of this one. "Hell, noooo."

"Oh, well, that's a shame… Anyway, I would like a bottle of champagne brought up to my room, please."

"Of course, would you like me to run through what we have? There are three labels to choose from."

"The Veuve Clicquot I think. Two glasses, please, and will *you* deliver?"

"Good choice." The way she said '*you*' made him uneasy. "It'll be myself or Callum." Callum entered the bar, mid yawn, to start his shift.

Steve finished the conversation, saying they'd deliver as soon as possible, and put the phone down.

"What was that about?" Callum said, rubbing his eyes.

"Room 104 wants a bottle of champagne taken to her room. Do you want to do it, or shall I?"

"Nah, you go. I'll man the fort."

Steve placed the champagne flutes on a tray lined with a cloth napkin and fetched a champagne bottle from the fridge, resting it in an ice bucket.

"If I'm not back in ten minutes, send out a search party," Steve joked.

Steve found the room, and balancing the tray on one hand, knocked.

The door opened, and Steve's eyes widened momentarily at the sight before him. He reined in his surprise, to look unfazed.
Marilyn.

The woman had opened the door, dressed in only a bronze, silk negligee. Without her mask, Steve guessed she was aged around her mid-fifties. The heavy make-up and blonde hair tied up made it hard to tell.

"Oh good," she said, smoothly, "it *is* my superhero." She winked. "Please can you put it on the table by the window?"

Steve paced towards the table, noticing the curtains were still drawn, the lighting low, and a smell of bubble bath. He also spied the blonde wig and white dress draped over one of the lounge chairs. *Definitely Marilyn.*

"Open it, please," she said. Steve heard her lock the door. *Oh, shit.* His hands fumbled with the foil because he was concentrating more on the woman heading towards him. She unclipped her hair, so it swished around her shoulders. She had a good, curvy figure, hence the Marilyn costume suiting her, and the gown revealed the swell of her breasts. He spied a hint of lace underneath. *Thank God she was wearing underwear.*

Okay, so he was used to women chucking themselves at him, only he usually had a couple of bodyguards to help with the affray. And usually the women were a lot younger.

He got the cork out and managed not to spill any of the champagne, pouring a glass and handing it to her.

"Pour one for yourself."

"Thank you," *remember your manners,* "but I can't, I'm on duty."

"You're not a police officer. One glass won't harm. They won't miss you for a bit. Will they?"

Steve fiddled with his glasses. He felt like Laurel, or was it Hardy? How did he get himself into this mess? And more importantly, how was he going to get out of it?

She poured the second glass of champagne and handed it to him, giving Steve the once over, with a flirtatious pout. The woman was checking him out. She wasn't unattractive, and yes, he needed to find a woman, but she was possibly twenty years his senior.

"I should be going. The bar will be getting busy." Steve put the flute down.

She picked it back up and handed it to him. "Take a sip, don't let me drink alone. These business trips get awfully lonely."

"Um, so you're here on business? Not here to see the city?" It was Friday, usually all the business bods had checked out this morning.

"I need to be back for a meeting early Monday, so decided to stay on. Might pay Bath a visit, it's such a beautiful city. You could come with me..."

She brushed his waistcoat, her manicured fingers adorned with gold rings and gemstones, toying with a button. *None on her wedding finger, though.* Steve took a step back.

"Sadly I've got to work this weekend." He edged around the table, mentally organising his escape route.

"I feel like I know you." Her eyes narrowed.

Oh, please do not recognise me.

He nervously pushed his glasses up for good measure. "Well, if that's all, I'd better be going."

"Oh, um, I'm having problems with the television. Could you see if you can get it to work?"

"Sure." Steve cringed, and hoped it didn't show behind the smile he had plastered on his face. He went to the TV, found the remote control and turned it on. There was nothing wrong with the damn television. "What channel would you like?"

"Oh, could I have the radio through it?"

"Of course."

While Steve flicked through to find the radio – he knew some of the stations were set – she hovered by his side, holding both champagne glasses. "See, while you're here, you might as well finish your drink."

Steve took the glass, sorely tempted to gulp it down. It might calm his nerves. How far did customer service go? He didn't dare be rude and have a complaint made to Ruby, but at the same time...

The telephone started ringing.

With a puzzled expression, the woman answered it. "Hello? Yes, yes, he's here... okay, I'll let him know. Thank you." She put the phone down, and disappointment etched across her face and in her tone. "Apparently you're needed downstairs. The manager is on the warpath. If you're not back at the bar, your colleague said something about you being sacked."

"Oh, right." *Thank you, Callum!* Steve dropped the remote control on the bed, placed the glass by the television and was at the door faster than Superman could save Lois Lane.

"She sounds like a right bitch. Maybe I should complain?"

"No, no, don't do that. Enjoy the rest of your stay at Durdham Lodge," Steve said, hurriedly, and darted out of the door. In the safety of the lift, he wiped the beads of sweat from his forehead with the back of his hand.

Back downstairs in the bar, Steve grabbed Callum's shoulders and shook him gratefully. "Thank you, thank you, I could kiss you!"

"Let go of me! What did I do?" Callum pulled a face.

"You rescued me from room 104."

"That was me, actually." Alice stood the other side of the bar, and in his relief, he'd not noticed her.

He grabbed her head in both hands and kissed her forehead. "Thank you! But how'd you know?"

"Oh, I'd given Ms Jones a massage earlier, and a manicure. All she'd gone on about was the new guy behind the bar." Alice mocked the woman with facial expressions, changing her tone of voice. "How hot he'd looked dressed as Superman, how he was kind of dorky but cute."

Dorky but cute? Maybe the glasses were working.

"Oh man, *Ms* – as she prefers to be called – *Jones* – and I'm sure that's not her real name – has frightened more bar staff from this hotel than I can remember," Callum said, laughing.

"You knew about her?" Steve turned on Callum, his cheeks flushing with anger.

"Yeah, she's a regular to the hotel, but hey," he held his hands up defensively, "I didn't realise that was who the champagne was for. When Alice asked where you'd gone, I told her the room number—"

"And so I quickly made the call."

"How can I ever repay you?" Steve teased, hugging her.

"You could take me out tonight, Stuart?" Alice beamed. "I really want to see the new Thor film that's just come out, and I've got no one to go with as my mate has stood me up."

"Oh, right," Steve said. He hadn't expected a date. But Alice was more the kind of girl to date, than *Ms Jones* upstairs. He had to start somewhere. "Of course, what time shall I pick you up?"

＊＊＊

"You're going out with Alice?" Ruby said, her tone mixed with surprise and possibly disapproval. She stood outside the bathroom watching Steve gel his hair.

"Yeah," Steve said, relaying what had happened earlier during the day with Ms Jones.

"Maybe I really should ban that woman."

"Yeah, maybe." Steve frowned at Ruby. He'd experienced some scary situations in his time involving women, and that one would be added to his 'close call' list, mainly because he hadn't had a bodyguard to bail him out.

"Okay, I'll look into it. She can't harass my staff. I can't do anything about it if no one tells me though. It's the first I've heard about it."

"Callum said Pete knew."

"Pfft! Pete! That explains everything. He's wet behind the bloody ears."

"Right, how do I look?" Steve posed in front of Ruby.

"You're forgetting one thing." She handed him his glasses from the bathroom shelf.

"Damn it."

"You have to wear them," she scolded with a stern look to match.

"I know, I know." Steve put them on. The glasses did help remind him to be Stuart.

"Right, have you got everything?"

"You're not Mum, but yes, I booked the tickets when I got home."

"It's crazy to go when the films just started showing. I always wait a couple of weeks."

"Apparently she was supposed to be going with a friend this

109

weekend, and I do owe her." Steve was rather surprised Alice had suggested the action movie *Thor: The Dark World*. He'd anticipated some romantic comedy – which he would have equally enjoyed of course. But he always loved a good action movie. Plus, romantic comedies could set the wrong atmosphere for a first date. If the girl started weeping at the sad bit, did you hand her a tissue, put your arm around her? What then? Action movies were safer. He'd just have to watch her drool over Chris Hemsworth.

"So it's not a date?"

Steve shrugged his shoulders. "I think it is." He'd certainly taken care in his appearance, choosing the best shirt from his limited wardrobe.

Steve borrowed Ruby's car, throwing any rubbish cluttering the footwell into the back, and collected Alice. Her face didn't look any different than at work, as she always wore her make-up heavy due to her job, but tonight, her chestnut hair loose, resting below her shoulders and softened her features.

"I didn't know what to wear. Hope I look okay," she said, sliding into the passenger seat wearing skinny jeans.

He'd chosen to wear jeans too. They weren't dining in a fine restaurant, they were grabbing a bite to eat, then going to the cinema. She could have been wearing a black bin liner and still would have looked stunning.

"You look great. You always look great."

"Thanks, Stuart" Alice beamed at him.

Someone like Alice would fit right in with his lifestyle.

"Where do you fancy eating?" Steve said, as they strolled around the restaurants in Cabot Circus unsure whether to hold her hand or put his arm around her shoulder.

"What do you want to eat?"

"I don't mind, honestly. I'll eat anything. I'm a man."

Alice giggled. "Okay, Frankie and Benny's because I like their pasta, and you can have a manly steak if you want."

"What the lady wants, the lady gets. Frankie and Benny's it is."

Steve held the door open, allowing Alice to enter first. They were quickly seated in a cosy booth with their drinks order taken.

"Seriously, thanks for this afternoon. Not sure what I would have done without your phone call," Steve said, looking over his menu.

"She comes to the hotel once a month. Sometimes she's no trouble, sometimes she's a pain in the arse." Alice closed her menu.

"If a guy tried it on with one of you girls, it would be a different story."

"I know." Alice giggled. "But you survived, so best put it behind you. It's all fun and games working in a hotel."

The waiter returned with their drinks; Alice a glass of white wine and Steve a coke filled with more ice than required. He then took their food order and left them again. Steve found it hard to know what to talk about. Although Alice was attractive, he couldn't decide if he was attracted to her. He was, of course he was, but he wanted to find someone who he connected with, minds as well as bodies. Laughter. Great sex wasn't that great if you couldn't laugh with that person too.

This was only the first date, admittedly. However he didn't have much time; he'd have to treat it like speed-dating.

The food arrived, and as they devoured the food – he was starving – Steve kept the conversation on Alice, trying to find out more about her. He got the full run down of her life's history, almost. How long she'd worked at the hotel, and how long she'd been single. She liked talking about herself. And other people too.

"All the chambermaids are shagging the waiters," she said. This wasn't the first time Steve had heard this, Callum talked about it too. "I could tell you some stories. Sometimes it takes a bit longer to get a room ready for the next guests." She chuckled. "I think..." she paused, as if in thought, "Brett and Lydia had something going at one point."

"Really?" His interest spiked. It was none of his business... But hadn't Brett showed a liking towards Ruby? So his concern was as a big brother.

"They say they're just friends, but I'm not convinced."

The waiter cleared their plates, and Steve glanced at his watch.

"Did you want a dessert or happy with popcorn in the movie?"

"I can't eat another thing else." Alice patted her stomach. "We better go so we can get good seats."

Steve caught the waiter's attention and paid the bill. He didn't push anything more about Brett and Lydia. He didn't want to know, or seem to Alice as if he was prying.

After some time queuing, Steve sank into the cinema chair. They were wide and comfortable, with plenty of leg room, which meant Alice wasn't sitting too close to him.

Or should he raise the arm of the chair, so they could cuddle... Would she expect a cuddle?

It was only a first date, and the whole evening had felt more like friends out together, than a nervous couple. Maybe Alice couldn't see the 'tenth sexiest man' in front of her. Were the glasses actually working?

Before turning her phone to silent, Alice showed him her Facebook profile. She'd tagged herself in Cabot Circus watching *Thor: The Dark World*. "Unfortunately I can't tag you. Are you on Facebook?"

Steve switched his own phone off as he shook his head. *God no!* Ruby had toyed with the idea briefly about setting him up on Facebook, but then agreed best to stay off social media as a precaution. "I don't have time for Facebook." Other people did his real Facebook for him. Marie, his PA liked to keep track of any fan pages, and he had an official page maintained through his publicist.

During the trailers, they made small talk, agreeing or disagreeing about other movies they'd like to see – not necessarily together. He hid his anxiety, relieved his face didn't flash up on the screen. Perfection had been out during the spring and his next movie wasn't due out till the following year, but there was always the fear that they might run the trailer. When the film started, he relaxed fully. Two hours without having to make small talk with Alice, and two hours of getting involved in a story, his favourite subject.

Sometimes Steve liked to watch the movies his agent had put him forward for, and he'd been unsuccessful in getting. Not necessarily to torture himself over it, but he wanted to see what that actor had that maybe Steve didn't, look at the things he needed to improve on. Assess the other actor's qualities.

Alice didn't budge throughout the whole movie. They'd both laughed at the funny parts. The credits rolled at the end, and Steve made to get up, but Alice grabbed his arm to stop him. "We have to stay till the end. Usually something happens," she said.

Steve nodded, and settled back into his chair. He could still feel the warmth of her hand on his skin.

"Did you enjoy it?" he asked, aware that others were leaving around them, though some stayed too. Probably a stupid question, as Alice, like him, had been engrossed in the movie.

"Yes, loved it. It followed on from The Avengers nicely. Loki really is a bad guy you love to hate, isn't he?"

After all the credits, there was an extra scene when Thor returned to Jane, in true superhero fashion, embracing in a passionate kiss.

Alice sighed, "Sadly, only in a film, huh? Now you can take me home, Stuart."

Outside Alice's house, Steve left the car running so the heaters kept blowing.

"Thanks for a wonderful evening," she said, unclipping her seatbelt.

"No, thank you. I had fun." Going to the cinema wouldn't be his ideal first date as it's hard to get to know someone sitting in silence for two hours, but the evening had been enjoyable. They'd managed to talk over dinner and the film had been entertaining.

"So did I. Gosh, is that the time?" she glanced at her watch, "I've got work tomorrow." She leant across and kissed him on the cheek. "See you at work."

Steve waited to make sure Alice entered her house safely, then drove off. There had been no 'let's do it again' or anything like that. Was he disappointed? Maybe Alice liked to keep it cool, and was waiting for him to ask again.

How he felt about Alice he wasn't sure. Only time would tell.

Chapter 10

An icy November had arrived, dry but cold, and in the following week, Steve saw little of Alice. Either their shifts didn't mesh, or she was incredibly busy in the spa. He managed to clear the air with Lydia though, especially as he regularly caught her in the canteen if she arrived early for her shift. It enabled Steve to joke around with her; usually teasing she had a smudge on her nose. Her fingers frequently had black ink marks, so she was easily convinced. His curiosity continued, wanting to know what else was in the sketchpad she carried. He'd notice her tuck it away underneath the reception desk at the start of her shift, with a couple of 2B pencils with chewed ends resting on top of it. He asked a couple of times if she'd added anything to it and if he could see, but she was still reluctant to show him. What would the little boy look like? Another cherubic child, with his electric-blue eyes?

He'd even pull funny faces, or use his best smile, if he passed her on reception, but she still refused, flustered, adjusting her headset, ignoring him, though the corners of her mouth would twitch where she tried to hold in a smile, or laugh.

His evenings were filled by playing Xbox with Callum and Brett, albeit remotely. Steve found it fantastic, how they could meet up online and play together. He'd become addicted. Currently they were blasting their way through a shoot 'em up called *Battlefield 3*.

"As it's Friday, who's up for a few beers and maybe even a club?" Callum stood zipping his coat outside the locker rooms. "Could do with giving the Xbox a bit of a rest." He chuckled.

"Oh, yes, sounds like a good idea to me." Alice joined him.

"Yeah, I could do with a drink," Brett said with a sigh, rubbing the back of his neck.

"If Ruby's game, I'm game," Steve said. "Lydia, you coming?"

Lydia shook her head as she buttoned her coat. "I've got some stuff to do, and besides it's not really my thing."

"Oh, come on, let me buy you a drink." Steve slipped his own coat on. It was a rare occasion for them all to be finishing together. Before Lydia could refuse again, he grinned and said, "Go on, please. It is Friday."

"Okay, but I need to go home and change."

"Me too." Alice popped her head over Steve's shoulder, holding onto his jacket. Conscious she was close, he moved. Although he liked her and she always smelled of exotic, alluring scents, he wasn't keen on her invading his personal space.

"Let's meet up at nine thirty, then," Callum said. They agreed on a pub to meet up in Bristol and who would pick up who in a taxi.

Steve noticed Ruby walking towards them, already with her coat on.

"Coming out with us tonight, Ruby?" Brett shuffled in, to walk beside her. Callum stifled a yawn.

"Oh, yes, okay, if Stuart is, I will." Only Steve heard Ruby stutter over his name.

"Of course I am."

***

Ruby and Steve arrived at the pub before everyone else. Their taxi was running early, whereas the others were running late, according to Callum's text message.

Steve bought them both a drink, and being a busy, popular bar, found a place they could stand and wait. He hated wearing the glasses; they tended to steam up the minute he walked into somewhere hot, coming in from the cold, and they smudged quickly if he touched them.

He had never imagined he'd be able to stand in a trendy bar and not get recognised. It was like no-one would believe the actual actor, Steve Mason, would be standing there drinking bottles of Bud with the rest of them. Which, he gently reminded himself, he should not drink too many of. He did need to keep his wits about him.

Marie had called before they'd left, saying the media were going mad over some other actor, another heartthrob in LA. Luckily, a big movie release meant press coverage, and the rest of Hollywood could relax for a bit. She reassured him that he wasn't being missed – there were enough celebrities out there for the papers and magazines to gossip about; they weren't speculating on a missing Steve Mason – and to enjoy the peace.

Reality seeped back into his life as she also informed him a new version of the script had come through for his film, and she would forward a copy of it to him in the next few days.

Callum arrived and chinked his pint glass against Steve's bottle, bringing him back to the here and now. The music seemed louder as Callum shouted over the noise.

"All right, Stu?"

Steve glanced around; only Callum and Brett had arrived. "Where are the girls?"

"They are making their own way here. You know how long it bloody takes them to get ready."

Brett stood next to Ruby, awkward and quiet, while Callum bobbed to the loud music. Steve found himself tapping his foot and taking it all in. He couldn't remember the last time he'd been able to hang out in a pub like this. Brett wasn't wearing his glasses – and yet he was blind without them, apparently. Steve wished he could take his damn things off – he didn't need them, full stop.

Lydia joined them. Steve grinned at her, for a moment lost for words. She wore a figure-hugging jumper-dress with leggings, and knee-high boots, which added a couple of inches to her height. In the hotel, Steve was used to her in an unflattering uniform, like his own, and going home she tended to wear long floaty skirts, hiding the shape of her legs, and her figure. This outfit accentu-ated a superb figure he hadn't taken much notice of before. When Alice flounced and flirted in front of him, Lydia often fell into the background. That's why he liked the quiet time he usually got with her before starting their shifts.

"You look great," Steve uttered the first words he could find in his scrambled brain. Well, he was supposed to be an amateur.

"Oh, thanks, but it's really warm in here. It might not have been the right choice." She fanned herself. With the bar getting busier and people bustling about, someone shoved Lydia into Steve. Reacting quickly, he put his arm out to catch her, his hand resting on the small of her back. As he breathed, her citrus, sweet perfume filled his lungs and he revelled in her softness against his hard form.

"Oh, sorry." She stepped out of the brief embrace, looking at the floor and not into his eyes.

"Nothing to be sorry about." He shrugged with a jolt of disap-pointment as she moved. Had it been that long since he'd been close to a woman?

Alice bobbed in front of him whilst handing Lydia her drink, quickly shaking him out of his thoughts. "Hello, gorgeous. Sorry we're late." She managed to nuzzle into the group, getting between Lydia and him.

"Shall we get another in?" Callum waved his empty glass at Steve and Brett. Both men nodded. Steve spied a shelf lined with half-drunk drinks and beer bottles, and ditched his bottle there, pretending it was empty. He had to remember to take it steadily. He wasn't used to drinking like Brett and Callum were, and the beers were stronger, too.

They had one more drink in this bar, then moved along to another. Alice linked arms with Steve; she probably needed the assistance considering the height of the heels she was wearing. Callum strolled, weaved, actually zigzagged ahead to search out the next drinking hole while Lydia hung back with Ruby and Brett. Did Lydia have a thing for Brett as Alice had suggested?

As they walked, there was an occasional bang and the sky was lit up with a flash, and then red, green and gold lights fanned out, or whites with purples; the remnants of fireworks from Bonfire Night, which had been earlier in the week. Steve associated fireworks with the Fourth of July now. He shivered, watching the sky for the next display, and stuffed his fists into his jeans. Clouds of mist formed as he uttered an 'ah' with Alice, confirming the coldness of the night.

The next bar they entered vibrated, the bass drumming through them, wall to wall with people. Frustrated, Steve quickly de-misted his glasses and put them back on. The large dance floor in the middle was crammed, and scantily dressed women walked by gawping men, including Callum who nudged Steve and Brett for approval.

They stayed in this bar because of the atmosphere. Everyone was having a good time, the music was upbeat and as he finished a beer, another was shoved in his hand. How long they'd been there, Steve didn't know. He was drunk, or on the way, because he didn't give a shit. So much for trying to take it easily. Caught up with the flow of enjoying himself and relaxing, he'd been keeping up with Callum and Brett and lost all thought about control. But he didn't care; he was enjoying himself. His whole body relaxed, he chatted to girls. This was how he'd find his Miss Right. Alice didn't bother him now, being close to him, he'd lazily move his hand around her waist. His cheeks ached from laughing, his whole body bounced with the beat.

Lydia talked to Ruby, not that Steve could hear, and Ruby

nodded. Then Lydia waved good-bye. He waved too. What time was it? Steve glanced at his watch. Too early to be leaving, just past midnight. He looked up, searching for Lydia, to convince her to stay, but she'd gone.

Damn it, had she got in a taxi okay? Should he check?

Alice pulled at his arm. "Come on, let's dance!" She took his drink out of his hand, placed it on a shelf near Brett and dragged him on to the dance floor, Callum following, Lydia soon forgotten.

Busy dancing, Steve had lost track of the time. When Ruby tugged on his sleeve, he lowered himself so she could speak into his ear over the music. "Bro, I'm going now."

"No you can't go. The fun's just started."

"I'm shattered." Her expression said so too.

"Okay, okay, I'll get you a cab."

"It's fine. Brett's going to make sure I get one safely." Brett stood beside her, Steve realised.

"Then you'll come back, right, Brett?"

"Yeah, yeah, sure."

Steve, Alice and Callum danced. And danced and danced. With one good tune after another, Steve let any inhibitions go. He liked dancing, always had done, and he was good at it, too. He wasn't born with two left feet, like Callum, who lacked the rhythm but hid it well by jumping up and down.

Callum went berserk when a rave tune blasted out and Alice disappeared from Steve's side. He watched her flirting and dancing with some guy, similar in age. A small element of relief flooded over him. Although a beautiful girl, there was something about Alice that didn't tick all his boxes. Not that he had boxes, but although they got on, he found her hard to talk to. Although they had similar tastes in films, he couldn't quite find the right topics of conversations, and they didn't share the same sense of humour. The things he found funny would go over her head.

He was nudged whilst dancing, and ended up bumping into someone else. A blonde girl, with full, glossy lips, large eyes framed by black kohl, and gorgeous tits. She appeared to be dancing with girlfriends, not a boyfriend in sight, so Steve took an interest and danced with her, Callum tagging onto a friend of hers. He tried not to stare at her assets that bounced beautifully in front of him, but he couldn't stop thinking about them.

Oh yes, he was drunk. Happily drunk.

He weaved an arm around her tiny waist, and they danced together, hips gyrating, sticky, sweaty bodies pressed together. Then, his mouth found hers, blotting out the beat of the music, finding their own rhythm.

***

"Looks like we left at the right time," Ruby said, shivering, waiting in the taxi queue with Brett. "It'll be a nightmare later on."

"Here, have this." Brett took off his jacket and wrapped it around her. Thankfully, the taxis arrived quickly, and the queue moved fast.

"Cheers," she said, smiling. "Won't you get cold?"

"Nah, I've drunk enough beer to keep me warm."

She giggled nervously. Brett placed his hands in his pockets, but stayed close. He was lying. She could see goosebumps on his neck.

"You can leave me if you like, and go back in the warm, to St-Stuart and Callum." *God, she'd nearly said Steve – again!*

"No, I'll make sure you get in a taxi first." He fiddled with his pierced ear, then looked at his watch. "Actually, would you mind if I share your taxi?"

"What? And leave your best friend?"

"Callum's a friend, and he's contagious. You can't help mucking around with him when he jokes about, but I can live without him." He winked and as he smiled, surprise hit her, noticing those little half-moon creases around his mouth were attractive. She broke her gaze from his lips, hoping he didn't realise she was blushing.

A taxi pulled up and Brett opened the back door to allow Ruby to get in.

"I won't bother going back in. Callum will look after Stuart," he said.

"Yes, of course, get in." Ruby shuffled over the back seat, making room for Brett. "But who's going to look after Callum?" Luckily, with wine inside her, confidence overcame a shyness she didn't realise she had around Brett, allowing her to joke, because strangely, the close presence of Brett sent her insides warm and fuzzy.

"Alice?"

Ruby snorted. "Yeah, right, my brother is doomed." She reeled in embarrassment, but carried on anyway, trying to put the slight worry she did have for Steve to the back of her mind. Maybe Brett hadn't caught the unladylike snort? Instead, she kept the conversation light, because her brain couldn't engage in anything more serious – they'd talked earlier, and got to know each other a little better. She'd found out there was more to her sous chef than his Xbox gaming.

Funny how when you get to know someone, they appear more attractive... handsome.

She'd never thought of Brett before in that way. Although in what way? Did he fancy her? Maybe he was just being friendly and gentlemanly, making sure she got home safely, and this meant nothing.

It probably meant nothing.

But she was glad he wasn't staying behind. Which meant he wouldn't find another woman... Ruby swallowed at the thought. What a ridiculous pang of jealousy, why would she be jealous?

"Where do you want to go, kids?" the taxi driver said impatiently, swivelling around.

"Oh, um," Ruby stuttered, realising she'd been away with the fairies. "I must be tired." Between them they gave the driver instructions, Brett adamant Ruby should be dropped off first, even though he lived closer.

Ruby didn't want to stare out the window and watch the streets pass. She disliked the silence between her and Brett, too. Glancing at Brett, she met his gaze and smiled, then blushed.

"So..." She paused. "How long have you been single?" They had brushed over this conversation earlier, but now it was quieter in the taxi, Ruby felt compelled to know more.

"Lost track now, just before I got the job at Durdham Lodge."

"You've been there six months."

Brett nudged her. "Keeping track of me."

"Not at all." Ruby giggled. "I just have a good memory and you do a fine job. Is she the reason you changed jobs?"

"No, that was purely to further my career," Brett beamed. "But we did share a flat together."

"Is that why you moved back with your parents?" She couldn't remember who had told her this – Brett or Steve. The idea that he didn't have some bachelor pad where he could take girls back suited her. But at the same time... was he a man over mothered?

Brett fiddled with his earring. *Hmm... I wonder if he has a tattoo.* Ruby gave herself a mental shake as Brett sighed. "Partly, but also, although I didn't want to move back home, it made sense. My mum and dad convinced me actually. They live close to Durdham Lodge, and I can save money for a deposit, so I can buy a house of my own."

Ruby's inebriated mind wandered to where Brett's parents might live – a big house in Clifton?

"Yes, renting is a waste of money." Steve hated that she rented her little house. "It's a means to an end, and you have a secure job now."

"Well, I really want to invest in my own restaurant – oh, maybe I shouldn't have told you that as my boss." He blushed as he confessed his intentions. But Ruby found it admirable that he had ambitions.

"Oh, don't be silly," Ruby tapped him playfully with the back of her hand. "I don't want to be there forever, either." Though what she wanted to do, she wasn't sure.

When the taxi pulled up outside her house, Brett jumped out, mumbling to the taxi driver about waiting for a minute, and opened Ruby's door for her.

Ruby stumbled out of the car – *wine and heels don't mix* – and Brett instantly steadied her.

"Have you got your key?" he said in a caring tone, still holding her.

Ruby fumbled in her small handbag and found it, showing him. He grinned.

"Did you want to ... um, have coffee?" Ruby said, nervously. Why was she asking him to come in?

He stood close, his hand holding her elbow, his eyes not leaving hers. With her heartbeat ringing in her ears, she focussed on his lips, the curves around his mouth, then remembered why she was warm and why he had goosebumps on his arms.

"No, no ... I'd better get home, too."

Ruby was surprised at how disappointed she felt. She was only inviting him in for coffee, she berated herself. Nothing else. Absolutely nothing else.

"Oh." She dropped her gaze, breaking the spell, and slipped off his jacket, handing it to him. "Thanks for the loan."

"No problem." He shrugged his coat on and placed his hands in the pockets.

"Right, well, good night," she said, walking towards her front door. "Thanks for seeing me home." Had he wanted to kiss her? Was she disappointed that he hadn't?

Stop being ridiculous and get in the damn house.

***

"Shhhh!" Steve placed a finger over his mouth, trying to shush the woman, who was already undoing his pants – he meant trousers. Somehow, his key scraping around the metal lock, he inserted it into the keyhole. Would he manage in the bedroom department, if he couldn't even manage this simple task? Oh, hell, yes. Blondie was nibbling on his earlobe, hands groping inside his stretched boxers.

Oh, that felt good. That felt very good.

What was her name? He'd asked her name, but could he remember it? Hell.

Oh, yes, he was very much going to hell tonight. And back. He hadn't felt this horny since... *don't think about Erica!*

They kissed, tongues now doing the dancing, and groping in the darkness, he led her into the lounge. Probably not quite a good idea to go upstairs... just in case Ruby heard.

He threw his jacket aside and they got comfy on the sofa. Underneath him, she whimpered and moaned as he stripped her top off, shedding his own shirt. He gave a squeeze of her round breast in its lacy encasing, and then he dug into his back pocket, finding the couple of condoms he'd collected from the vending machine in the men's loos. His mouth nuzzled at her neck, around her collarbone, sucking, nibbling her smooth flesh, finding his way to a luscious breast.

Okay, I really should be taking my time here, but what the hell. A quick roll in the hay would do him good. He hadn't had something like this sort of fun in a very long time. They were both drunk, they were either going to go all night or be a fifteen minute wonder. She didn't have the faintest idea who he really was, hadn't hinted. Steve had managed not to forget to use the name Stuart, though he had stumbled over it.

This was exactly the medicine he needed.

He had two condoms; he'd be slower next time.

Steve hitched her skirt up, then tugged at her knickers. Quickly, she raised her hips to aid their removal, her thumbs tucked inside his boxers, pushing at his trousers.

"What the hell is going on?" The lights went on, and Ruby, in pyjamas, scruffy haired, stood hands on her hips, wearing an expression fit to explode. "Steve, I think I should have set some ground rules."

Fuck.

Blondie swiftly un-straddled her legs, pulled up her knickers, tugged her skirt down, and then covered her breasts with her arms.

Steve stood, zipping up his flies, fast.

"You bastard." Blondie slapped him.

"She's my sister!" Steve said, desperately, rubbing his sore cheek.

"You said your name was *Stuart*."

"It is." He glared at Ruby.

"Get her out," Ruby said, pointing to the front door, her face flushed with anger.

"Hang on! Hang on a minute. We're only having a bit of fun."

"In my house!" Ruby was not calming down. "You'll thank me later."

"Will I now?" Steve gritted his teeth. Taking orders from Ruby was starting to grate on him now. Especially when she was ruining *his* fun.

"Leave. Now," Ruby ordered the young woman. Steve stood in front of her.

"All right, Ruby," he growled. "I'll call her a cab. Just calm down."

"Calm down. Calm down?" Ruby stormed into the kitchen, and the woman, whose name Steve for the life of him still could not remember, found her top and put it back on. Her cheeks were flushed and her eyes glistened, ready to burst into tears. Ruby was slamming cupboard doors in the kitchen and making one hell of a racket, which made Steve's head pound. He'd sobered in his head, even if his limbs were still slow and drunk.

"I'm sorry, I made a big mistake," he said to the woman, combing a hand through his hair, then pulled out his mobile and dialled the cab firm.

Steve and Blondie waited outside Ruby's house. He had his hands shoved into his pockets, she hugged herself – it was so damn cold. Steve still hadn't got used to the cold. Oh, how he missed the warm LA evenings. Blondie, silent with anger, wouldn't let him near her to keep her warm, so luckily, he didn't have to wait long for the cab to pull up. She sneered at Steve, emphasising the guilt he felt, then got in the car. Steve leaned into the window and handed the driver twenty pounds that he'd counted out. "This cover it?" The taxi driver nodded. "Please take her home and make sure she's safe."

"Sure, mate."

Steve sighed heavily, watching the taxi drive away, then looked at the house, knowing he had Ruby to deal with inside. Why hadn't he gone to a hotel, for fuck's sake?

"You stupid bastard!" Ruby greeted him as he closed the front door. "We have not gone out of our way to hide your identity so you can shag all and sundry."

"I've got to test the water." He threw his glasses onto the coffee table, sick to the back teeth of them.

Ruby shoved him. "Test the water!" She cursed at Steve till she'd run out of expletives.

"Ruby, please..."

"You test the water by taking them on a date, going out for dinner, not just shagging the first thing that takes your fancy. And, and," she jabbed a finger into his chest, not even taking a breath, "what if she'd worked out who you were? Do you want her selling her sex story to the press? Because they'd buy it, Steve. Every. Gory. Detail."

He swallowed, rubbing a hand over his tired eyes. She was right. "I'm sorry, okay. I've had too much to drink, got carried away. I was reckless. It won't happen again." Way too stupid on the drinking. Callum drank like a fish and Steve was out of practice. Besides, he knew better than to drink too much. He'd seen the damage it did in Hollywood to young actors, and the stories the press released because of it. But stupidly, one drink had led to another tonight.

"It had better not."

Ruby stormed back up the stairs, her feet thundering loudly on each step. Steve turned off the lights, and wearily walked upstairs, into the bathroom. He splashed cold water onto his face, cleaned his teeth, then – how he really hadn't imagined the evening ending – got into his bed, alone.

Chapter 11

Saturday 9th November

Steve groaned, as sunlight peeked through the gap in the curtains and right into his eyes. Squinting, he checked his cheap watch; it was somewhere around ten in the morning. His mouth felt like sandpaper, and tasted like manure, his head thudded painfully with every pulse and hurt more when he opened his eyes. Next time, if there ever was a next time – Steve didn't see himself doing this again in a hurry – he would drink a pint of water before going to bed.

Downstairs, Ruby clattered and banged. Still evidently pissed off.

He showered, hoping it would clear his head, and shaved, so he'd feel more presentable. Ruby's insistence that he kept the shadow to a minimum meant he was shaving at least twice a day. At the hotel he took in an electric razor and on breaks would go to the locker rooms to shave. Luckily, the line of work he was now in meant he needed to look presentable, so other staff didn't see it as abnormal. In fact, only the other day, he'd caught Pete in there also shaving, and cursing about it.

All this effort to find the woman of his dreams.

Obviously, he hadn't said that to Pete.

Last night would have been nice, a one-night stand as an anonymous human being. But Steve couldn't have those anymore. Not that it was his thing, but he'd had a couple of one-nighters when he'd been a lot younger, in the days when he could be a free spirit. In fact, even back then, a one-night stand wasn't what he'd planned. He'd usually hoped to get to know the woman the next day, go on another date, but for one reason or another it never transpired.

Damn, why'd he forgotten about Ruby and what her reaction would be? He should never have come back here with... and he still couldn't remember her name.

It had felt good though. Was he finally getting over Erica?

Feeling only a tiny bit better – well at least he felt clean and didn't smell – he threw a fresh T-shirt over his head, pulled on some baggy jeans and ambled down the stairs, taking things very slowly. His feet and calves ached from the dancing, and his pounding head didn't aid his balance.

"Morning," he said quietly and then winced as Ruby slammed another kitchen cupboard. "Any coffee going?"

He'd bought a machine at last, and was pleased to see the jug full. He grabbed a mug from the cupboard, making a lot less noise than his sister, and poured himself a coffee. The smell alone woke him up, brain coming alive. Ruby continued to put washed up items away, without making conversation with Steve. If Ruby's anger was visible as a mist, the kitchen would be foggy. And its colour would be red.

"Why are you still in a mood?" Steve sipped his coffee, the liquid welcome in his mouth, the heat settling his stomach.

Ruby turned and glared. "Because I can't believe you'd be so stupid."

"Oh, Ruby, I'm not going over this again. I'm sorry, okay. You have no idea how sorry I am." However much the coffee tasted good, he disliked the atmosphere. He dumped the coffee down the sink, leaving the mug on the side. He could afford to get coffee elsewhere.

"Where are you going?"

"Out!" He'd get breakfast in the high street. "Until you change the record."

The walk would do him good, too, as he certainly couldn't run after a night like that.

Making sure he had his wallet, he slammed the front door behind him.

"Everything all right, dear?" Ruby's neighbour was putting some paper in her recycling bin. "I might be deaf, but I can feel a door slam."

Steve smiled, forced somewhat, but there was no need to be rude to Daphne. "Ruby and I, well, I did something—"

"It is hard when you haven't lived with someone in such a long time. You're used to your own space."

Steve nodded and waved a goodbye. Maybe that's what he needed; his own space. He strolled down to the high street, knowing the café would be open, and he could have a fry up – the perfect hangover cure. He'd run an extra mile another day to compensate for the saturated fat. Every cold breath slowly cleared his head. By the time he reached the café he was ravenous.

He ordered the big breakfast and a coffee, then grabbed a free newspaper from a rack and found an empty table in the corner.

Tucked away in the back, Steve sat for over two hours, filling up on coffee. Even though the waitress wore a wedding band, she still flirted and gave Steve the most attention compared to the other customers.

Sometimes he wished he hadn't been born with his looks. They caused him trouble. Usually a girl would not stop staring, then her boyfriend would get jealous, and blame Steve. Those were his younger days. There had been days too, when he encouraged the girls. Then, finally, his looks had helped him get parts in films. Okay, so he'd like to think he was good at acting too. He was. Directors and producers, and even the critiques had commended him for his natural comic ability; he made his characters whole and believable. He had a certain charisma on the screen. The camera liked him.

But he didn't kid himself, his looks had eventually got him through the door of Hollywood.

***

Half an hour after Steve had slammed the front door shut, the doorbell chimed.

Ruby was not in the mood for a sales call. She really needed to put one of those signs up. The ones that said politely, 'I'm poor, I don't wish to buy anything, now sod off.'

"Yes!" she answered the door angrily. Oh, God, now she wished it was a sales person. They would have been so much better than the slime standing on her doorstep. She scowled. *Bastard alert!* "What do *you* want?"

"Hello, Ruby. Nice to see you, too."

"Cut the chit chat. Why are you here?" Stupid question. She knew exactly why Terence Smythe, her ex-boyfriend, was here. Had he spotted Steve in the area? Terence was the one person who definitely couldn't find out that she had her brother visiting. He worked for the local press, Bristol Gazette, and had used Ruby a couple of years ago, as Steve started getting famous. Terence made Ruby believe he was in love with her, when all he wanted was inside material on Steve.

"Can I come in?"

"No, I'm about to go out." She grabbed her car keys, handbag and slipped on her boots. She had no make-up on, wasn't even sure she'd brushed her hair, not that it needed brushing much being this short. A plus side when trying to get out of the way of journalists – obviously. At least she'd got dressed before he'd showed up, otherwise she'd be going out in her pyjamas. She had to get Terence away from the house before Steve returned.

She locked her front door, and stormed towards her car, the little shit following her.

132

"Have you seen these pictures? Your brother seems to have found a new girlfriend. Care to comment?" A moment of panic swept through Ruby. Had someone recognised him in the club? Or had the girl last night been a set up? All sorts of thoughts and fears entered her mind as Terence flicked through some glossy magazine until he came to the page, and then presented it to Ruby. Steve – or someone who looked like him thanks to the blurry quality of the covert picture – on a beach with a beautiful, bikini-clad, young lady, and looking extremely loved up, splashing around in the water. Ruby kept her expression stern, but inside she smiled. At least he didn't think Steve was actually in Bristol.

"No comment. Steve hasn't been in contact lately."

"No invitations to meet his new girl?"

"Terry, Steve is half way across the world. I'm not interested. What he does is his business. Now bugger off." She got in her car, slamming the door, wanting to trap the man's evil hands in it, so he'd never type again. She turned the keys in the ignition and revved the engine.

She crunched the car into reverse, so angry at seeing the two-faced bastard again, all the hurt and misery rising inside her. Evidently, her feelings for this man were not as buried and forgotten as hoped. Her whole body trembled with shock and fear, hating the confrontation. She gripped the steering wheel hard, fearing she wouldn't be able to turn it. Terry had made her learn that she also needed to keep Steve's identity a secret in her life. The only way she'd find a decent guy, to love her for her, was if they didn't know about Steve. Otherwise how could she trust them? How did she know they weren't after Steve's money? Or his story... She blinked back tears. For God's sake, don't start crying now.

She'd trusted Terry, and look where it had got her? She thought she'd found someone to share her secret, share her brother's fame, and be proud that he'd made it. Instead, Terence had used every word she ever told him against her and Steve. Not that Steve knew of course. He'd probably break the man's neck. Her mother had urged her not to react, too. The whole affair was swept under the carpet before Mum had died. All would come out in the wash otherwise, and it wouldn't be good for Steve. Give the press an inch, they'll take a yard, her mother had said. Yeah, Ruby imagined the headlines, "Mason's Sister Murders Journalist Ex-Boyfriend." Okay, so that was a crap headline – she didn't want to be a bloody journalist – but the storyline certainly wouldn't have gone in Steve's favour. The press liked to dig up dirt, even a speck of dust in the family's closet they would try making it into a skeleton. The smallest of things blown out of proportion.

Now she drove along the road, unsure where she was heading. Steve had left in a huff, but she couldn't stay at the house, she needed to draw Terence away. She'd get lost at Cribbs for a bit. Retail therapy would do her the world of good. Not that she had the money.

***

With his head clearer, which had improved his mood, Steve strolled back home, hoping Ruby would be in a better frame of mind, too. He felt icy spots of rain as he walked, the sky growing greyer. He picked up his pace, eager to make it back before the sky truly emptied like it was threatening.

"Oh, damn." He checked his jacket pockets, slapping at them, then his jeans pockets. Every single pocket. He'd forgotten a goddamn door key. Dialling Ruby's home number on his mobile did not ease his nerves. She wasn't answering. And lo and behold, he saw her car was missing from the drive. He phoned her mobile. That too went direct to voicemail.

"Hey, Ruby, in my rush, I forgot a door key. Can you let me know when you'll be back? Thanks."

In typical November style, the rain started coming down heavier. Cold. He kicked the front door, turning up the collar on his jacket, the eaves over the front door, just keeping him dry. Then, just to top Steve's day, the heavens really opened. He hadn't seen rain like it in a very long time. He ran across to Daphne's door and rang her doorbell. Steve thought why the hell not. The old woman probably didn't get many visitors, she might be grateful for the company. And he'd be grateful for the shelter. She took a few minutes to answer and he worried he was disturbing her afternoon nap.

"Oh, hello, it's you." Then Daphne frowned, looking at the rain, and then Steve, getting wetter by the minute, and said, "Everything all right, young man?"

"Hi, Daphne, I forgot to take my key, I was wondering—"

"Of course, come in, come in! I was about to put the kettle on." Daphne opened the door wider and quickly ushered him in.

"I'll make the tea, you sit down," Steve said, wiping his feet on the mat.

"No, no, it's my house and you're my guest," Daphne replied sternly. "Go sit down and warm yourself up. I insist."

Removing his jacket and hanging it over the banister to dry, he followed Daphne into her lounge and settled into an armchair in front of her gas fire. He knew when to do as he was told. Many older people didn't like to lose their independence. She may have been slower than Steve, but she was still able.

Daphne brought out a tray with two cups and saucers, a teapot covered in an old-fashioned, burgundy coloured, woolly tea-cosy and a plate of biscuits.

"Milk?"

"Yes, please," Steve said.

"Sugar?"

"No," he said exaggerating the word playfully, "sweet enough as I am." He winked.

Daphne chuckled, croakily with old age. "Good, because I'd forgotten to put it on the tray." She held out the plate of biscuits. There was a mixed assortment. Steve took one, a plain digestive.

When he saw Daphne dip her own into her tea, he did the same.

"So you've upset our Ruby, have you? Where you been to?" Daphne asked in her very strong Bristolian accent.

"Just to the café down the road. Came home worse for wear last night. Haven't been out like that in such a long time. Anyway..." Steve waved it off. Daphne didn't need to hear about his and Ruby's issues. She wouldn't really understand, not knowing Steve's true identity.

"Like I said earlier. You're both getting used to each other. How long you been away?"

"Fifteen years."

Daphne laughed, more with shock. "Heavens, you're both strangers really."

"I'm trying to make it up to her, but can't really think how."

"I'm sure she's grateful really, for you just being you and being here, love."

"Thanks, but I'm still not sure it's enough."

Daphne leaned forward, placed her cup on the tray. "You know, tell me to mind my own business, but don't you own your mother's house?"

Steve frowned. How did she know? And why hadn't he thought about the house? Being so busy with work, and this pretence of being someone else, he'd forgotten about their old family home.

"Ruby told me some time ago that she'd moved because she couldn't afford to live in her mother's house. I think it was when I nagged her that she should be buying not renting."

"Yeah, I've been paying the bills, and making sure it's looked after."

"Is it bigger than next door?" Daphne's house was identical to Ruby's in layout, only the other way around. A mirror image, except for the chintz and china. "Might give you both some breathing space. I never believed Ruby wanted to leave the place, just maybe it reminded her too much of the past, of her mother, or even you?"

Steve's mind worked overtime. Daphne had come up with an

excellent idea. He let her chat away about the good old days as they drank their tea. When they'd finished, he took the tray out to the kitchen, telling Daphne to sit tight, even switching her television on for her. He'd found the perfect thing he could do for Ruby.

"Not a word to Ruby about the house," he said, winking.

"Don't worry, Steve, your secret is safe with me," she replied.

Steve frowned with surprise. "My name's Stuart," he stammered.

"Of course it is, dear." She tapped her nose. "It's okay. I won't say a word. I put two and two together earlier. I'm not as deaf as everyone thinks."

"Earlier?"

"I'll let Ruby tell you." She went to get up but Steve held up his hand, to gesture for her to stay sitting, and then he showed himself out. Thankfully, the rain had ceased – for now.

He immediately dialled Marie.

"Do you even know what time it is here, buster?" Marie sounded sleepy, and angry, and refreshingly American.

"Sorry, Marie." He hadn't thought of the time difference, just the need to get things in motion. And when he set his mind to something, it had to be done right away. "Please can you send me the number of the contractors looking after my house here in England? I've not got my other phone." He looked up to his bedroom window, visualising exactly where he'd left it, on the small desk. He left it switched on in case the real world contacted him, charging it up regularly. "And send it to this number, not my usual mobile, I mean cell phone."

"Okay. Gosh, you're sounding all British again. So darn cute."

Steve rolled his eyes. "I've had to work on regaining my accent, for my disguise."

"It's James Bond." She laughed. "How's that going, anyway?"

"Good. How's my double?"

"Oh, don't you worry about him. In fact, take a look at this month's issue of *Hello*. And you might even be in *OK*."

"I'll take a look, just please send me that number, as soon as."

"I deserve a raise."

"Thank you."

***

Waiting for Marie to get back to him, Steve walked down to the corner shop, where he'd become a bit of a regular. The guy behind the counter who Steve would idly chat to about the football appeared blind to the fact that Steve could actually be famous.

"Don't worry, those are for my sister," Steve said, pointing to the *Hello* and *OK* magazines as the male shop assistant scanned them. Steve had tucked them under two other magazines; *FHM* and *GQ*. He thought he'd throw them in to disguise the fact he was buying women's magazines – the ones he really wanted. *Being a Hollywood actor in disguise sure did make you paranoid.*

He paid for his shopping and sat on the wall outside the shop, flicking through the magazines. There wasn't a major feature or anything, just more in the gossip columns, but there they were, photos of him, or rather his stunt double, basking in the Caribbean sun. Whoa! Basking in the sun with a very attractive young woman. A 'mystery brunette' as the magazine quoted. Marie really was trying to keep the press at bay, wanting to get the message loud and clear: Steve was over Erica.

Was he over Erica?

He'd hoped she'd be the woman he'd marry, have children with, although he knew their relationship would be tough, both being actors. But they'd have made it work. Steve would have tried. He'd had this idea – what he realised now as pure fantasy – that they could have worked together, followed each other from set to sets of different filming. They'd take it in turns to make a film, whatever. He'd been prepared to do anything to make it stick.

But as quickly as the fire had lighted between them, it had died. Well, it hadn't died for Steve, only Erica. The press had caught hold of them planning to marry, which they'd never officially announced. It had been leaked. She'd decided she didn't want marriage, didn't want kids – yet. Maybe he could understand her apprehension about starting a family; Erica was still young, in her prime, and at the height of her career. But marriage? There was the crux of it, she hadn't loved him enough to get married.

On his walk back up to Ruby's house, Marie's email with the agent's details came through to his phone. Steve made some calls, and caught a taxi to their old family house.

As he got out, he swallowed down the shock at seeing his old family house. He had visited it briefly for their mother's wake, but other than that, he'd hardly been home in fifteen years.

He didn't remember it looking so rundown. He certainly hadn't noticed at the funeral, but then his mind had been on his mother's death. Was its run-down state purely due to a lack of residents over the past years, or had it been fifteen years of not having any help with the upkeep? The sills needed painting, the blue front door had faded. The front garden was sparse where bushes and flowers had died with neglect. It was mainly lawn but that was weedy and too long, cut too early before the winter had set in.

When Ruby decided she could no longer live in it, after their mother's death, he'd taken over its charges. The furniture had gone into storage and the house left empty. He hadn't liked the thought of renting it out to strangers. However, he hadn't realised how quick a place could become rundown with no-one living in it.

Looking at the sorry state of the building and the attention it needed, he realised he had some work to do. It was time Ruby came home.

***

"Where've you been?" Ruby answered the front door, frowning with concern at Steve.

139

"Out and about," he replied, shrugging off his jacket.

At least Ruby seemed calmer than this morning. He walked into the lounge and Ruby sat back down on the sofa, picking up her book.

"But you've been ages."

"I forgot my key." Steve wasn't going to tell Ruby about the house yet. He'd wait until it was ready, or almost ready. Then he'd surprise her. "I got breakfast in the high street, then came back and you were gone, so I had a chat with Daphne – and tea and biscuits," he emphasised. "Then went for another stroll." He slung the magazines on the coffee table in front of Ruby. "I'm in the gossip columns of *Hello*. And a small photograph in *OK*."

"I know."

"You know?"

"Yeah, a journalist from the Bristol Gazette knocked on my door, hence I went out to lead him away from here, in case you came home."

"Oh." Steve frowned. This explained Daphne knowing who he really was. The old girl was switched on. "What did you tell him?"

"No comment." She grinned, then her expression sobered. "Does this mean you have to leave?" She sat up straighter, throwing the book aside, and started flicking through the magazines.

Steve laughed. "No, it means my plan is working. He is my stunt double, but I asked if he'd do this for me. I wanted to get away, escape to the UK without the press following me, so Marie suggested we pay for him to take a holiday in the Caribbean." Steve shrugged, then chuckled. "If it works, I might ask him to do it more often."

"Oh, right." Ruby found the page and read the small feature. "Wow, he does look like you... when your hair was that bit longer. I didn't really look at the magazine closely when Terry presented it to me. Terry showing up has worried me. We've got to be careful, this journalist knows I have a famous brother. If he sees you, your cover will be blown. I know he only works for the Bristol Gazette, but the bastard is ambitious."

Steve nodded, dread sinking in, hating the idea of having to watch his back. Had he become complacent? Everything had been going well. Though, he found the less you acted like a star, the less people believed you were one.

Ruby smirked, still reading the article. "Says you've found love again with a secret woman."

"Yep, apparently so." He smiled again. This storyline pleased Steve. What would be Erica's reaction if she read it? *Scratch that, she probably won't care. She's moved on. So should you.*

"Yeah, that's why Terry was sniffing around. Wanted to know if I knew anything."

"Who is this Terry?"

"No one." Ruby continued to flick through the magazine.

"Ruby?"

"It doesn't matter," she snapped.

"Okay." Steve held his hands up, knowing when it was best to back off, especially when it came to Ruby. He was learning, and he didn't want to ruin the mood. "At least the press think I'm in the Caribbean, so it should keep the heat off me here for a while longer."

"Good," Ruby looked up at him, "I know I was mad, and everything, but I don't want you to leave me." Ruby's bottom lip wobbled, her eyes glistened and she swallowed.

"Hey, no way." Steve slumped onto the sofa beside her, hugging her closely. "I want to spend time with you, Roo. I want to make up for not being here." He kissed the top of her head, like he remembered his father used to do, though she wasn't four anymore.

"Phew! For a moment I thought I'd scared you off."

"Take a lot more than you blowing a gasket to get rid of me." Steve reached for the remote control and turned on the television. "So, shall we watch a film tonight, or play on the Wii?"

"Wii. I want to beat you at tennis."

"Deal." Steve turned on the Wii and handed Ruby a controller.

They were soon standing in the middle of the lounge, playing tennis, Ruby cheering and goading him when she won a point. They laughed; last night's argument and this morning's tempers forgotten.

An hour into the game, Steve frowned, swinging his Wii controller. "You know, we could do with a bigger screen." He regretted taking Ruby on, she was seriously whupping his ass at tennis.

"I can't afford a bigger TV."

"I can. Let's go shopping tomorrow. I'll buy you one."

"Steve, haven't you heard of 'if it ain't broke, don't fix it'?"

"Yeah, I know. But I can buy you a new one."

"There is nothing wrong with this TV."

"You could have a flat screen, high definition, it would look great. Blu-ray..."

Ruby rolled her eyes. "No, Steve," she said firmly.

"Go on. I want a bigger TV."

"Doesn't anyone say no to you in Hollywood?"

Actually, they didn't. If he wanted something, he got it.

Ruby sighed. "I don't want you spending unnecessarily. Besides, you shouldn't flash your money around, remember? Act normally. Otherwise I'll have to set you a budget, to appreciate having a limited income."

"No one need know."

"What about Callum and Brett if they come over again? They'd definitely notice a flashy new TV."

"I only want to treat you."

"You're treating me by spending time with me. I mean, how many celebrities would stay home, play Wii and eat takeaway pizza – cold – when they could be high flying it in some posh Michelin-star restaurant, with a high class date?"

"I'm having fun." And he was. Amazing how you appreciated the little things in life when it was so hard to have them. Everyone expected a celebrity to choose the high life.

"Even though I'm beating you?" Ruby's serious expression softened into a sneaky smile.

He nudged her and set another game up. "Yeah, but next you've got to play me at golf."

Chapter 12

Sunday 10th November

"I'm going shopping!" Ruby called up the stairs, slipping on her coat. It was about half past ten in the morning. They'd played Wii till the early hours, hence the late lie in.

"On a Sunday?" Steve replied groggily back. "And didn't you go yesterday?"

Shit! Yes, she had. "Yeah, I need to take something back, and it's mildly quieter than on a Saturday, especially if I go early."

"How long are you going to be? Will you be back for dinner? I'm cooking, remember?"

Ruby had a rare whole weekend off, and she'd promised Steve they'd make the most of it together. But she had a plan.

"Of course! I'll be back way before dinner. I wouldn't miss it for the world." Ruby rolled her eyes, not that Steve could see her sarcastic expression, grabbed her car keys and handbag. "Bye!" she yelled, shutting the door behind her.

She got into her car and started the engine. Paranoid Steve would be looking out his bedroom window, she drove off, deciding she'd make her call once she was at Cribbs Causeway.

Parked, she fumbled for her mobile phone and dialled.

"Hi, Lydia, it's me, Ruby."

"Hello."

"I was wondering if you wanted to call in and swap books today."

"Today?"

"Yeah, you're not working are you?

"No. It's my day off."

"Well then, come over." Ruby realised she didn't want this to seem too set up after all. "I'm shopping at the Mall, but will be home in an hour. You're not doing anything are you?"

"Oh, no, not really, just having a relaxing, do-nothing type of day."

"Well, pop over around twelve, then."

Ruby gave Lydia instructions on how to get to her house, guilt eating away at her with her lie. But Lydia needed a push, in the right direction. She'd hoped Friday night might have turned out better, but Lydia had gone home early. And Steve had been a jerk. Call it women's intuition, or something like that, Ruby knew Lydia had a thing for Steve. She was certain of it. It was like a gift, Ruby thought to herself. She'd got two friends, Ellie and Joe, together whilst at college. They hadn't even realised they were perfect for one another, and Ruby, having an inkling as she liked to think it, convinced them to go to a charity ball together and the rest is history, as they say. They'd ended up marrying and starting a family. As far as Ruby knew – she got a Christmas card every year – they were still happy.

On this alone, Ruby believed she was a good match-maker.

Besides, what did she have to lose? Or Lydia, or Steve, for that matter? Steve had been here over a month, he needed to pull his finger out. Unfortunately, nothing had happened at the Halloween party, and in hindsight, maybe she shouldn't have made him work. But she'd let him enjoy the party, allowing him to be more relaxed in his work, to talk to all of the guests as he'd served their drinks.

"See you later." Ruby ended the call and dropped her phone into her bag. "Time for some retail therapy." She'd killed time around the Mall yesterday, but she had every intention of being longer than an hour. She'd worry about the state of her credit card later. Now where had she seen that dress?

***

Lazy Sunday. Steve heard Ruby shut the front door, meaning he had the house to himself. He stayed in bed half an hour longer, feeling cosy and warm under his duvet. Besides, when did he get to snooze in bed till eleven a.m. usually? When he finally did surface, he showered and shaved, cursing as he cut himself – there was a downside to this normality lark, shaving every morning was tiresome, he longed for his designer stubble. Okay, so he probably could have left it this morning, but he was into a habit now. Or was it more a ritual? Once dressed, and removing the small patches of tissue from his chin – you'd think practise meant being perfect by now – he moseyed to the corner shop, then came home and flicked through the Sunday papers, drinking coffee. It had started raining while he was out – *did it ever stop?* – making him decide he'd wait until the rain eased before going for a run. The food Ruby was giving him – decent home-cooked recipes from Mum – was doing him in. It was the portion size rather than the quality of food. However, at the weekends they tended to be lazy and opt for takeaways. Today he'd cook. He hadn't cooked a roast in a very long time, but he'd learnt from the best – their mother.

The one thing his mother had done from an early age was not wait on him hand and foot. She'd taught him the basics, from putting the washing machine on to cooking some simple dinners. Maybe she'd fretted about him moving to LA and starving to death, unable to fend for himself. In his late teens she would say to him, "I'm training up a future husband." *If only that was the case.* His mother had certainly taught him to be clean and tidy, and to look after his appearance. Yes, Steve Mason knew how to iron – not that he did it now, of course. Well, he was doing it now, living with Ruby and being Mediocre Man. But his Hollywood lifestyle led him to have a housekeeper and a personal assistant. He didn't have time for chores, whether he knew how to do them or not. Why do them if you didn't have to?

The doorbell rang, and Steve frowned, looking at his watch.

Who the hell could that be? Maybe Daphne. She'd been calling occasionally as Ruby had been offering out Steve's services to hang a picture, carry something heavy.

"Oh," he said, opening the door. "Hi." He was surprised to see Lydia standing there. Steve's attention was drawn to the huge heart shape on the baggy jumper. She was also wearing skinny faded-blue jeans and brown leather boots, with her handbag across her shoulder.

"Hi, Ruby said it would be okay to come over, I've come to exchange books. Is she back yet?"

"No, not yet, but come on in." Steve realised he didn't have his glasses on, so as soon as he shut the door he hunted them out and put them on.

Complacent, complacent, complacent. Mediocre Man error.

Lydia removed her boots and followed him into the lounge.

"Tea or coffee?"

"Oh, I wasn't going to stay long."

"Go on, you can keep me company for a bit." Steve winked.

"Tea then, please. I'll wait for Ruby. She shouldn't be long, should she?"

"I don't know with Ruby." Steve shrugged. "The bookshelf's there, I'll get the kettle on."

Steve knew how Lydia took her tea, they made it enough for each other at work, usually taking it in turns. He came out with a steaming mug and put it on the coffee table. He refilled his coffee, too. Lydia stood behind the sofa peering at the books. Steve gave her an appreciative glance before squeezing past the sofa and joining her. There was something about those slender legs and her beautifully round bottom hugged nicely by the jeans. Her hotel

147

uniform definitely didn't do her figure justice.

He did find Lydia attractive. Quietly intelligent, and very artistic, she had the most wicked giggle when he got her going.

Trying to deter his attention from Lydia and the way her jumper slipped off her shoulder revealing her collarbone, he pulled a Stephen King off the shelf, flicking the pages. Why hadn't he noticed it before? "This is mine."

The bookshelf ran the length of the wall, and up to the ceiling, rammed with books, CDs and ornaments. He looked through the CDs. Some of them were his too. That's where his The Stone Roses had got to. He'd left for the US with the bare minimum.

Resting against the back of the sofa, he started reading the book.

"Are you all right?" Lydia asked. "You look like you've seen a ghost."

"I didn't realise Ruby had kept this stuff."

"Oh, what while you went travelling?"

That lie had stuck then. Steve gave himself a mental shake and put the book back.

"So do you swap books often?" he asked, picking up another book, wanting to change the subject.

"Oh, no, I gave Ruby something, and she insisted we swapped. Told me to come over today."

Steve nodded. *Why today?*

"She said she'd be back. Must have got caught up or something." Lydia's cheeks flushed pink, and she turned her attention back to the bookshelf, looking flustered. Steve shook himself. He'd been staring at her. Steve jumped over the sofa, towards the stereo and put on the CD then rejoined Lydia, happy, with The Stone Roses in the background on low. The music took him back to his teenage years. He resisted singing along, not wanting to scare Lydia. He may be good at acting, to the point he hoped one day to get an Oscar, but he'd never win a GRAMMY with his singing. He would never get cast in a musical.

"So what books do you like?" He nudged her playfully.

"Anything really. Romance, fantasy, or something unusual."

"Stephen King?" He waved the book he held in his hand at her.

She screwed up her face. "I'm worried he'll be too scary. Oh, but I haven't read this one." She grabbed a book with an orange cover off the shelf. "*One Day*... have you read it?"

Steve shook his head. "I've heard it's got a sad ending."

"Don't tell me that," she said, eyes widened, and she clutched the book. "I wanted to read it before I watched the film. Books are always better than the film, don't you think?"

"Ah, yes..." Steve hesitated. Did he want to get onto the subject of movies? "There's usually more in a book that can possibly be fitted into a movie."

"I know, it's such a shame sometimes. I always like to see the director's interpretation of the book, but I like to read it first to make my own pictures up in my head. I much prefer books over films generally, anyway."

"I know what you mean."

"As soon as Daniel Radcliffe started playing Harry Potter, he was in my head as Harry as I read the last books."

Sitting on the floor, they talked about books, pulling one out from the bookshelf, reviewing it and putting it back, discovering books they'd both read, what they liked and disliked about them. Steve steered the conversation away from movies, and kept it on books or even music where he could, for fear of letting his knowledge about filming slip out. They devoured more tea and coffee, and biscuits – Daphne had rubbed off on him.

"Oh, look at the time, I need to get the dinner on," Steve said, glancing at his watch – two hours had flown by. Having a late breakfast, he'd skipped lunch, plus drinking and chatting with Lydia had quashed his appetite. But where was Ruby? Maybe she'd run into an old friend, or worse, that Terence, but she'd told Lydia she wasn't going to be long... Or was she staying away on purpose? "I need to get the beef in the oven."

Lydia smirked. "Don't you sound so twenty-first century guy, or has Ruby got you trained?"

"I'll have you know I make a fantastic roast dinner, and with that remark, you've now got to stay and try it."

"Oh, no, I can't, really." Lydia put her nose into *One Day*, blushing again.

"Have you plans for this afternoon?" Steve hoped she didn't.

"No, not really, but I don't want to impose..."

Steve grabbed the book. "Oh, you won't be. That's settled because I'm not taking no for an answer."

"Hey, that's the book I was going to borrow." Steve stood up, and held the book high, Lydia unable to reach even on tiptoes. Her body was agonisingly close, with a hint of her perfume, Steve wanted to land his lips on hers, but thought better of it.

"I'll give it back when it's time for you to go." He raised his eyebrows, and held the book out. She reached out to grab it and he snatched it away. "Later."

"Right, well," she cleared her throat with a lady-like cough, "I'd better help you with this dinner." She rolled up her sleeves.

Steve turned up the music so they could hear it in the kitchen, and started preparing the food. Lydia peeled the vegetables while he danced around putting the beef in the oven, making her laugh.

"You know, if we're having beef we should have Yorkshire puddings," Lydia said. "Where will I find the flour?"

"Don't call me flower." He gently nudged her with his hip, his arm brushing her shoulder. "Or petal."

She rolled her eyes, and listed on her fingers. "Flour. Eggs. Milk."

Steve reached past her, searching the cupboards. He really enjoyed being so close to Lydia and out of the hotel. They hadn't stopped talking or laughing. She'd almost lost her nervous edge around him, too.

"You don't know where it is?" She giggled.

"I've only lived here a few weeks, Ruby likes to move things around."

"Just to keep you on your toes, right?"

"Why else?" He grinned cheekily. "She's strange like that." He pulled a face and Lydia giggled. "She's a bit like the bad guy in *Sleeping with the Enemy*. Likes the labels facing the right way... you haven't even seen the towels in the bathroom."

"This is your sister we're talking about." Lydia giggled more.

"I reckon Mum brought home the wrong baby."

Finally, he found the flour and before handing it to her, he opened it up, and gestured she look inside, which she did. Perfect. He grinned as he puffed the bag, then laughed as dusts of flour flew in her face.

"You... rat bag!" she said, a dusting of flour on her nose and cheeks.

"Rat bag?" Steve threw her a tea towel. "Wow, I'm hurt." He clutched his chest and feigned his agony. "I mean, even Ruby doesn't call me *that*."

She slapped his upper arm, and he caught her wrist, pulling her closer. His heart hammered. How could messing around in a kitchen be so sexy? Lydia's eyes met his.

"What does she call you then? And why?"

Steve liked the flirtatious tone to her voice. And he didn't want to ruin it. Steve was not going to divulge Friday night's mistake, and all the names Ruby had called him. No way. Not now he realised too, remembering Lydia had left early, because he'd invited her out and then totally forgotten about her. Idiot.

"Ruby's mouth is dirtier than a sewer. You'd be shocked."

Lydia's mouth was slightly open, lips moistened, full lips he wanted to kiss. He lent forward, his thumb brushing the last remains of the flour from her cheek... Electricity buzzed between them...

"Hello! I'm home." The front door slammed.

Ruby.

Still smiling, Steve released Lydia as she gave a little jump, and Ruby came in to the kitchen. "Oh." She paused, her surprised expression softening. "Oh, I am sorry, Lydia, I totally forgot I'd asked you to come over. I bumped into a friend; we got chatting and ended up having coffee. So sorry." Ruby poked Steve. "He looked after you, though?"

"Yes, of course I did."

"Maybe I should go ..." Lydia's gaze darted to the floor, not meeting Ruby or Steve's eye, while she dabbed her face with the tea towel.

"No, you're not going," Steve said quickly, holding up his hands. He wanted to hold her around her waist, pull her closer, but worried Lydia wouldn't be comfortable with that. "I said she could stay for dinner," he said, directing it to Ruby. "Well, it's more like an early dinner."

"Oh, yes, of course." Ruby nodded eagerly. "Uh, Lydia, you know you've got flour all over you?"

Lydia giggled. "Stuart puffed the bag in my face."

The name stung Steve with disappointment for a moment. He'd wanted to hear her say his name. Why it mattered, he didn't know. Any romantic intentions he did have with a woman would have to start out with a lie. This was the nature of his disguise. *A very thin disguise.* Would they accept him when they found out the truth? Would someone like Lydia be interested in a Hollywood hunk, or prefer plain old Stuart? He was caught between a rock and a hard place. If he told women the truth, he'd never know their sincerity. Stripping away his fame and fortune left Steve bare, but it was a lie. What if he fell in love and she felt cheated? Would he be left heartbroken again, as Erica had left him?

And why was he thinking about this with Lydia standing in front of him?

Stop thinking and worrying too much.

"And you've still got a spot on your nose." Wetting his thumb, he wiped her face, his knuckles brushing her cheeks, and an excited pulse jolted through his body and down into his groin. *Damn it.*

Oh, boy, you are in trouble.

"You put it there." Pink faced, she whipped him with the tea

152

towel. "Right, well, if I'm staying, I'll carry on with the Yorkshire puddings." Lydia turned back to the task in hand. "Have you got a bowl and a whisk?"

Steve pulled a gormless 'I don't know face' and shrugged, allowing Lydia to nudge him again, and Ruby took over, apologising all over again for not coming home earlier. As the kitchen was too small for the three of them, Steve leaned against the doorjamb watching the two women work.

Had Ruby set this up? She seemed to be stumbling over her story about suggesting swapping the books then meeting this so-called friend and forgetting Lydia.

Lydia? Really?

He did like her. There appeared to be something more natural between them than what he had with Alice.

Maybe he should take her out and see what happened... Test the water the way Ruby suggested.

But they worked together, what if it went wrong?

Shit, Steve, you're hardly there as a career move – in a few weeks you'll be gone. So what if he worked there? It's part of the disguise. He'd leave if things got awkward. The whole point of doing an ordinary job was to meet ordinary people under ordinary circumstances – and it was working.

But maybe he'd wait a bit and see how things panned out. Could be nothing, besides Lydia may already have a boyfriend. That jolted him.

Nah, she would have mentioned a boyfriend at work, Steve reassured himself. Lydia had talked about her house and never mentioned living with anyone, not even a housemate. Alice was the one with flatmates, Lydia had a cat... didn't she?

Time to take more notice of Lydia.

Could he afford to take his time over this? He had to be back in Hollywood for the Oscars, then he'd begin filming his next movie, and there would be all the promotional tours for *Nothing Happened*. And he wanted to have some sort of relationship, really make sure it was real before he came clean about his true identity. Maybe he should just grab that damn bull by the horns.

The quicker he found out Lydia wasn't the one, the quicker he could move on, and keep searching.

This wasn't going to work, was it? You don't look for love, it finds you. If he forced this into something it wasn't, both of them could wind up hurt.

But he could still take her out on a date... This wasn't a marriage proposal. Just a date.

"I thought you were supposed to be making this dinner?" Ruby said, eyeing him suspiciously. "Typical bloke, hands over as soon as he can."

"No, no, no..." Shaken from his reverie, Steve held his hands up defensively. "I was letting you two get on with the Yorkshire puddings. My job is done for the moment. I'll turn the potatoes once you're out of the way."

"We're out of the way." Ruby grabbed a bottle of red wine from the mini wine rack that filled the gap perfectly between the cupboards under the sink and the washing machine. "Glass of wine, Lydia?"

"Oh, I'm driving – so just a small one."

Ruby pulled three glasses out and filled them up. "Or you can get a taxi."

"But I have work tomorrow."

"I can come get you – in your car?" Steve said, taking his glass of wine and handing Lydia hers.

"I'll see if I get a taste for the wine," Lydia laughed as she spoke, then took a sip.

Ruby set the table while Steve checked on the food, then he shooed the girls into the lounge so he could prepare his master-piece. Okay, so, a roast dinner.

When he opened the oven, he was reminded quickly he had his glasses on, as they steamed up, blinding him. He swiped them off his face, so he could continue. Bloody things. How do people

154

cope? If he ever needed glasses, he was getting contact lenses. Before taking the plates to the table, he remembered to put the damn things back on.

As they tucked into their meal, he was pleased to hear Ruby groan with delight.

"Tastes like Mum's roast potatoes," Ruby said after swallowing. "You know what this means? Mum was cooking them that way, well before Jamie Oliver." He grinned.

"I can't take the credit for the Yorkshire puddings though." He pointed happily with his elbow at Lydia.

"No you can't." Lydia nodded, tucking into her food. "So, Stuart, what else can you cook?"

He rarely cooked, he had people to do it for him, or was wining and dining at some fancy restaurant. He usually made a sandwich, or breakfast, but that was about it. Maybe he should share the responsibility of cooking more with Ruby, get some practice in.

"Not a lot, not since he's moved in with me," Ruby said, maybe seeing he was struggling with words. "But at this rate, you're cooking Christmas dinner." She raised her glass and they all chinked.

Christmas.

He'd get to spend it with Ruby.

He hadn't thought of that.

Chapter 13

Thoroughly enjoying the evening, Steve topped up the wine glasses, including Lydia's, to the point she giggled and said, "I definitely need to take a taxi home." He'd forgotten she was supposed to be driving.

The three of them had chatted over dinner, then played on the Wii – Steve thought this would keep up his nerdish image – and then Ruby put on a DVD. Having let their beef go down, the three of them ate apple crumble and custard whilst watching the film.

Too busy watching Lydia out the corner of his eye, perched the other end of the sofa, Steve couldn't concentrate on the film. He wanted to be sitting next to her, cuddling. His interest in Lydia had certainly piqued, but was it only because he hadn't been close to anyone in a while?

When it was time for Lydia to leave, Steve walked her out to the taxi and paid the driver in advance.

"You don't have to do that," Lydia said, reaching for the passenger door. Steve had reached for the handle too, and placed his hand on hers. She giggled, taking her hand away, allowing Steve to open the taxi door for her. With his other hand, he gently rested it on the small of her back as if to steady, protect, or help.

"Yes, I do. I got you drunk." He looked down at her, studying her face, her lips parted, and he started slowly lowering his head...

"Right, well, I'd better go." Lydia pulled away, breaking the eye contact, and quickly got into the taxi before Steve could react. Damn perfect opportunity to land a kiss, and he'd missed it. Or she'd bolted.

He waved as the taxi drove away then returned to the house. Steve took the wine glasses out to the kitchen, Ruby followed. "Hey, sorry, I can't skip a good Die Hard film, and totally forgot I should have left you two to it."

"No, why?" Steve wore his best innocent expression.

"Oh, but I thought you were getting along, you know?" Ruby raised her eyebrows inquisitively. "When I arrived home earlier..."

"Oh, that. We were just having some fun."

"Exactly. That's what you need, Steve. Fun. Not some casual shag." He winced. He had hoped she wouldn't bring up Friday night's diabolical ending again.

"Yeah, well, whatever happens. Best it happens slowly, right?"

"Not too slowly though. You've only got till January, and we're already into November."

Now Lydia had left, he did feel deflated. He kissed the top of Ruby's head and made his way to bed.

It wasn't easy to get to sleep; he had visions of Lydia curled up on the sofa. At one point their feet had accidently touched, as he spread the length of the couch. He liked how her blonde hair hugged her neck, flicking up at the back, naturally messy. He wanted to feel it between his fingers. He liked the way she tucked strands behind her ears, and the way her cheeks dimpled with her smile.

He never thought he'd feel so strongly about Lydia after one innocent day. One very fine day. He had a major crush, thanks to today, and he now worried she wouldn't feel the same. But then, she never met his eye, and always played with her hair nervously or chewed her thumb tip. And she'd blush the most gorgeous pink if he teased her or looked at her too long.

Maybe she did feel the same.

He needed to work up the guts to ask her out. Which was ludicrous! He usually never had a problem chatting up a woman. He was Steve Mason, could have any girl he wanted – when it didn't matter.

His sensible half said *don't rush this, take your time*. The other impatient half was screaming *you've got less than three months, go for it*.

***

Bleary-eyed, and stomach churning from the wine the night before, Steve ran downstairs. He'd hastily pulled on a grey T-shirt and some sweatpants to answer the door. Who'd be knocking at this time of the morning? Though it wasn't too early, Ruby had only left for work.

Steve answered the door to a cheerful postman wearing shorts – in November? The sun was weakly shining, but had the Brits gone mad? What was it with them as soon as the sun poked its head out? Or was it just postmen?

"Good morning. Package for Stuart Fisher." The postman held out a large padded envelope.

"Oh, yeah, that's me," Steve said, remembering he'd told Marie to send the script to his new pseudonym.

The postman offered his pen, and Steve scribbled a signature. A fake one. He signed it 'S Fisher', which was his real name, after all.

Being rudely awoken by the postman ruining his lie in, Steve decided to get showered, shaved and dressed, and to make the most of the morning before he collected Lydia. Lydia worked a later shift on reception today, and so Ruby had agreed Steve could match her hours. To keep his mild hangover at bay, he spent breakfast reading the script, getting to know his new character, checking how much had been edited, whilst drinking copious amounts of tea. He'd got back into drinking tea since coming home, mainly

158

because the staff coffee at the hotel was cheap and tasted it.

Steve drove Lydia's car, a maroon Volkswagen Beetle, to pick her up for work. The old 'Herbie' kind, in its original state, no modifications like lowered suspensions, and in very good condition, Steve thought as he viewed the interior. The engine made that lovely ticking piston sound all old Volkswagens had – like a loud sewing machine. Too used to automatics, it took Steve a couple of crunches with the gearbox to get used to the gears – which he wouldn't tell Lydia about – but it ran smoothly for a classic. Although he'd driven extra carefully, he was still relieved he'd made it to Lydia's without incident. He didn't want to have an accident in her car. That would be sod's law.

He walked happily up to her front door and rang the bell.

"You forgot your book," Steve said, handing *One Day* to Lydia when she opened her door.

"Oh, thanks." She took the paperback, placed it in her large handbag and locked her front door.

Steve arrived at the car first, and in autopilot, opened the driver's door, thinking he was on the passenger side.

"Don't you think it would be best if I drove my own car?" Lydia said, frowning at him playfully.

"Oh, yeah, sure." Thinking quick, Steve opened the door wider and bowed as if making out he'd opened the door for her, and not made the mistake about which side the steering wheel was actually on. "Opening the door for Her Grace." Lydia giggled as she slid into the seat. He shut the door, then jogged around the car to the passenger side.

The left side. Must remember the left side. He kept doing that, and Ruby kept teasing him.

"So how's your head?" Lydia asked as he buckled up.

"Fine. Why?"

"We drank a lot of wine last night. I'm still feeling slightly woozy."

"We only did three bottles between us."

"There were only three of us!"

"We drank them over the course of the evening, and dinner. I feel great." Maybe a tiny bit ropey. Tired mainly, and he wondered if that was due to lack of sleep. Maybe he should have gone back to bed for an hour after the postman had called.

They walked into the hotel together. Callum, who stood in the back corridor, gave Steve a know-it-all wink.

"We've got fifteen minutes, shall we have a cup of tea before we start?" Lydia asked, retreating quickly to the canteen, her face flushed.

"Yeah, I'll be with you in a minute," Steve said.

"You sly old dog, Stu." Callum slapped him on the back. "You and Lydia hey? Did you go out last night? Stay over at hers? You lucky—"

"No, no, no." He waved his hands, gesturing to Callum to simmer down. "It's not like that. She stayed for dinner – with Ruby and me. Ruby's guest, not mine." Steve adjusted his glasses, then scratched his neck, his face heating up. He wasn't blushing was he? Did Clark Kent ever blush? "I picked her up in her car, because she'd got a cab home." *Cab? Sounds so American – remember to say taxi.* "Ruby had to come in earlier, as me and Lydia are on the late shift."

"Oh, right," Callum said, unconvinced. "So what's she like? They say the quiet ones are the worst. I didn't think you'd be into Lydia, with Alice wanting to jump your bones."

"I don't know," Steve said, keeping his voice low. "She's a friend, Callum, drop it."

"You really should put Alice out of her misery you know, and just do her."

Steve cringed. Callum had such a way with words. "Alice is way out of my league." Steve rolled his eyes, trying to be convincing. If he was looking for a bit of fun, Alice would be it. But to be honest, Steve found the way she flounced around and flirted more and more aggravating, and a turn off. Albeit she was beautiful, but there was no chase.

Steve Mason could get a dozen Alice's. Easy.

Besides, Steve and Alice had been out once, and nothing had come of it. He didn't think Alice was interested.

"Oh, what happened with that blonde girl you left with on Friday? Cor, Stu, you don't hang about."

"Nothing happened with the blonde girl." Still didn't know her name. He had hoped Callum would have reminded him then. "I put her in a taxi."

"You got in with her."

"And I dropped her home." He would not go to hell for a gentle white lie, would he?

Steve led Callum into the canteen, shoving him in his chair, still talking about how Steve really should shag Alice.

"Alice went home with some other guy, Friday," Steve said, trying to recall the last hours of Friday night, or Saturday morning.

"Yeah, but—"

"Shut it, Callum," Steve hissed, spying Lydia walking towards their table with two mugs of tea. He didn't want Lydia thinking he was crude and callous about how he made love to women. Callum was young, and joking really – he hoped. Alice wasn't so bad.

When Lydia sat down, Steve changed the conversation. Before they knew it, they'd finished their tea and were all off going their separate ways within the hotel.

During a quiet spell in the bar, Steve refilled the fridges and cleaned the shelves. He was in the small storeroom behind the bar when Alice disturbed his concentration, knocking on the open door.

"What happened to you Friday night?" she asked. Her scent filled the small room. The tight confines of the room meant she stayed close. Heat prickled up Steve's back.

"Nothing." Steve swallowed. "What happened to you?"

"Oh, I met some guy, he was okay. I didn't go home with him, if that's what you're thinking. Don't believe everything Callum tells

161

you." His arm brushed hers, as he reached up for some crisps. "So, how was your date? Worth it?"

This conversation all over again. He was grateful they were having it with Lydia unable to hear their discussion. "I put her in a cab. Nothing happened." Truth. Although if Ruby hadn't turned up, it would have been a very different story.

"Did you fancy going out tonight, on a date, again?"

Steve rubbed the back of his neck, and took a deep breath. "I don't know, Alice. We work together," lie, lie, lie, "and I don't know if it would be such a good idea." After spending one day with Lydia, innocently, just as friends, everyone else blended into the background. Alice wasn't ugly, far from it, but he didn't find her attractive. Whereas Lydia ... He could close his eyes and visualise her profile. His heart back-flipped. Creamy clear skin, long dark eyelashes, and lips that had him transfixed – he wanted to know what those lips felt like. Then, there were the little lines at the corner of her mouth as she smiled. No make-up hiding her imperfections, not that she had any. Not that Steve could see. Nor did he care.

Alice worked at her appearance, harder than she probably needed – underneath her make-up was still a pretty woman. Perfectly manicured, fashionable and chic – which she needed to be in her line of work, admittedly. Steve got that. But she was just a little bit too polished for Steve's liking. He'd found that they ran out of things to talk about.

Would Alice fit into Steve's real world? More than likely ... But Lydia? He wasn't so sure. That's what worried him.

"Shame." Alice shrugged. Steve thought he saw her lower lip quiver, but she held her head high and walked out of the storeroom.

Steve caught up with her before she left the bar area. "Hey, I like us being friends, and well, I can't believe a girl like you would be interested in a guy like me."

Flatter her, Steve, use the good old Mason charm.

"What?"

162

"You're a beautiful girl. We're not even in the same league."

"Stuart, change the frames – they're way too big for your face, get a better hair cut, and you'd be surprised." She patted his cheek and walked out.

Steve gulped. Great disguise.

***

Ruby stared at the paperwork in front of her. She hated Mondays at the best of times, but with the wine drunk the night before, her forehead pounded. As she reviewed the figures, staff rotas and orders, unsure which to tackle first, she took a sip of her coffee, and almost spat it out, forgetting it was still hot. Quickly swallowing and scalding her throat, did not improve her mood.

She looked out of her office over the great view of the hotel grounds, her mind drifting to Friday night. It was unusual to be invited out as one of the team. God, she hated being Miss Whiplash, which she'd overheard Callum say many a time to Brett. But she was the boss, sometimes she had to be, well, bossy.

Did Brett think of her that way?

Why did she care what Brett thought?

Get a grip, Ruby!

On Friday he had joined her in the taxi, and even paid the fare. They'd fumbled a nervous goodbye outside her house.

Had she wanted Brett to kiss her?

God, Ruby, this is about finding Steve the one, not you.

She'd got to know Brett more that night. They'd found a quiet corner, because neither fancied dancing, and they'd talked while slowly getting drunk.

He wasn't that much younger than Ruby after all. She'd assumed he was about Callum's immature age of twenty one. He was ambitious, too. In the taxi, he'd mistakenly confessed to wanting to run his own restaurant.

Well, if he got another job that would solve the working with one another issue.

But wouldn't it be nice to have your own business? Be your own boss...

Ruby, start thinking about work, or you'll be looking for another job, too.

She chucked her pen onto the desk, it flew off the other side and she huffed. Picking it up, frustrated further, she placed it on the desk, then went out to walk around the hotel. She took a deep breath. Concentrate.

After calling in at reception, then the restaurant (hoping for a sneaky peek of Brett, but he was busy), Ruby entered the bar, witnessing Callum and Steve mucking around, wrestling with one another. Thankfully, no guests were present.

She coughed, bringing both their attention on to her.

"We're running a four star hotel here, Callum, isn't there something you should be doing? Stuart, can I have a word, please? In my office?" See, that wasn't so hard. Didn't forget to call him Stuart.

"Yeah, sure." Steve whipped Callum with a tea towel, then followed Ruby. His smile dropped when he saw her scowl of disapproval.

"Take a seat," she said, entering her office. Steve jokingly started to wheel the chair out. "You know damn well what I mean. Sit!"

"Whoa. What's up?" He hopped into the chair and wheeled it with his heels towards her desk. He was always so full of life, and happy, it annoyed her at times. Ruby closed her office door and then sat behind her desk.

"Steve, I know you need to have fun while you're here, but remember I need you to work too. I brought you in here so Callum thinks I'm telling you off, and treating you fairly."

"Oh." Steve sighed, scratching the back of his neck. The look of frustration that he couldn't run his hand through his hair for all the gel products made Ruby chuckle.

"Is this your toughest part yet?" she said. Really, she'd wanted to chat, catching him misbehaving had given her a good excuse to call him into her office. Though, she was still annoyed he'd been taking the piss.

"I'd say, and I'm not even being paid. I can't wait to grow out these damn spikes."

"Hey, you're doing great with the Clark Kent disguise, just you know, don't muck about too much. This job is as much your disguise as the glasses and the haircut."

"I've been meaning to ask," Steve leaned on Ruby's desk with his elbows, his expression stern, "have you got Superman on DVD? Maybe I need to refresh my memory. And I'm talking the Christopher Reeve version here. The real superman." A cheeky grin etched across his face. "None of the remakes."

She rolled her eyes, shaking her head. "Get back to work, Fisher. Time is money."

***

Steve carried up a room service order and every time it made him nervous to imagine what might lie behind the door. However, today, after talking to Ruby, his mind was busy. Mediocre Man wanted to become Mr Motivator. Deep down he wanted to get Ruby out of this hotel. She might be the manager, but she didn't own it. Ruby had bosses of her own she had to report to. There must be something she'd rather do if she didn't have to worry about money. He wanted to help her follow her dreams, give her the support Mum had given him. It would have to be another conversation for another day.

He trotted down the stairs, then paused, noticing Lydia and Brett laughing together, the front desk separating them. Was Alice right, did they have a thing going on? Then Brett, chuckling a 'see you later', headed back towards the restaurant, leaving Lydia on reception scribbling into her pad. It really was a quiet afternoon, and was everyone fumbling around trying to find something to do. Hopefully it would liven up in an hour, after five, when the business guests would arrive for their overnight stay.

As he approached, she'd caught his eye and shut the pad.

"What you drawing?"

"Nothing."

Before he could tease, Ruby had joined him, coat on and handbag over her shoulder. "I'm going home. I'll come collect you later."

They'd agreed he'd better work his full shift rather than slope off.

"No need, I'll give him a lift, Ruby," Lydia said, softly.

Steve stood perplexed. He'd been craving some private time with Lydia, and wondering how to get it, and she'd delivered it to him. "You sure? You don't have to," he said.

"Yeah, of course, it will save Ruby coming out later." She smiled nervously.

"Okay, great, I'll crack open a bottle of wine when I get home then." Ruby rubbed her hands together gleefully. "See you later. Now less chatter, everyone."

In silence, they watched Ruby leave, then Steve clapped his hands. "Right, I'd better get back to work."

Steve couldn't wait for the shift to end so he'd get a whole ten minutes alone with Lydia. Okay, so it would be in her car, but after yesterday, he wanted it. He'd take what was given. Thoughts of Lydia swirled around in his brain, and the only way to clear them, put them in some sort of order, was to talk to her, to see if these thoughts were rational or not. It was the only way to find out if she was into Brett. He should take this opportunity, bite the bullet, and ask her out on a date.

Chapter 14

"Thanks for the lift," Steve said as Lydia pulled up outside the house. The journey had ended too quickly. He wanted to sit in the car longer, but knew that would be just plain weird. But he had to ask her out. Shouldn't he? He couldn't believe how his heart rate had increased with the anxiety. He worried sweat was beading along his hairline.

"No problem," Lydia replied. She glanced at him then looked at the road ahead, hands still clutching the steering wheel as if to drive off any minute. Was she eager for him to get out of the car?

Then hesitantly she turned to face him, and they spoke at the same time, "Stuart—"

"Lydia—"

"Oh, you first." She blushed.

"No, you. Ladies first and all that."

She took a deep breath. "I was wondering... um... if you'd like to go for a drink?" The last of her words spilled out quickly, Steve had to concentrate for a moment to register what she'd asked.

"Wow, okay."

"Not right now, tonight. But another night? If you're not busy..." She nervously tucked her hair behind her ears, and drummed the steering wheel, as though she didn't know what to do with her hands.

Steve shook his head, smiling. "I'm not busy. I'd love to."

"Oh, great." Then she frowned, her excitement lost. "What were you going to say?"

"Oh, uh, I was going to ask you the same thing." He laughed.

"Right, well, uh... what night?"

"Tomorrow?" He winced at her surprise. "Too keen?"

She giggled. "What about Thursday?"

"Thursday is cool." Three days away. Could he wait three days? "So am I taking you out, or are you taking me out?" he teased.

"Oh, I'll pick you up."

"No, I'll come get you."

"But you don't have a car."

"I can borrow Ruby's."

"But I asked you."

"Only because you beat me to it."

She giggled. "Stop looking at me like that."

"Like what?" Steve pulled a face. He knew her weakness, he could put on the smile and sparkly-eye look, and Lydia would be Play-Doh.

She shook her head, giggling. "I'll see you tomorrow at work."

Steve planted a swift kiss on her cheek, and strolled to the front door, his insides wanting to burst with excitement. Hell, he was thirty-five, not a spotty teenager, but he had a date with Lydia, and she'd asked him.

"Someone's happy," Ruby said, poking her head around from the kitchen.

"I've got a date with Lydia."

"For a minute there I thought you were going to say Alice, and she's a bit vain. Two vain people in a relationship, not good."

"I'm not vain." Steve resisted the urge to glance in the mirror hanging in the hallway.

"Have you seen how long it takes you to do your hair in the morning?"

"That's because a certain sister insisted I have spiky hair." Steve followed Ruby through to the kitchen, and breathed the cooking smell of tomatoes, garlic and herbs. "Oh, smells good. I'm starving."

"It's my version of spag bol. I've had mine, yours is simmering. Just bringing the pasta up to the boil now." She handed Steve a glass of red wine. "Sit. I'll dish it up."

She brought out the food, with heaps of parmesan, and placed it in front of Steve. His stomach grumbled with emptiness. Ruby sat at the table nursing a red wine while Steve ate.

"So do you like Lydia?"

Steve nodded and swallowed. "Yes, why?"

Ruby shrugged. "No reason. I just hoped she'd be your cup of tea."

"We haven't gone out yet."

"But you get along at work."

"Yeah."

"Better than Alice."

He hardly saw Alice to be fair, tucked away down at the spa. On the one date they'd had together, it certainly hadn't left him wanting to see her more. He took that as a sign, following his gut instinct.

Ruby gestured around her chin, and Steve wiped bolognaise sauce off his face. "Yeah, Alice and I don't have a lot in common – or at least I run out of things to talk about with her. She reads glossy magazines not books. She's into manicures, pedicures and stuff like that – obviously. It's her job." Ruby gave him a disapproving expression. "She's not that bad. Don't believe everything Callum tells you," Steve said sternly, finding himself repeating Alice's own words, wanting to defend her.

As for Lydia... inside he felt like an excited child, his birthday and Christmas had come at once; he was going on a date with her. Why did that sound so good in his head?

Act cool. Super-cool. Fonzie cool... hmmm... Did Ruby have any old videos of Happy Days hanging around?

Lydia sat at her breakfast bar in her small kitchen, drinking tea and sketching, her dinner plate pushed aside. Pencils, paper, and various art materials sprawled across the surface. Her fingertips were now blackened with pencil smudge as she worked on another portrait in her favourite Moleskine notepad. Stuart's face embedded in her brain meant she could easily close her eyes, imagine his handsome profile and then draw it. She'd spent the past few weeks, since his arrival at the hotel, taking sneaky peeks while he was working to draw him. It started when she'd been trying to give one of her characters those eyes, but she couldn't stop at his eyes, ending up doing a new portrait of Stuart. She loved his profile. The strong jawline and cheekbones.

She'd never known an instantaneous crush before – well not since she was sixteen – but this was it. Could this be the love at first sight sort of thing people talked about?

He had a wonderful smile, and gorgeous, bright blue eyes that held her mesmerised. She fell under a spell if she looked at them for too long, like Mowgli when Kaa, the rock python, turned on his charm in the Jungle Book. Only the other day, while working on a painting, trying to get those beautiful blue eyes into one of her characters, she'd dipped her paintbrush into her green tea as her mind had wandered on to Stuart. When he looked at her for too long, it always sent heat up her spine and into her cheeks; an involuntary, unstoppable reaction from her body whenever he was close and paying her attention.

She couldn't stop thinking about him, it was maddening, having conversations with him in her head, ones where she got to tell him how much she liked him, or where she made him laugh, smile, or want to kiss her. It was interfering with her work, too. She couldn't focus on her illustrations, and ended up playing games on her iPad rather than use it to create illustrations – which had been its purpose for the extravagant purchase. Procrastination at its worst!

She'd never find an agent if she didn't get a portfolio together.

Would she ever get to use any of these rehearsed conversations?

Then, she'd braved it one day, and asked if she could study the colour of his eyes. She'd taken off his glasses, got so close to him, feeling his breath on her cheek, as she studied his blue eyes.

How she'd held it together she'd never know. He appeared not to notice the extremely embarrassing level of heat radiating from her.

Quiet, shy, innocent Lydia, wasn't so innocent really. Somehow, tonight, she'd found the strength and guts to ask him for a date. She'd wondered, as he was a little clumsy, if he was shy, so thought she'd make the first move. Though, thinking about it, the way he teased and joked with her, was he shy, or just hiding his confidence?

She looked back at her drawing, and as she concentrated drawing his eyes, his best feature, hidden by those ridiculous glasses – they were too big for his face – she fretted she'd been too forward in the car.

He had said yes, remember.

She'd been thinking about him all day, and after Sunday, which had been lovely, truly lovely, she didn't want the opportunity to slip through her fingers. Stuart was unlikely to stay working with his sister for long. Lydia got the impression the job was a stepping stone, something to get him back on his feet after travelling for so long.

After the disastrous Friday evening, she'd been in two minds whether she even stood a chance of a date with him. With Alice about – who was far more pleasing to the male eye – there really was no competition. Alice could win over Lydia, hands down – or at least that's what she'd thought. Alice had a way of making sure she got the attention, and Lydia had been pushed aside. Callum had let slip that Stuart had taken Alice to the cinema a couple of weeks ago, riddling Lydia with jealousy, wondering if Stuart had gone home with Alice on Friday night. She'd been glad to hear nothing had gone on with the two of them. Then, with the set-up on Sunday, which she was sure of now because Ruby was not the sort of person to forget appointments, she'd decided to get to know Stuart better.

Maybe she would hint about going for a meal, rather than go to the cinema, so they could talk and really get to know one another.

She'd stopped drawing again. Lost in her thoughts, staring into space – well, into her washing machine. Stop fretting, she told herself, it is the twenty-first century. A woman can ask a man out.

Chapter 15

Thursday 14th November

Steve could just see reception through the doors, and Lydia, behind the desk, if he stood at the end of the bar.

Tonight he had a date with Lydia. While he emptied the dishwasher and wiped the glasses, he dreamt of different scenarios.

Ruby approached, shaking him out of his reverie. "Can you relieve Lydia for me please? She needs to take her break."

"Yeah, sure," Steve said, putting the polished glass on the shelf. Any excuse to get a quick chat with Lydia.

He arrived at the desk as Lydia put down the phone. "I'm here to relieve you," he said like a sergeant, even giving a little salute, making Lydia giggle.

"Oh good because I'm parched."

"Hello, gorgeous," Alice said, winking at Steve as she approached the desk. She stood near Steve, but if he moved, would it make it look obvious that he was uncomfortable? "Lydia, an engineer is coming to fix one of the treadmills in the gym. Can you just send him down when he arrives, please?"

"Yes of course. Stuart, you got that too? In case he comes when I'm on my break."

Stuart gave Lydia a thumbs up.

As Alice left them she gave Steve a flirtatious smile, and Lydia mumbled something along the lines, "She could have just called reception." Then, she looked at Steve, "The desk is all yours, although it's a shame you can't join me for tea."

"Another time, now skedaddle," he said, as the phone started ringing again. "Good afternoon, you're through to reception." Steve rolled his eyes and Lydia saw, giggled, then walked away, happy he was competent at his job. He'd been doing this for over a month now, and it was very rare he got stuck answering the questions guests threw at him.

Putting the phone down, he noticed Lydia's sketchpad under the desk – she'd left it behind. Glancing over his shoulder, he watched Lydia disappear through the double doors, leading to the staff canteen. He waited for the doors to swing close. He pulled the sketchpad out, then pushed it back under the desk, knowing he shouldn't look. He didn't have permission. Lydia had specifically not wished to share its contents. Yet, he was curious. He pulled it back out, glanced at the double doors – still closed – and brushed his thumb against the pages. Should he? Shouldn't he? What did she have to hide? If he knew the contents of the pad, he might be able to convince her she was good. Steve internally battled, but his curiosity won and he sneakily browsed through the pages. His heart raced with fear of being caught, worrying she'd return remembering she'd forgotten her sketchpad. Another glance, the coast was clear, and no one came to the desk, so he kept flicking through the pad.

Cherubic drawings. Why couldn't she show him these? Cherub-like animals too. Then Steve.

He stopped. There, in front of him, were sketches of himself. Side profile of his face mainly. Some of his eyes. When had she been drawing him? There was nothing cherubic about these, yet they were beautiful.

The drawings were brilliant. Portraits in pencil or black ink, or even biro. They were accurate, though he did look boyish thanks to his haircut – he'd gone back to the barbers yesterday morning for another trim.

Is this what he looked like when he smiled? When he was happy? He looked happy in all of them.

How long had they been there, though? When she'd snapped the other week, when he'd gone to look, were his pictures in there then?

Steve's arms trembled, he glanced again, still no sign of Lydia, so he put the pad back and busied himself behind reception. Ten minutes later, Lydia returned.

"Did I miss anything?" she said, resuming her place behind the desk.

"No it's been really quiet." Did he confess? Or would that piss her off? He didn't want to do anything to jeopardise tonight.

You are stupid; you've already done that if she finds out. She'd asked you not to look.

Forget about the damn pictures.

***

Steve showered, gelled his hair, tweaked it and tweaked it some more. His date with Lydia was rapidly approaching and he'd never felt this nervous in his life, not even when auditioning for a movie. Or at least it was a different kind of nerves. He couldn't decide. They were going for dinner at a local pub, so he donned jeans and a long-sleeved shirt out of his new wardrobe. God, if the press snapped him in this would he have some explaining to do.

They really don't care what you wear – you're just worrying over nothing now.

"You look fine," Ruby said, leaning against the bathroom door. He checked his appearance in the mirror again. Yeah, he looked good. If he did turn up looking more like Steve Mason, Lydia would probably run a mile – or just freeze.

"You don't mind me borrowing your car?"

"Of course not."

"Only you won't let me buy one." He grinned cheekily.

"What's the point? You'll be flying back off to LA before you know it." Ruby sounded sombre.

"Hey, I've got a while yet. And I could let you buy a new car. It could be your choice, and I run around in your old one."

"No! We've talked about this Steve, I don't need anything."

Steve opened his mouth to argue, but a vibrating, rumble came from Steve's bedroom, interrupting them.

"What's that noise?" Ruby frowned. Steve shared a puzzled expression, then like a light bulb appearing above his head, he realised it was his phone. His cell phone. Not the one Ruby had made him buy which contained all of about six numbers, including a taxi firm, which rested in the pocket of his jeans. He ran into the room and grabbed the phone; he had left it on the desk to charge. He hadn't liked the idea of turning it off altogether in case people in the 'real world' did need to get hold of him. He winced, seeing the caller ID and answered the phone. This was someone from Steve's very real world.

"Where the hell are you?" Steve's agent bellowed down the phone. Maybe he should have let it go to answerphone. "You were supposed to be back in LA weeks ago."

"Karl, I'm sorry, I was supposed to call you. Didn't Marie send a message?"

"Yeah, she did, and I told her to tell you not to be so fucking ridiculous. I've got gigs lined up."

Steve didn't get that message. Marie was probably trying to give him more time. His PA had definitely earned a raise. "I told you I needed a vacation, Karl."

"Yeah, and I said take two weeks, not two months!"

"I need a longer break, I need to spend time with my sister. It's not like I'm needed or anything... am I?"

"I had a chat show lined up, photo shoot with Celebrity Style. It's the Oscars in February, remember?"

Steve rubbed the back of his neck, wincing at the thought of being a pain in the ass. He didn't want to be known as one of those celebrities, and he didn't want to lose this agent. He was a good agent, and had become a good friend. And would another agent touch him if he got a bad reputation? He wasn't that big in the Hollywood industry yet. He'd heard of famous actors crashing and burning due to their wrong attitudes. Besides, he liked keeping Karl happy. Karl had been the one to put Steve on the road to success, so he felt indebted to him. They were a team.

"Look, Karl, just this once, please? I'll be back in time for the Oscars, I promise. But I need more time. I really need this break. What with the split from Erica ... And I need to make up time with Ruby."

"Marie did mention your split with Erica taking its toll, but shit, Steve, you're a star now, you're going to have to get used to your heart being broken. Actually, you should be the one breaking hearts. You should be on your third wife by now. It's Hollywood, that's the done thing."

"I don't want three ex-wives! Look, I want to stay until Christmas. I need the vacation and I haven't spent Christmas with Ruby in fifteen years. Then, I am all yours in January." It would mean cutting his time short.

"You'd better be," Karl snapped, then his tone lightened, "Admittedly, you've worked hard these past few years, I don't want you burning out and ending up in rehab. Okay, Christmas, then I want your ass back in LA. I'll have to cancel the chat show and the photo shoot."

He threw the phone back on the desk.

"So?" Ruby stood there, arms folded. "Do you have to go back, or do we get Christmas?"

"We get Christmas." Steve nodded with relief. Hopefully his guilt for letting Karl down would dull. Yet, the reality that he would have to return shortly after Christmas didn't make him feel great.

"Right, well, you'd better go. Otherwise Lydia will wonder where you are." She brushed his shirt, almost motherly, and handed Steve her car keys. "You don't have long now, Steve, so stop dithering and get a move on."

With November here, and appearing to fly past, he had just over a month at the most. Steve had to return to LA after the Christmas holidays otherwise he would be kissing his career goodbye, and his agent.

Time to see if Lydia was the one.

***

A roaring log fire greeted Steve and Lydia as they entered the cosy pub, making them forget it was winter outside. Both shivered, rubbing their hands, as they found a table in a secluded corner, close to the fire. If it had been daylight, Steve knew that there was a great view to be seen from their window, looking out onto the Severn Estuary.

"This is nice," Lydia said, gesturing to the room with its solid beams and open fire.

"Yeah, I used to come here years ago. It's changed a lot though."

The Golden Lion in Portishead had once been a regular watering hole for Steve and his pals. He was pleased when Ruby confirmed it still existed and served great food. She'd also said it had been refurbished a couple of times, the managers had changed, and the regulars had moved on. No one would recognise him – he hoped.

"So how are you finding work?" Lydia said, once settled, sipping her wine. He could see by the slight tremble in her hands she was nervous. "Is it hard working with Ruby as your boss?" She timidly giggled.

"Oh, no, not at all. Ruby and I have some catching up to do, so it's rather nice."

"Will you be looking for other work?"

"How do you mean?" Steve frowned, thrown by her question.

He picked up his lager and took a sip. Had he hinted at leaving? That hadn't been his plan. Though the time would come eventually when he'd have to leave. And it would be sooner rather than later.

"Well, I get the impression Ruby's done you a favour, I didn't think you'd be staying long. What did you do before you went travelling?"

"Oh, well, I've been travelling for so long, I've lost touch with what I used to do..." Steve realised he hated lying.

"Which was?"

"Oh, Lydia, I kinda bummed around for a while." Actually, he'd worked his ass off since the day he moved to LA. And before that, paper rounds, working in corner shops, washing cars, flipping burgers, anything to save up for his flight over. "It's embarrassing what I did before..." He couldn't meet her gaze, concentrating on the bubbles rising in his glass.

"You can tell me. I won't tell the others, if that's what you're worried about. It can't have been that bad, could it?"

He looked around shiftily, thinking hard, then whispered, "I was... an estate agent." Unable to meet her gaze, he chided himself, hating the fact he was lying to Lydia,

Lydia laughed, making him feel at ease.

"See I told you it was bad."

"Not at all, I thought you were going to say something far worse."

"Worse? Like what?" Steve grinned.

Lydia shrugged. "I don't know. Double-glazing salesman?

"Oh, God, that is worse." They laughed. Damn, he liked her laughter. "And I'm not that good at selling."

"But you sold houses?"

"Houses sell themselves really. Either a person loves a house or they don't." He assumed, anyway. Nobody bought a house they didn't like. Okay, some hideous looking houses probably gave the estate agent extra work.

"So why don't you go back into selling houses?" she asked once she'd stopped giggling and sipped her drink.

"Because I hated it." This in the trade was called improvising. He'd never been an estate agent. Not even played a part as one. All he had was daytime TV and all those property programmes as research, and he hadn't watched many. Sometimes they were on in the morning whilst he got ready for the late shift at work.

"So where did you travel to then?"

Oh, hell, he really should have thought about some background more seriously. He and Ruby had winged it, and then nobody had really asked further. Where had he been with the film sets?

"Australia." He did spend a couple of weeks there. Not filming, but when the money had started rolling in, he'd managed to get some trips to places he wanted to see, tying in with a couple of chat shows and interviews. Besides, anyone who travelled usually did Australia. He could have easily been there a year. Australia could explain his now fading tan, too.

"Oh, I would love to go to Australia. Tell me all about it."

Unlike Alice, who talked about herself and gossiped about others, Lydia liked asking questions about Steve, wanting to know more about him. On the plus side, the conversation flowed, on the minus, it meant Steve found himself telling a white lie here and a white lie there to please Lydia. But he could hardly tell her the truth... yet. Though he had to stop himself spilling his guts. He hated lying to her. Every time she called him Stuart, he wanted to correct her, and say he was really Steve.

If this relationship blossomed... how soon should he tell her the truth? Ruby hadn't thought this through... neither had Steve.

Lydia put her knife and fork together and pushed her cleared plate away. Erica would have only ordered the salad. But then she wouldn't have sat in a cosy pub in Portishead and ordered the smothered chicken with chunky chips. One, she was a vegetarian, and two, Erica had to stick to a strict diet thanks to the career she'd chosen.

Lydia wasn't fat. She had a superb figure, which Steve could not stop fantasising about, imaging her curves pressing into him.

"So, have you seen how Brett acts around Ruby?"

Steve frowned, although thankful Lydia had changed the subject from him to Ruby. "I have wondered, but then I just thought it was Brett being Brett, nervous around Miss Whiplash."

"He never calls her that. Callum does."

"Come to think of it, a while back they did seem cosy on the sofa together when the guys came over for a boys' night in."

"And Friday night, he stayed with her the whole time I was there."

"He got her home safely, too." Guilt stabbed at him again. "I'm sorry about last Friday. I invited you out and then ended up forgetting about you."

"Not hard with Alice about."

"I forgot about Alice, too," Steve said, chuckling, trying to make a joke of it.

"Well... it doesn't matter." It looked as if Lydia wanted to forget Friday night as much as Steve did. He was thankful she shook her head and waved it off. Steve enjoyed watching how her hair flicked around her neck. "But anyway, I think he likes Ruby."

"Alice reckoned you and Brett had a thing..." Steve swallowed down fear that this could be true. Although, Lydia was not on a date with Brett.

Lydia laughed and shook her head. "The gossip in that hotel. All you have to do is talk to someone of the opposite sex and you're dating. No, Brett and I are just friends, and that's how I've noticed how he is with Ruby."

"I'll have to watch out for him then," Steve said, putting on a stern voice and a silly Popeye pose with his arms.

"Oh, how big brotherly." Lydia giggled.

"What about you? When are you going to show the world you're a great artist?" Steve leaned forward, resting his elbows onto the table. He took Lydia's hand and rubbed her palm with his thumb.

"Illustrator. Soon... I want to send them off to some agents. I want to get commissioned. I'm just putting a portfolio and a website together."

"What made you want to become an illustrator?"

"I've always loved drawing, but I always thought it would be my hobby. Then, never really knowing what to do, I decided I should try to turn my hobby into a living. This would be the perfect day job. Something I enjoy, love, rather than, like at work where half the time, I'm bored out of my brain. But it's regular and pays the bills, so I have to stick at it for the time being."

"Illustrating would be your dream job?"

"Yeah, I'd love to do children's books, but I'm not the writer, I'm no good with words, at least writing them down. Kids' stories are so hard. Knowing what to write, what they'd understand. I tried having a go, and just couldn't do it. Ideally, I want to illustrate the stories with my characters."

"So..." Steve smiled, cheekily, "when are you going to show me the contents of that sketchpad. I want to see your drawings." He'd seen them, of course, but he wanted her to show them to him, then his conscience would be cleared. "You know, we've dated once now. I should see them."

"Oh, um, one day." Her gaze dropped, withdrawing her hand from Steve, and she fiddled with the coaster on the table, turning it on the table.

"Lydia, you have nothing to be ashamed of. What you did show me were great. I want to see more. I'm interested."

"I know. I need to get over this hurdle, but let me do it in my own time. It's half the reason I haven't submitted anything yet. I'm worried about the rejections."

"Rejections toughen you up." Did he know about rejections. "Your skin will thicken, but they will love your drawings." He reached out and squeezed her arm reassuringly. "So, shall we get dessert, or just coffee?"

He didn't want tonight to end, but it was getting late. He'd have to take her home soon.

"Maybe a coffee for me. I'm stuffed. I couldn't eat another thing."

Coffee arrived, and Steve wanted to know as much as he could about Lydia. "So, you know my family – Ruby – what about yours?" Steve said, offering Lydia a chocolate mint that had come with the coffee.

"Oh, I'm the youngest of three," Lydia said, taking the mint, and placing it by her coffee. "I have an older brother – he's getting married next year and an older sister, the oldest, who is married with two young children – two nieces."

"Do you see your nieces often?"

"Yes, I spoil them rotten." Lydia grinned. "I try to help out with babysitting when I can." Tick, Steve thought mentally. She likes kids. "Actually, I've got to babysit in a few weeks – would you like to come with me and keep me company? Oh!" Lydia blushed. "Maybe that's a bit presumptuous. You might not want another date."

"Don't be silly. Of course I do." He caressed her hand, dying to touch her again.

"We could get in pizzas, watch a film," she said happily. "It's Emma's thirtieth birthday and her husband, Paul, wants to take her out. They don't get out much together. I agreed to it ages ago."

"Sounds like a date."

***

Steve parked up outside Lydia's house, behind her maroon Beetle. He got out and followed her up the steps to her front door. Keys in her hand, she stood on the top step, and turned to face Steve who was on the lower one. They were the perfect height. He didn't need to look down, she didn't need to look up. Lips parallel.

"I'd ask you in for coffee ... but ..."

"No, no, I don't want to come in ... yet," Steve said, pushing a strand of hair out of her face. "I want to do this right. You'll go out with me again, won't you? I've had so much fun tonight, you won't believe how great it's been to just talk, and listen."

She smiled shyly. "I've had a great time, too."

"Good. Plus, I think I'd better see you some more before I meet your sister."

"My sister?"

"Yes you asked me to help babysit, remember?"

"Oh, yes. I did."

Steve edged forward, lips an inch away, then gently cupping her face, he kissed her, softly. For a brief moment, she opened her mouth and welcomed his tongue. The kiss was exquisite. Lydia wrapped her arms around his waist, gently gripping his shirt. Blood raced to Steve's groin so fast it surprised him. He pulled away and sighed, not wanting Lydia to feel his growing erection. She kept her eyes closed for a moment. Everything in the world seemed perfect.

"Tomorrow night, or Saturday?" he asked.

"Does tomorrow sound too eager?" She tucked some hair behind her ear.

"Absolutely not." He grinned, then kissed her again, this time resisting his tongue tasting hers, because he really would find it hard to go home. He stepped down and walked to Ruby's car and waved. "See you at work tomorrow, too."

She looked at him puzzled, and he realised he'd done it again. He was the wrong side of the car. In his happiness, and feeling aroused, dream like, he'd been on autopilot. He slung off his jacket, chucked it inside as if he'd deliberately gone to the passenger side, and then went round to the driver side, trying not to show he was actually cold. It's November for heaven's sake. He waited, making sure she was inside her house safely, then drove off, his body thrumming with excitement.

Chapter 16

Monday 18th November

Ruby needed to do her usual rounds, make checks with the staff – sometimes she felt like a doctor on a hospital ward, only everything wasn't so clinical, thankfully. She closed her office door behind her and headed towards reception wondering if one of the girls would need relieving for their break, and stopped. Cold fear crept up her spine.

Terence. What the hell was he doing here?

Instantly her heart pounded, Terence hadn't noticed her, too busy being smarmy with Lydia, so she darted down the corridor and into the bar, closing the doors that usually remained open behind her. Steve stood with a tea towel slung over his shoulder – too casual for Ruby's liking – at the coffee machine, frothing hot milk.

"Quickly, get out of sight, until I say you can come out."

"What?" Steve frowned with a puzzled expression, glancing over Ruby's shoulder towards some guests who sat patiently at a table. They'd actually stopped talking and stared at Ruby as if she was nuts. "I'm in the middle of making coffees," Steve said calmly.

"Terry is here," Ruby hissed and Steve stiffened. "And he must not see you. Get Callum to take over."

Ruby rushed back out of the room, smoothing her jacket, and then ran her fingers through her hair in attempt to look cool and collected. Taking a deep breath, she approached the reception desk.

"Oh, Ruby, I was trying your office," Lydia said putting the phone down. "This is Terence Smith—"

"Smythe." Terry corrected Lydia.

"I know who he is. What do you want, Terry?"

"That's not how you should talk to your guests." He smiled, showing off perfect teeth Ruby would like to knock out – if only she had a baseball bat handy.

"Are you staying in this hotel?"

"No."

"Well then, that's how I talk to scummy journalists who happen to also be my ex-boyfriend."

Ruby saw Lydia blush. Luckily Lydia knew when to make herself scarce, realising it was none of her business.

"Ruby, I've not come to argue, I've come to see how you are and make it up to you. I wondered if you'd join me for lunch."

Ruby scowled. She no longer trusted a word uttered from this man's mouth, however handsome his face; he'd lost his appeal long ago.

"I have to work."

"What about in your own restaurant?" He gestured to the Avon Restaurant that was set off from reception. She had to get rid of Terry as Steve couldn't hide forever in the bar's storeroom. However if she tried to get rid of him too quickly, would he think her actions were suspicious?

"You can have an hour of my time," Ruby replied sternly. "But I have some business to attend to first, so get seated and I will join you in a minute."

Terry nodded, seeming pleased with Ruby's decision, and walked off towards the restaurant.

"Who was that?"

Ruby turned to see Alice leaning against the desk, giving Terry's backside an appreciative glance. Admittedly, the man did look good in a suit, only he no longer appealed to Ruby. Amazing how someone can turn ugly when you knew what they were made of inside; deceit, greed and a shallowness that ironically ran deep. He was like an exotic fruit, which was filled with maggots.

"None of your business. What are you doing here?"

Alice, astounded by Ruby's sharp tone, held her hands up defensively. "Lydia called me to reception."

"Oh, sorry." Ruby felt awful. She dealt with much worse in the hotel and always kept her head. She needed to stop acting like a headless chicken and gain control of the situation.

"Yes, your Decléor rep is over there on the couch." Lydia pointed to a woman who looked every bit a beauty rep, and Alice, giving Ruby a '*see*' expression, went to meet her visitor.

"Lydia," Ruby said, noticing Terry entering the restaurant, and Alice moving out of earshot, "get my car keys out of my office, then find Stuart – he may be in the storeroom – and tell him to go home." Lydia nodded but wore a puzzled expression. "You have to trust me on this one. Terry is an ex, and I don't want my brother knowing he's here – he might cause a scene."

"Oh, I don't think that's Stuart's nature," she said.

"Please, Lydia, tell him Ruby thinks it's best he stays at home. I'll mind the desk until you come back."

"No need, Maxine's off her break now." Sure enough, Maxine approached.

"Lydia, wait, actually, take the rest of the afternoon off too, and take Stuart out."

"Are you sure? What about reception?"

"Maxine will manage, and I'll cover if needs be."

"Okay, well I only had a couple of hours to go. You're sure?"

"Yes! Now go." She ushered hastily.

Maxine's confused expression said it all. "Don't ask," Ruby said. "I'll be in the restaurant for an hour. In fact, come get me out after an hour, tell me there's an important call, anything. And I'll

187

help cover afterwards. I promise."

"I am just a small cog in this large wheel, I'll do whatever you need me to do." Maxine shrugged. "Go get him then. Whoever the hell he is?"

"Right." Ruby took a deep breath, and headed towards the restaurant and the torturous hour of time ahead of her. If they weren't dining in her restaurant, she'd hope Terry choked on a bone.

Seated at one of the tables in the conservatory, Terrance looked up from the menu as Ruby paced towards him and grinned, too smugly for Ruby's liking. Did he know Steve was here?

He stood as Ruby took her seat, in true gentleman style, however she knew he was far from gallantry.

"I've ordered a bottle of champagne—"

"You're paying for it."

"Of course, and I hope you'll join me."

Christophe, the waiter arrived, placing an ice bucket by the table with a bottle of champagne chilling inside it. He opened the bottle with control, and let Terence sample it. Terence nodded his approval and the waiter poured a full glass. He went to pour one for Ruby, but she held her hand over the flute.

"I've got to work... but..." she did have to endure an hour with Terence. She might need the alcohol to help calm her nerves. "Oh, what the hell, seeing as you're paying." She narrowed her eyes on Terence, taking her hand away from the glass. Christophe poured her some champagne.

"Christophe, please could you bring me a glass of iced water, too," she asked the waiter as he was about to leave the table. She would need to remain sober. Not only because of work, but because this sly bastard might try to slip her up.

"So, why the visit, Terence?"

He glanced up from the menu, almost surprised by her question. Was he stupid?

"I was in the area, and thought of you."

188

"We both live and work in Bristol, Terry. It's been three years."

"Yes, I know, but when I saw you the other day—"

"Stop!" Ruby held her hand up. "You used me, remember that?"

Terry took a sip of his champagne, possibly to gather his slimy thoughts. "Ruby, it wasn't like that." Yes, slimy thoughts.

Fortunately, the waiter arrived back at the table so Ruby bit her tongue.

"Are you ready to order?"

"Yes, I'll have my usual, Christophe. Tell Brett it's for me. Charge *him* full price though, as he's paying." She gestured towards Terry.

Christophe nodded. "And sir?"

Lamb, I bet he has the lamb.

"I'll have the lamb, thank you."

Ruby hid her smirk behind the menu. She'd got to know this man so deeply. He'd let her, deliberately of course, so that he could get every gory detail about Steve.

"As I was saying," Terence continued once Christophe had left the table, "I did love you."

"Terence, I will not sit here for an hour and listen to this drivel. What the hell do you want?"

"I want to spend some time with you." He reached across the table and placed his hand on hers, instantly sending ice along her neck, prickling. She snatched her hand away.

"I don't feel like that about you anymore." He might still be a handsome man, but she found him far from attractive. She knew what he was capable of. The lies. The hurt of his betrayal still ran very deep within her, and if she wasn't careful, it would resurface. She had loved him. He'd conned her so believably.

Ruby changed the subject, and with the food served, the conversation faltered slightly. If Ruby ate in the restaurant with business partners, Brett always ensured she had a small portion of the chicken dish she loved so much, as she didn't like to have a large meal at lunchtime. But with Terry in front of her, she had found it very hard to concentrate on the food and ended up leaving half of it.

As Christophe cleared the plates, Terry was true to his word. "Well, have you heard from Steve?" he said casually.

"There, finally." Ruby finished her glass of champagne. She'd stuck to the one glass. "No I haven't."

To Ruby's surprise Brett appeared at the table with Christophe beside him. "Was everything okay with your meal, Ruby?" His brow furrowed, looking concerned.

"Yes, it was fine thank you. Why?"

"You left half of it. You never leave half of it."

Ruby chuckled. "Unfortunately I don't have good company. He put me off my food. Sorry." She placed a reassuring hand on Brett's arm, something she felt more comfortable to do nowadays, as he was friends with Steve. *Oh, please don't mention Stuart.*

"Would you like him removed from the hotel?" Brett said, and Ruby admired his assertive tone.

Brett always prepared her food to her special requirements. She'd always thought it was because she was the manager, but now she started to think it was a bit more than that. He'd become very protective, suddenly.

And was Christophe cracking his knuckles? He stood beside Brett as if ready to be his right-hand man.

"Yes, once he's paid the bill. But get Doug to escort him off." Doug was one of her security guards. A beefy guy who took no messing. She dabbed her mouth with the napkin then stood from the table. "Do not answer any questions he may ask. And I mean *any*." She winked at Brett, then strutted out of the restaurant, glad to be wearing a pair of heels that clipped the slate tiled floor in the conservatory, making her feel sassy and in control of the situation. Inside she jingled like a bag of nerves.

Only, please, no one breathe a word about 'Stuart'.

***

"That was odd." Lydia said, still puzzled over why Ruby would give her the afternoon off. Steve knew why, but he could hardly say he's a reporter sniffing around to find gossip on Ruby's Hollywood-Actor-Brother.

They'd taken Lydia's car as Ruby had given them both the time off. Steve's long legs were still cramped in the old Volkswagen, but at least the old girl had character as it thrummed.

"I mean, you're not the sort of guy to start a fight... are you?"

"No," Steve laughed nervously, "of course not." *Only on well-choreographed film sets.*

"Then why didn't she want you meeting her ex?"

Ex? Steve didn't realise that. He hoped his surprise was masked. "Ruby must have her reasons. Maybe the guy would wind me up to the point I would punch him."

Lydia gave Steve a disapproving look.

"Apparently he treated her roughly."

"How roughly?"

"Oh, not like that roughly. I mean, he broke her heart."

"Oh." She nodded her understanding.

"So, let's not dwell on it." After another fabulous date on Friday night, and brief encounters at work during the weekend, Steve was feeling very comfortable with Lydia "Let's make the most of a sunny November afternoon. Bit chilly, but at least it's dry." Which made a change. There was too much rain in England.

"Well, I haven't had lunch."

"No, me neither. Let's head for the waterfront. We can pick up a bite to eat and watch the boats on the river."

"And go for a walk."

Steve smiled. He liked Lydia. So early on really, yet they seemed to fall into step with one another. He felt at ease in her company, as if he'd known her years – but in a good way. "Yes, and a walk. Maybe you'll let me hold your hand?"

"I might, if you play your cards right, Stuart."

"You let me on Friday night." They'd walked from the restaurant

191

in Clifton to a pub, and he'd taken her hand into his as if it was the most natural thing to do. And as it had been cold, he'd tucked her hand with his into his jacket pocket.

Lydia chuckled. "So I did."

Hand in hand they walked until they found somewhere near the river to get a light lunch and frothy cappuccinos. Sitting by the window, they could chat whilst watching the world go by. The sun had sneaked out from behind the clouds, and spread warmth through the glass. It was turning out to be a fine day. One fine day with Lydia was worth a thousand with Erica... or any other woman for that matter, Steve thought, happily.

As they chattered, having their coffees refilled, Steve decided to keep the conversation on Lydia, to alleviate his guilt of telling lies. "Your drawings are impressive, Lydia," he said, wiping his hands on a paper napkin. "How much time do you spend on them?"

"Every free minute."

"And when it's quiet at work."

"Oh, I tend to only touch up some of the sketches at work, tweak them. I usually start them at home."

"What, even the ones of me? – I mean of my eyes..." *Big mistake*. Lydia looked at him questioningly. He held up his hands. "Okay, I'm sorry, I confess, I looked in your sketchpad," he said, jovially, but Lydia's expression hardened, her face flushing red.

"Stuart, I told you not to look in that pad." She pushed back from the table, her chair scraped the tiled floor, and she wouldn't meet his eye.

Leaning forward, he took her hand gently, tugging to get her to meet his gaze. "Hey, Lydie, please don't be mad at me," he said, softly. "Your drawings are amazing, you have a real talent. I'm so flattered you've drawn me."

"I asked you not to look," she said, angrily.

"I know I shouldn't have looked but I was intrigued, I want to support you."

"Support me?"

192

"Yes, if we become a team, which I hope we will – I know it's early days yet," he shrugged, "then I want to help you with your career. I'll understand if you say you can't see me because you need to finish an illustration. Things like that."

Lydia softened, and he drew her in for a kiss, tenderly cupping his hand around her neck.

When he released her, she smiled. "Stuart, that's really sweet."

"Come on, it's a fine day out there. If I'm forgiven, let's make the most of this sunshine," Steve said.

"You're forgiven."

He paid the bill, then coats buttoned, they linked arms and strolled along the waterfront, becoming tourists for the day in the midst of the city.

Chapter 17

Saturday 23rd November

The week passed in a blur; working, dating Lydia, and playing Xbox or Wii with Callum and Brett. Life could not be more normal, and less stressful, if he tried. He was surprised at how much he wasn't missing the thrill of acting, which usually gave him a buzz, making him feel challenged and alive. Maybe it was because he'd been living peacefully, unrecognised. That's what he wasn't missing. The fact he could live without the fear of the press being at his heel was surprisingly relaxing. He couldn't have lunch out in Hollywood without someone taking his photo.

But was his life really normal? Ruby fretted occasionally about money, when a bill would come in, counting the days till her next payday. Admittedly, she stopped doing it in front of Steve. She knew his answer would be to write her a cheque in a flash or transfer the money. Was this why life was so relaxing? No money worries, yet in hiding from his own reality. The only 'real life' reminder he had was when he started going over his lines in the script for his next movie.

Steve also sneaked out to their old house to see how the builders and decorators were coming along. Soon he'd be able to show Ruby its transformation, and hopefully convince her it was where she belonged.

Walking back from the corner shop one Saturday morning, thinking about the house, Ruby, Lydia, and how he'd have to return to his real world, how that weighed heavy on his shoulders, he noticed the poster in the bus stop had changed.

Erica Kealey, dressed in leather and wielding a machine gun, looked provocative and sexy advertising her next film. Her husband-to-be, the hero of this movie was standing beside her. This was Hollywood.

Steve studied it, realising he felt unaffected by this picture. He admired it. Erica was a beautiful woman. She appeared taller and stronger in this picture than she looked in real life. But she no longer stabbed at Steve's heart, that pang of emptiness and love lost didn't happen.

He was over Erica Kealey.

Lydia was equally beautiful, and she didn't have the money or resources like Erica, and she made him laugh. She allowed him to be himself, not the alter ego of Steve Mason whom everyone had to see on chat shows, or in glossy magazines. Okay – so he'd had that with Erica behind closed doors – sort of. It was only now, looking back, he could see how wrong Erica was for him. Lydia brought the best out of him, whereas with Erica, he'd had to work hard in the relationship. Everything was easy with Lydia. Okay, he couldn't deny the initial attraction he and Erica had, but underneath the surface, that's all it had been. They may have worked in the same circles, but it was obvious they were two very different people. Unlike Steve, Erica had been born into stardom, having an entourage from a young age. She didn't know of the struggles and money worries ordinary folk worried about on a daily basis. And he had started to forget, too, as a wealth of money can easily do.

Lydia didn't need bodyguards, an entourage – though she might when – if – Steve made his romance with her public. He swallowed down the worrying thought. He'd cross that bridge when it came to it. It was important to use this time to get to know

Lydia, fully, before taking that leap. Their romance might fizzle and there'd be no need. It's why he hadn't yet made love to her. They were both eager. He assumed Lydia felt the same, the way she kissed him goodbye, not wanting to let go. It got more difficult every night he had to leave her. He was fit to burst. Even though his head said he needed to rush through things – Christmas was rapidly approaching – he didn't want to. It wouldn't be fair on Lydia. He hated lying to her. He'd hinted he wouldn't be in the job long, maybe to reassure her this affair wouldn't affect her job if things did go wrong. But he didn't want to take their relationship to the next intimate level until he was truly sure. Maybe this way there'd be less fallout if things did go wrong. He didn't need details of Lydia's and his relationship getting into the sordid paws of the press.

In these past weeks, Steve had time to think. Reflect. Erica and he had had a whirlwind romance. The press had glamorised it, 'Hot New Couple Alert' and all that trash, and new to the rollercoaster ride, Steve hadn't liked the jerk when it stopped and Erica stepped off. She'd been in the limelight longer than Steve, and had learnt to cope with a public break-up.

Arriving at his front door, he slotted the key into it and entered, the smell of bacon and eggs greeting him. He patted his grumbling stomach. He needed to train harder. Ruby was feeding him too well. He threw his glasses aside on the coffee table.

"Oh, just in time for breakfast." Ruby called from the kitchen. As he sat at the table, dumping the papers and magazines he'd fetched from the shop, Ruby pushed a fried breakfast under his nose.

"You're too good to me."

"Well, don't get too used to it. But I like you being home, so I thought I'd spoil you. But you tell a soul and I'll kill you." She was waving the tomato sauce bottle at him. He grabbed the brown sauce already on the table. "I don't want word getting out that I'm actually domesticated. Someone might try and make a wife out of me."

"You'll make a great wife."

"Pfft." Ruby pulled a disbelieving face and went back into her kitchen. "Someone's got to learn to put up with my bossiness first."

"True." He chuckled. He knew his sister was confident and strong-willed, but they weren't bad qualities; it meant she could handle herself and not be walked over by some git. Except Terence, but Ruby had learnt from that incident. No, he didn't have to worry about her – too much. Swallowing his food, he asked, "Will you help me go through my script today?"

"Oh, do I have to?" Ruby pulled a face as she sat down at the table with her own breakfast.

"I can't ask Lydia, can I? However much I would like to."

Ruby sighed. "All right. Of course I will. When do you think you'll tell Lydia the truth?"

Steve scratched the back of his head. "I don't know. I want to, but then I want to make sure she feels strongly about me."

"Have you two...?" Ruby raised her eyebrows questioningly.

"Ruby!" Steve scolded. "A gentleman should never kiss and tell... but no, I've been waiting – it's only been a couple of weeks. I don't want to hurt her. I want to make sure I do love her first."

"And that she loves you?"

"Yes."

***

Tuesday 26th November

Steve thought he was having a really good day at work until he answered the phone on the bar, and heard Ruby hiss "Terence is here. Hide," while at the same time, Callum, stood right beside him, and said, "Cougar alert. Incoming."

Should he be concerned about Terence showing up twice in just over a week? Did Terence suspect something or was he just pursuing Ruby?

Steve glanced up to see Ms Jones, aka Marilyn heading his way. "Ruby, I've got to go. I'll keep out of sight, I promise." Ruby's reporter ex-boyfriend seemed the least of his worries right now. He slammed the phone down. *Great, and he was supposed to be taking his lunch break with Lydia in a minute.*

"Callum, I'll go do that stock take and don't disturb me," he said, loudly.

"I don't know what you're worried about. For an older women, she's hot."

"You chat her up then."

"I would, but she doesn't fancy me."

Steve ducked out of sight into the store cupboard where he could hear the conversation at the bar.

"Oh!" Ms Jones said. "Where is your colleague?"

"He's doing a stock take. Can I help, Madame?" Callum stumbled over what to call her. *All mouth, no action, Callum. He won't chat her up.*

"That's a shame... I'll have an Americano, please."

"But Stuart's British."

Steve stifled a groan.

"Pardon?"

Callum chuckled. "Forget it... would you like the coffee taken up to your room?"

"No, I'll sit in here. Put it on my room bill, please."

Steve rolled his eyes – he was stuck. As he heard Callum shuffle about, using the till then the coffee machine, Steve wondered how the hell he was going to escape without being noticed. Hard, because the only way out was through the bar. He couldn't even dive out via the back door onto the decking.

"Hi, Callum, is Stuart about?"

"Oh hi, Lydia," Callum said loudly, Steve presumed he thought he couldn't hear. "He's stock taking."

"Hi, Lydia, ready to go?" Steve appeared from the stock room, smiling. He tried to look as if he'd been working hard. "I'll finish the rest of the stock take later, Callum."

"Of course you will." Callum shook his head.

"Oh, there you are." Ms Jones stood up from her table to greet Steve. "I wondered if you'd like to join me for dinner this evening." There was a twinkle in her eye. Did she know who he really was? Surely not... Steve straightened his glasses on his face. *Act dorkily.* "As you know, I'm all alone in this hotel."

Lydia frowned, and Steve grasped her hand firmly. "I'm sorry, flattered as I am, I have a girlfriend and we're going out tonight." Lydia beamed, and Steve tugged her arm, "Let's get some lunch, sweetheart."

Ms Jones gave Lydia a dirty look.

Steve rushed out of the bar, and then remembered Ruby's call. Cautiously, he looked around, checking the coast was clear. Hopefully Ruby had the reporter hidden away in her office. Alice walked out from the spa, heading towards Ruby's office. There were raised voices coming from inside. He wanted to help but knew it would make matters worse. Quickly, he jerked at Lydia's hand and pushed through the double doors, striding along the corridor, eager to tuck himself away in the staff room.

"Why are we walking so fast?" Lydia said, running to keep up with him.

"I'm hungry."

***

Terence had knocked at Ruby's open office door, and leaned casually in the doorway, as she finished her warning call to Steve. Lydia had given her the heads up that he was in the building.

"I was going to meet you at reception," Ruby said, coldly, scowling, her hackles up.

"It's okay, I told the receptionist I'd find my way to your office."

"You'd snoop about more like." *Ruby shut up. You're acting like you have something to hide. Which you do, and he'll cotton on.*

"Ruby, I was in the area, and thought I'd pop in to see you." Terry took the seat opposite Ruby's desk – uninvited. The man really had a nerve. Ruby would not be taken in by this guy's charm. She'd lost all trust in him a long time ago, and it would not be returning any time soon. He might look hot with his good looks and flashy suit, but underneath his falsely warm exterior ran an ugly cold-hearted liar.

"But I no longer wish to see you." Ruby interlinked her fingers in front of her, leaning on her desk. All business, no messing.

"Please don't be like that. I made a mistake all those years ago."

"It's been three years, Terry. I can even give you to the exact day you hurt me. You can't walk back into my life as if nothing happened." Ruby stood up from her chair as her fist thumped her desk and her blood pounded around her body with rage.

"Tell me what I need to do to get your forgiveness?"

"Nothing. I don't trust you."

"Is everything okay? I heard shouting." Brett poked his head around the door. When he spotted Terry smiling at him from the chair, Brett's expression hardened, and he entered the office, making more of a presence.

"Everything is fine, we're catching up on old times," Terence said, grinning at Brett. Too annoyingly cool for Ruby's liking.

Brett frowned. "Ruby?"

"Terry was just leaving – weren't you?" She glared at Terence, her hands still forming fists.

"I'll show him out," Brett said. He looked impressive in his chef whites. Twice now he'd rescued Ruby from Terry. Terry stood, and Brett stood a remarkable couple of inches taller than him.

"Ruby, what can I do to make you forgive me?" Terry pleaded. He'd grabbed her hand in the moment, trying to soften her will. Ruby paused at his touch, good times flooded in to her mind, good memories, then the heart-breaking horror which had followed. Her heart hardened. Terence had had his opportunity, Ruby would be a fool to give him a second chance. *She deserved Brett – better – she meant better.*

"No, get Doug to make sure he leaves the property," she said, coldly to Brett. "I wouldn't want you getting your hands dirty."

"Oh, hello, are we all having a party in Ruby's office?" Alice entered, bubbly and looking her usual striking self. She gave an appreciative smile towards Terry.

"Terry was just leaving," Ruby said, sternly, and Brett took the hint to escort him out of her office. Ruby didn't like the way Terry had smiled back at Alice as he'd left.

"What can I do for you, Alice?" Ruby's words were still laced with anger. She needed to calm down.

"Someone's in a bad mood."

"You'd be too if you were being harassed by your ex."

Chapter 18

Saturday 30th November

Lydia snuggled into Steve, as they sat in a café on a well-worn sofa, sipping mochas. Olivia and Rosie, Lydia's cute nieces, sat opposite. Each sucked through a straw thick banana milkshakes and nibbled chocolate chip cookies.

Steve had just shared another fabulous date with Lydia. He'd also shared it with a chatty five-year-old, Olivia, and a giggly, butter-wouldn't-melt, three-year-old, Rosie. Both with blonde hair and blue eyes like their aunt. When Steve had suggested the theatre, and then found this time of year he could only book a pantomime at the Bristol Hippodrome, Lydia had asked if her nieces could come too.

"I can call it an early Christmas present," she'd said. "And Paul and Emma could use the time for Christmas shopping."

They'd also agreed it would be a good practice run for when he babysat with Lydia next week.

And so, now at the point Steve would do anything to please Lydia, he'd booked the matinee performance. It had been so much fun, booing and hissing at the baddie, and it had brought back some childhood memories of Christmases with Mum and Ruby. He now had a lovely memory to treasure with Lydia too, who had participated fully with the show alongside her nieces.

With November coming to a close, it meant Christmas was rapidly approached. Everyone buzzed with excitement and shops were decorated and full of gift ideas. The hotel now had a huge Christmas tree in the reception, adorned like something out of a Dickens' scene. Everywhere you went, you couldn't miss it, the festive season was drawing near. The café they sat in also had a large Christmas tree already up. Steve had totally forgotten Thanksgiving, which had been two days ago, glad that it was one less thing to worry about. He'd received a couple of emails, forwarded from Marie, to wish him a happy Thanksgiving, but he hadn't seen any invitations from his friends and associates in LA, as he normally did to remind him of the occasion. Maybe Marie had dealt with them as he was out of the country. Or maybe, he realised, they were only acquaintances in the business, rather than good friends, if Marie felt she needn't forward on the messages.

Either way, he didn't care. Life would get busy with the run up to the launch of the film, plus the making of a new one, so he was savouring every relaxing, mundane moment. Not that being with Lydia was dull. He just felt at ease, peacefully happy.

Originally, he'd considered taking Lydia to the cinema, but decided against it. He had managed to get away with it on his date with Alice, but didn't want to risk his chances with Lydia. He had some paranoia about going to the cinema, fearing he'd see his next film's trailer. With his next movie, *Nothing Happened* out sometime next year, he had good reason. He didn't need to be sitting there, trying to remain anonymous, with his face flashing up on the big screen. It was an action comedy, and he was the leading man. You wouldn't miss his face on the screen.

With a three-year-old perched on his lap for the majority of it, Steve had appreciated the live performance instead. Theatre – not panto – was something else he wanted to do as an actor – one day, to be on stage and having to get it right first time. No cuts, edits, to make you look better. You couldn't laugh, and lose it (unless it was panto) – there was no bloopers reel for the DVD – and then take another shot. You had to remember your lines.

As he and Lydia discussed the pantomime afterwards, laughing with her two nieces, he tried not to sound like he knew what he was talking about when it came to acting. He wanted to move the subject on, fortunately Lydia's niece helped.

"Auntie Lydie, I need a wee wee." Rosie looked at her aunt desperately, holding herself between her legs.

"That's okay, sweetheart, I can take you." Lydia scooped Rosie up.

"I want Stuart to take me." Steve gulped. He loved kids, but he'd not had much practice with them, with no little people in his immediate family, he wasn't sure he wanted to take a little girl he'd only known a couple of hours to the toilet.

"No, I will take you," Lydia said firmly. Steve found it attractive. "Stuart can't go in the little girls' room."

"And they're much nicer that the little boys' room," Steve added, trying to aid Lydia's argument. "I'll guard your cookie." Steve threw a macho pose and Rosie giggled, holding her small, podgy hand over her mouth.

"Okay." She dramatically nodded. "Don't eat it."

"I won't."

"I'll be back in a minute," Lydia said, pushing Rosie higher onto her hip. "Will you be okay with Olivia?"

"Of course. Olivia was just about to tell me who her favourite princess is." Steve moved round to sit on the couch with the little girl, dressed as a princess.

"I told you silly, it's Cinderella." Olivia rolled her eyes. If it wasn't for the endearing voice and the fact she wasn't much taller than three feet, she could easily have been fifteen with the attitude.

"Oh, yes you did."

"Oh, no you didn't." Olivia laughed. It had been their little joke after watching the pantomime. "Can I call you Uncle Stuart?" Olivia looked innocently into his eyes.

Steve sobered. "Oh, um..."

"You're going to marry Auntie Lydie, aren't you?"

Steve chuckled, rubbing his hot palms down his jeans. "I don't know. It's very early days. We've not been seeing each other long."

"Cinderella only went to a ball, and she married Prince Charming afterwards."

"Yes, good point. It's just that some relationships take a little longer." Steve patted the little girl's hand, then found his mocha for comfort.

"What's a relationship?"

Steve swallowed. He did not need this conversation to lead to the point of birds and bees. That certainly was not his domain. *Nip in the bud. Now.* "Um, well, it's when two people want to be together."

"Why?"

There it was; the dreaded why question. Lydia had dealt with most of those over the afternoon. "They want to be together because they love each other – like your mummy and daddy."

"And you and Auntie Lydie."

"Yes, yes, hopefully," Steve said nervously. The whole point was to find someone to spend the rest of his life with, even marry, but confronted by the reality of it with a five-year old made Steve anxious. Was Lydia the one? Would he really ever know?

"What did we miss?" Lydia appeared, lowering Rosie onto the sofa beside her opposite.

"Stuart's going to marry you!" Olivia blurted, grinning triumphantly.

Steve didn't usually blush, but the temperature in the café had risen suddenly.

Lydia chuckled. "Oh, Olivia, I think it's a little early for me and Stuart yet."

"Why?"

Lydia and Steve laughed. "I'll let you answer this one. They're your nieces."

"Oh, thanks." Lydia pulled a face.

"I'll do what I'm good at... and get us another coffee. Same again?"

Steve escaped to the counter. When he returned with two more steaming mochas and more biscuits, the girls were happily, and quietly, colouring. Rosie had her tongue out, fully concentrating on her picture. Although occasionally interrupted by the little princesses with questions like 'do you like my drawing?' their focus enabled Steve and Lydia to talk about things they'd like to do – together, which pleased Steve. He wanted to walk a beach, hand in hand. The golden coastline of California, but he didn't hint at it. Lydia was thinking more of the sandy beaches of Cornwall. They dreamily discussed sitting in coffee shops in different European cities, watching the world go on around them. These things they would do, Steve promised himself. He'd make her dreams come true.

Steve wanted to know everything about Lydia. They'd only touched the surface with their discussions as new romances usually did, scared of saying something to put the other off. So far, their interests were similar; from the way they liked to relax by reading rather than television, to similar views on life. And silly things like brown sauce always with fried eggs and bacon.

"Because tomato sauce is just yucky," Lydia said wrinkling her nose, and he would remember that adorable image for the rest of his life.

"No it's not," Olivia said, looking up from her picture. Steve had forgotten the two girls were there, they had been so quiet concentrating on their colouring. "I like it with fish fingers."

"Me too." Rosie squeaked.

"Ah, yes, tomato sauce with fish fingers is the best," Steve said, giving the little girl a thumbs up.

"I think on that note we best get you two back to your mummy and daddy," Lydia said.

Both girls started complaining and moaning.

"Be good, you two, or Stuart won't come and help me babysit."

Lydia turned to Steve. "You still want to keep me company?"

"Of course." He stroked her hair, and kissed her head. "As long as it's not this weekend."

"No, next week," she said happily, toying with his hair and running her fingers around the back of his neck. The sensation sent delight to his soul.

"I wouldn't miss it for the world. And I get to see these two cuties." He reached across the coffee table and tickled each of the girls, and they giggled. Then, Steve kissed Lydia chastely, remembering they were getting too snug on the sofa in the café. They were in a public place. Plus their five-year old and three-year old chaperones thought it was disgusting to see a boy and a girl kissing.

"So what's so special about this weekend?" Lydia said, gathering up coats and bags. Steve helped Rosie into her puffy pink coat.

"I've got an early Christmas present for Ruby, and I promised we'd go buy a Christmas tree." Plus, he needed to get Lydia a special Christmas present, but what to buy?

"You're such a good big brother, Stuart."

Every time she said his name, it reminded him of the lie. The disguise had worked, letting someone get close to him. But it was still a lie. Ruby and Steve hadn't thought this through.

"Lydia?" Should he come clean? They were so close now.

"What?" She looked at him, probably sensing the seriousness in his tone, her tone equally sober.

This wasn't the place, or the time. Everything was perfect; he didn't want to ruin a good day. What if she reacted badly? They were in a public place and Olivia and Rosie could get upset.

"Nothing, sweetheart. I had a good time today."

"So did I."

Chapter 19

Sunday 1st December

"Come on, Ruby, aren't you ready?" Steve called up the stairs. It was the first Sunday in December – they were going Christmas tree shopping – a family tradition.

When his head wasn't busy, he'd drift off in his thoughts, remembering how fantastic his day had been with Lydia yesterday. Over the past few weeks, they'd taken it slowly. He hadn't done anything really past first base. They were both ready to take the next step but he wanted to make sure they'd got to know one another well enough before he took things further. There was a nagging voice inside his head not to rush this – although he did need to, as the weeks ticked away and January hurried towards him. He only had till early New Year at the latest, then Hollywood would beckon. But he wanted to feel sure Lydia was the right woman and that she loved him like he loved her.

He did love her. She was his first thought when he woke, and his last before he slept.

Nothing was going to disturb his good mood today. Excitement bubbled inside him, too. He wanted to treat Ruby. Christmas with Ruby. Nothing was going to spoil it.

"I'm coming!" She ran down the stairs, jumping the bottom one and pulled on her boots. "I want to get a real Christmas tree this year, if you're staying for Christmas. Can we do that today? Please?"

"Yes, yes, but first I want to show you something. It's an early present."

"Early one? I haven't even thought about buying you something yet. I mean, what do you get a man who's got everything?"

"I haven't got everything." What he wanted most was a woman in his life. A soul mate, a wife. Something money couldn't buy; true love.

He unlocked Ruby's car and got in the driver's side – he would drive today. It had taken him a while, but he was now walking around to the right side of the car to get in. Luckily, he hadn't made that mistake too much with anyone else about – except Lydia. But then she fuddled his brain.

"Where are we going?" Ruby asked as Steve reversed the car off the driveway.

"You'll see in a minute."

"So what would you like for Christmas?"

"Christmas dinner with all the trimmings, and spending it with you. That would be perfect," Steve said.

"I'll make sure I wear a bow." Ruby giggled.

"Well, and maybe if Lydia could be there too..."

"You and Lydia really have hit it off." She clapped her hands excitedly.

"We really have. I just hate lying to her, though. I want to tell her the truth."

"Wait a bit longer, Steve. Things can fizzle out very quickly."

Yeah, he knew that, too, but he couldn't wait to get more intimate. To show her how much she meant to him.

"Right, close your eyes," Steve ordered, stopped at a set of traffic lights, focussing on Ruby. She was important too. Her happiness needed to be attended to, just as much as his. When he went back to Hollywood, he wanted the knowledge that Ruby was secure and happy.

"Why?"

"Just do it or you'll ruin the surprise." Ruby squeezed her eyes shut, screwing up her face, and satisfied, the lights turning green, Steve drove on. "Keep them shut. No peeking."

"How long do I have to keep them closed for? I'm feeling queasy."

"You are not. You just hate surprises."

"I don't hate surprises. I'm just impatient."

Steve pulled into the driveway of their old family home. "You can open them now."

He watched Ruby as she open her eyes, and saw them widen. She raised her hands to cover her mouth that gaped open. He grinned.

"Wow," Ruby said, staring at the renovated building. Fresh paint and a landscaped garden made all the difference.

"Come and see inside." Steve ran up to the front door, unlocked it and they walked inside. It still smelt of paint and polished wood floors.

"You got all the furniture out of storage?" Ruby rubbed a finger along the bureau in the hallway. She wouldn't find dust. Steve had had the place cleaned from top to bottom. All the furniture was polished, and had been restored where needed. Ruby wandered from one room to the other. Her eyes glistened. Steve had a lump in his throat. It brought back wonderful family memories, and some cheerless ones, like losing Dad. But these memories made a person, happy or sad. When he needed that sorts of feeling in his acting, he always thought of his father. Channelled the emotion of his death, the funeral, to bring to life what he needed on the screen. And that way, he'd always remember his father, too, keeping his memory fresh.

"I'll make us some tea, then you can see upstairs." He'd kept the kitchen well-stocked; it helped the builders and decorators to work better if he provided tea and biscuits.

"When did you get all this done?" Ruby took a chair at the kitchen table, while Steve boiled the kettle.

"Well, it started the day I was locked out of your house, and Daphne put the idea into my head. I haven't really done anything, just made a few calls."

"Steve, what if the press find out you're here?"

"Don't worry about it. The contractors were none the wiser."

"I do worry about it. Terry showing up has me rattled."

"I can't believe you dated a journalist. Were you mad?" Steve remembered, Lydia had let slip he was an ex-boyfriend.

"I didn't know at the time. The bastard lied to me, to get information about you."

"Oh." He placed his hand on her shoulder, and gave her a reassuring squeeze. "Sorry."

"Mum knew about it. And helped me pick up the pieces. I'm over it."

Steve sat at the table and handed Ruby a mug of tea. "If he knew anything, I think we would have seen trouble by now. He's bought the story I'm sunning myself in the Caribbean with a new woman, so don't worry about it. Biscuit?" he said, opening a tin.

"I suppose you're right." She delved in and pulled out a chocolate bourbon. "Wow, you really were keeping the contractors sweet." Steve devoured a digestive in two bites. "So, now the house is done up, are you going to sell it?"

"No! Of course not."

"So what are you going to do with it?"

"I want you to live in it, Ruby."

"What?"

"Okay, you don't need to keep all the furniture, if you don't like it. I know some of it is old fashioned. It was Mum and Dad's, and none of it is really antique, but I thought, the only way to tell if you like it or not was to put it back. I know the colour isn't exciting, but I got the decorators to paint the rooms neutral colours, so you've got a blank canvas."

"Wait, hold up!" Ruby held up her hands to stop him. "I don't want to move back to this house."

"Why not?"

"Too many memories."

"Good memories."

"Steve, this house is far too big for just me to rattle around in. Without Mum, I started to hate it."

"You won't hate it when you've got a family of your own. Mum would have wanted you in this house."

Ruby snorted in disbelief. "I've got to find somebody first."

"You will. Lydia seems to think Brett likes you."

"She does?" Ruby blushed, staring into her mug of tea. "I think he's just being nice."

"Look, promise me you'll think about it. Let me show you the garden." He grabbed her hand and they made their way to the back door.

Donning their hats and gloves, Steve showed Ruby around the back garden. The trees and shrubs had been pruned, flowerbeds dug over, winter pansies, cyclamens and primroses planted out. Daffodils, tulips and hyacinths would appear in the spring, to surprise her further. Even with the sun shining, the air was crisp and as they talked, mist appeared from their mouths like speech bubbles in a cartoon.

"Sometimes, I do wonder why you disappeared, Steve."

"I didn't disappear." Steve frowned, shoving his hands into his coat pockets. They stood under the sycamore tree at the end of their garden. Steve had made the gardener cut it right back; it had grown too large for the garden. When Steve had been a boy, he used to climb it. Struck by lightning, it had split a large branch off, perfect for climbing and making a den. "I had to knuckle down if I was going to make it. Mum understood."

"Yeah, I know. But I wondered if I'd done something, being much younger – were you jealous of me?"

"Hey, no, far from it. I loved being your big brother." He wrapped an affectionate arm around Ruby. "And Mum had tried to have a smaller age gap. She'd miscarried twice before you. Almost thought Mum and Dad had given up – not that back then I knew what they had to do to get me a brother or a sister." He laughed.

"She had told me about the miscarriages." Ruby's cheeks and nose were pink with the cold.

"And then, finally, she got her little girl," Steve said, tugging her rosy cheek as well as he could in his gloved hand. "Her wish granted."

"And then five years later Dad died."

"She had to cope; she had two kids she wasn't going to let down. It was hard at first, but luckily I was thirteen and able to help out."

"But then you took flight."

"Ruby, I knew you were about the age I was when Dad died. I knew you'd both manage without me. You'd flourish. And I was twenty, wanting to follow my dream, and regain some freedom. I could see I no longer needed to be the big supporting brother. Mum realised that too." He wasn't sure he could admit that at twenty, with the world ahead of him, wanting to follow his dream took a more selfish approach. He'd outgrown his twelve-year-old sister.

"I do sometimes wonder if Dad be would be alive now... you know, if it hadn't been for the car accident."

"He'd be sixty-five, drawing his pension."

"But he smoked heavily back then, didn't he?" Ruby asked and Steve nodded. "Cigarettes could have killed him too. But at least I'd have better memories of him. I play the same ones over and over in my mind, sometimes, worrying I'm going to forget what he looks like. I look at photos of him, old black and whites, him looking like you do now, but I can't see it in my mind."

"I feel the same about Mum. At least you had the last fourteen years with her. I missed those."

"Bringing me back to this house wasn't supposed to turn us miserable, was it?"

"No." Steve chuckled. "Come on, let's get this Christmas tree and decide where we're going to put it."

"Here?"

"Yeah, why not? Come on, Ruby? I would really love to spend Christmas here. It would mean a lot to me."

"I suppose if you want Lydia over, my little house is a bit small to entertain friends. But won't she find it strange?"

"How do you mean?"

"Well, how did we afford to get this done up? You're not supposed to be splashing your money around."

"They don't know how much work needed doing. Don't worry about it. Let's spend Christmas at home, Ruby."

***

Friday 6th December

Before Steve knew it, another week had passed and he felt ready for another weekend to begin, understanding that Friday feeling. He had just over two weeks until Christmas.

Lydia had already left the reception desk, finishing slightly earlier than him. Tonight they were going to her sister's to babysit.

Was tonight the night? He really wasn't sure how fast to move. But considering Christmas was around the corner he needed to act fast, or faster, and things were hotting up between the two of them. They both yearned for an intimacy they couldn't perform in public. He craved to feel her naked, soft body against his, wanting to explore her every curve...

Obviously, he wouldn't be able to do anything while they were babysitting Lydia's nieces. But what about after?

Brett entered the locker room, and started to change. Steve threw on his coat. Now, if Brett was to take Ruby out, then the house might be free.

"Hey, Brett, um..." Steve wondered if this was a good idea. But sometimes a guy needed pointing in the right direction. "I'm out with Lydia tonight, so Ruby's home alone. Maybe you could, you know, take her out or something… it's Friday night after all?"

Brett instantly glanced at the floor, then frowned at Steve, shoving his hands into his pockets. "Do you think she'd like that?"

"Yeah, why not? You two seem to be getting along, right?"

"I think so. Just we work together, I wasn't sure if she was really interested or not."

"You like her, don't you?"

Brett hesitantly nodded, maybe wary of the big brother approval.

Steve nudged Brett. "You won't know, pal, until you ask. And take it from me; a girl prefers to be asked." *The fact Lydia asked you first is neither here nor there.* "And if I know Ruby, she'll be too bloody stubborn to actually ask you."

"Yeah, that's true." Brett laughed. "Okay, there's a new film out she mentioned wanting to see. I'll ask her out."

"Good luck." Steve winked and walked away without a backward glance, smiling to himself, his job done.

***

Tucked away in her office, away from the hubbub of reception, Ruby rubbed her eyes gingerly, remembering she had mascara on and not wanting panda eyes before leaving work.

She felt content that Steve and Lydia were out again tonight, and that her brother might have found his happiness, and her plan may have worked. Then with the crunch of reality, Ruby leaned back in her chair and closed her eyes. There was so much paperwork to be finished and sometimes not enough hours in the day to do it. Bloody useless meetings with area managers and suppliers this morning had written off half of her day. Did she stay and finish it, or leave it for Monday? She had a weekend off, so she should enjoy it. Steve would be out. She could make the most of the house to herself. Although she loved having him home, she enjoyed the quietness of living on her own without having to listen to him moaning about the TV being on because he wanted to read through his script. She could watch whatever she liked – not the football. *She liked EastEnders.*

She spied Brett heading towards her office, uniform off, and coat on, about to go home. She combed a nervous hand through her hair, to make sure it was smooth. Quickly, she opened her drawer, where she knew a small compact mirror was to hand and subtly checked her make-up.

God, she was an idiot. What had got into her?

"Hey, Ruby," Brett said, resting against the doorjamb, "okay if I come in?"

"Yeah, sure, take a seat." Oh hell, did that remind him she was his boss? She hated that she was his boss. She wanted them to be on equal terms.

Her heart hammered inside her chest and all of a sudden her office became very hot.

Then her telephone rang, and she gave a nervous apologetic smile, and Brett nodded his acceptance she had to pick up the phone.

She hesitated, then said, "Ruby-uh-Fisher speaking." *Argh!* She'd forgotten how to answer the phone with Brett sitting in front of her.

"Ruby, one last chance. Let me take you out." *Terence.* Her blood boiled.

"Terry…"

As she said his name, Brett stood, mumbling, "You're busy, I'll leave you…"

She cupped her hand over the mouthpiece. "No, no, wait, please." Then she spoke more firmly down the phone. "Terry, I'm not interested in anything you have to say. Goodbye." She put the phone down, with relief. "Sorry about that."

"He doesn't want to leave you alone."

"He can't take no for an answer…" She could hardly tell Brett why Terry was really pestering her. "So, anyway, you came to see me, what can I help you with?" Ruby tried to look and act as relaxed as possible. It wasn't working.

"It's not about work... I wondered if you wanted to catch that film tonight. We could go for a bite to eat first."

Was he asking her out... on a date? Or was this just friends? "Um ... is anyone else going?" *Had Terry addled her brain?*

The corners of his mouth twitched, as if trying to hold in a smile. "No," he said, with a hint of friendly sarcasm. "But I can invite them if it would make you feel more comfortable."

Ruby quickly shook her head. "No, no, no!" She didn't want sodding Alice or Callum ruining this. "I'd love to. Of course. Yes." The paperwork could definitely wait. Terry was history. She hadn't been able to stop thinking about Brett, silly fantasies in her head, since they'd shared a taxi home. And since then, whenever in his presence, she'd dry up and act so shyly around him, burying herself in her work.

Ruby Fisher, shy? Never. But apparently so in the presence of the man she fancied.

Fancied?

The only conversation she could drum up was work related whilst in the office. This would be a good opportunity to get to know him. He was asking *her* out! She'd make sure she got a glass of wine down her, and that would drown the nerves, and her shyness.

He grinned, and his whole demeanour relaxed, as if relieved. "I'll pick you up at seven-thirty?"

"Perfect."

"I'll book the tickets, then we won't have to queue and it will give us more time to eat."

"I look forward to it."

"See you later," he said, then strolled out of her office. Ruby thought she heard him mutter a *'yes!'*

Ruby sat dead still for a moment, recovering, taking a deep breath, hoping to regulate her breathing. Her heart, still pumping blood around her body faster than was probably normal, slowed and her office cooled. Then, frantically, she finished what she'd been doing, organising her paperwork, tidying her desk and putting the unwanted papers into her tray. You never know, she thought, Pete, her ever useful assistant manager might deal with some of it for a change. Or pigs might fly. She'd be more than likely dealing with it next week, but she didn't care as excitement bubbled inside her.

Grabbing her handbag, she dashed out of her office. She was getting out of here. She had a date. Serious amounts of maintenance on making herself look wonderful was required. Shave legs, new polish for toenails... the list was endless. *Oh, God, and what should she wear?*

As Ruby drove out of the hotel grounds, her worries about what dress to wear were forgotten. Alice had walked out the front of the hotel and was getting into a sleek, silver car. Ordinarily, Ruby wouldn't have a problem with this, only the driver of the showy car had been on the phone to her only ten minutes ago.

Terence.

Chapter 20

Steve's head might be working out whether Lydia wanted the same things as he did, but his heart was already falling. They'd put on a DVD - *The Avengers* – but didn't watch much of it. Not even the Iron Man Robert Downey Jr or the muscular Chris Evans in his Captain America Lycra suit could distract Lydia. The cuddling led to kissing, but he was conscious they were babysitting her nieces and if Rosie or Olivia did venture down, they shouldn't see anything inappropriate.

He had a very good relationship with Lydia's nieces. He wanted to keep it that way.

"Do you want this?" Lydia asked.

"This?" Steve frowned. "Kissing you, yes, I want." He kissed her again, wanting his tongue to find hers, but she pushed him away playfully.

"No, silly," she giggled. "You know, cosy nights in front of the telly, kids upstairs asleep. Do you want it, too?"

"Oh," Steve said, sarcastically, as if cottoning on, making Lydia giggle more. When her expression sobered, anxiety etching into a frown, he quickly reassured her. "Absolutely. Why'd you ask?" Lydia had confirmed it herself, she wanted the same things in life as him. Another tick in the box, Steve thought, trying to refrain from smiling too much. Sometimes he felt like Dick Dastardly rather than Superman the way he was executing his plan – well, Ruby's plan – and Lydia was doing exactly what he wanted; falling for him. Falling in love never seemed so easy.

"Oh, well, maybe I'm too practical for my own good, but I don't see the point in being in a relationship if we're going off in opposite directions. And I like you, Stuart, a lot." She nervously chewed her bottom lip. Steve wanted to kiss her, but resisted, pulling her closer. She touched his face, gently stroking his temple. "And I wanted to make sure we both sought the same things, before it was too late... and one of us got hurt."

"Lydia, I like you a lot too, and I hope we can have this," he gestured to the comfy sofa, the lounge full of family portraits, "together, too."

But could he provide it? His life would not be as private as ordinary Stuart's. Lydia was private, even shy, until she learnt to open up and trust. Would she accept life in the Hollywood fast lane?

"Wow, most blokes would get freaked out so early on discussing something so heavy." She sighed with pleasure, snaking her hands around his neck, pulling him towards her for a reward, a kiss. His words had obviously pleased her.

Stroking her hair as he released from the kiss, he said, "I'm not *most blokes*. Believe it or not, however strange this may sound, I'm looking for the perfect – no not perfect," he shook his head, screwing up his face, "the right woman to settle down with, for the rest of my life."

"Oh, Stuart, that's lovely."

Sprawled out on the sofa, the film forgotten in the background with the volume turned down, he kissed her thoroughly, his tongue exploring her mouth. Soft, unhurried, sensual caresses. Her legs wrapped around his, tightening, pulling their bodies as close as they could fully clothed.

Steve wanted her naked. The next step was for him and Lydia to fall into bed and make love as if they were virgins, exploring each other's bodies for the first time. He couldn't wait much longer.

And neither could she. But they had to. Her family could return any moment, and with the girls upstairs, one of them was bound to wake up and stumble in on them. Instead, Lydia would have to suffer his hardness against her jean-clad thigh. He risked his hand seeking her soft breast, slipping under her blouse, gentle, tender touches, and her breath shortened, hot on his cheek.

The front door slamming shut separated them. They sat up, both running their hands through their hair, and giggling, straightened their clothes, like naughty teenagers almost caught in the act.

"Hey," Paul said, cautiously entering the lounge, holding Emma's hand.

"Girls been okay?" Emma asked.

"Haven't heard a peep after I bathed them," Lydia said, switching off the television with the remote. "They had a story and went straight to bed, good as gold."

"Great." Paul nodded, hands slung in his pockets.

"Right, well, we'll be off. Leave you to it." Lydia jumped up from the sofa. Steve needed more time. He was still very conscious that he had an erection the size of Mount Vesuvius. Hoping his un-tucked shirt would cover his slowly softening arousal, he stood up and shook Paul's hand and kissed Emma quickly.

"Nice meeting you both."

"Yes, hope to see you again, Stuart," Emma said, giving an appreciative nod to her sister. "We heard so much from Olivia and Rosie. Thank you for taking them to the panto."

"It was fun. They're cute girls," Steve said, and Lydia squeezed his hand appreciatively.

Once the door had closed behind them, Lydia launched herself back into Steve's arms and her tongue was plundering his mouth with determination. Reluctantly, Steve broke off.

"Let's at least get to the car," he said, pulling out the car keys and tugging at Lydia to follow him.

"Shall we just do it in the car? I don't think I can wait."

Steve laughed, deep from his belly, sensing Lydia had to be

joking, but he'd play along. "Let's get off your sister's driveway first, huh?"

"Blast, you're right." She clicked her fingers. "Drive to mine."

"You're sure?"

"Yes, even if Ruby's out, she'll come home eventually. Might as well stay at mine – where we won't be disturbed," Lydia said seductively, grinning.

Steve drove Lydia's Beetle, occasionally looking out the corner of his eye, catching Lydia chewing her lip, staring at him lustfully. He needed to concentrate on the road ahead, not the beautiful, horny woman sitting next to him. She didn't touch him, probably equally afraid he might crash the car, but it didn't stop his groin from aching with desire.

The minute he pulled the car up outside her house, and turned off the ignition, he half expected her to clamber awkwardly across the handbrake and onto his lap. Instead she leaned across, cupped his face and pulled his mouth to hers.

While they fumbled, and giggled, Steve had a nagging feeling that they should get into the house. He was constantly watching his back and was confident the press weren't onto him, but even so, he wouldn't need this hitting front pages – mucking around or not. He wanted Lydia private in his life for as long as possible. And there could always be one sneaky bastard somewhere trying to catch him out.

"Lydia…" he said between breathless kisses, "we should go inside. I'm assuming I'm invited in for coffee."

"Sod the coffee," she purred, nibbling his earlobe, sending hardening heat into his lap.

He opened the car door, and she released him, and somehow hit the horn, so it blasted. She giggled.

"Great, wake the neighbourhood," Steve teased. "Now we've definitely got to take this inside."

"I was never *really* going to do it in the car with you."

"I'm relieved."

Lydia threw her handbag and door keys on the floor, as Steve closed the front door behind him, and holding Steve's hand, led him up the stairs and into her bedroom. Steve subtly tapped his back pocket to check he had his wallet on him, knowing it contained a couple of condoms. Since dating Lydia, he'd made sure he was prepared for this moment.

Although he'd wanted to act cautiously with Lydia, he also realised there was a certain urgency. Hollywood weighed heavy on his shoulders, and was always at the back of his mind, unless thoughts of Lydia scrambled his head... especially when she nipped at his neck.

She kicked off her shoes, losing a couple of inches in height, and he tugged her towards him, pressing his hard body against her softness.

"I've fantasised about this moment for weeks," she said, her hands struggling with the buttons on his shirt. He removed her blouse.

"Weeks, huh?" He slid his hands around her back, unclasping her bra. The swell of her breasts naked against his chest was divine. It had been a long time since he'd held a woman in his arms like this. Too long.

Okay – so he'd held a woman in front of a camera, but not like this. He hadn't been with anyone since Erica had walked out on him. Hollywood didn't allow that either, a woman on the rebound, not unless you want it plastered in the gossip magazines.

"Practically the moment you walked into reception." Lydia fell back onto the bed, he crawled on top of her, soaking up her almost naked form – only her black lace knickers hid what he craved. He licked and sucked each breast, until the nipple hardened. She whimpered impatiently, but he was going to take his time and savour every moment. It felt important he did this right.

With all the pent-up sexual energy they both had, he didn't want to disappoint.

Her nails dug into his back, and she bit his shoulder as he kissed her neck. He licked and kissed, until he reached the black lace. He teased, biting gently at the fabric, knowing his teeth softly grazed her most sensitive parts. Her hips hitched.

"Please, take my knickers off," she moaned, trying to assist with their removal.

His fingers teased the lace, tugging at the fabric.

"Rip them."

He grinned wickedly. Quiet, shy Lydia was demanding he rip her underwear. Secretly she was a fox. He tore at them with his teeth and fists, throwing the black lace aside, then with gentle thumbs, he parted her, rubbing, stroking. His own impatience grew, wanting to taste her, feel her heat on his tongue, give her the pleasure she deserved.

And he knew, he wanted her and only her, forever.

Her fingers combed his hair, while he explored her heat, sucking, tasting, until her body trembled and she moaned. The tug at his hair, told him she wanted him back with her. Her eager mouth found his immediately. Blindly, he reached for the wallet he'd thrown onto the bedside cabinet and riffled out the condoms.

"I can't get enough of you," she whispered. "I want you inside me."

Those words alone hardened him further. He wanted to bury himself inside her, and stay there for eternity. He had a male need for sex, but this was better, he knew they'd be making love, yet he was still too afraid to actually utter that four letter word.

Slowly, he sank into her, liquid hot, and with every thrust, he fell further, deeper, wanting, hoping, Lydia would be the one.

She felt perfect in his arms. Lydia wasn't like Erica; he could grasp, savour her. She was beautiful. Their bodies fitted. Hard against soft. Man beside woman.

"Stuart..." Lydia whispered as they rocked, deeper and slower, bringing her closer and closer to another orgasm. The name hurt, like a punch to the gut. He almost faltered. He wanted to hear *his* name called from her lips. How upset would she be when she learned the truth? He would have to tell her. Soon.

As she came, her nails dug into his buttocks, pushing him in harder, knowing he too could release. Speeding up, thrusting faster, harder, he cried out with sheer pleasure and clung to her, bringing her body tightly to his, as the waves of pleasure thrummed through him.

He'd never made love to a woman like it. It had never meant so much. They belonged to one another.

Satisfied and clammy with exhaustion, they cuddled. The scent of sex lingering around them. Lydia fell asleep in his arms, but although exhausted, his head wouldn't let him sleep. He wanted Lydia to know the truth, but when could it be best to tell her? Would she forgive him for lying? Would she understand why he had done it?

Steve watched her sleep, tangled in the sheets, peaceful and relaxed. He stroked her back gently, loving the swell of her breasts pressed against him and the warmth of her thigh, hooked over his.

Was Lydia the one? He wanted her to be, but it just felt too easy, falling for her. He really didn't think this plan of Ruby's would work. He'd envisaged spending quality time with Ruby mixed with maybe a few dates, but he never imagined he'd meet *the one*.

When Ruby had first introduced him to Lydia, he'd thought her pretty, but nothing outstanding. Just the girl next door. Quiet, reserved and polite, with a wicked sense of humour – she seemed to laugh at Steve's jokes a lot. That was the important thing. But every day, she'd blossomed, as he got to know her better. They shared similar interests. Not that they'd done very much together, but they'd talked enough about stuff. Maybe he needed to date her a bit more, to make sure. Be certain before he confessed all.

It had been a month. How long did it take?

And currently how he felt, with the heavy ache in his chest where his heart beat, he couldn't bear the thought of being parted from her.

In the bedroom, Lydia had turned into a sexy minx, the sex

they'd just shared wasn't shy or polite. It was damn well fantastic. She'd be the perfect wife on his arm in the limelight. She wouldn't do anything that would give the press ammunition, and behind closed doors, she'd possess Steve with her passion. Steve remembered the exquisite feeling of her nails trailing along his back, digging into his shoulders, and ass. His body started to respond to the memory, his arousal growing, hardening again. He stroked her breasts, kissed her neck. She gave a sleepy moan, pulling Steve in tighter. He found her mouth, dragging her out of her drowsy state, and was soon making love to her all over again. Gently, slow, sensual.

Chapter 21

December sunshine sneaked through a gap in the curtains, waking Steve. He squinted then rubbed his eyes, gaining his bearings, remembering where he was. He grinned with delight, recollecting what they'd done all night and his groin stirred as sexual arousal echoed through his body. Lydia wasn't in the bed but he could hear a shower running somewhere. Now did he venture in and see if he could join her, or would that be too eager?

They'd had mind-blowing sex last night – twice, so sharing a shower couldn't be overdoing it, could it? He didn't have any more condoms though – which was a problem. Big problem. Two was the limit in his wallet. Which was stupid. He'd make sure he carried the whole box from now on. A big box.

Lydia might be back into her reserved state, too. He'd let her drink the wine at her sister's. She hadn't got drunk, but she'd softened and lost her nervous edge which he found she carried when he was close by. Well, lost her nervous edge was an under-statement; she'd been a completely different woman in some sense. Discarding the memories of the vixen he'd held in his arms last night, he had to remember the relationship was still fresh, they were still at the exploration stage, treading on eggshells, worried you might say the wrong thing and end the attraction.

Or worse, fart.

Maybe he would enjoy the Saturday lie in, and wait to see her reaction when she returned.

A small, brown tabby cat jumped on to the bed and rubbed his head contentedly against Steve's foot under the duvet. It purred, pawing and circling on the duvet until it was comfortable at the end of the bed, then started washing itself.

He closed his eyes. He could lie here and keep the cat company... or go find Lydia. Wet, soapy images of Lydia's body plagued Steve's mind.

Ah, hell. He pulled back the sheets and the cat meowed its disgust at being disturbed. Steve ignored the cat, slipped on his discarded boxers, and strolled towards the bathroom, adjusting his underwear to remove the tent effect.

Lydia's place was smaller than Ruby's, he thought, as he arrived at the bathroom door, which was open... Inviting him in?

"Lydia?"

"Come in," she called. He heard the water turn off and she pulled back the shower curtain. "Could you hand me a towel, please?"

He stared for a brief moment, left speechless by her luscious, soaked figure. Her hair was slicked back smoothly and her breasts dripped water. He could easily lick every droplet from her creamy skin. He blinked and grabbed a towel, holding it out as she wrapped into it. "Thank you," she said, then kissed him. "You look so different without your glasses."

He swallowed, his heart leaping with fear, and reacted by touching his temple. His glasses had been lost in their passionate clinch last night. Trawling through his lust-filled memory bank, he was hoping they were on the bedside cabinet where he'd placed his wallet. This morning he'd totally forgotten about them. He glanced in the mirror. Christ, he needed a shave, too.

"Can you see without them?"

"Oh, yeah, first thing in the morning, I forget I need them, till I put them on." He scratched his head nervously.

"Right, well, have a shower, Handsome, and I'll get you some breakfast." She kissed him hard, leaving him craving her more. "I'll fetch you a towel."

Steve turned the shower on, removed his boxers and clambered into the bath. He grabbed the bar of soap and started lathering up, ridding his body of the scent of sex. He rubbed soap over his face, feeling the roughness of his stubble. Would Lydia recognise him?

As he rinsed the soap from his face, he heard the curtain pull. He looked, squinting, soap stinging his eyes, and Lydia mischievously grinned, still wrapped in a towel.

"I could so easily join you," she said. He wanted her to. Just the purr of her voice stirred his erection.

"You'll have an opportunity. For now, get my breakfast on, woman," he teased.

"Right! For that," her towel dropped and she stepped into the bath, "you'll pay."

He chuckled, then, as her mouth reached his, he relished in her body pressing into his, water trickling over them. Her hand found him already hard. Blurred by desire, his brain scrambled to some awareness, eventually a small voice got through and he pulled away. "No, Lydia, I haven't got any more condoms."

Her blue eyes gleamed at him, a smile etched on her face. She knew how to toy with him.

"Lydia?"

"Shhh..." Pushing her wet hair out of her face, she knelt down and took him deeply into her hot mouth. His mind, obliterated of all sense, was lost to Lydia.

There was a thud in the bath, something slipping away. Steve had dropped the soap.

His hips moved with her. And closer and closer he got.

Crying out, whilst trying to keep some control, he came, and an electric energy pulsed through his core. Once the pleasure had passed, he released his hold of her head, realising he'd clutched fistfuls of her hair.

"I'm sorry, I didn't hurt you?" he gasped, finding his strength as he helped her up to join him.

"No, you were fine."

He claimed her mouth, unsure if he was feeling lust or love for this woman, or both. His arms snaked around her, pressing her breasts against his hard torso, every part of their bodies that could touch did. One hand combed through her hair, gripping firmly, holding her head, while the other searched down the curve of her back and found the swell of her backside, pulling her close to him.

Finally, he allowed her to withdraw from the kiss.

"I must make you breakfast," she said softly. He groaned, a little out of disappointment as she climbed out of the bath, retrieved her towel, grabbing a smaller one for her hair. He remained under the hot water.

Pulling the shower curtain back across, he turned the temperature down. Really, he needed it cold, but he wasn't crazy – besides it was too late for a cold shower now. However, if he were to regain any of his senses he needed the water cooler.

Once he finished showering, he donned yesterday's clothes, and found his glasses, which he reluctantly put on, then headed down the stairs. He tried to flatten his hair forward so it looked dorky. It needed another cut if he were to retain his disguise. And it didn't matter how much he rubbed his jaw, it wouldn't remove the stubble.

Lydia's duck-egg blue lounge housed a squidgy, darker blue two-seater sofa and armchair, with a mix of scatter cushions. The well-worn suite sat tightly around a television to allow for a small desk to be situated in the corner, which was strewn with sketches, inks, pencils and paintbrushes. All evidence of an artist. Along the other wall was a walnut bookshelf, full like Ruby's. By the window, he spied her small Christmas tree, white lights twinkling, and a garland, thick with artificial holly and berries adorned the mantelpiece. Dotted about were other little Christmassy ornaments. Steve felt a pang of guilt. He'd promised Ruby they'd decorate their house today. They had bought a real Christmas tree last weekend, but it was time to put it up now, get the house ready for the festivities. Hopefully Ruby would understand that he couldn't turn down superb sex with Lydia – after all it had been Ruby's idea to find a partner, and he had to move fast. He wanted to spend as much time as he could with Lydia.

Hopefully Brett had taken the hint to ask Ruby out.

"Tea or coffee?" Lydia called from the kitchen. He could smell bacon and eggs, and hear the sizzle as he approached.

"Coffee, please – and make it black. I think I need a strong one after that shower." He took a silver stool at the breakfast bar in Lydia's modern, yet small kitchen-diner, designed to optimise space, and watched as she cooked, her cat circling and rubbing her ankles.

"Not now, Kipper," she said affectionately to the cat. "I should never have given you bacon." Lydia picked up the cat and put him out, opening the back door.

"That should give us some peace." She put a mug of black coffee in front of Steve and nuzzled into his neck, murmuring something about him smelling nice. Automatically, he fed his arm around her narrow waist and tugged her close.

"This is nice. I could wake up to this every morning," Steve said, hopefully.

"Not every morning is a day off, though. Not sure we'd have time for that sort of shower before work."

"You'd just have to make up for it in the evening." He kissed the top of her head. "Or set an earlier alarm."

"Would I now?" She gave a little purr. It registered with Steve. He searched his memory. Where had he heard it before?

"Hang on. Were you Catwoman at the Halloween party?"

"Might have been." She winked, and purred again. "I thought you knew."

"If I'd known, missy, me and you would have been in bed weeks ago." He grabbed her bottom, loving its firmness, and pulled her closer, his excitement and sheer horniness stirring, again. It was what this woman did to him.

"Oh, blast, the eggs..." Lydia leapt over to the stove, turned the gas down and flipped the fried eggs onto toast waiting patiently on two plates. She pulled the bacon and sausages out of the oven, hissing and sizzling, and poured on some baked beans, which she'd fetched from a silver microwave. All the time Steve appreciated the view of her curvy figure, remembering how good it had looked in the rubber costume. Lydia placed the loaded plate in front of Steve, handing him a knife and fork, then sat beside him. "Sorry, I've got no tomatoes or mushrooms. I hadn't really planned last night."

"Hey, this looks great." Steve was going to need some serious work-out sessions in the gym before filming. He'd have to warn his personal trainer to set a strict exercise regime up at this rate. "As I've just found out I've slept with Catwoman, I'll let you off the tomatoes and the mushrooms."

"Cheeky." She nudged him. "I was wondering... if you can stay all day?" Lydia met Steve's gaze, then concentrated on her breakfast.

"I would love to."

"Great, we could do something nice. Or just lounge around ..."

"I'm liking the lounging around idea, maybe you could get that catsuit back on..."

"I'm sorry, I gave it back to my sister." She gave him a warning glance.

"Damn shame." Steve pretended to grimace with disappointment. Then it dawned on him; Ruby. "Actually, before we make plans, let me make a call to Roo first." Steve winced apologetically, stroking her arm. "I promised we'd put the Christmas decorations up this weekend and get the tree in. We haven't done it together since we were kids, you know?" For a moment he worried he'd given too much away. But maybe it wasn't an abnormal statement. He'd never really thought of a story of how long he'd been travelling, plus, he tried avoiding telling lies to Lydia where he could. He wanted as much truth between them as possible. At Christmas, if all things continued as they were, he'd tell her the truth. After last night, he was more than certain he wanted her in his life.

They had to at least give it a go.

"Oh, of course."

Steve finished his breakfast and as Lydia cleared the plates, he dug into his jeans pocket for his mobile phone. There wasn't much battery left, he'd need to charge it. There weren't many numbers on this phone, so it didn't take him long to find Ruby's and call it.

"Hello," Ruby finally answered, groggily.

"Hey, Roo, it's me. I'm with Lydia and she wanted to do something today. But I said about the Christmas tree. Can we do it tomorrow?"

"Oh, yeah, sure. That's fine. That would suit me, too."

"You okay?"

"Yeah, yeah, still in bed. Bit of a late night."

"All right, okay... I'll see you tonight."

Steve grinned at Lydia, as he put his phone away. "It suits her to do it Sunday, too, so I'm all yours."

Lydia had refilled the coffee mugs, and put them on the breakfast bar. She eased herself between Steve's legs, as he remained on the stool, and removing his glasses, she circled her arms around his neck, pressing her breasts against him. She nuzzled his neck, grazing her teeth over his skin, making him rumble a groan of delight.

"Good," she whispered.

***

Ruby put her phone down, sighing, and she was pulled tighter into her sleepy partner's hold. It was well past eleven and they were still in bed.

"Who was that?" Brett's breath, warm on her shoulder, caused the hairs on the back of her neck to rise. It brought back last night in exquisite detail, sending sexual delight through her body

233

to every nerve ending.

"Just my brother," Ruby replied, snuggling in closer. "I wasn't the only one to get lucky last night."

Brett started kissing her neck and shoulder, his palms gently cupping her breasts. She could feel him hardening against her hip as he rubbed her nipples to buds. "You're about to get lucky again this morning."

She turned, her mouth finding his, and between the kisses, mumbled, "I hope so."

Last night had gone so well. Brett had picked her up, already reserving the VIP seats at the cinema, and letting her choose the restaurant for dinner. The night ended with them snogging in the car outside Ruby's house. She hadn't intended on sleeping with him, it had just kind of happened. Both of them were unable to tear apart from one another. And the same was happening right now.

Between them they wriggled until she was underneath. She stretched out, opening up the drawer in her bedside unit and fumbled for a foil packet, then passed it to Brett. She always kept some there, handy. Not that she regularly brought a guy home, but sometimes it happened. A woman needed to be prepared.

"I've fancied you since the day you interviewed me," Brett said, rolling the condom on. He hovered over her.

"Really?" Ruby blushed. "I thought you thought I was some ice woman. What do you call me? Miss Whiplash?"

"That's Callum, and I always tell him to shut up. Though you can whip me as much as you like." He bent to kiss her, but, as Ruby's eyes widened, stopped.

"What? You're into that kind of stuff?" Ruby said, surprised.

Her expression must have been anxious, because Brett chuckled, shaking his head. "No, not really. I was joking."

She clasped his bum, impatience growing, wanting him to make love to her. "Phew! Though... I don't know... never say never and all that."

"I'll do whatever makes you happy."

As they joined as one, she wrapped her legs around him, using her ankles to pull him in closer, and he grasped both of her hands, pushing them into the pillow either side of her head. He kissed her thoroughly, his tongue in rhythm with his thrusts. Slowly, withdrawing almost all the way so she felt its tip, he plunged back into her and sent ripples of pleasure through her body. She'd never made love like it. Or couldn't remember it ever feeling this good with anyone else.

Pushing himself up onto his palms, and deeper into her, she reached with her tongue, circling, licking his left nipple. He moaned, closing his eyes. Last night she'd discovered it was pierced, and loved the sensation of the metal ring on her tongue. And he seemed to appreciate it too. Brett was lean but solid – she'd worried he looked skinny with his chef whites on – but get the guy naked, he was so damn sexy.

Once both satisfied and dizzy from the rush of the climax, they lay there puffing and panting, exhausted from their exertion, and Ruby breathed, "And I thought this was about Steve."

Brett raised himself onto his elbow. "Who's Steve?"

***

"I so thought you'd want to – you know? – shag Alice."

Steve nearly spat his coffee back into the mug, but managed to swallow and looked up from reading the newspaper, startled by Lydia's abrupt words. She rarely swore for a start. The word 'shag,' albeit not a true swear word, had sounded harsh from her mouth. "What? Why'd you say that?"

"Well, she's gorgeous, and bubbly, and you know, she's got great... assets."

"Yes, she has got..." Lydia's eyes narrowed at him, "*okay-ish* tits." Lydia was branding a sharp knife, admittedly for cutting up chicken breasts, but even so, Steve wasn't stupid. Actually, he didn't fancy

Alice – even if she did have great tits – and legs – *remember, she wasn't the one wearing the catsuit.* Maybe initially, because she did have that wow factor – she was extremely pretty, too. "But she's a bit much for me. I like the quiet life." Now he was lying. Well, he did like the quiet life; only he no longer got it with cameras pressed in his face wherever he went. With Lydia though, he would maybe be able to attain some semblance of it. She might bring him down from the celebrity lifestyle and give him the normality he needed, even craved for in his life.

They hadn't gone out in the end, deciding to stay in and make the most of each other's company. This way they could get cosy on the sofa, whereas in public, they'd be restricted. Not everyone wants to watch two lovers cavort. Even Kipper had turned his tail up at the two of them. And Lydia seemed to want to touch Steve, a lot. In places that wouldn't be acceptable in public. Which Steve didn't mind at all, as it meant he got to touch her back. But he was going to have to rectify the lack of condoms situation soon.

Now, Lydia was putting a lunch together for them. They'd spent the morning cuddled on the sofa chatting, and kissing.

"I just thought you wouldn't be interested in me."

Getting off the stool, Steve pulled Lydia into him, she dropped the knife – thankfully – but held her hands up awkwardly, having touched the raw chicken. "Believe me, when I say this, you are perfect." He kissed her as she blushed, then let her get back to preparing the chicken, unable to resist affectionately tapping her backside.

"Stuart, that's really sweet."

She might have well stabbed him with the knife. Every time he heard that damn name, guilt cut into him.

The implications of what would happen if Ruby's plan worked hadn't been thought through. He hated that this relationship had started on a lie. So, okay, there were no guarantees. It might not last, but it would be the same with whoever he met. The thought of going home tonight actually hurt. Would she feel the same?

Chapter 22

Sunday 8th December

Steve hauled the eight foot Christmas tree through the back door, leaving a trail of needles behind. *So much for non-drop needles.* He'd just spent half an hour cutting off the bottom, and getting it into the Christmas tree stand outside in the cold. His knuckles ached from the icy air. He'd been thankful it hadn't rained as predicted. Family tradition usually meant the tree was put up the second weekend before Christmas, but Ruby – and Steve – had been too excited to wait, so arranged to do it a weekend earlier. This way, too, Steve could convince Ruby to move into this house sooner, rather than later.

He'd spent the whole of yesterday with Lydia. Today, Sunday, was Ruby's day. Although his phone would occasionally ping with a text from Lydia, which he craved to answer immediately. Oddly enough though, Ruby's seemed to be doing the same too. He'd catch her stopping what she was doing, glancing at her phone with a smile on her face.

Now, Ruby stood on a stepladder, hanging decorations from the ceiling, going from one corner to the next. They had the stereo on, playing a Christmas CD – currently Shakin' Stevens was singing *Merry Christmas Everyone* – and Ruby was singing her heart out to the lyrics. Not a bad effort either. Her voice wasn't hurting his ears.

"I loved Shakin' Stevens as a kid," Ruby said, upon noticing Steve enter the room, hauling in the tree. "Even though he was before my time, Mum would always play his albums."

Steve had a suspicion he might have been named after Shakin' Stevens, not that Mum had ever admitted it. "Is this where you want the tree?" he asked as he dragged it into place.

"Oh, yes, in front of the window so the pretty lights will show outside."

Steve nodded, centred the tree in the bay window, and unclipped the mesh holding it together, fanning it out so that the branches dropped. He had outside lights to put up too, Ruby had insisted. They'd gone barmy buying Christmas decorations, had spent a damn fortune. At this rate, they'd be here till midnight decorating the place. But hey, he didn't know when he'd get to do it again, with his work schedule and everything. He wanted a proper family Christmas with Ruby.

Once happy the tree was in the right place and the best part of it faced the room, he checked the multi-coloured fairy lights worked, and whilst they were still on, he started wrapping them around the tree. Ruby stopped pinning up the foil decorations and joined Steve, hanging baubles and tinsel. They'd gone for the traditional colours of gold, red, and green.

The aroma of roast beef wafted in from the kitchen. Ruby went to check the cooking and returned holding two glasses of steaming mulled wine.

"Remember Mum used to always drink mulled wine while putting up the trimmings. She'd let you have a glass, but I was only allowed warmed blackcurrant," she said, then breathed in the spicy scent before sipping. "Mmm..."

Steve drank his mulled wine, savouring the warmth it provided. They really were reliving their family Christmases and it felt good.

After the last bauble was placed on the tree, Steve grabbed the fairy to put on top, and climbed the stepladder, placing her in pride of place.

"There," he said. "All done."

Ruby approved, giving him a thumbs up. "Let's have dinner, then we can finish the rest off afterwards."

"Yeah, I'm hungry and the smell of that beef is making my mouth water."

Steve laid the table in the dining room. The table was old, nothing special, yet it did have some sentimental value. If Ruby wanted to get rid of some of the old-fashioned furniture, he'd help her purchase what she wanted. He wouldn't take no for an answer, either. He would help with the expenses.

One thing had been bothering him lately. He'd set up a fund for Ruby when his money had started pouring in, and well, she needed a new car, lived in a tiny rented two-bed terrace...

As they both tucked into their roast beef with Yorkshire puddings and perfect, fluffy roast potatoes, Steve decided to broach the subject. "Ruby?"

She swallowed then replied, "Yes?"

"I've been sending you money for the last couple of years, increasing it as things got better." Steve tried to sound subtle, curious. "If you don't mind me asking, what are you spending it on?"

"I'm not spending it."

"Why not?"

"I don't know. I just wanted to try and manage on my own."

"Ruby, the money is there so you can enjoy life, relax a little."

"I am relaxed." Her knife clattered as it hit the plate.

"You could do something you enjoy, not spend all hours in the hotel."

"I do enjoy my job."

"Really?" Steve raised his eyebrows in an *I-don't-believe-you* way.

"Oh, okay, I've never known what I wanted to do – unlike you. And that job came along, I'm good at it. It pays the bills."

"The money I send you could easily pay for the running of

this house."

Her eyes narrowed. "I told you why I didn't like living here. It reminded me too much of Mum."

"But I would love you to live here."

"Steve, I'm not sure. When you're gone, it'll be just me."

"Brett seems a great guy – I'm assuming that's who you were with yesterday." Steve grinned.

"How'd you ...? Yes it was, but we've only just started going out. So don't get us married off yet. It really is early days. Like you and Lydia, only you don't really have as much time as I do. How's that going by the way?"

Steve washed his food down with some red wine, nodding. "Good. I feel damn guilty every time she calls me Stuart though."

"Yeah, sorry, I didn't think of that. I'm sure if she really loves you, she'll forgive you."

"I hope so! Anyway, you're changing the subject." He pointed his fork at her.

"No I'm not."

"We're talking about this house. Mum would have loved you to bring up your own family in this house. I believe it was her plan all along."

Ruby clicked her tongue. "Hey, don't start with all the emotional blackmail shit. Don't ruin a good day."

He held his hands up. "Okay, okay, but let us spend Christmas here – no point bothering with the decorations otherwise. Maybe on Christmas Eve we could have a little party. Get Brett and Lydia over, maybe Callum and Alice." They'd all become friends. Real friends, which meant a lot to Steve. "Maybe start making some new memories in this house?"

Ruby placed her knife and fork together, leaving one roast potato and some veg. Steve nicked the roast potato, even though he knew full well he shouldn't. Luckily, there weren't any Yorkshire puddings left, or he'd be going for those too. He'd run an extra mile tomorrow. He'd been checking his weight and muscle tone, and regularly running, so he hadn't completely lost it. He kept telling himself he'd have time to get some intense gym work in before filming.

"Okay," she said. "That would be nice, and the six of us in this house would be much comfier than my little rabbit hutch of a place. Maybe Daphne would like to come too."

"We'd better get the decorations finished with then."

"I'll load the dishwasher and clear up the kitchen, while you get those outside lights up."

Steve groaned. He'd been dreading that particular job. "Okay, and later we'll discuss you moving in here, and looking for a new career."

Cutlery clattered as Ruby huffed. "I like my job."

***

While he'd finished hanging the lights outside, Steve managed to convince Ruby to move some of her things into the house during the week.

"We might as well make the most of the house looking festive," he'd said. With just over two weeks until Christmas, he hoped between them they'd create new memories, and Ruby would decide to stay.

Steve wanted her to stay.

He didn't like the thought of selling the house, as there were good memories for him held between its walls. It was an option though, to let Ruby choose a new home, if that's what she preferred. His life was in LA. He couldn't dictate to Ruby if it was going to make her miserable.

For now, this house was bigger. They weren't tripping over each other. It meant he got to stay in his old bedroom – though it had a fresh coat of pale olive green paint and lacked the posters stuck over the wall by his bed. Star Wars. His first crush had been

Princess Leia. The room was larger and comfier than the box room at Ruby's two-bed end-terrace. Once he was gone, he thought Ruby could convert it into a study.

"No I can't do that."

"Why not?" Steve said, frowning as he hung his clothes up in his old wardrobe. His suitcase containing the clothes he'd hauled across from LA still remained unpacked, shoved under the bed. He needn't have brought most of it – he'd only worn the underwear and socks.

"Where will my big brother stay when he comes to visit me – regularly?" She nudged him as she helped hang some clothes.

"You may have a point. Might be nice to hole up here, rather than a hotel. I will visit you more often. I promise."

"It can be the guest room. Your room," she said. "I can make my old bedroom the study, as it's that bit smaller. Although, I'm still not sure about sleeping in Mum's room."

"Roo, it's your house now. You need to make it yours." At least she was coming around to the idea of staying here, which pleased Steve.

***

Monday 9th December

Ruby should have been doing her work; there were Christmas parties and dinners to oversee, orders to fulfil with the run up to the busy festive season. Instead Ruby perused a couple of home improvement magazines perched on the cream leather couch in the hotel's spa. The scent of the place helped you naturally relax.

Now the house was decorated for Christmas and it was clean and tidy, she was coming around to the idea of remaking the house her home. She hated to admit it but Steve was right. It no longer had its old decor to remind her of the days when it was Mum and Ruby living there. If she chose some furnishings she liked, it would feel more like hers, and a different home. Renting the little two-bed terrace, albeit cosy, wasn't cost-effective, especially when she had a perfectly good home with no mortgage. So while she waited in the spa, she looked for some inspiration on colour schemes and furniture.

Ruby hadn't specifically gone to the spa to flick through the magazines. She wanted to see Alice who was currently in a treatment room with a client – so Yvonne, another beautician, had told her. Five minutes later, Alice appeared, smiling and calm, talking to a middle-aged woman, whose rosy face and towel imprint on her forehead gave away that she'd had a massage. Ruby waited for Alice to finish with the client then stood up. Yvonne had returned to the front desk.

"Yvonne, could you give me a minute with Alice, please? I need a word in private." Ruby said.

"Yes, sure." She grabbed a handful of fluffy white towels from the rack and headed down towards the female changing room.

Alice frowned, perplexed. "What have I done wrong? Please don't tell me I've had a customer complaint. I can't think who'd complain."

"It's not work related."

"Oh." Alice's shoulders relaxed.

"I want you to stay away from Terence." Ruby had said it. Her heart already raced with the potential of confrontation.

"Why?" Alice said, angered. "It's nothing to do with you who I see. Jealous, are we?"

"Not in the slightest, but he'll use you, Alice."

"He said you'd get jealous."

"He's using you to get to me," Ruby said, her voice raising. "Don't tell him anything about me." How did Ruby tell her all Terry was interested in was news about Steve? How could she ask if she'd mentioned 'Stuart'?

"Don't be ridiculous."

243

"Did he ask about me?" Ruby snapped. "Did he?"

Alice's gazed dropped to the ground, unable to meet Ruby's.

"Did you tell him anything about me, Alice?"

Yvonne returned, witnessing Ruby and Alice, both hands on hips and glaring at one another. Ruby gestured she still leave them, and Yvonne turned on her heel back towards the gym.

"Alice?"

"No I didn't, okay. But I learnt a few things."

"Will you keep them to yourself?"

"Maybe," Alice said too smugly.

Ruby's eyes narrowed, her heart beating so fast she thought it might explode. "If you want to keep your job and ever work in hospitality again, you'll keep your trap shut."

A couple of young women, both giggling at each other in their own conversation walked through the double doors into the spa.

Alice grabbed Ruby's arm as she was about to walk away, her voice softening, "Ruby, I'm not a complete bitch. Your secret's safe."

Chapter 23

Thursday 12th December.

It was late afternoon, and Steve and Ruby were heading home from work. Steve was driving. He was starting to get used to Ruby's little car.

"Where are you going?" Ruby said, frowning. "Why are we going this way?"

"As we got away early, I thought we could take a detour to Cribbs Causeway."

"Why?"

"Didn't you say you'd like some new towels for the bathroom?"

"Yes..." Ruby replied hesitantly. "But it could wait."

Steve spent the next couple of hours encouraging Ruby to splash out on some new furniture, pictures and ornaments. Surprisingly enough, it didn't take Ruby long to see things she liked, and was making Steve carry the heavy load around John Lewis. Then Marks and Sparks... Once Ruby got the taste of shopping, there was no stopping her.

"Don't use your credit card," Ruby said, placing her hand over his. "I'll use mine."

Twigging that Ruby's paranoia had set in, he agreed. "But I'm paying your credit card bills."

"There is no need."

"Yes there is. It's my present to you."

They'd argued all the way home in the car – which was rammed full of new furnishings. He relaxed, knowing she had the money he'd been sending her. He also had a warm, satisfied feeling that Ruby was coming around to the idea of staying in the house. Yet, as they unloaded the car, something still felt off...

"You okay, Roo? You seem kind of distracted," Steve said, watching his sister going away to another planet inside her head. Whilst shopping she'd been snappy and not quite concentrating at times.

Ruby sighed heavily, rubbing her forehead. "It's Alice. I saw her get into a car with Terry on Friday night. I confronted her on Monday, and I think she knows about you. She didn't actually say, and I wasn't going to clarify, in case we were both talking about different things. But what if she told Terry my brother was working at the hotel?"

Steve hugged his sister reassuringly. "If she'd said anything to Terry we would have found out by now, wouldn't we? Don't worry." He'd seen Alice a couple of times during the week also, and she hadn't acted any differently around him either. Or had she? Maybe he just hadn't realised until now, given this piece of information. No, Alice always flirted with him.

"Okay, I'll try not to."

An hour later and with what felt like half of John Lewis in their lounge waiting to be shelved, placed or hung up around the home, the doorbell rang.

Steve checked his appearance in the hallway mirror before grabbing Ruby's car keys from the hook that hung beneath it – she still wouldn't get a new car – and answered the door, getting a cold blast of air.

"Hiya, Brett, Ruby's in the kitchen," he said. "She's fretting about cooking you dinner. You might want to put her mind at rest."

"She shouldn't panic. Even if it's burnt to a crisp, I'll still tell her I love it."

Steve couldn't smell burning, so Brett wouldn't have to pretend too hard. Ruby was a good cook. "She's worried that because you're a chef and you'll be picky, so she wants to get it right."

With a warm smile, Brett said, "I'll go give her a hand."

Steve winked, then called out, "See you later, Roo. Off to see Lydia, I might not be back." He wouldn't feel guilty if he didn't come home, because he was certain Brett would be staying over.

"Okay," she called along the hall.

Tomorrow Lydia and Steve were on a late shift. Ruby had managed to fix the rotas so that Steve could see as much of Lydia as possible. He had an inkling Ruby was matching her own shifts to Brett's too. Working in a hotel was never Monday to Friday, nine to five; it meant working some unsociable hours. It wasn't surprising that some of the younger staff were all 'shagging', as Callum so politely put it – usually sounding miffed because he wasn't getting any invites from the chambermaids. And neither was it surprising that those who wanted more than a roll in the hay were single. Knowing January was only around the corner, he was keen to see Lydia as much as possible – and Ruby for that matter – without looking like they were living in each other's pockets. She needed her time to do her illustrations after all.

Impatient to see Lydia, Steve ran out the house into the depressingly dark evening, towards Ruby's car, turning up his jacket collar. The icy heavens had decided to open and cold rain stung his face. From inside the misty windscreen, Steve saw a man huddled under an umbrella fighting with the wind. He was sitting on the garden wall of the house opposite, pulling his jacket tighter around him, looking like he was waiting for someone. Steve frowned, but didn't take much notice, too busy thinking about getting to Lydia's. He didn't envy him stuck out in this weather and hoped the poor guy's ride turned up soon.

Steve arrived at Lydia's. The door opened before he could knock and Lydia threw herself into his arms, kissing him thoroughly. He kept both hands behind his back.

"Where have you been?" she said, cupping his face.

"Sorry, Ruby took forever picking co-ordinating cushions. Plus I stopped for wine." He held up the bottle of Shiraz. "And flowers." Grinning, he held out the yellow roses in his other hand.

"Oh, thank you," she said, taking the roses, fingering the tissue paper wrapped around them.

She pulled him into the house, shutting the door behind him. "I will let you off as you come bearing gifts. I've made us dinner – I didn't fancy going out in the cold and wet – plus it will be manic with Christmas parties and shoppers. Thought we could stay home and keep each other warm."

"I like that idea." He put the bottle down, weaved his arms around Lydia's waist from behind, and kissed the back of her neck.

"Besides, you'll be taking me out next week," she said, placing the flowers on her coffee table.

"Why, what's happening next week?"

She turned in his arms, her fingers teasing the hair at the back of his neck while she kissed him again. He groaned appreciatively.

"It's my birthday."

"Your birthday, too huh? Your mum didn't plan that well – two daughters with December birthdays."

"Mum's birthday is in March." Lydia winked knowingly and Steve nodded.

"And... how old will you be this birthday?" he asked hesitantly.

"I'll be twenty-six." He hid his surprise. For some reason he'd thought she was older, but then her older sister had just turned thirty. Lydia carried a maturity about her.

"What would you like for your birthday?" He nuzzled her neck.

"You – with a bow on."

"What kind of bow?" He edged her towards her sofa, where they fell onto it and cuddled, kissing. He imagined turning up naked except for a bow tie, or even a large silk ribbon. He would have to think of a special present too, but nothing too flash. He wanted to tell Lydia the truth, but would wait a bit longer. Part of him couldn't bring himself to do it yet, worried what the reaction may be initially. *This* was so good. Making out on her sofa as if they were teenagers. People acted strangely around him when they saw him as the big movie star. He wanted Lydia to become so comfortable with him, she'd see why he'd done it. Why he'd hidden the truth. And it would all be fine, he was sure, if he told her. As long as she didn't learn it from someone else. Though who would tell her? He'd managed so far to be undetected. Marie was keeping him posted. His double was doing a superb job at keeping the press happy.

Yeah, he was convinced Lydia would love him no matter what. He didn't want to doubt it.

"Can I smell burning?" He pulled out of the kiss, but kept his hand under her T-shirt savouring her softness.

"Oh crap!" Lydia pulled away. "You always distract me and make me burn things." She ran into the kitchen, and Steve followed, bringing the flowers with him to watch her save the dinner bubbling away on the hob.

"It's fine. I love things burnt."

***

"Right, you cooked, I'll wash up," Stuart said, placing his cutlery together on his empty plate. Lydia giggled at the way he jovially pushed up his sleeves. He had an amazingly cheeky, sexy grin, and blue eyes that made her blush in an instant.

"Leave them," she said, tugging at his arm.

"No I can't, it'll help me let my dinner go down." He took the plates to the sink and turned on the hot tap, squirting some washing up liquid into the bowl. Lydia admired his jean-clad bum. His clothes made him appear more dorky than he actually was, but it charmed her. He wasn't shallow or vain about his appearance.

It meant Lydia stood a chance too. If Stuart dressed to his full potential, he could have his pick of women, and Lydia would be too lost in their shadows for Stuart's attention.

"Okay, but don't be long, I'm dying for a cuddle." She kissed him on the cheek then hurried into the lounge, switching on the stereo. She fussed quickly, puffing the cushions and drawing the curtains, making sure they were closed properly. Much to her cat's annoyance, even though she loved Kipper dearly, she shooed him off the sofa. There wasn't room for the two of them and the cat – even though the cat would argue differently. To make it cosy, she lit a few candles around her mantelpiece and turned off the ceiling lights, so her Christmas tree lights and the candles created a soft glow in the room. Satisfied, she went back into the kitchen to find Stuart drying his hands.

"Ready?" she said.

"Ready."

They snuggled on the sofa together and she hoped everything was perfect for their cosy night in. She scrambled for her stereo remote, and turned up the volume of her favourite CD, which was still in the stereo. She'd been playing it like mad and hadn't tired of it yet. With a smile, she pulled Stuart into a kiss, and they cuddled, resuming their position from earlier.

If she was looking for faults in Stuart – which she wasn't – she couldn't find any. The man ate her food and always complimented it, too. He always touched her; and even the slightest stroke along her arm sent her dizzy with emotion. He wasn't afraid to cuddle her and show her how much she meant to him. At least she hoped this was what he was doing. She'd never felt so connected to someone. Although she didn't have many boyfriends to compare with, she had enough experience to know that this feeling was different. This could well be real. And wow, he was a fantastic kisser.

As she relished his kiss, she pulled him on top of her, snuggling down amongst the cushions.

"Who's the band playing?" Stuart mumbled while kissing her

neck. "I think I've heard this song on the radio."

"They're called *Abandoned* – this is their debut album." Lydia tugged at Stuart's shirt, getting her hands on his flesh, brushing the hair around his navel with her palms. As the music played, they explored each other, kissing and caressing, as though it was new to them all over again, slowly peeling clothing off each other. Her skin tingled with sexual excitement, pooling deep between her thighs.

"I love this song..." Lydia said, hearing the song she'd been waiting for. "Stuart, make love to me, to this song..."

All day she'd imagined having sex on her sofa with Stuart while this band played in the background. The male lead vocalist had an unusual voice, which she had loved the minute she'd heard it on the radio.

When she'd first heard it, she'd been drawing, and had since found the music very inspirational for her illustrations. Hence she'd bought the album as soon as it came out and had played it continuously since.

Stuart didn't disappoint. To the lyrics of her favourite song, a love song for Jessica, they started making slow, sensual love. The words were poignant. She believed it was their song.

"I'm liking this track, too," Stuart whispered in her ear, his breath warm on her neck. The lyrics had him too. "It's always going to make me think of us on this sofa every time I hear it."

She squeezed him tighter, desiring him, kissing him wholeheartedly. She too would remember this moment on her sofa. And she knew she was falling in love. Just like Jessica.

Chapter 24

"Ruby, you've got to help me. What shall I get Lydia?"

"Oh, hell, I don't know."

They marched along inside Cribbs Causeway, the winter sunshine beaming through the glass roof. The large frosty Christmas decorations dangling from the ceiling sparkled with the light. They browsed at every shop they passed. As Ruby had work later in the afternoon, they'd arrived early on Saturday morning, before the unbearable Christmas rush.

Steve had booked the restaurant, so that was all taken care of – now he needed to find a gift. He couldn't buy something too flashy – one day he'd spoil Lydia – however he wanted something to show he was serious about their relationship.

He looked at earrings. Admittedly, they did range in price and he could pretend they weren't real diamonds, but the box would give it away.

Steve rubbed his temple and adjusted his glasses. "I don't know what to buy, and how much to spend."

"Well, aren't you going to tell her at Christmas? So the present could be less restricted." Ruby had stopped outside another jewellers.

252

"Yes, but won't that look bad if I lavish her with gifts, after telling her my true identity? She'll think I'm posing. Or buying her love. I want something with thought and meaning. And although I hope she's the one I will ask to marry me, isn't it a bit soon? I could scare the woman off. We may both be head over heels, but we're still learning about each other."

"Well, for her birthday you could buy her some clothes. Or what about a sketchpad, or a picture? There's a gallery along there." Ruby pointed.

It was so difficult to buy a present for someone he felt strongly about, because he hadn't been in the relationship long enough to truly know her. He worried the present might not be right. He wanted to find something that encompassed their relationship so far, and spoiled Lydia a little...

"Let's keep walking, and maybe I'll be inspired." Steve huffed, pushing his hands into his pockets and hunching his shoulders. Slouching, so he looked self-doubting, like Clark. Start standing too tall, looking self-assured and people noticed him. Especially women.

Steve started to lose his patience as the shopping centre got busier and busier. Finally, he decided that for her birthday he'd buy her some underwear. He had had the sense to check her sizes in the week. There was a nice boutique, and the way Ruby was sighing at all the pretty lingerie, he knew it was a good choice.

"The Americans call them *panties*. After fifteen years I'm still not used to that word," Steve said in a low voice, leaning into Ruby and pinging a pair of black lace knickers at her cheek.

"Panties sounds so kinky, don't you think? They're *knickers*," Ruby said, snatching them off him and putting them back, giggling.

Normally, Steve wouldn't go shopping with his sister for lingerie for his girlfriend, but he had little choice as Ruby was the only one who knew his secret. And she would be honest with him. Ruby helped him choose, giving her 'too slutty' or 'too flowery' comments. In the end, he'd gone with powder-pink satin, trimmed

253

with lace, as he knew the colour would suit Lydia, and the underwear was practical, but sexy too. The way Steve felt about Lydia, she could be wearing a black bin liner and still make it look hot. The image of the mysterious Catwoman flashed up in his mind, and now he knew the owner of that beautiful body it made his heart quicken with even more excitement.

"Boyfriend treating you early?" said the assistant, smiling knowingly at Ruby, as she folded the garments and put them into a gift box, with tissue paper and scented beads.

"Oh, no! No! He's my brother – these aren't for me." Ruby blushed, holding her hands up defensively, and Steve chuckled.

"I've got a new girlfriend. My sister here was giving me a helping hand, I'm no good with these things," Steve said, adding a nervous tone to his voice, and pushing the glasses up his nose for effect. If the role of Clark Kent ever came up again, he really should audition.

Outside the shop, the Mall was now rammed with shoppers, Steve sighed. "I think I'll come back and get Christmas presents another day. I'm all shopped out. Don't know how you do it. Fancy a coffee?"

At least he had Lydia's birthday present. He knew every girl liked sexy underwear, and he would benefit from it too. He couldn't wait.

∗∗∗

"Your phone's ringing again!" Ruby called from upstairs. She was getting ready for work. "It's the Bat Phone. Shall I get it?"

"No." Steve groaned. He stopped hanging the picture Ruby had bought on their shopping spree earlier this morning and ran up the stairs – two at a time – to fetch the phone. He didn't get to it in time, so listened to the message which just said, "Call me as soon as you get this, it's urgent." Karl sounded harassed. What did he want this close to Christmas?

"Hey, Karl, what's up?"

"Just a reminder that Monday you need to go to London. It's been in the schedule to do some of the ADR for *Nothing Happened*."

"What? London? Not Monday. Please." Lydia's birthday.

He'd forgotten all about being required for recording dialogue. The background noise whilst filming on location meant the dialogue didn't get picked up and they had to go into a studio to put the voices back over on some of the scenes.

"I tried telling them you're on an extended vacation, and could they rearrange it for January, it's Christmas and all, but they're insisting. The studio is in London, and was scheduled months ago, so at least you don't need to fly anywhere. It was in your diary, Steve." Yes, it probably was, he just hadn't been checking this cell phone regularly, or checking in with Marie, who held his diary. "They want you for two days, three max. Everything else is scheduled for after Christmas."

Steve ran his hands through his hair, his face screwed up as he tried to work his way out of this one. What was he going to tell Lydia? He *had* to go – he was under contract.

Damn it!

"Okay, I'll be there. I'll call Marie to sort out travel, etc. Thanks, Karl."

Steve threw the phone onto his bed, and went downstairs.

"Your agent, right? Your voice went all American while speaking to him," Ruby said, slipping her handbag over her shoulder, then her expression sobered. "Has someone died? You look white as a ghost."

"I've got to go to London for a few days."

"Okay."

"It means missing Lydia's birthday."

"Ooohhh." Ruby winced. "That's not so good."

"What am I going to tell her, Ruby?"

"You could come down with a virus? Flu? That can drag itself out. Man-flu especially."

"I'm serious. What if she wants to come see how I am?" he said.

"You're highly contagious and the doctors recommend no visitors?"

Steve palmed his forehead, as if hitting himself would help. "Shit, I'm not ready to tell her the truth. I only have tomorrow. I have to leave Monday morning – early."

"Could you tell her the partial truth; you've got to go to London and can't get out of it?"

"Why would I need to go to London for something I can't rearrange?"

Ruby drummed the table with her fingertips, thinking. Steve imagined the cogs turning inside her brain. He too was thinking of a decent excuse.

"What about a job interview?"

"But I haven't told her I was looking for a job."

"You could say you'd been keeping it a secret because you didn't want to jinx it."

"But what job? I've portrayed myself as some sort of hippy with the travel bug. A high flying job in London, really?"

"Don't have a go at me! I'm just trying to think of something."

"It was your damn idea to hide behind this disguise!" Steve clenched his fists, banging the table.

"And it worked didn't it? Do you think you'd have had these opportunities to meet Lydia otherwise?" Ruby's voice had raised, her hands on her hips. Her expression was stern, all made up and dressed for work in her suit.

Steve took a deep breath to calm himself. There was no point arguing with Ruby. He was angry with himself. Couldn't his real life leave him alone until after Christmas? He loved his life and career, but at the moment he was enjoying this normality with Ruby and Lydia. The little things in life that he now took for granted. Everything was going so well with Lydia, and now he was going to miss her birthday. Which was his reality, with his life and commitments – he'd been missing special occasions for the last fifteen years.

"Look, I've got to get to the hotel. I'm running late now." Her car keys jingled as she fetched them out of her bag. "I'll have a think and we'll discuss it more tonight."

Steve nodded. Ruby kissed his cheek, leaving a sticky lipstick mark, and closed the front door, leaving Steve to stew over London and what he would tell Lydia.

The job interview sounded like the best idea. He wouldn't be lying about going to London, and he wouldn't be lying that he couldn't rearrange it. The fewer lies he told Lydia the better. But what sort of job would he be going for?

He'd call Marie, get a train booked. He couldn't take Ruby's car. Then, he'd work out what he was going to tell Lydia. Maybe Marie might have some inspiration.

London. He needed to be discreet there too. He really didn't want the press getting wind he was in the UK. He'd have to have Marie plan something so it looked like he was heading back to the States for Christmas.

***

Ruby hurried into work, thoughts of Steve having to leave for London tumbling around her head. Would he get photographed in London? Would that trigger further suspicion for Terry? At the time, this had all seemed such a good idea, but she hadn't contemplated the levels of stress it would cause. If Ruby didn't have a few grey hairs after all this, she'd be surprised.

How depressing – grey before she was thirty.

Ruby craved coffee. She might be able to focus better with some caffeine inside her. Making her way to the staff kitchen, Alice walked towards her, immaculate in true beautician style, as usual. Alice would fit instantly into Steve's high profile life, Ruby immediately thought. She imagined them photographed together, photo shoots for *Hello* and *OK*. They would be the perfect couple – on paper.

"Hey, Ruby, I'm glad I've bumped into you," Alice said, nervously, blocking her path. Ruby frowned. She'd been avoiding Alice where possible, which was absurd as she was the boss. It felt easier to put her head in the sand, and hope that the less she saw of Alice, the more the truth about Steve would be forgotten. Maybe Alice didn't really know the truth...

"Look, I've been doing some thinking, and I don't know what *Stuart*," Alice emphasised his name – *she knows*, "is hiding from—"

"Alice, I'd prefer we didn't talk about this in the middle of a corridor." A couple more members of staff passed them to start work. Ruby didn't need this broadcast to the whole hotel. "Can we go some place quieter?"

"I'm just saying, I know how it feels – a bit. I have to be always made-up otherwise people think I look ill. If I don't look good, they presume I'm a crap beautician..."

"Alice, not here." Ruby walked, guiding Alice to her office. Coming from reception, Lydia headed towards them carrying a large bouquet, an array of pink flowers. Ruby had only ever received flowers at work once before in her life. Could that same person be pulling the same trick twice?

"Is that for the spa?" Alice said, frowning. "Larger than usual aren't they?"

"No silly, they're for you." Lydia giggled.

"Me?"

Ruby scowled. Alice took the flowers, cradling them in her arm like a baby, searching for the card. Alice blushed. Her make-up hid her face, but Ruby noticed the flush of red in her neck. "Let me guess, they're from Terry?"

Alice nodded sheepishly.

"Terry?" Lydia said, turning to Ruby. "Isn't that your ex?" The expression on Lydia's face said it all. *Awkward*. It's certainly what Ruby would be thinking. However, Ruby wouldn't give a shit if

Alice wanted to date Terry if Steve wasn't around. But he was, and Lydia couldn't find out the truth this way. It had to come from Steve.

And however much Alice was an attractive woman, Terry only wanted information.

"Lydia, I think there is someone waiting for you," Ruby said as jovially as she could muster. Luckily, there was a resident stood at reception. Ruby pulled Alice into her office and closed the door.

"This has to stop. He'll use you, Alice. Ignore his calls," Ruby hissed, as soon as she'd shut her office door.

"I will. I promise."

"And don't even thank him for the flowers."

"What shall I do with them?"

"Usually, when it comes to Terry, I would say burn them, but then it's such a waste." They were beautiful flowers. "Leave them in the spa, so every time you look at them, you can remember Terence Smythe is an arsehole."

Alice nodded sombrely still cradling the bouquet.

"Oh and Alice?"

"Yes?"

"Whatever you've learnt about my brother, please, please, please keep it to yourself – at least until after Christmas. You have to understand that no one would act the same around him if they knew who he really was."

"I understand. Really, I do."

***

Sunday 15th December

"Hey, Lydie."

"Hey," Lydia replied sleepily down the phone.

Damn, he hadn't realised she'd still be in bed. He loathed that he had to do this over the phone, but Marie had booked him on an early train for Monday morning, to get him into London for a prompt start.

"I'm sorry to call you so early in the morning, but I know you're busy today." She was visiting her sister to celebrate her birthday with her family, Steve remembered, but at the time, thinking they'd be seeing each other on Monday, it hadn't mattered not being together over the weekend. "But I'm going to miss your birthday tomorrow."

"Oh, no."

"I'm really sorry. Really sorry. You don't know how I hate doing this to you. But something's come up and I've got to go to London..."

"London? Why London?" Steve hated that she sounded alert, much more awake. She spoke with genuine intrigue, "Stuart, you can tell me, please... why are you going to London?"

He regretted he had to fabricate so many lies. This wasn't who he was. He paused, taking a breath. "I was keeping it a secret, but I applied for a job, and well, I've got an interview – but it's at their headquarters in London."

Marie hadn't been much help at all; she'd simply agreed a job interview would be the best reason for going to London.

"What company?"

"Er... I'll tell you about it all when I get back, okay?"

"Oh, right, well that's fabulous. Really. I understand."

"Really? You're not mad?" This woman truly was a keeper. "I'm so sorry..."

"Hey, no, why would I be mad? I understand you've got to do this – you can't work with Ruby for the rest of your life. I have a birthday every year," she said, lightly. "And it's not like it's a special one."

"I promise, honey," Steve coughed, clearing his throat, realising his accent had slipped into a more American tone, "I'll call you as soon as I'm back and I'll take you out. I'll get Ruby to drop your present off."

"You bought me a present?"

"Yes, of course..."

"Oh, I want you to give it to me. I'll wait till you get back – there is no rush, honestly. How long are you away?"

Steve winced. God, would she believe this? "Might be three days," he said hesitantly.

"Three days. Some job! Oh, you really will miss my birthday," she said sadly.

"I'm really sorry. It's sod's law."

"Yes it is. But I understand you've got to do it. Really, I do," Lydia said, more positively. But Steve had heard the disappointment in her voice. "You must tell me about it when you get back. Gosh, Stuart, why didn't you say something?"

"I wanted it to be a surprise." He grimaced, glad she couldn't see his expression. *I'm such an asshole.*

"Good luck. Miss you already."

"I'll miss you too."

Steve put the phone down and felt sick. Physically sick. His stomach was heavy. His mouth felt dry, his tongue could sand walls. Lying to Lydia left him riddled with guilt. The more he dug himself in this huge hole of lies, he found it harder and harder to get himself out. He had to tell Lydia the truth, and soon. He prayed she would forgive him and understand why he'd done it. Because he wanted her in his life more than anything now.

Chapter 25

Monday 16th December

Steve rubbed his pounding head, catching his reflection in the elevator. It had been a gruelling first day, trying to get back into character, remembering the scenes. He'd worked his butt off, determined to get the recordings right. Tucked away in the studio had meant more privacy. He'd managed to avoid any press so far. From Paddington, a car had been waiting which had taken him straight to the studio. He didn't know if it had been raining or sunny all day, until seven o'clock that evening he'd stepped foot on the wet pavement, and jumped into another car to take him to his hotel. He had to hand it to Marie, she was a damn good PA.

He opened his hotel door, slotting the key card into the wall to switch on some lights. He dropped his bag on the stand and as he loosened his tie, he checked his mobile. The phone Lydia would send a message to.

He smiled. She'd replied to his brief text this morning that had wished her happy birthday and announced he'd arrived safely in London. Lydia had made him promise to do that. He became sombre when he read her reply:

'GOOD LUCK!'

If this worked out between him and Lydia, he promised himself, and her, although she didn't know it yet, that he'd never lie to her again. Only white lies for surprises, of course. But nothing like this.

He slipped off his shoes and made himself comfortable on the bed, propping up the pillows then hit the call button for Lydia. It didn't ring for long.

"Hello, you!" she answered.

"How is my birthday girl?" he said, the warmth in her voice remedying the stress of his day, and a little of his guilt.

"You'll be pleased to know I have been thoroughly spoilt by my family."

"Good to hear. What are you doing tonight? I'm so sorry I can't be there. I feel terrible."

"It's okay," momentarily she sounded disappointed, "I really do miss you though."

"I miss you too." That was the truth. He'd never known anything like it. He wondered if his feelings for Erica had been as strong, compared to what he felt now.

"Anyway, don't feel too bad, I'm sure you'll make up for it," she purred, sending a quiver of excitement straight to his groin. "Ruby and Alice are coming over, bringing a Chinese takeaway and some DVDs with them." Her tone was bubbly and she really didn't seem annoyed with him. "So, how was your day, how did the interview go?"

Steve leaned his head back and stared at the ceiling – as if that would give him inspiration – and tried not to exhale a groan.

"Lydie, I don't want to talk about it. I might jinx my chances."

"Have you got another interview tomorrow? Or are you coming home?"

He had more work tomorrow. "No, I have to stay for another day at least. Today was just the aptitude tests."

"That's good news, isn't it? They wouldn't bother interviewing you if you hadn't passed the tests."

The Devil was possibly clearing out a spot in Hell right now for Steve as he spoke. "Yes, yes, I suppose so."

"So what is this job? Tell me."

"Uh... it's a sales job... for a national company..." he said cautiously, "They have offices in Bristol." *More lies. Would Lydia still forgive him when she found out the truth?* He was riding on what he'd told her about once being an estate agent – hopefully she believed he was good at sales.

"Oh, what's the name of the company?"

Damn, should never have mentioned a company. Schoolboy error.

Steve sat up quickly, turning to get off the bed, and hit his temple on the silver spotlight reading lamp which hooked over the bed. "Ow!"

"Stuart... Are you all right?"

"Yes, yes," *I'm just looking for inspiration.* He glanced out the hotel window; not a company name to help him. He opened the mini-bar... Schwepps, Coca-Cola, Heineken, Piper-Hiedsieck champagne... "I'll tell you all about it when I see you." If he made up a name, it would be just his luck she'd Google the company.

"Are you going onto Big Brother and you can't tell me about it?"

"No—"

"You're not being interviewed by Sir Alan Sugar are you?" she giggled.

He laughed and shook his head. "No, I'm not being interviewed by Sir Alan either."

"I'm imagining someone like him though. All these rounds of interviews and everything, sounds so daunting. Will you be in front of a panel?"

"Lydie, I'm sorry, I'm tired..." How did he change the subject? At this rate, he'd get an award in compulsive lying if he didn't stop now.

"Okay, I'm sorry, I know, you don't want to jinx it." She still sounded excited and giggly. At least Lydia didn't do diva strops.

"Tell me about your day? What have you been up to with your day off?"

"Oh, I got some illustrations finished. My portfolio is nearly ready to send off to publishers and agents."

Steve relaxed back onto the bed, and closed his eyes to alleviate his headache, and let Lydia talk about her drawings.

***

Wednesday 18th December

Only a week until Christmas, Steve thought, trying to relax as best he could in the back of the car, returning from London. The seatbelt rubbed at his collar, and resting against the headrest, he sat too upright. Yet, he was glad to be chauffeured, as the drone of the tyres on tarmac and the radio low lulled him into a sleepy state. He couldn't keep his eyes open. It had been three demanding long days, and a shock to the system – the hotel work seemed easy in comparison.

Due to the dark winter mornings and evenings, he'd arrived early and left late under the cover of darkness, staying hidden within the studio. He hadn't seen the light of day and had worked his ass off to get his lines right – enabling him to leave London at three p.m. today. Seeing clips of him as his character on screen helped him to focus. *Nothing Happened* was about a guy down on his luck, trying to prove to his friends and family, and the police, that a suspicious photo is all rather innocent. There were more sessions scheduled for January, so he'd check with Marie about those for future arrangements. By then, he would have told Lydia the truth, and wouldn't need to sneak about.

She could come with me and share my hotel bed...

His head rolled forward, startling him from his sleepy state, and he stared out of the car window, the murky countryside filing past. The driver had been paid for his discretion and wasn't the talkative type. The overweight man, in his mid-fifties, kept his eyes on the road and drove. Too uncomfortable to sleep, Steve thought about his plan of action. He would shower and begrudgingly change back into his disguise of Mediocre Man, with his high street clothes and ridiculous glasses – he hadn't missed those. He certainly had missed his tailored suits and how much more comfortable they were though. Then, his first port of call would be to make it up to Lydia. Before leaving for London, he had rearranged the restaurant reservation. So close to Christmas, he wasn't sure how he'd managed it, but they'd been accommodating, although Steve and Lydia had to be seated early. But if she opened her present first, he couldn't promise whether they'd make it to dinner. They could spend the whole evening in her bed. He would be happy with that.

Remember Lydia deserves to be spoilt first.

Unfortunately Steve had been snapped by some photographers as he'd entered the studios yesterday morning, but Marie had press releases ready to explain why Steve Mason was in town, confirming he was returning to Los Angeles in time for Christmas. A limo had taken him to Heathrow, where another inconspicuous car had collected him, making the switch, while his double boarded a plane.

He smirked, shaking his head. Would they notice the Caribbean tan he now wore on the plane, compared to the photos snapped of him looking a lot paler entering the studios?

Christmas Eve was only six days away, Steve kept worrying. He'd tell Lydia by then. He wasn't sure what he was going to say, or how he would to do it, but she had to learn the truth. He agonised over how she would react. She was the one for Stuart Fisher, but would she want to be the one for Steve Mason?

Steve wanted a future with Lydia. For the past three days, she was all he had thought of. The way her delicate fingers were stained with inks and paints, and how she usually wore a smudge on her cheek or nose unknowingly. How she laughed with him, sharing silly jokes; the way her blonde hair felt smooth as he combed his fingers through it; the way their bodies melded together perfectly when making love...

He loved her and he needed to tell her. His heart ached as if it had been ripped from his chest, stamped on a few times, and put back upside down, he missed her so much.

How would he cope when he returned to LA? Would she come with him? He rolled over ideas in his head, how he'd set up a studio for her in his apartment so she could do the thing she loved – her illustrations.

Lydia was in his every thought, always on his mind. The minute he woke, she'd be in his thoughts. The ADR had kept him busy, but as soon as he had a moment's rest, he'd lapse into thinking about her, checking his phone to see if she'd text him. A yearning to want to see her, hear her voice, kiss her, touch her, make love...

God, he hoped she loved him too. He couldn't suffer a broken heart twice, could he?

He grew impatient, thinking this car journey was insufferably long. He rubbed his eyes and looked at his watch. Then, with relief, he saw a motorway sign for the M5 junction, only one mile away. They weren't far away now. Soon he'd be home and soon he'd be back with Lydia.

Chapter 26

Steve pressed the doorbell, and as he heard the door chime, he hid behind the large bouquet of flowers he was holding. The door opened and he appeared around them.

"Boo!"

"Stuart!" Lydia lunged at him. The name threw him just as much off balance. He wobbled, regaining his equilibrium on the step where he stood, holding the flowers out so she didn't crush them as she smacked her lips onto his. He held a gift bag in his other hand, and tried the best he could to tighten his hold on her. It felt wonderful to have her back in his arms.

"I'm happy to see you too," Steve said, when she'd pulled out of the kiss. "Happy birthday, I'm so sorry it's late."

"It's all right, I understand you had to go away for an interview." Lydia grabbed his shirt, kissed him again then pulled him inside. "Oh, you smell so good. I can't believe how much I've missed you."

"These are for you, to say I'm sorry," he handed the bouquet over. "And this is your birthday present."

"Have I got time to open it now?"

"Yeah, sure, but the restaurant's booked for seven." He'd showered and changed in record time to get there, knowing they had to be at the restaurant early.

He admired Lydia as she tore at the wrapping paper like an

excited child, her blue eyes complemented by the sapphire blue evening dress she wore. She'd straightened her blonde hair, so the layers chopped and swished as her head moved. He wasn't sure how he was going to manage keeping his hands to himself all evening. His groin already ached in approval.

She pulled the matching underwear garments from the box and smiled coyly.

"Thank you," she said, smiling, her eyes wide with a knowing excitement.

"I hope I got the sizes right. I wasn't rummaging through your underwear drawer, honest." He held up his hands, grinning cheekily. "But one morning, well, you know, your underwear was just lying around... so I thought I'd check."

"No, it looks perfect." She smoothed the pink satin between her fingers admiring the lingerie. "Unfortunately, I don't think we have time for me to try anything on."

She put the garments back into the box and stroked along his clean-shaven cheek, cupping his face, kissing him. As she pulled out of the kiss, her teeth grazed his tongue. He growled sexily, as it sent excitement straight between his thighs.

"Lydia," he said warningly, "we've got to go out."

"I'm sorry, I'm such a tease, but I've missed you so much, Stuart."

There it was again. Stabbed with guilt, his stomach turned cold.

She wiped the lipstick off his lips. "I better go touch up." As she disappeared upstairs, Steve spied a newspaper open on the coffee table. His heart pounded, blood ringing in his ears. Page seven, and there he was, going into the London studio, opening the damn door. He was glad he was wearing shades, but the headline was obviously questioning how long he'd been in the UK. Had Lydia read this? He heard her coming down the stairs and rustled the paper closed, pushing it away. He quickly relaxed back on the sofa, arms behind his head, hoping he didn't look like a naughty child caught in the act. He concentrated on getting his breath back to a less erratic state. If she'd put two and two together, she'd have said something, wouldn't she? Maybe he should talk over dinner.

"Ready?" he said, standing up, holding out Lydia's jacket to help her into it.

"Yes, thank you."

Steve drove them to the restaurant in Clifton. He'd chosen a place that wasn't too flashy, taking heed of Ruby's advice not to splash his money around, but something with a little class and uniqueness to make the evening special. Unfortunately, they were only serving a Christmas menu, but that would have been the same two nights ago.

"Hey, it's the problem I have with my birthday being so close to Christmas," Lydia said, sipping her glass of Prosecco as the waiter served the starters. They'd both opted for breaded brie wedges with a warm cranberry sauce.

"Maybe in the future, we can celebrate your birthday in June. Have a second birthday."

"Oh, Stuart, that's sweet."

"If it's good enough for the queen, it's good enough for you." He beamed, raising his champagne flute.

For their mains, they'd both opted for roast beef as they'd be eating plenty of turkey soon enough. As they tucked into their dinners, everything was swimming along nicely. The conversation, the flirting, like Lydia slipping off her shoe to give a little shin rub with her toe. He'd asked the questions, letting her talk, hoping to avoid probes about where he had been for the past few days. But it was inevitable.

"So, tell me, how did you get on in London?" Lydia asked once the waiter had cleared away their plates. She flicked her hair out of her face, and leaned onto the table, her breasts pushing together, emphasising her beautiful cleavage. "You haven't mentioned it all night."

He shrugged. "Lydia, I don't want to talk about it. Tonight is about you."

"Oh, go on, how do you think you've done? You were there for the three days. So you must have done well."

Steve took a sip from the one glass of sparkling wine he was allowed to have and had to make last. What could he say? Maybe he needed to prepare Lydia. He still couldn't quite bring himself to tell her the truth. Not here anyway. Because if someone overheard then it would be autographs, photographs...

No, he needed to do it privately. Just the two of them.

Holding her hand, he gently circled his thumb in her palm.

"What is it?" she said, frowning.

"Let's say I get this job. It would mean I have to travel..." With his anxiety, sweat beaded around his hairline.

"So?"

"Well, I could be away months at a time. Would you come with me?"

"Stuart, I don't know... We've not been seeing each other that long. I don't think I could afford—"

"Hey, I'd support you. I'll be earning enough." He tightened his grip around her hand, reassuringly. "You could concentrate on your drawings, on getting published."

"But what if it doesn't work out? Where would that leave me?"

"I wouldn't leave you without. I'd make sure you were provided for." She frowned. "Okay, okay, just think about it. Because..."

"Because?"

"This job, if I get it, means not being in the UK much."

"Okay... but I thought you said they had offices in Bristol."

Damn, shit, bugger! He really needed to remember his lies.

"That's where I'm based from, but there's a lot of travelling involved."

The disappointment in Lydia's face made Steve need to elaborate more. He wasn't doing this to get away from her. Far from it. "Look, I applied for this job before anything happened with us."

"I know. It's okay. Really."

The waiter arrived with their desserts, allowing Steve to change the conversation to something where he didn't have to fabricate the truth. He'd chosen the raspberry pavlova, and Lydia had picked some chocolate indulgence, both agreeing they'd eat enough Christmas pudding over the festive period.

"This is good, you need to try it." He scooped up a small portion of meringue and strawberries, holding out the spoon to Lydia. Delicately, she took his spoon into her mouth, then nodded and licked her lips agreeably. He hadn't meant it to be erotic, but the slightest glimpse of Lydia's tongue sent desire through his bones.

After the meal, Steve pulled up outside Lydia's house.

"You're coming in, right?" she said, tugging at his tie. "I've got to try on my birthday present…" she purred in Steve's ear.

"Try and stop me."

They kissed, stumbling into Lydia's house. All night Steve had wanted this. He'd feared he'd blown it, mentioning working away. Lydia had gone quiet. But now, she eagerly tugged at his shirt, while he unzipped her dress. It dropped to her ankles, revealing black lace.

"You know, why don't you show me your present another day? I'll just take my time with this tonight." He tucked a thumb into her knickers, a rumble releasing from his chest.

"Okay, it'll be your Christmas present."

***

Saturday 21st December

Today was the shortest day of the year; winter had truly arrived, and with the sky filled with grey clouds for most of the afternoon, it made it feel even shorter. With it already dark outside, technically Steve hadn't seen daylight. Depressing. Today he missed the LA sunshine.

The weekend was hectic with the run up to Christmas. The majority of the guests were staying for a weekend break to do shopping in Bristol. Tonight was the last Christmas party at the hotel too. There was so much to organise; moving the furniture, uncovering the dance floor, more balloons were arriving. Steve hadn't stopped all day. The hotel rooms would be full tonight, the majority of the guests were choosing to stay over rather than get a taxi home.

He had finished his shift and was waiting for Callum. The last people he served were a young couple in their thirties. They both wore wedding bands, so Steve assumed they were married to each other. Although these days, you never could tell. By the amount of carrier bags the man held, they'd obviously been Christmas shopping.

Steve closed the dishwasher and approached them at the bar.

"What can I get you both?" he said.

"I think I'll have a glass of your house white," the woman said. "Or is it too early for wine?"

"As my sister would say, it's never too early." Steve grinned.

"I'll have a bottle of Bud," the husband said.

Steve served the drinks, and took the payment. The wife looked at Steve quizzically, as if studying his face. Having been in London and spotted by the press, did he look too familiar? The couple whispered. Paranoia set in, and Steve fiddled with his glasses and remembered to slouch in his stance. He decided to go back to his work, and clear away glasses. Luckily, Callum came bouncing in full of Christmas cheer to relieve him.

"Ho, ho, ho, sorry I'm late."

"No worries, I've got to wait for Ruby anyway. See you Christmas Eve if not before?"

"Can't wait, mate." Callum beamed.

Steve changed out of his uniform, and wandered back to Ruby's office.

Ruby was running him back to the house, freshening up, then returning to help with the party tonight. She'd given Steve the night off. He offered to help, but was relieved in some ways she refused it, because he felt shattered.

"I'm sorry, I've got so much to do." Ruby fretted around her office. "Could you do me a favour, and take these down to the spa please?" Ruby pointed to two small boxes. "They got delivered to my office, but they're supplies Alice ordered."

"Of course." Steve lifted up the boxes, surprisingly heavier than expected, and made his way to the spa. There was no one at the spa reception desk and rather than leave the boxes, he thought he'd wait for a moment. Steve grabbed a magazine, and got comfy on the cream leather sofa. *Good, no pictures of me.*

A women emerged, in her late twenties, red faced and sweaty. She wore gym clothing and trainers, so she'd been in the hotel's gym. She wiped her face with a towel and then drank water from a bottle. Steve took no notice, and carried on reading.

"Excuse me, but you look familiar. Do I know you?" the woman had approached Steve.

He closed the magazine, and fiddled with his glasses for good measure. His second dose of paranoia for the day washed over him. He stood up, which didn't help matters, because the woman then had to look up to meet his gaze, showing his impressive true height. He tried to slouch and shook his head, "No, sorry, I don't recognise you." He pulled an apologetic expression and hoped he looked dopey. "I work in the hotel, maybe you've seen me in the bar?"

"No, that's not where I've seen you."

Steve shrugged.

"I know who you are!" the woman said, excitedly. "You're Steve Mason."

"He gets that all the time." Alice. She'd appeared from nowhere. Steve had been so focussed on the woman, his heart pounding, he hadn't noticed her. "I keep telling Stuart he should play his double. He'd get loads of money," Alice said jovially, giving Steve a nudge with her fist. He chuckled.

"Such a shame. You really look like him. I was going to ask for your autograph."

"No sorry, I work in the hotel bar. Never been to Hollywood. Not me."

The woman appeared convinced and after she left the spa, Steve stood silent unsure about what to say to Alice. Did she know? Awkwardly, he said, "Ruby asked me to bring these boxes to you. They're heavy, so would you like me to move them?"

"No, that's fine. It's the shampoo and body wash for the gym showers. I wondered when they'd arrive."

"Okay, right, Ruby might be waiting for me, so I better go. Thanks for that... you know, then, with the woman."

Alice winked. "Not a problem. I understand."

Steve nodded. "Oh, and remember our Christmas Eve party."

"I wouldn't miss it."

Chapter 27

Christmas Eve

Steve made Daphne a cup of tea, just how she liked it, and brought it into the lounge, dodging a low-hanging Christmas decoration. Since Lydia's late birthday meal, the week had flown by. Work at the hotel had been hectic, and Steve had failed to find the opportune moment to talk seriously to Lydia. In fact, really, he'd been a chicken, which wasn't Steve's nature at all, but the importance of Lydia being in his life had made him lose his nerve. What if she rejected him?

"Are you sure you don't want something stronger?" Steve said to Daphne handing her the teacup. "We have sherry."

"The mulled cider is good." Alice raised her glass.

"No, dear, thank you. Maybe later."

Apart from Daphne, the whole party had agreed to wear their garish Christmas jumpers; the louder the better. Steve, wearing a navy blue jumper with a reindeer's face on the front Ruby had found him, returned to the kitchen, to where Ruby and Brett were preparing the buffet. His stomach rumbled as he took another small platter of party food into the dining room. With Brett's assistance, they'd dished up a variety of delicious canapés from smoked salmon parcels to honey glazed sausages. None of it was ready made or supermarket purchased; Brett had made everything from scratch. The one thing Ruby had insisted on was having an orange poked with cocktail sticks of chunks of cheese and pineapple – a party favourite. Lydia, Alice and Callum chatted amongst themselves in the lounge, with drinks in hand, making Daphne welcome.

"It used to be a family tradition on Christmas Eve to have a buffet tea and play games, so I hope this is okay?" Steve placed a homemade pizza cut into thin slices onto the table, squeezing it between egg sandwiches (another family tradition) and a bowl of stuffed olives – those may have been shop bought.

Steve remembered the look of dismay on Brett's face – the master chef – when he'd insisted having egg sandwiches. These were presented as delicate fingers, crusts removed, with a scatter of cress, whereas Mum would have cut them into triangles and wouldn't have cut the crusts off as it would have been a waste. There was enough to feed the whole street. Steve could see he'd still be eating this in January. Would he have room for turkey tomorrow afternoon? It was just like Mum to make sure there was a good spread laid out.

Finding matches, Steve lit a couple of Christmas candles Ruby had dotted around on the table, then glanced at Lydia talking to Daphne and Alice, and a wave of anxiety flushed through him. Tonight he had to tell Lydia the truth, then he would tell the others, too. Ruby had agreed. His nerves eating away at him left him not feeling so hungry – but someone had to eat this food.

Lydia excused herself and joined Steve's side, linking her arm through his and smiling.

"Doesn't all the food look great? Like a Nigella Christmas buffet," she said. He weaved his arm around her waist and squeezed her closer. "Brett could be our very own celebrity chef one day."

Ruby came out carrying a dish full of seasoned potato wedges. "Right, everyone, come and tuck in. Grab a plate, and take what you want. You're not leaving until it is all gone. And there's pudding

277

to get through too."

"Are you sure you don't want any help?" Lydia said.

"No, no, start eating. Besides I actually think I'm getting in Brett's way."

"Anyone need another drink?" Steve held up a champagne bottle, realising that entertaining could be stressful. In LA, when he'd held a party, he'd had caterers in and they did all the hard work, worrying if guests had enough food and drink. His guests all shook their heads. "Well, all the drinks are in the kitchen, so help yourself otherwise."

Callum, in a bright red jumper with a snowman, reached the table first and started loading food onto his plate. Lydia assisted Daphne.

"What game shall we play first? Twister?" Steve said mischievously glancing at Daphne.

"You young 'uns can," Daphne said, chuckling. "I think my twisting days are over. I'll spin the wheel."

"Not spin the bottle?" Steve winked.

Daphne laughed more. "You're so cheeky. I do like charades though."

"Oh, yeah, we could team up," Callum said, his plate piled high with an array of food.

One by one, they returned to the sofas, placing their plates on their laps, eating, drinking and chatting. It was so normal, and the kind of party Mum used to throw when Ruby and Steve were kids. Family and friends visiting, the evening ending with them all sat around the table playing a game of cards for real money, albeit just coppers.

"Mmmm... Brett, Ruby, well done on the food." Alice raised her glass.

"Brett did it. I assisted."

"Yes, no wonder the restaurant does so well," Lydia said.

"He wants to run his own restaurant," Ruby said, rubbing his arm proudly.

Brett popped a sausage into his mouth and shook his head.

"And you're happy to be losing a good member of staff?" Alice looked from Ruby to Brett questioningly.

"Well, the hotel can always find another chef. I wouldn't want to stop someone following their dreams." Ruby looked at Steve then. "Besides—"

"Ruby could actually run the restaurant for Brett, and let him concentrate on the kitchen sides of things." Steve had suddenly thought of a solution for Ruby.

She glared at him. Not main beam, but a look that said 'not so fast.' "We'll see. It's early days for me and Brett, remember. And I was going to say, it might be healthier for our relationship if we didn't work together."

"I'd love you to join me, Ruby." Brett kissed her forehead. "You could manage front of house."

"We may have lost our sous-chef and manager." Alice chuckled, elbowing Callum, who couldn't respond because he had stuffed his face gleefully with all the delicious food.

"It's early days. Don't you lot spread rumours around the hotel, please." Ruby almost went into boss mode.

"Right, let's get this party started." Steve stood up, about to turn up the music a little, a Christmas party songs CD inserted and ready to play.

The letterbox rapped loudly.

Ruby looked at Steve, confused, then through the lounge and out the window. Her eyes widened.

"Oh shit!" she said standing, food falling from her plate.

"Fuck!" Steve hissed.

Daphne stood, surprisingly spritely for her age, and took the plate slipping from Steve's hand while muttering, 'Oh my dear, why now?'

Lydia looked at him, confusion etched on her face. She hadn't noticed the gang of reporters outside the house, their presence lit up by the streetlamps. A crowd trying to peek through the front

279

window to get a good look, with the odd flash from a camera. Thank God, the Christmas tree took up most of the window. "Stuart?"

"I'm sorry," he said, gently cupping her face with his hands and filled with an unbearable sadness that he hadn't spoken to her before this moment. This was the worst possible way for her to find out. "I was going to tell you. Tonight."

"Tell me what?"

"Steve Mason! We know you're in there!"

Steve jumped away from Lydia as if touching an electric fence.

"How do you feel about Erica Kealey marrying her latest leading man?"

"Why the stunt double in the Caribbean?"

Ruby tried to draw close the curtains. "Steve, the tree's in the way!"

"What's going on?" Callum said, bewildered.

"Leave it, Ruby!" Steve snapped, ignoring Callum. Think. What the hell should he do? How had they found him? Why Christmas Eve? He raced up the stairs, where he knew his cell phone was and dialled Marie. He needed a safe passage out of the house, that way Ruby and everyone would not get sucked into this.

"Marie, sorry to disturb your lunch. The press have found me. They're banging on Ruby's door now. You need to get me an escort organised and a flight out of here, please," Steve said to his PA, giving her the address details.

He rubbed his forehead, a headache already forming at his temple. He threw his glasses across the room in anger and heard a crack.

"I'm sorry, Marie, but you're going to need to get me home on the first plane to LA." He explained the situation.

"I'll get you an internal flight from Bristol to somewhere other than Heathrow, where they'll be expecting to see you."

"Thanks, that's a good idea."

"Suppose you're in too much of a rush now to buy me a present from quaint old England?"

"Yeah, sorry."

Once he'd ended the call with Marie, he grabbed his wallet, passport and anything else important he could carry in his jacket. His clothes and other belongings would have to wait. He needed to travel fast, and light. As he rummaged, he caught a glimpse of his Christmas jumper in the mirror. He heaved it over his head and found a more suitable sweater. He didn't want to turn up in LA wearing a reindeer. He really wasn't in the mood.

He thundered down the stairs to hear Ruby bellowing through the closed front door.

"Haven't you bastards got anything better to report on? It's Christmas Eve for fuck's sake! Piss off to your families. You—"

Steve pulled her away from the door. "Don't give them ammo, Ruby."

Tears welled, then trickled down her cheeks. "But this means you're leaving. You have to go. We don't get Christmas."

He hugged her tightly, closing his eyes, which he could feel prickling. He didn't want to leave her either. Not yet. He hadn't realised how much he'd wanted to spend Christmas with Ruby up until this point, when he now couldn't have it. "I know."

The banging at the door and the kerfuffle outside continued. Men peered through the window.

"Should we call the police? They're trespassing after all?" Alice said, her mobile phone at the ready.

Brett placed a hand on her arm. "No, not yet," he said softly. "It might make matters worse."

Releasing Ruby, Steve turned to the five faces gawping at him, speechless. Plates abandoned. The food untouched.

"Lydia, I'm so sorry, I was going to tell you. In fact, I was going to tell you all tonight." Steve took her hand, trying to pull her into a hug, but she stared blankly at him. "I love you. You have to believe me."

"It's all a lie? A lie. Your name isn't Stuart?" She grimaced, meeting his gaze.

"No, what I feel for you isn't a—"

"How could you?"

"No, Lydia, I love you." Before his very eyes he could see he was losing her. She hated him. What had he done?

"Leave me alone!" Lydia yanked her hand out of Steve's grip and barged past Ruby. Frantically she started to unlock the front door, but Ruby grabbed her hands away, blocking the door, Steve following.

"Don't go out there. Not yet!" Ruby yelled, pushing at her, as Lydia fought for freedom and sobbed.

"Lydia, please," Steve begged. "Ruby's right."

"Stay away from me!" Lydia screamed, shoving Steve, tears streaming. She bolted past him and up the stairs.

His head was spinning; his gut felt like it had been wrenched up through his throat. He started after her, but Ruby clutched his arm. "Leave her, Steve. Let her calm down. I'll talk to her." A door slammed upstairs. He prayed Lydia would stay away from the windows, wouldn't look outside. He didn't want her to see the amount of press he could draw. He closed his eyes, taking a deep breath. In through the nose, out through the mouth. Calm down. Think.

"Everybody, in the kitchen," Steve ordered, helping Daphne. Brett grabbed a dining room chair and took it with him, to seat her comfortably. "I'm sorry, it's probably best to wait in here where they can't see us." As a precautionary measure, he drew the blind by the window over the sink. Even though it was dark outside, it looked out to the back garden, and he wouldn't be surprised if a bastard got over the back gate.

Everyone was silent, dumbfounded. Even Callum was speechless. Brett put a protective arm around Ruby as they leaned against the work surface. Steve continued to rub his forehead.

"I'm sorry, guys," he said. "I was going to tell you all."

"Let's have a cup of tea," Alice said calmly, sounding completely out of character. She would be suggesting Vodka usually. "Daphne, tea?"

Daphne nodded. Alice soon had the mugs on the counter for those who wanted tea, pouring the steaming water and handing them out. Daphne got the first one. Steve refused. There was an uncomfortable silence in the kitchen for what felt like nearly twenty minutes. Everyone afraid to speak, not knowing what to say, what to ask. He knew they all wanted to ask him something, but were all in a state of shock. Even Callum remained quiet and withdrawn.

From their point of view, Steve thought, this probably was a very surreal moment in their lives.

Steve muttered softly, "I'm sorry," probably for the umpteenth time. He couldn't look any of them in the eye. Only Ruby. She would wipe a tear away every time one escaped. He could tell she was trying to hold it in.

Daphne patted his hand and softly said, "We know you didn't mean any harm, dear."

She was attempting to make him feel better, but it wasn't working. Steve was racked with guilt over Lydia. Feeling remorse, he glanced up at the ceiling wondering which room she had taken refuge in above them. What was she thinking? He hated that he couldn't talk to her, couldn't convince her that he was sorry. The fact he wasn't going to say goodbye properly pulled him apart. His chest felt tight, and his body empty, drained of all sense and feeling. Nothingness.

Why couldn't he have had a couple more days? A couple more hours even?

Anger bubbled inside of him, which he would not release until he was safely tucked away in his apartment in LA.

Loneliness was creeping back into his heart.

Eventually, there was a heavy thump at the front door, making both Ruby and Steve jump. Everyone looked towards the front door, instead of their feet.

"Mr Mason, we're your escort," a gruff, deep voice shouted

from behind the door.

Steve hugged Ruby tightly again, her tears making his cheeks wet, and they both made their way towards the front door.

He was about to open the door, confront the press, but the thought of not saying goodbye to Lydia hurt so much. Emotion and pain swirled inside his chest. He took the stairs two at a time, and reached the landing. His bedroom door was the only one shut. She was in his room.

He gently knocked. "Lydia, please let me say goodbye." There was no reply. "Lydia? Please, honey, I love you."

He rested his hand on the door handle, warring internally whether to open the door. His hesitation cost him, as he heard a bang behind the door, as if she'd thrown herself against it, blocking his entrance. "I don't want to speak to you." The anger that laced her words stung, straight to his heart.

"Lydia, please, let me in."

"Go away. I never want to see you again."

Steve rested his forehead against the door, closing his eyes, before they betrayed him, and prayed. Praying that she didn't mean it. She was angry. She would calm down and forgive him, wouldn't she?

"Steve," Ruby called calmly up the stairs, "you've got to go."

"I'm sorry, Lydia. I really am. If there was anything I could do to change this. I would." He slowly turned, and with a heavy heart, lumbered back downstairs.

"Goodbye, Ruby. I'm so sorry. Please talk to Lydia." He glanced again at the stairs, hesitating. "I'll come back as soon as I can."

"Go!" she ordered, wiping her face, losing control of her tears. "I promise I'll talk to her."

"I'll call you." Steve nodded, then opened the front door – photographers flashed cameras, questions shouted all at once. Most asked why he was in Bristol, what was he doing, who was he with? It all blurred, becoming numb with the assault.

Two intimidating muscle men in black suits – like bouncers outside a club, almost as wide as they were tall – ushered Steve with force towards an awaiting black car with blacked out rear windows. Another car waited behind it. Two other men were pushing cameras out of the way and clearing the path. One of the men with Steve opened the passenger door. Steve quickly ducked inside the car, the bodyguard joining him. They'd moved him so fast, the car sped off before he could think. He didn't even have a proper look at the house – the home – he was leaving behind. Glancing out the back window, the other car followed with its passengers – his men in black.

His heart heavy, he closed his eyes. When would he see Ruby and Lydia again? What a shitty way to say goodbye. Leaving the ones you loved always hurt. God, did he love Lydia. And dear God, this was the worst way he'd wanted her to find out who he was.

But this was show business. The show must go on. The press didn't care about who got hurt.

Anger surged through his body. His fist clenched and he ground his teeth. His whole body tensed. He wanted to punch something, but years of training made him take a deep breath, and breathing out, he released the anger. But it didn't alleviate his emptiness.

Chapter 28

When Lydia knew it was safe to move from the bedroom door, she sat down on the double bed, her arms wrapped around her knees, occasionally wiping away a tear. Tears, that however much she tried to hold in, wouldn't cease falling. Typical; she had found his bedroom. Pale olive green walls. A couple of shirts hung over the solid oak wardrobe door. The X-box and a small television sat patiently in one corner. His discarded Christmas jumper lay on the floor and his glasses were crumpled in the corner; one lens popped out. The rage inside her fought the urge to collect the jumper up and snuggle it, to smell his scent. She could even get into his bed, and wrap the duvet around her and bury her head in his pillow. But she needed to forget, not remember. It wouldn't comfort her.

She could hear the commotion outside. It had got louder as Stuart – Steve had left the house.

She felt hurt and used by – who was he? Steve Mason.

Really the Steve Mason?

She certainly wasn't Erica Kealey.

Now she felt stupid for not even recognising him. How had she not when they'd been so intimate? All the things they'd done – in her bedroom and bathroom! She buried her head into her hands. Oh, God! In her defence, she wasn't one for keeping up to date with celebrities. She didn't pore over glossy magazines like Alice.

She didn't have the time.

So why hadn't Alice realised?

He'd duped her too.

Or had she realised? She flirted around Stuart – Steve. *Whoever he was.*

Lydia's anger surged again, as intimate memories flooded her mind, mixed with longing and regret, the coldness of reality that it was all over. *Do not hug his pillows.*

She didn't understand why he'd lied.

Why would someone who could have anything and everything disguise themselves?

She understood he'd been maybe trying to have some quiet time with Ruby. But the job? The glasses? Even some of his terrible clothes. She'd found it cute and quirky, and one of his adorable traits, but, she shuddered; what had it all been for? Some game?

The more she thought about it, the more it fuelled the fire of rage inside her.

***

Ruby stared at the front door Steve had just closed behind him. Gone. And when would she see him again? He promised to return, but when? When would his schedule allow it? It could be a year, two years...

Unstoppable tears leaked from her eyes. She felt an arm slip around her and bring her into a cuddle, but her mind was numb as she rested her head on Brett's chest.

"Ruby, this wasn't me, by the way, before you think it was," Brett whispered, anxiously, stroking his fingers through her hair. "I made you a promise. I swear, I didn't tell a soul."

She hadn't even contemplated that Brett had leaked the information – she'd confessed all on the morning she'd let Steve's name slip; it had felt brilliant to share her secret. But then who had?

She glared at Alice.

"It wasn't me either! I swear, Ruby." Alice stood defensively, eyes wide. "I realised he had to be hiding for a reason, and I liked him too much."

"But I warned you about Terry," Ruby shouted, stepping closer to Alice.

"I didn't tell him anything. I promise."

"You didn't mention I had a brother working at the hotel – at all?"

Alice shook her head, then her hands flew to her mouth and she started to shake. "Oh, God, I don't know. I don't think so. Ruby, I swear I didn't know when he first picked me up. I promise, I stayed away once you'd warned me."

Ruby blinked. With rage building she wiped her face and yanked the front door wide open, searching the crowd of reporters. Some cameras flashed, but most were moving on now that the prize had left. And there he was; Terence.

She tore after him, barging photographers out of her way, pushing and shoving.

"You bastard. You. Fucking. Bastard!" she screamed. Hate, anger, tears flooded to the surface. "It was you. You couldn't leave it until after Christmas." As she came face to face with him, her fists clenched, seething, she punched, but she missed. She was being lifted, carried, dragged away from him. She fought the arm holding her back. "I want to kill him! Let me go."

"Ruby!" Brett yelled. "Ruby. Inside the house now. Before you make things even worse for Stu – Steve."

She hated the smug smile on Terence's face. She hated it so much she wanted him dead, painfully, breaking every bone in his body, dead.

"You bastards! Haven't you got families of your own you should be with?" she screamed as Brett heaved her back into the house, Callum helping, pushing cameras out of the way. Then, hauling Callum in and pushing a reporter back, Brett slammed the door shut. He placed his hands on his knees and panted from the exertion Ruby had put him though.

"Callum, away from the window," Brett snapped. "Alice, get him away."

Alice, trembling, burst into action, pulling at Callum.

Ruby, slumped on the sofa next to Daphne who gave her a pat on her knee, watching as Alice and Brett dragged the tree out of the window, baubles swinging and some dropping, a glass one shattering, and then between them shutting the curtains. Pointless. The bastards would have got what they wanted. And Steve was on his way back to LA. His home.

She should have drawn the curtains earlier.

"I'm sorry," Ruby whispered to Daphne, fearing the old woman really shouldn't be subjected to something like this in her time of life – especially Ruby's language.

"Don't you worry, dear. If I was thirty years younger I'd have been out there with you swinging for those horrid men. I wish there was more I could do."

"Here, get this down you." Alice handed Ruby a glass of red wine, and she thankfully took it with trembling hands, and gulped some down. Alice knocked back her own. Ruby needed to calm down. This wasn't doing the situation any good, wouldn't change the matter either. She needed to talk to Lydia, as it was essential she understood why Steve had done it.

"When I first saw him, I thought he was a catch, and I did think he looked familiar," Alice said, mainly to Callum and Brett. "Then, when Terry took me out on a date, I put two and two together." Ruby was still in a trance, trying to get back to the reality of the situation. "I really should have tried harder to shag him."

Callum snorted.

"So where does the name Mason come from?" Callum asked, once he'd recovered.

"It's their mother's maiden name," Brett answered for her. Ruby nodded, sipping her wine. "Ruby, maybe you should eat some food."

She shook her head. "No, I must talk to Lydia," she said softly, her voice hoarse from the screaming, and her throat tight from trying to hold in her tears. She listened for movement upstairs, but there wasn't any.

"So why was he pretending to be Stuart?" Alice asked. Callum shrugged, tucking into some of the food at the table. At least someone was eating.

"It was my idea," Ruby muttered. "My stupid idea."

***

Lydia had heard the front door open again. There was screaming. Ruby was swearing her head off. Lydia spied out of the window, using the curtains to hide her face. Ruby was ferocious, running at one reporter. Lydia recognised him, but where from?

"Oh, he came to the hotel that time," Lydia whispered. That's why Ruby had sent Stuart – Lydia still thought of him as Stuart; Steve felt completely alien – her brother away that day.

Lydia carefully watched as Brett hauled Ruby back indoors, the flashes of cameras lighting the street. Even Callum had shoved a few of the reporters who stood on the pavement by the front garden. The usually quiet, narrow road was swarming with paparazzi, like wasps, hovering around the house. Or vultures, wanting to pick flesh from the bones. Cars were parked on pavements and neighbours stood on their doorsteps, confused at the commotion. What would the neighbours think? Where were the police to move these cretins on? Lydia felt disgusted and appalled how these so-called human beings could show so little respect for someone else's property, squashing bushes, trampling the grass. Good job it wasn't summer.

Evidently, her anger towards Stuart must be calming if she was thinking about Ruby's garden.

Lydia listened, and carefully kept watch. She'd wait until the coast was clear then leave. She really didn't need this sort of attention. Steve Mason probably didn't need this sort of attention either. He'd obviously wanted to keep her a secret.

Had he been getting a kick out of it? Was that why he'd done it?

Tears streamed down her cheeks. She sobbed, unable to stop herself. In some ways she didn't want to stop. She wanted to cry until all the pain disappeared. The thought of never seeing Stuart again, never being held, kissed or made love to by him again... it was all over.

There was a knock at the door, making Lydia hug herself tighter, sitting on the bed.

"Go away."

"Lydia, it's Ruby, please can I come in?"

"No."

Ruby opened the door. Her face was puffy and blotchy from crying, probably a mirror image of Lydia's. "Sorry. It's my house, and you need to hear me out."

"You knew about this." Lydia shouted, tension flooding her body. "You knew! Why'd he do it? Why'd you let him do it?"

Ruby sank onto the corner of the bed, and sighed heavily, then looked Lydia in the eye. In the dim light the lamp by the bed provided, Ruby looked how Lydia felt – utterly miserable. "It was my bad idea, Lydia."

"He's a grown man, Ruby. He knew what he was doing. Why did he pretend to be..." God, she still couldn't bring herself to say his real name, "Stuart?"

Lydia watched as Ruby ran her hands through her hair, scrunching into fists, as if pulling at it, as if causing herself deserved pain.

Ruby filled her lungs, then breathed out slowly before she looked at Lydia. "He came over in October, unhappy. He'd broken up with Erica Kealey, and was reeling off how he'd wanted to be married by now, but questioning who would love him for him, and not his fame and fortune." Lydia stared at the pale, freshly painted olive green wall, but listened. "And I came up with the idea of a disguise. Strip away his assets, his swanky clothes, his designer stubble – God, you should have seen his face when I made him get that bad haircut." Ruby chuckled, and Lydia found it briefly infectious, imaging the faces Stuart – Steve – could pull.

"Then, I decided he needed a job, because lazing around in a four star hotel he would get noticed, and in my house, he'd meet no one."

"So you thought he could work in one instead?" Lydia's words were laced with sarcasm.

"I thought some of the staff, especially Brett and Callum, would make friends with him, and get him out socialising, and meeting someone. And he did meet someone, Lydia. He met you. And I know he loves you." A tear trickled down Ruby's cheek, and Lydia felt her own eyes stinging. She swallowed to halt her tears. "And I didn't bring him to the hotel to intentionally meet you. You two hit it off all by yourselves."

"But Ruby, he's not Stuart. I loved Stuart..."

"Lydia, everything you saw was Steve. Everything. You saw his whole personality. Just without his money and fame."

"But that's just it. I won't fit into his lifestyle."

"You will. Trust me. I'm sure you two can make this work."

"I don't know. I need time to think." Lydia stood up and walked towards the window, sick of talking, sick of thinking about it. Her heart had just been ripped from her. Suddenly her love for someone felt gone. Yet, it hadn't disappeared. She loved Stuart. *Stuart*. Not Steve. Her love for him ached in her chest. She missed him already. Only now, he'd lied to her, meaning her trust in him was lost. "I bet everyone's laughing at me for not realising. Did the others know?"

"No! Of course not. I told Brett, but only the other day... And Alice had worked something out due to Terry sniffing around—"

"Alice!"

"But I'd sworn her to secrecy, otherwise no one else knew." Ruby stood from her perched position on the bed, too. "Lydia, he was going to tell you tonight. He was going to come clean with you earlier, but he chickened out, worried about your reaction. He loves you. Lying to you was eating away at him. He doesn't want to lose you."

Lydia peeked through the curtain. Dark, with no moon, it had started raining, the wind blowing it against the window. The weather represented the mood of the house. A few determined reporters and photographers lingered outside under umbrellas – hopefully this weather would get rid of them too. Lydia wished the wind would take them, like the scene in Mary Poppins, all the hopeful nannies swept away, then she'd be able to go home. That's all she wanted. Her own home, her own bed.

Lydia wrapped her arms around her waist defensively, stepping away from the window, fearing she'd be seen by one of them.

"Lydia, I suggested this for me as much as I did for him. It meant I got to spend time with my brother. I haven't seen him properly for fifteen years." Ruby sniffed, and wiped relentless tears with her palms. "Please don't blame Steve. If you can't forgive anyone, then make it me."

"Can you call me a taxi, please? I want to go home."

***

Brett helped Ruby clear up the disastrous Christmas Eve festivities. Daphne, Alice and Callum had helped, but feeling the need to be on her own, Ruby had sent them home. Alice and Callum shared a taxi, taking Daphne with them, promising they would see her home safely.

This would go down as possibly one of her worst days ever, bar Mum dying.

"Do you want me to go too?" Brett handed Ruby a cup of tea.

293

She was curled up on the sofa, with the television on low, staring at the Christmas programmes. If she'd been in a better mood she'd have been laughing at the jokes. But she felt too miserable to laugh. Steve had been wrenched away from her early. No proper goodbyes.

She'd envisaged waving him off at Heathrow Airport. Not this. She dreaded the papers and what would be in them on Boxing Day. Luckily, there were no papers Christmas Day. What mess was Steve going to face?

They'd both dreamt of him re-emerging in LA, and claiming he'd had a long holiday in the Caribbean and no one being the wiser. She wanted Terence to pay for this. Painfully. Excruciating pain. She'd never felt hate for a man like it.

"Ruby?"

"Huh?" She realised she hadn't answered Brett. "Oh, no, no, I don't want to be left alone." She reached for his hand. "Please stay if you can. I will apologise now for not being much company."

Brett smiled, and nudged her over, to join her on the sofa. "I totally understand, and I want to be with you. It pains me to see you this upset and I can do nothing to stop it."

Ruby nuzzled into his shoulder as he wrapped around his arm, cuddling her. This was what she needed. Closing her eyes, her other senses heightened. She could hear his heart beating and he smelled like a mixture of home cooking and his musky aftershave. His firm hold comforted and soothed her.

Ruby's mobile rang its annoying tune and she jumped, wondering briefly, where she'd left it. Groggily, she grabbed it off the coffee table, and answered it quickly, fearing it would go to answer phone as it never rang for long enough.

The caller ID displayed 'Steve'. He was ringing from his old phone, not the stupid pay as you go she'd made him buy two months ago.

"Steve? Is everything okay?" She rubbed her eyes, and Brett watched silently.

"Hi, kid." There was a pause, Steve sighing. "I wanted to tell you quickly that I'm safe. My flight leaves for Dublin soon."

"Dublin?"

"Yeah, that was the best flight out of Bristol Marie could find me. I'm staying overnight – probably airside so the press can't find me."

"Oh, Steve, check yourself into a hotel. You can't sleep in an airport."

"I'll see. I'll be on the first plane to Los Angeles tomorrow, via Chicago."

"Quite a trek then."

"Thought it best to avoid Heathrow." He sounded as miserable as Ruby felt, but at least she had Brett to comfort her. Poor Steve didn't even know where he stood with Lydia. "I'll call you in a few days and make some arrangements. I promise I will come home again soon."

Ruby, who thought she was clean out of tears, started crying again. Brett handed her a tissue.

"Okay." Ruby closed her eyes, letting her tears fall. Please be no more than a year. She couldn't bring herself to tell him she wanted him to return soon. He didn't need the pressure. "I tried, Steve. I really tried to talk to Lydia for you. But I think she may need more time. I'll keep persevering though. I promise. At the moment she's angry and thinks you did it as a joke. I told her you love her."

"I know, Ruby. And I love you, too. Miss you already, bossing me about."

She laughed. "I love you, too. And miss you. Who's going to make me coffee in the morning?" Steve chuckled. "Just don't take too long to come home. I hate that I never got to give you your Christmas present." She looked at the tree – Brett had moved it back and tidied it up – with presents all placed around it ready for Christmas Day.

"Promise me you'll stay in our house, not that rabbit hutch down the road. That's the best present you can give me. It's your home."

"I will. I promise."

"Okay, I better go. Take care of yourself."

"You too."

Ruby threw her phone back onto the coffee table, grabbed another tissue out of the box Brett was holding, and blew her nose. Curling back into the foetal position on the sofa, Brett curled in behind her. He grabbed her hand and squeezed it.

"I'm here for you, Ruby. I know it's not the same, and you'll miss him. But I just want you to know that. Okay?"

"Thank you." Ruby snuggled closer to Brett. She knew Steve would be back, they'd regained so much, got so much closer, he wouldn't let the distance grow in their relationship again. But there was an empty space in her heart, a sadness because she didn't know when she'd see him again. His intentions might be good, but his schedule could get in the way.

However, she loved Brett too. He did fill some of that gap, making the ache that bit less painful. With his arm wrapped around her, cuddling and gently stroking her skin along her wrist, she felt safe and secure. Loved. Time would heal and everything would be all right. Maybe in a few months, she'd get brave and pluck up the courage to ask Brett to move in. Share this big house with her; make it a family home again, like Steve wanted, and as Mum would have wanted, too.

But she wouldn't rush it. She stared at the Christmas tree, and the presents that were scattered beneath it. This house wouldn't see a family Christmas yet.

***

What a way to spend Christmas Eve. Miserable, Steve settled down across some chairs in Dublin's airport, deciding he wanted to stay airside. He'd turned his phone off for now, fearing the battery dying. It was already low. He folded and tucked his jacket to make a pillow and held his arms around him to keep his hands warm. Great research if he ever played a part as a tramp. Someone else was attempting to sleep a few rows along, so this wasn't abnormal behaviour. Only for an A-list celebrity. Yes, he could afford a hotel, but at the moment, he didn't feel like answering any of the press' questions – he quite possibly wouldn't be very polite. He had a few choice words he'd really like to get off his chest.

Firstly, he needed to get his story straight in his head before talking to them, otherwise they would spin it into some mid-life crisis. Would wanting to spend quality, private time with his sister be viable enough?

He could hear the questions now, "Steve Mason, explain the off the peg suits and glasses."

He shifted. The seats, albeit padded, didn't remain comfortable for long. The lights were bright, and although the airport wasn't currently busy, there were people noisily meandering. Last look in the mirror in the gents loos told Steve he was highly unlikely to get recognised. He looked rough. He needed a shave. If only by morning he'd have a beard to fully disguise him – but unfortunately his facial hair didn't grow that fast. Even without his glasses, which now he wondered if he should have kept, he hoped he didn't look like himself.

Maybe he should just buy a book and sit in a coffee shop... His eyes were demanding forty winks. Closing his eyes felt like the only way to ease his throbbing head, and soften the ache in his chest.

Ruby, Lydia, Lydia, Lydia... his thoughts were like a big wheel, going round and round and not stopping. He missed his sister, his girlfriend, and his new friends.

He'd try counting sheep, clearing his mind, counting one sheep jumping the stile, then the next, and the next...

Abruptly, Steve stirred to a hum of Irish voices.

"Twenty euro's it's him," said a male voice.

"The man should have his privacy," a soft Irish female voice replied.

"Yeah, but what's he doing here?"

Steve heard a shutter noise. And looked up to see a young guy with spiky blond hair pointing his phone at him, taking pictures.

"Hey!" Steve said more angrily than intended, not happy about being woken up. What time was it? How long had he slept? You couldn't tell if it was night or day in the airport; the lighting didn't change. He had hoped it would be more like five a.m. or seven. Glancing at his watch though, he was disappointed to see it was only two a.m. He groaned, rubbing his stubble.

Standing around him were four young adults, around their late teens early twenties, each carrying a rucksack and geared for travelling.

"Are you Steve Mason?" another Irish girl asked quickly.

"What?" Steve almost didn't catching the question. His brain caught up. "Yeah," he replied groggily, realising as soon as he'd said it he should have denied it.

"Told you!" One nudged another and the group whispered between them.

"Please can I have your autograph?" The girl fumbled in her bag.

"What did you do with that picture?" Steve asked the guy still thumbing his phone.

The young man winced. "I've put it on Twitter."

"Great." Steve stood, and stretched out his aching back. A bed of nails would have been comfier. Next time, Steve, get a hotel. "Right, who wants coffee with me?"

"You're buying?" said the young lad holding the phone.

"Yes, I'm buying, as long as no more pictures go on the internet."

"You got yourself a deal, mister." He tucked his phone into the back pocket of his faded jeans.

As Steve walked towards the coffee shop, grateful it was open all hours. The four backpackers followed excitedly.

"You know, you don't look as good as in your photos," said one of the girls. Steve frowned, finding it hard to tune into the strong

Irish accent. He really needed that coffee.

"She means you look fecked, mister," one of the lads said.

"Gee, thanks."

Chapter 29

Lydia didn't return to work on her first day back after Christmas, calling in sick. She wouldn't speak much on the phone, and Ruby didn't push it. She knew well enough what sickness Lydia suffered and decided to give her time. Lydia would still need her job, and as Ruby felt partly the cause, she would be lenient. Lydia was not only a work colleague, but through Steve, they'd become closer friends. It pained Ruby to think they were both hurting.

Even Ruby hurt. She missed her brother. It felt like losing her mum all over again. Though she told herself frequently she was being silly because Steve was alive and well in LA, his normal life resumed – which was far from normal for Ruby. She would see him again, and he was at the other end of a phone. Mum was not. Although she'd spent the majority of her Christmas being comforted by Brett, it had still been crap. She'd longed for a family Christmas, and it hadn't happened.

"Have you heard from... Steve?" Alice knocked on Ruby's office door, her glossy, chestnut hair in a chignon and make-up immaculate, ready for another day working in the spa. Her question had been hesitant, as if still unsure to call him Steve or Stuart. She probably felt some guilt, that the messy departure of Steve was partly her fault, that unwittingly she'd let slip about Ruby's brother being at the hotel to Terry. Ruby tried to reassure Alice that she didn't blame her. Terry had duped Ruby once, so he could easily have done it again with Alice. He knew how to use his charm to get what he wanted. It didn't stop the whispering and rumours circulating the hotel, and Ruby was grateful of Alice's loyalty. Of all the people, Alice understood why Steve had disguised himself.

Ruby shook her head. "No more than I've already told you. He arrived in LA unscathed after a night slumming it in Dublin airport, and his agent and PA have been working to minimise the damage."

Callum stood beside her and nodded while Alice replied, "Okay, well, you know where we are if you need us, Ruby."

"Yeah, Ruby." Callum winked. "And tell him, I miss him."

"Ah, Callum, of course. I'm sure he's missing you, too." Ruby giggled. "We all miss him. Thank you."

The week plodded on, with still no sign of Lydia, so Ruby shifted the reception duties around. Fortunately, Maxine wanted more shifts. On a daily basis, Ruby phoned Lydia but it always went to her voicemail.

"Lydia, it's Ruby. Look, just phoning to see how you are. Call me if you need to talk. Your job is safe, I understand you need some time off. We're all thinking of you and want to see you back at the hotel soon."

Give her time, Ruby thought, putting her phone down, trying to shake off her own doldrums. The way Steve had suddenly left before Christmas, plus January's miserable arrival, had made it harder for her to concentrate on work. Ruby had not been in the partying mood for the New Year, she hadn't even bothered watching the fireworks at midnight on the telly.

January was a depressing month most years, but this year was exceptional.

Friday 10th January

"Come on, Steve, cheer up!" Karl handed Steve another glass of champagne he'd swiped from a passing waiter. Another Hollywood party, another celebration in the industry. Only Steve didn't feel like celebrating. The richly furnished room buzzed; live music, familiar faces, glitzy frocks, tuxedos and champagne. Steve usually enjoyed a party, but tonight it was closing in on him, as if he was stuck in a lift.

Lydia wasn't answering his calls. He hadn't seen her in over two weeks, hadn't heard her voice. The asshole who said it's 'better to have loved and lost, than never to have loved at all' obviously hadn't really loved and lost in Steve's opinion. Steve would rather not be feeling this miserable. He'd rather live in ignorance of how love felt. However, he would agree absence made the heart grow fonder, because he couldn't stop thinking about her. As soon as his life quietened down, and there was a lull in his schedule, Lydia would be the first person to pop into his thoughts. He missed her. But was she missing him, or was she back to her life, life before Steve? Had the drawings in her sketchpad changed from him to a new person, a new obsession?

Did she hate him, because he'd lied?

"I'm sorry, Karl," Steve said, sipping his champagne, trying to focus on his agent, and not everything else going on in the room. "Maybe I shouldn't have come tonight."

"No, you needed the night out, besides I have some good news."

"What news?"

"I've managed to get you on a chat show in England. You look like you need to go back."

"When? How soon?" Steve couldn't believe his ears. He'd wanted to fly back as soon as he'd landed to make things right with Lydia again, but unfortunately, it was all down to his schedule when he could return. But now it looked like Karl was making his wish come true. "Yeah, you could say I have some loose ends to tie up."

"Don't get too excited yet. I'm trying to pull a few strings as we say." Karl nudged Steve and winked. "What's the point of being in this business if we can't?" He laughed heartily, Steve found it infectious and started smiling, his spirits lifting. "They had someone drop out, and I figured you could do with some positive publicity. I'll let you know as soon as I know more."

"Thanks, Karl. You're a good friend."

"And a great agent," Karl chuckled. "You know, all those years ago, when I first saw your portfolio, I knew you had potential to be big."

"I'll always be grateful, Karl," Steve said.

"Hey, you and I go back a long way. I like you. A lot. Now stop before we start getting mushy."

Steve relaxed a little, maybe it was the champagne, or maybe because he wasn't very good at staying in a bad mood. Plus, he was in Hollywood, and his career was important to him. He needed to mingle and network, not mope about feeling sorry for himself.

"Right, I need to catch up with an old friend." Karl gestured to a couple of men in tuxedos, deep in conversation. He patted Steve on the back. "Have some fun, and I'll catch you later."

Steve nodded, resolved to enjoy the rest of the party. However, he didn't expect to bump into the one person he wasn't sure how he'd react to; Erica Kealey.

"Steve," Erica said, holding the hand of her new boyfriend – fiancé if the press were to be believed. *Assholes doing whatever it took to be the first for a story – had they invaded Erica's privacy to get the scoop?* "It's good to see you."

"Erica," Steve said. "You look great." And she did, in another stunning outfit that accentuated her slim figure. His insides jolted, but it wasn't for Erica. Seeing Erica heightened how much he missed Lydia and wanted her by his side.

"Thank you. You look fabulous, too," Erica said, politely. "This is Marco."

Steve shook Marco's hand, smiling, his best dazzling Hollywood smile. Marco was welcome to Erica. He didn't feel jealousy as he feared he might. In fact he felt happiness for them.

"I understand you were in England for a while," Erica said. Was she prying or just making conversation?

"Yeah, yeah, I wanted to catch up with my sister, Ruby." *And find the love of my life after you'd broken my heart.* But he was over Erica now. Really over her. But would he ever get over Lydia?

He certainly wasn't donning another goddamn disguise.

***

Sunday 12th January

The house was dark, and Ruby's landline phone was ringing. Initially she cursed, thinking she'd forgotten to put her mobile on silent, then, realising it wasn't her mobile, she'd hurried downstairs, still bleary-eyed. Fumbling, she switched on the lights, squinting at the initial brightness, then shivered because the house was cold. The phone silenced its annoying ringing as she picked it up.

"Hello," she mumbled sleepily, with a slight conscious effort to hide her impatience.

"Oh, crap, sorry, Ruby, but I really needed to talk to you."

Ruby caught the time on the clock in the hallway. Two a.m. Technically, no longer Saturday night, and more like Sunday morning.

"It's okay."

"She won't answer my calls, Ruby. She won't answer them."

Ruby rubbed her eyes, trying to wake up at the distressed sound of Steve's voice. If he was calling Lydia at this time of the morning too, she could understand why she wasn't answering the phone.

"If I've blown this… Shit, I don't want to have blown this. I think about her every goddamn day." Steve's American twang had returned. "I love her, Ruby. I love her. Lydia's the one."

"Steve, she's been off work the past couple of weeks, she's not answering my calls either, or returning them. We've got to give her time."

"Go round. Talk to her. Tell her I love her. I'll be back soon. When I know more details I will let you know, but you've got to make her see that I love her."

"Okay, okay." Ruby blinked, trying to clear the sleep out of her eyes.

"Shit, I'm sorry. Are you okay? How's things? Glad you're in *this* house."

"I made you a promise. Though occasionally I do go and check on Daphne."

"Send Daphne my love. And how's it going with Brett?"

Nodding with the phone tucked to her ear, Ruby sat on the bottom step of the stairs, using her free arm to hug herself. "It's going good. Actually, I don't know what I would've done without him. He's been my rock. He helped me take down all the decorations and tidied the house, too." She sighed. "I miss you."

"I miss you, too."

"However much I love hearing the sound of your voice, can I go back to bed now? I have work today." Ruby said and Steve chuckled. "I'll try and call in on Lydia soon and I'll let you know how I get on."

"Okay, thank you."

"Can't promise anything though."

"I know. But please try."

***

Wednesday 15th January

Ruby pressed the doorbell, then rattled the letterbox.

"Lydia, I know you're in there. Please let me in," she shouted through the letterbox. Unless she'd gone for a walk or caught the bus, Lydia's classic VW Beetle was parked outside her house.

Ruby stood outside the door, stamping her feet and waving her arms, patting herself. Why'd she pick the coldest night in January to do this?

"Lydia, I'm not going anywhere. In fact if you don't answer this door soon, you'll have to call an ambulance, I'm freezing my nuts off out here... If I had nuts that is..." Ruby trailed off. "Oh, please let me in! It's dark out here." And Ruby didn't like the dark, although at half five in the evening it wasn't so scary.

Ruby sighed thankfully as she heard the front door being unlocked, and Lydia's face peering around the door. A tabby cat shot from out of nowhere behind Ruby and darted inside the house. Lydia looked pale and sad, not wearing a trace of make-up, and yet her skin still looked flawless. A twinge of jealousy hit Ruby – she always felt she had to at least wear mascara and lip gloss – but she could see why Steve had fallen for Lydia. Ruby, deep down, had always hoped he would.

Still rubbing her hands, and stamping her feet to emphasise the cold, Ruby said, "Hi, Lydia, do you mind if I come in?" Lydia looked reluctant. "Please? We are friends aren't we? I need to talk to you."

Lydia sucked her bottom lip and nodded. "Of course."

They got the niceties over, the small talk, while Lydia made two mugs of tea. Then, perched on the sofa, cradling the tea to defrost her hands, Ruby decided to just go for it.

"You know why I'm here, don't you?"

"Ruby, I'm not sure I'm ready to talk about this. I feel like a fool." Lydia stroked her tabby cat.

"I want to say I'm sorry," Ruby said, "because this whole thing had been my idea. Lydia, you have to believe me, you were seeing the real Steve."

"But what if I don't want the Hollywood lifestyle?" Lydia replied. "What if I won't fit in?"

"You will. Or he'll keep you out of it. Other celebrities do, don't they?" Alice was probably the best person to answer that. Yet, Steve had managed to keep Ruby and Mum out of the limelight all his career. "Look, he didn't think he'd find an ordinary, nice girl, really, he'd always be thinking 'do they like me for my personality or is it my looks, fame and fortune?'" Ruby said. "I convinced him to strip it away – to be Clark Kent, hide his superhero. Lois was never interested in Clark – you realise?"

"I'm not Lois Lane." Lydia's raised voice made her cat jump off her lap.

"I know, but please believe me, he loved you. He loves you! You need to give him a chance. Please, Lydia, he's miserable without you."

Lydia sighed heavily and drank her tea. "I'm miserable without him, too."

"If it's any consolation, I miss him too." Ruby could empathise. She loved Steve unconditionally; he was her brother after all. And these past couple of months had been great, catching up, bringing the family together, able to talk about Mum, and even Dad. And most importantly, Ruby wanted Steve to be happy. Wherever he was in the world, it felt important he be happy.

"You know, I've watched a couple of Stu, I mean Steve's films. Just to check, to see how I missed it. How I couldn't have realised who he really was."

"Look, I was part of the deceit too, and the others didn't guess either."

"Alice did."

"Alice had help from Terry." The mere thought of that man made Ruby angry. "It was only after his probing that she put two and two together. So you don't have to feel stupid about this. This wasn't why Steve did it. He really enjoyed making friends with all of you at the hotel. To get to know you properly – you know, under normal circumstances." Ruby hugged the warm mug, thawing her fingers. "Please find it in your heart to forgive him. If you're miserable then maybe you're meant to be together? It wouldn't harm to try... and if you don't like it, it doesn't work out, you can come back to your crappy job and friends in Bristol."

"It's not crappy. You're not crappy."

"Thanks." Ruby laughed. "But you could follow him around the world, and be supported to do your illustrations. Steve could even help—"

"I don't want his support – or his connections."

"Sorry, sorry, I didn't mean it like that. But think about it. You could be with the man you love, not doing this shitty job in Bristol that you hate, so that you could solely concentrate on your drawings. And by the way, this hasn't come from Steve. I'm saying this. Think about it."

"Ruby! I'll become the person he was trying to avoid. The reason he stripped away that lifestyle and donned a stupid disguise. It looks like I'm only interested in his money."

"Yes, yes, good point." Ruby held her hands up. God, she really needed to convince Lydia. And she wasn't doing a good job. "But the point is, you fell in love with him thinking he was poor – didn't you? You wouldn't really care less about his money if he turned up broke tomorrow."

"No. In fact, I want Stuart back."

"Then think about it. Maybe answer his phone call the next time he rings, please?" Ruby stood up, handing Lydia her empty mug. "And come back to work – the others aren't judging you. At least come back to be reminded how shit it is, before you make a decision." They both laughed.

"I enjoy my job."

"Yeah, yeah, but you'd rather be drawing."

"Yes, and I haven't done much of that either lately. I've lost my inspiration and my muse."

Ruby squeezed Lydia's shoulder sympathetically. "Thanks for letting me in, and for the tea. Please think about what I've said."

***

Wednesday 22nd January

Ruby had been staring up at her calendar on her office wall when the phone rang. There was only a week left of January; she hadn't seen Steve in over four weeks, since disappearing out of the door Christmas Eve and into the throng of photographers to a limo whizzing him away. She hadn't spoken to him since he'd begged her to get in touch with Lydia.

What was he doing in the big old Hollywood world?

"Hey, Maxine, who is it now?"

"You'll love this caller," Maxine said, without waiting for Ruby's response, she put the call through.

"Hello, you're through to Ruby Fisher. How may I help you?"

"Hey, Roo."

"Steve!"

"Just calling to let you know I'm flying into the UK tomorrow to do some interviews. I'll be on a chat show live on Friday evening," Ruby listened as Steve spoke, his American twang sounding natural, "Anyway, can you get Lydia to watch it?"

"I'll try Steve, I'll try. Will I see you?"

"If you watch the show, you will."

"No, silly, are you going to come to Bristol? Will I see you in the flesh?"

"I can't promise, here is my plan..."

Chapter 30

Friday 24th January

Lydia perched on the edge of Ruby's sofa, feeling uncomfortable while she waited for Ruby to come back from the kitchen with the wine. Ruby had already brought out savoury snacks in little bowls but Lydia didn't fancy anything to eat. Anxiety crept up her backbone as she observed the room. With the Christmas decorations removed, the room appeared more spacious, even lighter. The front window, no longer blocked by a huge Christmas tree, had its curtains drawn, so no roaming photographers could peer in.

Family photographs including recent photos of Steve and Ruby were dotted about in frames on bookshelves or hanging on the walls amongst floral canvas prints.

She knew why Ruby had invited her over this evening. To talk about Stuart – Steve. She was still doing that. Lydia still couldn't get her head around the fact he was Steve Mason. *The* Steve Mason. Lydia had tortured herself, streaming his films through Netflix to watch him in action. She'd searched the internet for everything he'd made – she could find everything on YouTube. She couldn't believe she'd been so stupid, hadn't seen through the disguise. However, watching the films had made her miss him. She missed the touches, the kisses, the little loving gestures. The way he made her laugh by pulling crazy faces. They were able to talk about everything, yet nothing important, even comfortable in each other's silence.

"Right, here you are." Ruby entered, handing Lydia a glass of rosé. Ruby checked her phone before tucking it into her pocket, then nervously sat next to Lydia.

"You've got me here to talk about h – him, haven't you?" Lydia took a sip of her wine, then placed it on the coffee table.

"Sort of, yes." Ruby grimaced. "Look, I'll be honest with you. He's on a chat show tonight, promoting the DVD release of *Perfection*." Lydia made a move to get up but Ruby placed her hand on her knee. "I thought you'd like to see it. And it would be easier for you if you watched it with me – that's all."

Lydia gulped some wine down, hoping it would numb any feelings, eradicate the nervousness that had started trembling through her body.

"Drink up," Ruby said, raising her glass toward Lydia. "It is Friday after all. If you don't fancy a taxi ride home, you're more than welcome to stay in the spare room. This house feels so big without St—" Ruby turned the TV onto the right channel, then hit the mute button. "Just in case we get caught up with chatting and forget the time. God, Steve would never forgive me then."

"Steve put you up to this?"

"Noooo." But Ruby didn't sound convincing. Lydia frowned. "No, no, he told me about the show and I thought I'd watch. And I thought you might like to, too."

"You're a bad liar, Ruby."

Ruby sighed. "I am. Okay, so he did tell me and asked if I'd get you to watch it."

Lydia fidgeted, finding the strap of her handbag beside her and rubbing it, unable to look Ruby in the eye. Did she bolt or did she stay and watch? What would Steve say to make her change her mind? She'd been thinking of nothing else but how much she missed him. Now she understood; when he'd talked about that

311

job interview, he'd stressed he wouldn't be in the UK. He lived in Los Angeles. He travelled around the world filming, on different locations. Could she handle that? Could she deal with the swarms of press like Christmas Eve?

"Why did he go to London, Ruby?" She realised this was one thing she hadn't had answered.

"Oh, uhm, basically his agent called to remind him he had an appointment to do some ADR – voice-over work – in London for his new film that's coming out in the summer. It had been scheduled ages ago and Steve had forgotten all about it." Ruby shrugged. "He felt terrible about missing your birthday, please believe me."

"Oh." Lydia nodded. He'd gone to work. How stupid had she been? She'd even seen a photograph of Steve Mason in London in the newspaper. Why hadn't she put two and two together? Because it wasn't believable. Why would Steve Mason be interested in her, when he could have any woman he wanted?

"He tried hard to get out of it. But apparently he was under contract so he had to go. Lydia, he felt terrible about lying to you. I think he'd just dug himself in so deeply he didn't know how to get himself out of it – and then the press bloody well got there first. Life as Stuart was uncomplicated." Lydia nodded then sipped her wine, trying to digest the information, but unable to get her head around it.

"Look," Ruby said, rubbing Lydia's upper arm, "he loves you, Lydia. I know it."

Ruby glanced at the TV. "Oh, look, it's starting." She reached for the remote control, increasing the volume, and Lydia's heart rate increased at the anticipation of seeing Steve on the television screen.

As the show's host, in a flashy suit, introduced the guests for the evening, the camera shot to Steve backstage, waving and smiling. Her insides jolted with the surprise, her stomach back-flipped. No glasses hid his electric blue eyes, his hair was slightly longer, sexier, so she could run her fingers through it. Then there was his designer stubble and he wore a tailored suit, the colour highlighting his eyes. Yet, his smile was the same. Stuart's.

"Wow, he looks like a different person," Ruby mumbled, echoing Lydia's thoughts. Lydia was too stunned for words.

Both watched the show silently. Lydia forgot to tell Ruby to stop filling her glass with wine, both mesmerised, waiting for Steve to come onto the sofa. Ruby muttered impatiently under her breath, wanting Steve to appear. Finally he did, and as he strode towards the sofa on the stage and sat beside the young, pretty actress, Lola, who'd just been interviewed, wolf whistles and loud cheering came from the audience. And Steve – Lydia was getting it better in her head now this was Steve Mason – waved and smiled.

The presenter interviewed him enthusiastically; they talked a little about his new film releasing in the summer but mainly of *Perfection* coming out on DVD, and even showed a clip. Lydia, hit with jealousy, watched Steve kiss Erica Kealey.

"God, he's handsome," Lydia said, without even thinking. "He was born to be on the screen." She couldn't stop watching him. All the little mannerisms, how he rubbed his nose, held his hands together as he sat, the dimples in his cheeks as he smiled. Everything was there in front of her – exactly the same. No difference. Just the material things like his clothes had changed his image, how he looked.

"Yeah," Ruby said mournfully, "he got the sparkly eyes gene." And she chuckled, and Lydia couldn't stop herself from smiling. He did have sparkly eyes. "His American accent is back too. But it sort of suits him."

"He sounds sexier."

Ruby grinned and nudged Lydia. "See, glad you watched?"

Another guest emerged onto the sofa – this time a male comedian. The limelight was taken off Steve as he was interviewed, though Steve joined in, with the petite young actress in the conversations, sharing experiences. They all laughed and joked about fame, fortune, and television. You could see both guests were enjoying the attention and company of Steve Mason on the sofa. He exuded charm and serenity, and his good sense of humour shone as he laughed and joked with the comedian. The audience loved him too. They were all probably thinking what a lovely, down-to-earth kind of guy he was.

Now came the end to the show with some music to finish it off but the camera wheeled onto Steve first. Ruby hastily shared the remains of the bottle of wine between the two glasses. Lydia frowned. This didn't usually happen. The presenter was mentioning something about Steve Mason having a special message. Then the camera fell back onto Steve and he looked straight into the camera lens, as if looking right at Lydia. Her breath quickened.

"There is a special woman in my heart, and I'm really worried I've broken hers. Anyway, I wanted to say – on national television (that got a laugh from the audience) – that I love you. Words can't describe how I feel right now. The past few weeks I've been to hell and back not seeing you, not sharing my life with you." Steve kept his focus on the camera. "Anyway, in the hope that you'll forgive me, I've asked the band to play our favourite song."

The presenter announced the band, *Abandoned*, and Lydia's insides felt like a thousand butterflies taking flight. She watched in amazement as one of her favourite bands played one of her favourite songs. A song she and Steve had made love to on her sofa. Every time she heard this song it made her think of that wonderful evening the two of them had shared. She listened and realised the lyrics were changed slightly, to include Lydia's name rather than Jessica. He'd made that happen. Even Ruby whispered to herself that it was romantic.

The band finished, and Lydia blinked, releasing a tear, which she quickly wiped away, then gave her chest a rub, to ease the tightness that had gathered there. The cameras were back on the presenter who thanked his guests, and the camera panned to the long couch. Steve was still smiling and laughing, the audience applauding rapturously.

The young actress, Lola, sitting next to Steve nudged him and asked quietly, "That was beautiful. So, are you going to ask her to marry you?"

"Yeah, hopefully. One day," Steve responded quietly, looking at the woman, and not the camera.

Lydia gasped, bringing hands to her open mouth.

"Shit, I don't think he realised his mic was on," Ruby said as the presenter was back on the screen announcing next week's guests on the show.

As the credits rolled, Ruby, thankfully, remained quiet as Lydia's brain whirred silently.

Did she want to marry Steve?

Chapter 31

Steve, hands in his pockets, strolled into his dressing room to collect his belongings, wondering how Lydia would have reacted to seeing the band play their song. Before the show, Ruby had texted a confirmation that Lydia was with her. It had filled him with anxiety, knowing she could be watching. But he'd sucked it in, taken a deep breath, and had ploughed on with his speech, wanting to tell Lydia how he felt.

As he tucked his phone into his inside pocket, it vibrated and started ringing, funnily enough, the song that had just played.

"Steve, what the fuck were you playing at?" Karl bellowed down the cell phone. "You do realise we're going to have every woman in the country, across the world, responding to this." His voice rose to a squeak. "*I'm his special woman*. He loves me."

"It doesn't matter—"

"It doesn't matter!" Karl boomed. "You've caused a major headache for your personal assistant if nothing else. Fan mail from all over the world responding with a 'yes I'll marry you.'"

"What?" Steve stopped in his tracks, cold. The blood drained from his face.

"It's all over Twitter. Apparently, it was on camera, you saying you'd ask her to marry you *one day*. I haven't seen it yet – obviously. But Twitter's going berserk. Steve Mason is trending. I've just had Marie on the phone—"

"Shit." Steve combed a hand through his hair. He'd made Ruby get Lydia to watch the show, just to hear the song. Nothing more. Hoping it would bring back pleasant memories, and maybe win her back, slowly, get her to answer his calls. Baby steps, Steve had thought, would be the best way to deal with this, to convince Lydia. If he'd gone in, all guns blazing Hollywood style, he'd scare the crap out of her.

Steve glanced at his watch – the cheap thing Ruby had made him buy and wear. Back in LA, he'd put his Jaeger-LeCoultre watch back on his wrist, thinking he'd missed it, but he couldn't get used to the weight of it, and this reminded him of home, Ruby and more importantly, Lydia. It kept him grounded. Hastily, feeling sweat beading around his hairline and at the back of his neck, he checked he had everything and exited his dressing room. "Karl, I've got to get to Lydia."

His agent was yelling away as if he had to shout down the phone to be heard, when Lola approached him.

"Are you all right, Steve?" Lola asked, placing her hand on his arm.

"The camera was still on us at the end."

Lola held a well manicured hand over her mouth in shock. "Oh, I'm sorry, I didn't realise." She took out her iPhone and after some navigating, she nodded. "It is all over Twitter."

"I've got to get to Bristol. I've made a right mess of this."

"Gosh, it's all my fault for asking the stupid question." For someone so young and bubbly on the stage, Lola was intelligent and warm, sensibility emanating from her. "Look, I've got a helicopter ready to fly me up to Manchester. It can take a detour. Let's get you to Bristol."

"Do you mind? Because that would be great." He laid on his best smile. He could call Ruby ahead to get her to keep Lydia at the house – if she was there still.

"Of course not. The least I can do. Do you think the press will realise who your special lady is?"

"I hope not. But they might go to my sister's anyway."

"Let's get a move on then. I have a car waiting outside."

As the car sped to London Heliport, Steve quickly text Ruby to check whether Lydia was still at the house and to say he was on his way. Relief waved over him momentarily when Ruby instantly replied back.

"Yes she's here. I'll do everything I can to keep her here. Ruby x"

But he wasn't out of the mire yet. He wouldn't feel happy until he'd spoken to Lydia.

Inside the helicopter, which Steve kept calling a chopper, sounding so American – too much of The A-Team as a kid – he wanted to close his eyes. He'd had such a hectic day in London, this chat show being the last one. He'd had other interviews and commitments – all the pluses of being famous, not. It wasn't just one show a day, it was as many as you can squeeze in. Karl had lined them up. He'd done daytime TV, radio, a magazine interview. His schedule today had been tight; he'd been alert and bombarded constantly with questions, and now his body demanded rest.

How had he been so stupid not to realise the microphones would still be on?

Would Lydia forgive him? He was going to ask her to marry him one day, he even considered popping the question soon to convince Lydia he wanted her in his life for good, but he'd needed to win her back first, and he certainly didn't expect them to rush into marriage.

Lola had let Steve close his eyes for some of the flight, realising he was exhausted. But he hadn't actually slept – impossible inside a noisy helicopter. Closing his eyes had at least stopped the dry, itchiness of his eyelids wanting to close, allowing him to recharge his batteries. The helicopter landed at Filton and there was a car waiting for him. Lola had taken charge and got her people to organise everything. He'd been too dazed and tired, plus with the time difference in LA he hadn't been sure if he'd get hold of Marie or not. He thanked Lola profusely, and they'd agreed to keep in touch, celebrity style.

"I want a wedding invitation," Lola said, winking. He laughed, and waved, leaving her at the airport to refuel and head up to Manchester.

The car pulled up outside their family house, Ruby's home. The curtains were drawn, but the lights were on. So far no press hounds were stalking outside.

Would Lydia still be there? Would Ruby have managed to make her stay?

As he opened the passenger door, he surveyed the street and recognised Lydia's car. He told the driver to wait. He had an urge to send him away, but if things fell apart, he might need the ride, or a quick getaway. The man could hold on for a few more minutes. He'd get paid for his time. The driver nodded, and grabbed a newspaper from the glovebox.

Steve, taking a deep lungful of cold air to calm his nerves, strode towards the front door. Moment of truth. Would Lydia be his leading lady?

***

Ruby jumped when she heard the knock at the door. She sat alone on the sofa, Lydia was upstairs in the bathroom. After Steve's text, Ruby had done her best to keep Lydia here, even opening another bottle of wine, but she really was ready to go home now. It was coming close to midnight.

Would it be the press or Steve? Or had Lydia already called the taxi?

She was expecting Steve, hoped it would be, but who could tell? With what had been broadcast on national TV, the tabloids were probably going bananas for front-page news. And they knew where to come.

319

Deciding to err of the side of caution, before opening the front door, she used the old chain, sliding it across.

Maybe she should keep Steve's old cricket bat by the door in future, in case Terence ever reappeared.

Her hands trembled as she hesitantly opened the door, her heart hammering nineteen to the dozen. Immediately, she recognised Steve and squealed. She closed the door, ramming the chain back, then wrenched the door open, to throw herself around him.

"Oh, thank God, you made it."

"Good to see you too, Roo. So," he looked at her, fear in his expression, "is Lydia here?"

"I'm here."

***

Lydia was halfway down the stairs, when she saw Ruby hugging Steve by the front door. Her insides jolted – part pleasure for seeing him in the flesh, part fear for knowing what to say, how to react. *He lied to me, remember?* Ruby released her hold on her brother and he entered the house.

"I'll go put the kettle on," she said, walking into the kitchen. Lydia heard the door close. She didn't move.

"Hey," Steve said, smiling, also motionless.

"Hi," Lydia replied, unable to engage her brain to say something more coherent. God, she didn't know if she wanted to scream at him, or kiss him.

"You saw the show, right?" He still had his American accent. He wasn't disguising it. He stepped towards the bottom of the stairs, hesitantly.

Lydia moved down, only one step as she nodded.

"I'm sorry about the marriage thing. It wasn't supposed to be broadcast. It was a mistake." He edged closer tentatively. "I mean, I do want to marry you, but I don't think we're ready for that.

Lydia, I want you in my life..." He rubbed the back of his neck, his fingers combing his slightly longer hair. "I wanted you to watch the show to see the song, to remember what we had, in the hope you'd forgive me, answer my calls and we could get back on track. I really would like to spend the rest of my life with you."

"How can I believe that?" She wrung her hands. "I mean, I'm so... ordinary."

"You are far from ordinary. You are beautiful." He stepped towards her, but read the fear in her expression because he stopped, leaving one foot on the bottom step. "Lydia, please..." He held out a hand. "Ruby explained didn't she? I was never going to find someone with my fame clinging to me like a bad smell. You would never have relaxed in my company, been yourself..."

"I know."

"I hate the way you found out. I was going to tell you that day – I know I should have told you sooner – I was trying to find the right moment." He looked her in the eye. "Lydia, I'm sorry."

"I know."

God, she needed to think of something better than, 'I know'.

Her eyes prickled, tears wanting to fall. Were they due to happiness or sadness or both? Now he stood before her in the flesh, after weeks of daydreaming and remembering his handsome face, her emotions were overwhelming. She swallowed then took a deep breath to gain control.

She moved another step down, only five more steps to take. Suddenly, breaking the tension, she heard clattering in the kitchen and swearing. Ruby. Steve softly chuckled, hearing the commotion too and rolled his eyes, pulling a face at Lydia. The one he always made when Ruby was throwing a strop. She let out a giggle, cupping her mouth with her hand. A single tear escaped, trickling down her cheek. He was the same guy who had made her laugh over the past three months.

Steve didn't know what to do or say. On tenterhooks, he could only wait and be patient, and watch Lydia's hesitation. His heart pounded with nerves inside his chest. Standing in front of Lydia right now would mean winning or losing. If he could physically see a directional fork in his road, his fate, it was right here, now. Either he would be spending the rest of his life with Lydia, or without her...

If Lydia chose to be with him, he promised himself, and he would promise her, he'd do everything in his power to make things right, to make things special between them. He would show her every single day how much he loved her.

He wanted Lydia and no one else.

He would not fail her.

In that moment of tension, his sister banged about in the kitchen and swore in true Ruby style. Without thinking, Steve automatically rolled his eyes, and made a face that said, "Trust Ruby." And with that silly expression, Lydia had giggled.

***

Lydia rushed down the last few stairs, and launched herself into Steve's open arms. His lips found hers and he was the same man kissing her as before. His touch was identical. And she'd missed it. She pressed her whole body into his, so that as much of her touched him as possible.

"I've missed you," she said breathily, between his kisses. He even smelt the same. His stubble gently grazed her chin. She cupped his face, feeling the roughness. He always used to be cleanly shaven. Now his designer stubble was intriguing as the softness of her palms felt the scratching bristles.

"Ruby used to nag me to shave – sometimes three times a

day!" He laughed.

"Yes, you used to be quick to remove it even when you stayed over," Lydia said, still stroking his face, her eyes remaining on his. "I realise why now. You do look more like *him*."

"I am *him*."

"And where are the glasses?"

Steve chuckled, wiping dry Lydia's cheek. "I don't need glasses – yet. There wasn't a prescription in them, they were plain glass."

She kissed his lips, intoxicated, closing her eyes. He wrapped his arms around her body, up her shoulder blades, pulling her tighter to his body, sighing with the touch.

"God, I've missed you," he said, his tone grave and sexy, sending a warm fuzz to her core. "Does this mean you'll come with me?"

Lydia remained hesitant. It was such a leap. She realised she'd stepped away from him, unconsciously.

He looked up at her.

"Please, don't make me beg. I'll get down on one knee."

"But what about marriage? It feels all of a sudden."

"We'll have a long engagement – it'll keep the press happy." He reached out and gently stroked her hair, enticing her back to him.

"Oh, heavens," Lydia mumbled.

"Hey, hey," he tucked a finger under her chin and made her look up, "it'll be fine. I promise."

Ruby burst out of the kitchen. "So, do I open the champagne to celebrate, or do I make tea to commiserate?"

Steve took Lydia's hand and squeezed it.

"Champagne," Lydia said. "Definitely the champagne. I'm going with Steve."

Ruby hugged them both enthusiastically, too enthusiastic as she almost winded Lydia. "Great, great! Phew! Right where's my best crystal?"

"Actually, hold the champagne for now. We'd better go, Roo," Steve said, shaking his head. "The press might be here any minute, and I do have a tight schedule. I hadn't planned coming to Bristol, remember?"

Ruby's expression dropped, like a scolded child.

"I'm sorry. I promise, I'll be back, and we'll drink champagne till we're sick. But I can't stay now."

Lydia could see this was actually painful for the two of them. She held Steve's hand, squeezing it. Seeing the faintness of unhappiness flash across his face, she wanted to be the support he required, and be the friend to Ruby.

"Ruby, I will make sure he returns – you have my word."

"I'm so happy for you two." Ruby's eyes now glistened, trying to hold back tears. Ruby smiled forgivingly, and hugged her brother. "You'd better be back soon. And don't leave it so long, ever!" She playfully nudged him with her fist.

"I'll fly you out. You need to come see my place. Brett can come too."

"Yeah, yeah," Ruby said, then hugged Lydia. "Look after him for me. Make sure his head doesn't disappear up his own arse." Lydia laughed. "Or grow so big he can't fit back on a plane."

"Hey!" Steve grumbled then tugged Lydia's hand. "Come on, Lydia, I want to take you home." He hugged his sister goodbye again, whispering how much he loved her, then wrapping an arm around Lydia's waist, they walked out of Ruby's house together, united. Lydia was thankful there were no paparazzi. They left under the cover of the darkness of the night and into an unknown future together.

***

Wednesday 29th January

Steve relaxed contently into his seat, Lydia asleep beside him holding his hand. The stewards left them alone after leaving a blanket. Looking out the small porthole sized window on the aeroplane, the sky was dark.

Friday had not ended how he'd even imagined. He'd hoped Lydia would return his calls and they'd rekindle their friendship and love – he'd win her back. Maybe Lola had done him a favour, because he hadn't dared dream of taking Lydia home with him. They'd had to organise tickets, and inform the visa waiver programme seventy-two hours prior to their flight, but here he was, flying back to LA with Lydia. It gave them ninety days to discuss their future, experience living together. It would allow Lydia to get used to Hollywood, and if she decided she liked it, they could make the necessary arrangements for her to stay permanently.

They'd left Ruby's and gone back to Lydia's to fetch her some things, manically packing her suitcase, throwing in the essentials she'd need.

When Kipper had appeared from his favourite warm spot in the second bedroom, there had been a few tears.

"It's okay, Daphne will look after him, I'm sure," Steve said. "She'll spoil him rotten, and the company will be good for her."

Steve had contemplated staying at Lydia's but decided a hotel would be impersonal if the press showed up. He promised he'd take Lydia shopping and they'd arrange any belongings she wanted in LA to be transported. The rest would be put into storage, and her place rented out. They'd agreed that way she could return if she wanted to. If things didn't work out.

But they would.

He stroked her hair, her head resting gently on his shoulder. Thank God she'd agreed. He hadn't been sure what he would have done if she'd said no. Ever since that evening, knowing Lydia – and possibly the majority of the UK – had watched him say he wanted to marry his special person, he'd been on edge.

All that worry was for nothing.

He closed his eyes and daydreamed of setting up a studio for her in his apartment. There was room for a workspace where she could draw. His apartment boasted fantastic views of Los Angeles. Would they help inspire her, help her creativity? He couldn't wait to start sharing his life, and its madness with her. He'd protect her as much as possible from the paparazzi. They'd grow tired trying to find gossip when there wasn't any.

He was going to do anything and everything to make this work, make her see she hadn't made a mistake.

He felt ecstatic. He enjoyed his career, and now he had someone to love, who would love him for the real person behind the Superman persona.

His life felt complete.

Now he just had to work out how to ask her to marry him properly.

TURN OVER FOR AN EXCLUSIVE LOOK
AT THE FIRST CHAPTER OF TERESA'S
BRILLIANT DEBUT,

Plus One is a Lucky Number...

Chapter One

Sophie Trewyn needed an excuse. A good one. A week to go and she was still no closer to a decision. She hated being a coward, but she couldn't face this alone.

"Sophie, what's up? You're quiet tonight." James frowned at her as he drank his pint.

Roused momentarily from her reverie, Sophie picked up her wine glass. "It's nothing. I'm tired." She plastered on a smile.

They were sitting in the garden at The White Lion, where everyone – from Accounts to the techies on the factory floor – went on Fridays for a drink after work. Luckily, it was a warm, July evening, so they could sit comfortably outside. Otherwise the small pub, with its low ceilings and wooden beams, would be swelling under the strain of its increased patrons.

"Who's keeping you up at night? Someone I know?" James nudged her playfully.

"You know I'm not seeing anyone." She sipped her Chardonnay and tucked a wisp of hair behind her ear.

"Yeah, I mean, who'd want to go out with you? Pretty, intelligent –"

"Oh, please." Sophie blushed.

"Okay – forget the intelligent bit."

Used to his teasing, she laughed. James and Sophie were

design engineers, specialising in robotics. When she'd started at the company ten months ago, he'd taken her under his wing, becoming the older brother she never had and even introduced her to his girlfriend, Kate.

"Does Kate know you think I'm pretty?"

"Kate thinks you're pretty! She wants to set you up with one of her boring accountant types." Then, grinning, showing off boyish dimples, he added, "I keep telling her they'll be too outgoing, even for you."

She jokingly slapped him on the arm, finished her drink and excused herself, heading for the ladies. When Sophie pushed open the door she found a stunning young woman, cursing into the mirror whilst delicately dabbing the corner of her eyes with tissues. Sophie meekly smiled and hurried into a cubicle. Having enough worries of her own, Sophie didn't need someone else's problems, too. The woman continued her tearful rant to herself in front of the mirror. "Commitment-phobic bastard. You can do better than that arsehole, Bella. Adam arsehole Reid's loss, not yours!"

Sophie knew that name. Relief washed over her as she heard the door swish and Bella leave, and hoped she wouldn't be upset for too long. Men these days were not worth it.

With the amenities to herself, Sophie tidied her ponytail and reapplied some lip-gloss. Working in a male-dominated office, she preferred to keep a low profile, hair worn back, minimalist make-up. Sophie wanted to be noticed for her work, not the skirt she wore.

She stared into the mirror as Bella had just done, her head clouded with excuses to make to her best friend Cassie, and how she'd deal with Cassie's anger – albeit over the phone.

Coward.

If only it had been Kate who had set Sophie up with one of her friends …

Or maybe she could feign a terrible illness?

God, why'd she let it go this far?

Because I thought I wouldn't be going home alone. She'd had months to find someone, and she hadn't thought it would come around so quickly.

She sighed heavily. This was ridiculous. She couldn't stand in a pub loo worrying all evening, James would wonder where she was.

Walking towards the picnic bench, Sophie noticed fresh drinks on the table and someone sitting in her seat. The man – with mouth-watering good looks – had removed his jacket and loosened his tie, laughing with James.

Adam Reid – Bella obviously long forgotten.

His name often came up when James discussed his weekend jaunts with his mates. How could such good friends be the opposite ends of the spectrum? Unlike his friend, James wasn't a naturally smart dresser. Adam looked sophisticated with his crisp, white shirt, a contrast to James' faded dark blue polo shirt that hadn't ever seen an iron.

Adam glanced at her as she approached. He had short, sandy blond hair, expensively cut. She'd heard some of the women in the office talk about him being a real head turner. They weren't wrong. *Poor Bella.*

Poor Bella? More like poor Sophie.

Oh, please don't have a trail of loo paper stuck to my shoe like some Andrex puppy trailing tissue behind it.

She subtly tried checking her blouse was tucked into her trousers, and quickly brushed a hand over her hair. Why hadn't she untied it? She could understand why Bella had been upset. This man was a catch.

"Sophie, this is Adam Reid."

She nodded and smiled. "I know." She'd attended a couple of meetings which he'd been at, and could count – on one hand – how many words she'd spoken to him.

"Oh, sorry, I'm in your seat." Adam stood up, and Sophie had to look up into his blue eyes. They shook hands. He had a firm, professional handshake. She could feel the warmth from his palm in her own.

She shuffled along the bench as some of their colleagues moved from the table, and she gestured to Adam to sit. As he did, she caught a whiff of his aftershave and heat instantly rushed up her neck.

"Adam's an account manager in Sales and Marketing," James said. Hence, he looked smart and she and James didn't. Working in the design department allowed them a more casual dress code. *He must think we're a right pair.*

"I know that, too," she said, placing her handbag on the table. Some said he was the best in the marketing department supporting the company's biggest clients. Sophie wasn't going to forget his cool, confident attitude in a hurry. Adam Reid had dominated the meetings she'd sat in a couple of times. His smooth, deep voice, combined with his good looks, had made it very hard for her to concentrate on what he'd been saying. James once told her Adam had started on the factory floor. She doubted he ever got his hands dirty now, but it hadn't stopped her watching his strong, masculine hands, and picturing what they could do.

He rubbed his thumb along the condensation on his pint glass. *Stop looking at his hands.*

"Sophie works with me," James said to Adam.

"I'd worked that one out, James." Adam winked at her. "Aren't you lucky working with such a bright spark?"

"Someone has to work with him. I drew the short straw," she said, nervously smiling back, finding it very hard to meet his eyes and not blush. The bottom of her wine glass was easier to look at. "I've managed to put up with him for almost a year." Adam chuckled.

"Hey, you two!" James laughed and reached for his pint, but knocked Sophie's full wine glass over, spilling the contents on her handbag.

All three of them jumped to their feet. Cheers and laughter came from a neighbouring table. James righted the glass.

"Oh, hell, sorry."

"James," she huffed, as she scrambled to empty her bag onto a dry part of the table and shake it out. Some of the contents fell through the gaps of the picnic table and onto the ground. She mumbled a curse. Luckily her bag had got most of it, not her clothes - the last thing she needed, especially in front of Adam.

Adam reacted quickly, grabbing clean paper napkins from another table and soaked up the wine.

"What's this?" James picked up a card, battered and now soggy, from underneath the table. Sophie tried to snatch it, but he held it away from her.

"A wedding invitation." James looked at Sophie, then Adam, his eyebrows raised. "For next weekend."

"James, please give it to me." She tried reaching for it again, but he raised it so she couldn't grab the card.

Sod him for being so tall.

Lowering his arm, he read further. "'To Sophie Trewyn and guest'. You never said anything about this."

Sophie wanted the ground to swallow her up.. *Please don't let this be happening. Not here.*

"No, because I'm not going," she said coolly.

"Why? Aren't weddings supposed to be fun? All that free food and drink." He playfully grinned. "Isn't that right, Adam?"

"Yeah, so I've heard." Adam shrugged. "I'll go get Sophie another drink."

James nodded, and before she could say not to bother, Adam had walked off.

"So?" James sat down, giving Sophie an interrogating look.

Sophie, relieved that Adam had gone to the bar, rolled her eyes and sat back down at their table. She pulled tissues from her jacket pocket and started wiping her bag. "I have a mountain of stuff to do and I can't afford to take the time off from work either."

"Rubbish!"

"And well, they're not really close friends or anything."

Who are you kidding?

"It's an all day invitation, so you must mean something to them," James said.

Sophie looked down, unable to meet James' gaze. It galled her to admit this, even to James. "I'm not sure I can face going on my own."

"Oh." James' smile dropped. "You don't have an 'and guest', do you?"

"You know I don't," she hissed.

"Well, you should still go. Might find yourself a nice man."

Sophie cringed, but hoped her expression didn't show. "James, I'm too busy with work."

"Really?"

"Yes."

"Bollocks."

Sophie let out a sigh, glancing around the pub garden. Could anyone hear? "It's complicated." Then she lowered her voice, "I don't know if I can handle the 'why is a pretty girl like you still single?' speeches."

She remembered the family gathering last Christmas, all tucked around the dinner table about to tuck into the turkey. Her Aunt Veronica, with too much sherry inside her, started harping on at her. 'Isn't it time you found yourself a boyfriend, rather than follow that career of yours?' She hadn't let it rest all day. Her insides turned cold, even now. Not to mention the endless 'So how's your love life these days Soph?' from a variety of younger, male cousins. 'Still single, eh?'

Irritated, she snatched the wedding invitation from an unsuspecting James. She didn't exactly date much, but she couldn't admit that, could she? It wasn't that she was shy. In fact she used to be much more outgoing ... and why she had thought that she might have found someone to go with her. The months had whizzed by and her only social outlet was The White Lion on a Friday night. It was her own fault. She should have gone out more, accepted

James and Kate's invitations.

"I'd go with you, for the champagne and food of course!" James said, smiling. Sophie clicked her tongue. "But as you know I'm going –"

"Yes, to that bloody meeting in Manchester." Most of her colleagues were going next Friday and tonight they'd been talking about extending it to the weekend. Sophie wished she was attending. It would be the perfect excuse. But she'd actually booked the time off ages ago in preparation for the wedding. Months ago she'd psyched herself up, telling herself that she could attend it. Now it came to actually going, her confidence had gone. "Besides, I don't think Kate would appreciate you going away with me for a weekend."

"True. She likes you a lot, Sophie. But even Kate might find that difficult to swallow." He laughed. "But what if Kate went with you?"

Sophie smiled, understanding James' offer, though not particularly enamoured he was still pressing the matter. "You're sweet. Thank you, but it's not really a case –"

"Soph, come on. Would you go if you had someone to go with?"

"Um ..." Yes, she would. But did it sound pathetic? She frowned. Adam walked towards them carrying a glass of wine and a greying dishcloth.

"Sorry, queue at the bar," he said, handing Sophie her glass. She wasn't sure if it were true, yet was glad he'd taken his time.

James suddenly beamed. "Adam, you'll go with Sophie, won't you?"

Sophie nearly spat out her wine.

"What?" He stared at James, shocked – or horrified even? – stopping mid-wipe with the cloth.

Sophie waved her hands in protest. "Seriously, it's not that big a deal. I'll cancel." She took a gulp of her wine, Dutch courage was really required now.

"No, no, no." James placed his hand on hers and squeezed it. Once he had an idea in his head, he didn't stop or even listen.

"Adam, you'll do it, won't you?"

Sophie glanced around again, hoping no one would take any notice. Good job they weren't in the office otherwise she'd be the talk of the whole building. She imagined the sniggers.

"Just go along so she doesn't get all those awkward and annoying questions, you know, like 'why aren't you married yet? You're working too hard at that office.'"

Sophie laughed, and even Adam couldn't hold back a smile. James sounded exactly like an old lady, not dissimilar to her Aunt Veronica.

"Well, I'm not sure," Adam stammered. Unable to look Sophie in the eye, he picked up his pint.

Sophie sobered. Maybe he'd do it for someone prettier. And smarter. She hardly compared to Bella. Automatically Sophie brushed her hands down her trousers. She couldn't blame him. Adam was well out of her league. He played Premiership; she was way down in second division.

"Adam, honestly, don't listen to him," Sophie said, pointlessly dabbing the cloth over the table. "You don't have to. I'll say I'm not going."

"Rubbish!" James interrupted. Sophie quickly glared at him.

"James —"

"Go on," James cut in, ignoring her. "You'll charm the socks off the wedding guests." He grinned.

"Sophie looks quite capable of standing on her own two feet," Adam said, giving her a smile. It wasn't huge, but enough to make her heart flutter. He'd just made her feel like a million dollars. Maybe she should wear more makeup into the office after all.

Stop it.

Adam was right though, what was James suggesting? She didn't know Adam from … Adam. *Oh, God.*

"You'll be helping a lady in distress."

"I'm not in distress!" Sophie slapped her hand down on the table.

"Ah, James, shall we go get another pint?" Adam said, giving James a stern look, then his expression softened. "Sophie, would you like anything else?"

She shook out her bag and started putting the contents back into it. "Um, no, thanks."

***

"What do you think you're doing?" Adam scowled at James. He'd never heard of anything so ludicrous in all his life. They both ducked the low doorframe as they entered the pub. The warmth hit them, dry and stuffy compared to outside. "Not only did you just put me in a very awkward situation, the poor girl's embarrassed."

"Come on, Adam, she needs a date. Just go along, charm the guests, keep them off her back. You never know, you might enjoy the weekend." James leaned against the bar. "And Bella's no longer on the scene, so what's the problem?" Adam winced. Bella had wanted more than he was prepared to give. He was too busy with work. And his father expected nothing short of absolute dedication.

Adam ordered the drinks when the barmaid arrived, trying to think of arguments for not doing it. There were plenty.

"We hardly know each other."

James nudged him and laughed. "When has that stopped you before?"

"That's different! Besides, what have you told her about me?" Adam looked at him questioningly.

"Only what everyone else knows." James held up his hand defensively. "If she's ever listened to me jabber on," James winced, "then she might think of you as ladies' man."

"Oh, just wonderful." Adam shook his head.

"Look, you know I would have gone with Soph, but I'm at that damn meeting in Manchester – and you're not." James paused. "And even if I could, Kate loves Sophie, but I'm not even sure

337

she'd understand this one. Come on, help a mate out," James said, rubbing his hand through his unkempt hair. "Do it for me? You're the only guy I can trust to do this properly."

"I don't know." Adam slid his hands into his pockets. Why hadn't he stayed at the office this evening? He'd taken the opportunity to leave on time, rarely able to join the workforce down the pub on a Friday. Now he regretted it. First Bella, and now this.

"So, how good is she ... at engineering?" Adam said hesitantly.

James frowned. "She's a bloody good design engineer. Thomas will be making her chief engineer at this rate – obviously some time yet, she's only young."

"So we don't want to lose her?" Adam's forehead creased. Would helping Sophie actually benefit him, even if only in company matters?

"No, but what's this got to do ...? Adam, I'm asking you as a friend."

"I know, but I might need to call in a favour." He shrugged.

"Man, it's always about work with you. Well, you're probably both suited. The woman works all hours," James said. Then more sternly, "But she's the sort who'd help a friend out if that's what you're thinking."

"I don't know what I'm thinking. This is a stupid idea."

"She's great. You'll love her. You two might even hit it off." James sounded hopeful. Adam scowled.

"We've talked about this before. You know it's not for me, settling down. Not everybody wants what you and Kate have."

"How do you know if you don't try it? Dating a woman who's not afraid to chip a nail might do you good."

"Date?" Adam sighed and run a hand through his hair. The barmaid put the last pint on the bar and Adam paid her.

James continued frantically, realising his misplaced word. "I'm not asking you to sleep with her. In fact you'd better not - I'll bloody kill you! Sophie's a nice young lady, who needs treating properly." James looked at him knowingly but Adam's returned expression was horrified. "But truthfully, I think something's up."

"Oh, great."

"She needs someone there for moral support, for some reason. Like I said, she helps friends out, that's why I can't believe she's seriously thinking of not going." James nudged him. "Haven't I got you out of a few scrapes? If you're helping Soph out, you're helping me out," James added, looking pleadingly at him. "You're the only one I know I can trust."

Trust. There it was again. If James wasn't such a good friend …

The barmaid handed Adam his change and he sighed. "All right, all right, I'll do it."

James slapped his back and grinned. "You won't regret it."

"Famous last words those."

"Sophie is lovely."

"You keep saying that, but she's not really my –"

"The problem is you can't see beyond a woman's looks. You wait until you get to know her. Trust me."

Adam rubbed his forehead, and they headed back to the pub garden. "Why do I get the feeling I'm going to regret this?"

***

Well done, James. The one thing she would have liked to have kept buried deep in her handbag, was now the topic of the most embarrassing conversation at the pub.

Coward.

This could be the answer to her fears; only Adam Reid... *Really*?

While she worried about what James was telling Adam at the bar, she said hello to colleagues, not really listening to them and what they were up to at the weekend.

What would she be doing this weekend? Thinking about packing, or plucking up the courage to call Cassie?

Why hadn't James stuck with asking Kate? Or one of her

accountant friends? Oh, no, he'd asked Adam Reid from Sales and Marketing – a department she wasn't even familiar with, as her job rarely led her there. All she knew was everyone dressed in smart, slick suits and looked immaculate. They talked about sales figures, advertising campaigns and the big picture, while she and James knuckled down to the hard work behind the scenes.

She glanced around the pub. Some of them were here.

Sophie swallowed, conscious her throat was like sandpaper, and sipping her wine didn't help.

James and Adam walked towards her and sat down in silence.

What had James told him?

All nice things, surely? He's a friend. Though, how well did James know her, really? So they worked together five days a week, and went to the pub on a Friday evening, but Sophie didn't speak much about home, and what awaited her there. They talked shop most of the time, discussing their latest design project, or she let James fill her in on his weekends with Kate and friends.

"As I was saying," James looked at Adam, as if passing a silent message between them, "Adam will go with you to the wedding."

"You don't have to."

Adam smiled, in an 'I don't mind' kind of way. "So where's the wedding?" She became very aware of his blue eyes piercing through her at knee melting capacity. Good job she was sitting down.

"Cornwall, where I grew up. I'm supposed to drive down Thursday morning," she said nervously. "It would mean taking a couple of days off."

"See, mate, it'll be fun –"

"Shh, James," Sophie hissed.

"Okay, fine," Adam said, ignoring James. He frowned, combing a hand through his hair. Sophie could see he was still thinking about it. Had James bullied him into this?

"So, you will come with me?" She kept staring at the table, looking at James, anything but meeting Adam's eyes. Admittedly, this could be a good solution, although he still sounded hesitant.

"Yeah, I could do with a weekend away."

"You'll both have a scream!" James said, eagerly. "All you got to do is pretend to be her boyfriend."

They both stared at James and spoke in unison, "Boyfriend?"